Beverly Connor is the author of the Diane Fallon Forensic Investigation series. She holds undergraduate and graduate degrees in archaeology, anthropology, sociology, and geology. Before she began her writing career, Beverly worked as an archaeologist in the south-eastern United States, specialising in bone identification and analysis of stone tool debitage. Originally from Oak Ridge, Tennessee, she weaves her professional experiences from archaeology and her knowledge of the South into interlinked stories of the past and present. Beverly's books have been translated into German, Dutch, and Czech, and are available in standard and large print in the UK.

For more information about Beverly Connor visit her website: www.beverlyconnor.net

Also in Beverly Connor's
Diane Fallon Forensic Investigation series:

One Grave Too Many
Dead Guilty
Dead Secret
Dead Past

DEAD
HUNT

A DIANE FALLON FORENSIC INVESTIGATION

BEVERLY CONNOR

PIATKUS

PIATKUS

First published in Great Britain in 2008 by Piatkus Books
This paperback edition published in 2008 by Piatkus Books
First published in the US in 2008 by Obsidian, an imprint of New American
Library,
a Division of Penguin Group (USA) Inc, New York

A CIP catalogue record for this book
is available from the British Library.

ISBN 978-0-7499-0929-1

Data manipulation by Phoenix Photosetting, Chatham, Kent
Printed and bound in Great Britain by Clays Ltd, Bungay, Suffolk

Papers used by Piatkus Books are natural, renewable and recyclable
products made from wood grown in sustainable forests and certified
in accordance with the rules of the Forest Stewardship Council.

Mixed Sources
Product group from well-managed
forests and other controlled sources
www.fsc.org Cert no. SGS-COC-004081
© 1996 Forest Stewardship Council

FSC

Piatkus Books
An imprint of
Little, Brown Book Group
100 Victoria Embankment
London EC4Y 0DY

An Hachette Livre UK Company
www.hachettelivre.co.uk

www.piatkus.co.uk

*In memory of Dixie Lee Connor
and Charles C. Connor, Sr.*

DEAD HUNT

Chapter 1

It wasn't the sound of the steel doors clanging shut
behind her that bothered Diane Fallon about the
prison, or the flashing red lights, or the blare of high-
pitched horns that screamed their warnings when the
doors were unlocked. It was the smell, like no other—
the accumulated odor of hundreds of women caged
for years in close quarters.

Greysfort Maximum Security Prison for Women
looked clean—the gray-green walls were freshly
painted, and the tile floor of similar color was so
highly polished that Diane could see her reflection as
she walked down the hallway to the interview room.
But bad odors always come through, and even the
pine scent of disinfectant in the air carried with it the
smell of urine and feces.

Diane was accustomed to the unpleasant odors of
death. They held useful information. But she didn't
have to live with those odors as the prisoners and
guards did here. The thought of it was depressing.

A guard opened the door for her and motioned
toward a plain gray metal chair next to a table on the
visitor side of the interview room. Another dull gray-
green room.

The room was divided by a thick screen of wire so finely woven that only the tips of fingers might fit through the holes. Diane stood waiting beside the chair. She looked at her wrist, momentarily forgetting that she had been required to leave her watch outside.

Several long minutes passed.

Diane glanced at the clock on the wall behind her. It reminded her of a school clock—large and round, black hands and numbers on a white face. It clicked quietly as the sweep hand ticked off the seconds. Depressing. This was a place where time crept by.

She needed to be at the museum putting out the fire that was igniting all the local media. Why had she agreed to come here? The prosecution hadn't wanted her to. Nor had the detectives on the case. Frankly, she hadn't wanted to come.

It was not the first time she'd received a letter from an inmate put in prison by evidence processed by her lab. The letters were always long and often full of excuses and accusations. This one had been short and almost cordial. Three sentences.

> *Dr. Fallon,*
> *I know the last thing you want to do is respond to my letter, but there is something I need to tell you. I'm asking that you please visit me. I will understand if you can't.*
> *Clymene O'Riley*

Diane had almost filed it away without responding. Instead she called the lead detective in the case and left a message. It was the district attorney who called back.

"Out of the question," he'd shouted before she even said anything. His manner always irritated her, even during the trial. She had to keep reminding herself that they were on the same side. DA Riddmann. He had used his name to good effect during his election campaign.

"What is out of the question?" Diane had asked, though she knew the answer.

"Visiting O'Riley. That's what you're asking, isn't it?"

"No. What made you think that?" she asked. He had caught her in a bad mood.

"Detective Malone said . . . I just assumed . . . " He stopped. "What did you want?"

Nothing from you, she thought. She pinched the bridge of her nose, trying to discourage a headache. "I called Detective Malone to ask if he knew what Clymene might be up to."

He paused for several seconds. "I don't know. I've expected her to file an appeal. So much of the case was circumstantial."

He said it in such a way as to imply that Diane and her team had failed to provide convincing evidence. They hadn't.

"What did the letter say?" he asked.

Diane read it to him.

"Short," he said. "You think maybe she wants to confess?"

"I doubt it," said Diane. "Not to me."

"Of course it's the warden's call, but I would prefer you not to go," he said after another long pause.

"I have no intention of going. I only wanted to pass along the information and get an informed guess as to why she wrote me."

When Diane hung up the phone with the district attorney, she filed the letter and forgot about it. A week later she was sitting in her museum office when

Ross Kingsley, a profiler for the FBI, called. She knew Kingsley. When Rosewood police had been frustrated by a particularly gruesome murderer, they had called Kingsley. He had interviewed Diane after the murderer began calling her and sending her flowers.

Ross Kingsley was now interviewing Clymene O'Riley, a convicted killer and possibly a serial killer, a rarity in the category of serial killers—almost all of whom are male.

Kingsley surprised Diane. He wanted her to comply with Clymene's request for a visit.

"Why?" she asked.

"I want to know what she wants," he said.

"Why?" Diane asked again. She had more immediate concerns. She frowned at an Atlanta newspaper spread out in front of her with a picture of the museum and the headline: SCANDAL AT THE ROSEWOOD MUSEUM? One of her worst nightmares—negative publicity for the museum. At least it was deep inside the paper, not on the front page. She scanned the article as she listened to Kingsley.

"I think she's killed many more men than just her late husband. If poor Archer O'Riley had only known what he was marrying. I don't have enough proof to convince a jury, but I'm convinced she killed her previous husband, Robert Carthwright. And I believe she may have killed others—and so do you."

"You may be right, but what does that have to do with me? I only do crime scenes," muttered Diane. The article was no more than questions voiced by a reporter who had little information, and it was short—only three paragraphs. But this was just the beginning. It wouldn't take them long to start collecting stories on such a juicy topic.

"That's not exactly true and you know it. It was you who discovered her faked background. And those things your team did with the photographs were amazing."

"That's all part of crime scene analysis. My part is done." Diane was only half listening to what Kingsley was saying as she scanned the article. *Damn*, she thought as she finished.

"But the reason I want you to visit her is to see if she'll open up to you . . . tell you something, intentionally or otherwise."

"She hasn't given you anything?" asked Diane.

"Getting serial killers to open up is a long process. They are not trusting people and are always driven by their own agenda. I'm sending you a preliminary report on her."

"The DA doesn't want me to go," Diane said. She still wasn't convinced she should help Kingsley with his job—that's what it felt like he wanted.

"I've spoken with him. He's worried about her getting information from you that will help to overturn her conviction."

"She isn't even trying to get it overturned," said Diane.

"That's a little different too. She's much too quiet for your average serial killer—even a for-profit serial killer. You need to do this, Diane. There are more of her victims out there waiting for justice. I'm sure of it."

So here Diane stood in an interview room at the Greysfort Maximum Security Prison for Women waiting for a black widow. The sound of the door opening on the other side of the wire screen brought her attention around.

Clymene O'Riley was dressed in a bright, almost glowing, orange prison-issued dress. Quite different from the conservative suits she wore at her trial.

Diane had seen her wardrobe at the crime scene. The huge walk-in closet filled with clothes in a rainbow of colors and styles. She could visualize Clymene in front of her clothes rack looking for just the right outfit, running her hands along the suits and dresses, deciding what would make the best impression on the jury. Black? No, too obvious a play for sympathy. Not jewel tones—they subconsciously convey the impression of wealth. Pastels are too lighthearted. A tailored look? Yes, a tailored look in earth tones. The tweed is nice, and the brown wool. Perhaps the navy too—it's dark, but not black.

She had sat beside her lawyer in court, well dressed in wool suits and cream blouses accessorized with June Cleaver pearls, looking like the grieving widow of the man whose portrait the DA had resting on an easel.

Clymene's hair was still blond, but darker now and shorter, without the beauty-treatment highlights. It was combed back behind her ears. Her lean face had been softer at the trial, with gentle curves that made her appear vulnerable and feminine. She'd looked at the jury with liquid blue eyes and it had taken them two weeks to decide her guilt. Not because the evidence was only circumstantial, however much the DA tried to poor-mouth about the lack of hard evidence. The jury took so long because Clymene O'Riley simply did not look like the kind of woman who would murder her husband.

Even in prison clothes behind screen wire she didn't look like a murderer. Diane studied her face. It was a good face for her line of work—if indeed murdering husbands was her line of work. Diane suspected there was a string of dead husbands, but they knew only of the two and could prove only one.

Clymene had regular features, almost generic—if there is such a thing as generic features. Her nose was straight, neither too large nor too small. The same for her lips—not small, but not full lips either. Her eyes were almond shaped but not slanted in any direction, nor did they droop. Her face was perfectly symmetrical—that in itself made it interesting. It was a face that could be made to look beautiful or plain. She could change her hair and eye color and be a different person.

In addition to her chameleon-like attributes, Clymene's age was hard to estimate. From a distance she could pass for her late twenties or early thirties. A closer look showed she was older, but by how much was impossible to tell—she could have been thirty-five or forty-five. Diane didn't know how old she was. They didn't even know her real identity.

Clymene moved her chair forward and sat down. Diane sat in the visitor's chair and they stared at each other for a moment. Diane tried to read her face, looking for some sign of hostility, remorse, deceit— something. The woman simply looked interested. That was all. No daggers shooting from her eyes. No bared teeth.

"Thank you for coming," she said. "Frankly, I'm surprised you came. My profiler must have asked you."

She said *my profiler* the same way she would have said *my biographer*. Diane supposed that's what he was.

"What do you want?" asked Diane.

"I want you to check on one of my guards," she said.

Chapter 2

"You want me to check on one of your guards?" *Are you nuts? I don't have time for this,* Diane thought. She stood up to leave.

Clymene didn't stand, but she appeared poised as if she might be ready to chase Diane through the wire barrier if she tried to leave.

"Please hear me out," said Clymene. "I know this sounds strange."

Diane stood for a second, then sat down again. "All right, go on," said Diane. "I'm listening, but I don't have a lot of time."

"The reason I want you to check on her is to make sure she is all right," said Clymene.

"Do you have reason to believe she isn't?" asked Diane. Now she was getting concerned. *What was Clymene up to?*

"Yes and no. Let me explain," she said.

Diane eyed Clymene. Her profiler said she never exhibited any of the normal tells of a person who lies. She always maintained eye contact; she was always relaxed. She would be evasive, he said, but he could never find a pattern in her body language that said she was lying. Diane couldn't either. But that meant nothing. Sociopaths are good liars.

"Why are you concerned?" Diane asked.

Clymene smiled. Not a strained smile, but one that reached her eyes. "I guess that seems strange. But in the world I live in now I depend on—how shall I say—the kindness of strangers. That's the way it is in here. I own nothing—things are taken away at any moment and my living space turned inside out. I have to be alert to prisoners who suddenly go off the deep end because they received a letter they didn't like and decide to take it out on me. As I said—that's just the way it is in here, so kindness from a guard is important. It makes the quality of life a little better. It gives me some protection against the elements here. Grace Noel is a kind guard."

As Clymene spoke, her hands were flat on the table, her right over her left. Her nails were short and well manicured. Her voice was calm, her face pleasant, even though the bright orange color of her dress made her look sallow.

She showed no noticeable reaction to Diane's obvious impatience. Ross Kingsley said she was always self-possessed. She would get frustrated, but never angry. She would state her innocence, but only in response to a question or some statement from him. She wasn't like other prisoners. Ross thought she made it a point not to be like them.

"Why do you think Grace Noel may be in danger?" asked Diane. She wondered if there was a real danger or if this was a ploy—or threat.

"Let me start at the beginning," Clymene said. "Grace Noel is the kind of guard who likes to talk with the prisoners—some of them anyway."

Diane noticed that Clymene usually referred to prisoners as *them*, not *us*.

Clymene smiled. "I suppose I should say *us*," she said, as if reading Diane's mind. "Grace Noel is a plain woman, large boned."

"Are you saying she is overweight? How is that relevant?" asked Diane, growing more impatient. She shifted her position in the hard chair, thinking she needed to be tending to the problem at the museum.

"It is relevant. That's how she describes herself and . . . just let me explain. I work in the library and in the chapel. Noel talks to me while I'm working. You know, girl talk. A few months ago she was lamenting the fact that she was rarely asked out on dates. She was asking me things like how she should wear her hair—girl stuff."

Diane was having a hard time visualizing Clymene deep into girl talk and how this was leading to Grace Noel's being in danger. She leaned forward and rested her forearms on the table.

"One day," continued Clymene, "she asked me how I got so many husbands, and she couldn't even get a date." Clymene paused a moment. "I told her that I'd only had two husbands. She gave me the knowing smile."

"The knowing smile?" asked Diane.

"Once you've been convicted, to the entire world you are guilty of all charges and innuendos against you. No amount of denial changes anyone's mind, especially not in here." She paused again and smiled. "Of course everyone in here says they are innocent, which takes the credibility away from those of us who really are. Noel, as kind as she is, believes I am guilty not only of the crime for which I was convicted, but also of the rumors and accusations the DA and others have leveled at me."

"Rumors and accusations?"

"That I've had many more husbands and killed them all. I know that's what the DA believes—and so does my profiler," she said. "So that's what Noel believes. And in my capacity as a serial black-widow murderer I must have many wonderful secrets for capturing a man." Clymene's mouth turned up in an amused expression.

"That's what she wanted? Secrets to getting a man? What are you worried about? That she's looking for Mr. Goodbar?" said Diane.

"No. She had already met the man—a new member of her church. She wanted him to notice her, to be drawn to her. So I gave her the benefit of my expertise."

"Is this an admission?" asked Diane. "You have expertise to give?"

"For my trial I researched the kind of person the DA thought I was. Yes, I've become quite the expert." She shrugged. "I've also had two husbands and many boyfriends, so I figured I would give her some pointers and stay in her good graces—so to speak." She smiled at her own pun.

"What did you tell her?" asked Diane.

"To research the man of interest—find out what he likes and dislikes and become the person he wants." She shrugged again.

"Just how did this put her in danger?" Diane glanced down at her arm for her watch. Clymene seemed not to notice.

"Noel didn't know how to begin with such a plan and she wanted me to help her. I asked her to tell me all about him. This is what she told me. Eric Tully, that's his name, is an accountant. He likes camping, hiking, boating—anything outdoors. He likes country music, reality TV, and action movies—but he also likes poetry." Clymene arched a brow as she said the last statement. "His most recent wife died giving birth to his daughter, now five years old. Before that he lost a wife to leukemia, and both his parents died when he was a teenager. He's had a very sad life, Grace told me." Clymene leaned forward. "Too sad, I told her."

"What are you saying?" asked Diane.

"I'm saying that I recognized the kind of person I'd been reading about during my trial."

"Are you saying he's a serial murderer?" Diane was skeptical.

Clymene leaned back in her chair. "I told her I was suspicious of him, but she insisted that he was the man of her dreams."

"Did you help her with a plan?" asked Diane.

"Yes. It was just a basic plan that any girlfriend would come up with. Nothing in it was guaranteed to work."

"You can guarantee your work?"

Clymene eyed Diane for a long moment, then smiled again as if she found the conversation humorous. "Just a figure of speech. I mean there was nothing fantastic about the plan. But it worked. I was surprised."

"Why?"

"Not to put too fine a point on it, he is a handsome man; she isn't a beautiful woman. Like it or not, handsome men rarely choose plain women to marry . . . not without some ulterior motive."

This time Diane arched an eyebrow. She was thinking of herself. She had never considered herself beautiful, yet Frank was drop-dead gorgeous.

Clymene shook her head. "You're not plain. Your face is interesting and intelligent. I imagine you attract a lot of good-looking and intelligent men," she said.

Diane was disconcerted by the way Clymene kept reading her mind. *Is my face an open book?*

"You were thinking that you are an exception, therefore Grace might also be an exception," said Clymene, "But you're not an exception."

"To know that you would have to know who I date or who I'm married to," said Diane.

"You're not married and I know who you date. Don't look so suspicious; I didn't dig it out, my lawyer did. In preparing my case he researched everyone on the witness list so as not to miss any angle. You have to know that. He was an expensive lawyer."

Diane did, but she still didn't like the fact that Clymene knew so much about her. "Grace . . . and . . . Tully got together?" she said after a moment.

"Yes. They had a fast courtship and marriage. Another bad sign," said Clymene.

"You warned her?"

"Of course. Many times. She blew me off. When it became imminent, I told her not to take a honeymoon that involved being over water or near a cliff. She thought that was terribly funny."

"When was this?" asked Diane.

"She got married three weeks ago," responded Clymene.

"So why did you call me now?" asked Diane.

Clymene leaned forward again. "Because I overheard one of the guards say she's overdue and they haven't heard from her."

Chapter 3

"Why didn't you just ask the guards to check on Grace?" said Diane.

Clymene shook her head. "Not all guards are friendly. I was afraid they might see my warning as a threat against Grace instead of a concern for her."

They probably would, thought Diane. *I did.* "There are a legion of people you could have asked instead of me—what about your lawyer?"

"I'm between lawyers right now. The few friends I still have who visit me wouldn't have a clue about how to investigate. Of course there's Kingsley, my profiler . . ." She shrugged. "But all he's interested in is the book he's going to write about me. I thought about asking the minister here at the prison, but I don't believe he would take it seriously. He's a nice guy, but like many others, he thinks I'm a guilty sociopath. You seemed the best bet."

"And you believe I don't think you're a guilty sociopath?" Diane raised her eyebrows in surprise.

Clymene grinned. "I thought it possible your view would be that I can recognize my own kind and that perhaps I really do take the danger seriously."

As Clymene spoke she never took her eyes off

Diane. Ross Kingsley was right—she had no tells—at least none that Diane could see. Clymene was right about another thing. Diane did believe that she could recognize her own kind and, for whatever reason, she was indeed concerned about Grace Noel.

"All right, so I check on her. Then what? I can't watch after her," said Diane. She folded her arms as if emphasizing the point and realized how her own body language was so easy to read.

"I know you can't look after her. I am just asking that you see that she is all right now. Maybe you can get through to her where I couldn't."

Diane was shaking her head even before Clymene had finished. "No. I'm not going to interfere in her life. I'll only make sure she got back from her honeymoon safely."

Clymene nodded. "I understand. You might make sure the daughter is okay as well. She's not safe either. Despite what my profiler thinks, I'm not a sociopath, but Eric Tully is."

Diane unfolded her arms and leaned forward. "How do you know he is?"

Clymene shrugged and smiled slyly. "I read a book on sociopaths."

Diane knew that was true. Ross Kingsley's report said that Clymene was well versed on sociopaths and murderers. And it wouldn't surprise Diane that Kingsley wanted to write a book about her. He considered Clymene a more interesting form of black-widow killer—one entirely motivated by profit, not the usual type with a hyperbolic sense of romance addicted to finding the perfect Prince Charming.

Diane didn't know what category Clymene fit into and didn't really care. She did know—or rather strongly suspected—that Clymene had many more kills to her credit. Why she thought that was not easily explained. Perhaps it was the polished way she had killed her husband. She had come close to getting away with it.

As Clymene spoke, Diane listened to her speech patterns, trying to discover any clue to her origin. Not that Diane was any good whatsoever at linguistic analysis. But it was a mystery that Diane would like to have solved. Clymene told her husband that she had been on staff at the American University of Paris. But there was no record of her. She did speak fluent French, but her accent here and at her trial was southern United States, even though she said she was raised in various places in Europe. Rosewood detectives and the DA felt they had enough evidence against her without spending the money to track down her past. Clymene was an enigma.

Diane listened to the ways she pronounced her vowels and consonants, her syntax, the tonal quality of her pronunciations, hoping for a clue. Clymene did sound southern and Ross Kingsley said her French was flawless. He said he carried out one of his interviews with her entirely in French. He said he suspected she spoke other languages as well.

Language. It made her think of her daughter. Ariel had picked up languages with the same ease that she had learned how to swim. A bright light gone from the world—and Diane's life. Her hate for murder swept over her like a wave. Her face must have changed, for Clymene looked puzzled. It was the first time Diane saw an expression that she believed was honest. Clymene had been good at reading Diane, but she couldn't possibly follow the stream-of-consciousness thoughts translated into body language. Diane sensed that Clymene felt she had just lost her.

"What's your real name?" said Diane suddenly.

"Clymene O'Riley," Clymene responded.

Diane started to say they both knew that it was not, that truthfulness would go a long way toward generating some goodwill, but then wondered why she was even considering arguing with her. Diane's role was over the minute she stepped down from the witness stand. She was wary about following through on the request regarding Grace Noel. Clymene was up to something, but Diane couldn't imagine what. Whatever it was, Diane didn't plan to get pulled into it. She wished she hadn't gone so far as to ask for her real name. She'd known Clymene wouldn't tell her.

They stared at each other for several moments before Diane spoke. "What makes you so sure about Tully?"

Clymene had regained her composure—not that she had actually lost it; she was just momentarily puzzled. *How she must have been concentrating on me and my body language*, thought Diane.

"His story is too tragic and he is too willing to tell it," said Clymene. "He is overly charming. He patterns himself after a hero in a romance novel. His pursuit of outdoor activities provides the opportunity to get his victims in dangerous situations. His interest in poetry is designed to make people think he is sensitive. His interest in accounting is his excuse to handle the money in the relationship."

Clymene leaned forward again, supported by her forearms. The expression on her face was that of one imparting great knowledge.

"He's self-centered," she continued. "Grace would tell me about their dates. He would start out asking her what restaurant she wanted to go to, or what movie she wanted to see. Even as she told me about them, she didn't notice that one way or another they always ended up seeing what he wanted or going to his favorite restaurant. From her description I saw that he is indifferent to his daughter. Grace didn't notice because he keeps Julie well fed, well dressed, and pats her on the head occasionally."

Clymene paused a moment and looked down at her hands, then back up at Diane.

"His daughter is only five, but she knows how to clean house, wash dishes, and fetch and carry for her father. Grace sees it as playing house. But it isn't."

Clymene said the last with such gravity, Diane wondered if she'd had a similar personal experience and was projecting. On the other hand, Clymene had made a compelling argument.

"He never reads to his daughter and he never tucks her into bed. Grace sees this as something she can help him with—like he's just a guy simply out of his depth as a single father, not as someone with a serious character flaw."

"Why do you think he will hurt his daughter now?" asked Diane.

"I don't know that he will do anything now, but it's a time of big changes for them, when anything might happen. It's an ominous sign that no one has heard from Grace."

"All right. I'll check on them," said Diane.

Clymene relaxed back in her chair. "Thank you."

Diane sat for a long moment studying Clymene through the wire. For the life of her she couldn't think of what angle Clymene might be playing. And she definitely believed that there was an angle. Clymene had an agenda besides saving a prison guard from harm.

As she listened to her speak, Diane thought that

Clymene's personality felt slippery. She was someone you could never get to know. Diane couldn't put into words why she felt that way. It wasn't anything that Clymene did or said—it was like she was too polished. Had she rehearsed her meeting with Diane in front of a mirror? Or mentally, at night when the lights were out and everything was quiet?

"You're a good actress," said Diane. "Why didn't you take that up instead of murder?"

"You think I've been acting?"

She spoke without malice, but Diane could see she was puzzled. Puzzled, not angry. She never showed anger. That was one of the things Diane found suspicious in her behavior.

"I don't know," said Diane.

Clymene raised her eyebrows. "Then . . . what? Why do you think I'm a good actress?"

"I saw you in court and you were an entirely different person than you are here. I don't know if you were acting then, now, or if neither of these personalities is the real you."

In court Clymene had been demure. The shine in her eyes looked as if she was always holding back tears. There was little of the confident personality that sat in front of Diane now. It was only when she took the stand that any self-assurance showed through from the woman that looked more victim than perpetrator.

Clymene closed her eyes and opened them again. "I see your point. I confess, I was playing to the jury at my trial. Surely you can't blame me. I was fighting for my freedom. Don't tell me you weren't playing to the jury when you and your team came across like CSI television. Isn't that what the DA told you juries expected these days—to be dazzled with fantastic forensic analysis?"

Diane gave a small shrug, not willing to concede the point. But she was right. That's what juries expect these days. They want the fancy forensics, and that's what the DA had told her and her team.

"I wouldn't call the forensics we had dazzling. They were compelling," said Diane.

"You made it sound dazzling. It's not a criticism—a compliment really. How you took a dirty cotton ball and turned it into"—she gestured with a wave of her right hand—"into murder."

"We had more than a cotton ball laced with *Clostridium tetani*."

Clymene smiled. "Yes, you did," she said. "Scrapbooking."

Diane smiled back. That was the weakest link in their chain of evidence.

"How many ladies are going to think twice before they crop their family photos?" said Clymene. She actually looked like she was going to laugh.

"Is there anything else I can do for you?" asked Diane.

Clymene shook her head. "I appreciate your coming and being willing to check on Grace for me. She truly is a nice person who just wants a little romance and companionship in her life. She doesn't deserve what I believe Eric Tully has in store for her."

She seemed sincere. Ironic, thought Diane. From what they had discovered, that's all Archer O'Riley wanted when he married Clymene—a little romance and companionship in his life. What he got was murder.

Chapter 4

It was a civil visit, Diane thought as she left the interview room. Even Clymene's side trip into "I'm just an innocent victim" was done with humor. It felt to Diane as though Clymene still saw herself in complete control of her destiny. The thought didn't exactly worry Diane, but it did give her pause.

She hadn't for a moment believed Clymene was innocent. But she could see how other people might be persuaded by her. She knew Clymene had friends and supporters on the outside who believed her. Perhaps they were what the DA was worried about.

It wasn't the quality or the conclusiveness of the evidence collected by Diane's forensic team that was cause for concern in Clymene's conviction. It was the DA's inserting information into the trial about the death of Clymene's previous husband, Robert Carthwright. He'd died of an apparent accident while working on one of his cars. At the time, Clymene hadn't even been named as a suspect. There was evidence that a local handyman may have been involved, if indeed it was anything but the accident that it had been ruled.

But DA Riddmann's strategy was to persuade the

jury that the murder of Archer O'Riley was part of a larger pattern and that Clymene was more than just a onetime killer—that she was a serial black-widow killer. So he raised new suspicions about her culpability in the death of Robert Carthwright. He drove hard on the dark motives that lay behind her elaborate measures to hide and fabricate her past. And he coupled all that with extensive evidence of a sociopathic personality.

The hard evidence connecting Clymene to Archer O'Riley's murder was more than sufficient for a conviction, and bringing in information about her uncertain past and her previous husband's death would only present grounds for an appeal. Diane had thought it was a bad move. But the prosecution strategy was the DA's call.

Be that as it may, the scrapbook link wasn't as weak as Clymene liked to claim. Her lawyer had made much of it. If he could convince the jury of its absurdity, then the competence of the prosecution would be put in question and doubt cast on the validity of all the prosecution's evidence.

Clymene's scrapbooks were certainly not the main evidence, but for Diane they provided a powerful insight into Clymene's modus operandi. Ross Kingsley, the profiler, loved them.

Diane knew about scrapbooks through classes taught at the museum. Today's scrapbooks are far more elaborate than scrapbooks of the past. The philosophy behind the design of the pages is to have the viewer experience the content of the photographs at a deeper level than just looking at the pictures. The photographs themselves may be cropped, made into a mosaic, covered with velum, or treated in any number of creative ways to draw attention to them. A picture of kids building a snowman might be showcased amid drawings of snow-covered trees embossed with fine white glitter. A photograph of a beach scene might be shown on a page with tiny shadow boxes filled with sand and sea shells. Personal journaling on the pages can supply context and explanation for photos. But the idea always is to illustrate an underlying truth, because the pages are windows into personal history.

Clymene's pages were elaborately artistic and creative, but they were also fake. David, one of Diane's crime scene crew and an expert in photographic analysis, noticed it first. Clymene had digitally edited herself into photographs, Photoshopping herself into the lives of strangers.

One photograph alone might simply have been artistic licence, but her scrapbooks were built on dozens of photos in which she had systematically grafted herself into a false past. She had even created a five-generation photograph out of whole cloth. It was as if she might have scoured flea markets looking for discarded photographs to build herself a history. Clymene had created a family and experiences that weren't real, weren't hers.

The scrapbooks in and of themselves weren't conclusive of any wrongdoing. But added to the weight of the other evidence, they were more than suggestive. The fact that investigators were unable to find any family or history for Clymene before her marriage to Carthwright cast the purpose of the scrapbooks in a very grave light.

Clymene's scrapbooks were constructed around the interests of each husband. Robert Carthwright was a car buff—he particularly liked cross-country racing. One of the scrapbooks showed her participating as navigator in cross-country rallies throughout Europe—

most notably the Acropolis Rally in Greece—complete
with sightseeing photographs of ruins and quaint vil-
lages. She had used a photo-paint program to graft
her face or her whole body into all the pictures.

Archer O'Riley, the man she was convicted of killing, enjoyed amateur archaeology. One scrapbook
showed Clymene on various digs in Europe. Digs that
she was never on. David even found that faces in some
of the images were the same faces that appeared in
another scrapbook showing photos of other places and
other times. The digital editing had been good and
her pages elaborate enough to actually take the eye
away from the individual people and focus it on the
context. Clymene was good at creating illusions.

As Diane was let out of the maximum-security section she suddenly turned to the guard at the door and
asked whether the chaplain was in. She followed the
guard's directions and came to an office labeled REV.
WILLIAM RIVERS. She knocked on the door. It
opened immediately.

She faced a heavy-set man in dark gray pants, short-
sleeved white shirt, and tie who looked at her quizzi-
cally over an armful of papers. She imagined that it
wasn't often that people he didn't recognize knocked
on his door.

"Reverend Rivers?" she asked.

He looked at her badge. "Dr. Fallon . . . " He
wrinkled his brow. "Do we have an appointment?"

"No. I—I'm the director of the Rosewood Crime
Lab and currently working with Ross Kingsley, the
FBI profiler. I was wondering if I could speak with
you about a prisoner." Diane didn't want to get into
Clymene's request as the real reason for her visit, and
since Ross got her into this, he deserved to have his
name dropped.

Rev. Rivers nodded as he came out and closed his door. "Can you walk with me to the chapel? I need to put out these handouts. Who did you want to talk about?" Rivers breathed hard as he walked briskly down the hall.

"Clymene O'Riley," said Diane.

"Ah, yes. Ross has spoken with me about her before. He's taken quite a shine to her."

They reached the gate and the guard let them back into the high-security area. Diane didn't ask any questions until they got to the chapel. Rivers seemed to have a hard time breathing, talking, and walking at the same time.

"Here we are," he said.

Diane opened the door to the chapel for him and he proceeded to place his handouts on each desk. Rather than pews, the chapel had rows of metal and plastic classroom chairs—the kind with a table attached and a wire basket underneath. The chapel itself had the same shiny tile as the rest of the prison and the same gray-green walls. A single wooden cross stood behind a wooden lectern at the front. Vases of silk flowers—mostly roses, irises and lilies—sat atop tables that lined the walls. Rivers caught her looking at the room.

"Who would invent paint this color, huh?" he said. He shook his head. "Some of the women arranged the flowers. A local florist taught a flower-arranging class as part of our skills program." He looked at Diane and grinned. "She had written a nice proposal to the state. Anyway, it was something for them to do. Clymene O'Riley took the course. She did several of the arrangements you see here. What do you want to know about her?"

"Your opinion of her," said Diane.

Rev. Rivers finished placing his handouts on the

desktops and motioned for Diane to sit down. He turned one of the desks around to face her and sat down with a deep breath, as if laying out all the handouts had tired him. His light brown hair was disheveled and his brown eyes looked red and strained.

"She's an interesting prisoner. When she asked to work in the chapel she wasn't like the usual prisoner—she didn't tell me how she'd found the Lord and wanted to help do his work. We sat over there in those chairs." He pointed to two vinyl-upholstered wood chairs at a table by the wall. "She told me she was scared and wanted a safe place to work and if I let her work here she would listen to what I had to say with an open mind. I found that refreshing. She told the truth and promised me only what she could give. I've had women promise me they would become nuns." He laughed. "I tell them I'm Protestant, but I'll pass their desires along to Father Henry."

Diane smiled. "You are also a counselor here? Is that right?"

He nodded. "I'm here all day. We have a rabbi and a priest come to minister to the prisoners too."

Diane glanced down at the handout on the desk in front of her. It was instructions for filling out a job application. Rivers followed her gaze.

"With some of them, small skills like filling out forms, going for a job interview, and creating a budget help them get by on the outside. Clymeme has been a big help. She already has those skills. Sometimes we do role playing and the women pretend they are at a job interview. Clymene is good at interviewing and showing them how to improve. She's fluent in Spanish. I'll tell you, that's a big help."

"And did she listen to you with an open mind?" asked Diane.

Rivers nodded. "She did. She listens and asks a lot of intelligent questions. She's a smart woman. She actually understands everything I have to say."

"Do the other prisoners like her?" asked Diane.

He nodded. "They do. She writes briefs for them. Pretty good at it too. She's gotten one woman a new trial and another one visitation for her kid. That's really a good record."

It certainly was, thought Diane. Now she knew why the DA was so nervous. Apparently there was no end to Clymene's skills.

"And the guards?" asked Diane.

He shrugged. "They like her as much as they like any of the prisoners, I suppose. Probably more because she doesn't cause trouble. There are a couple of guards she is friendly with, I think. Guards are like the rest of us. Cynical. We hear and see a lot."

"You don't seem cynical," said Diane.

"I try not to be. Occasionally we actually get prisoners who are really innocent. It happens more than you think. I try to keep an open mind without becoming gullible. And I try not to take it too hard when they disappoint me. It's not an easy line to walk."

"I can imagine," said Diane, though he seemed to her like a man who felt disappointments deeply.

He shifted in his chair and stared a moment at the handout in front of him. After a moment he looked back up at Diane.

"I'm not familiar with the evidence against Clymene O'Riley. I get the impression from prison talk that it was weak." He gave a faint laugh that barely made it out of his throat. "Something about creative scrapbooking?"

Diane grinned at him. "Those illustrated her duplicity and pointed to an underlying scheme." Diane took a breath and explained in detail about the scrapbooks. Rivers bent forward, resting his arms on the desk, and listened.

"None were true?" he asked.

"Not that we could discover. Almost all the photographs of her were digitally inserted over a background. Those places we could contact—like the car rally in Greece and the archaeology digs—did not have her in their records and had no one who remembered her, though they could verify that her husbands had been there."

"I see," said Rivers. But Diane wasn't sure that he did.

"Clymene's scrapbooks were only secondary to the case," said Diane. "The key piece of evidence was the cotton ball, and it was a slam dunk."

Chapter 5

"The cotton ball?" Rev. Rivers sat up straight in the chair. "I don't know about that."

"Do you know how Clymene's husband died?" asked Diane.

Rev. Rivers frowned and looked at a vase of irises to his right. "Lockjaw, I think she said." He looked back at Diane. "Is that right?"

"Yes. Archer O'Riley flew to Micronesia to work on an archaeological dig. Clymene was supposed to be with him but developed a case of the flu at the last minute. She was to join him later. He arrived feeling sick, headachy, feverish, and a little stiff. He thought he was also coming down with the flu. The archaeology team sent him to a hospital in Guam. On the way he had seizures so severe that he broke one of his vertebrae and his arm was so swollen and inflamed the doctors were going to amputate it."

Rivers winced. "Tetanus is rare, isn't it? I can't say I've ever heard of anyone dying of it, despite all my mother's warnings about stepping on rusty nails."

"Yes, it's rare. Only about eight people a year die from tetanus in this country, out of a population of three hundred million," said Diane.

Rivers said nothing for a moment, as if he were searching for the right words. "She . . . she somehow infected him? You proved it? With a cotton ball?" He looked skeptical.

"One cotton ball about that big"—Diane made a circle with her thumb and index finger—"told the entire story. I've never had evidence that good before."

Rivers shifted in the small chair. A few of the buttons on his shirt looked to be in danger of pulling loose. He shifted again.

"I don't know the details of Clymene O'Riley's trial," he said. "All I really know is that she was convicted of killing her last husband and suspected of killing her first husband."

Diane started to say they didn't know if Robert Carthwright was her first husband or second, third, or tenth for that matter, but she let that go. The fact was, she didn't know. She did know the evidence supporting the Archer O'Riley murder and she felt it was important for Rev. Rivers to know it.

"Archer O'Riley died just an hour after they got him to the hospital," said Diane.

"Why was murder suspected?" asked Rivers.

"It wasn't right away. His body was flown back to the United States, where it was examined by his own doctor, who was concerned about the arm because the site of the infection was where his office had taken a blood sample in a routine checkup just days before."

"Naturally, he didn't want liability," said Rivers.

"Naturally," repeated Diane.

Clymene had gotten to Rev. Rivers. Diane could see it in his face—the way he blushed at leaping to her defense. She guessed that he hadn't realized it himself until now—until he felt called upon to defend her.

Diane imagined that it had been easy for Clymene

to win Rivers over, even though he was resistant to prisoners trying to pull the wool over his eyes. He was a man with meager resources, dedicated to making a difference among the prisoners. Successes were probably few and far between. Clymene hadn't told him what he wanted to hear, like so many prisoners do. She told him what he hadn't expected to hear. Making a promise, small though it was, and keeping it set her apart from the prisoners who made pledges he knew they couldn't keep. By his account, Clymene listened, asked questions, and participated in a meaningful way in his classes—actions above and beyond her simple pledge to keep an open mind. A small thing, but an important thing to Rivers. Clymene was good at calculating what was important to people.

Saying she was afraid and wanted a safe place to work was probably true. What was it Frank, her white-collar-crime detective-friend, said? Truth makes the lie believable in a con. Clymene was undoubtably good at using truth to her advantage—just as good as she was at making fiction seem true.

Diane saw now what Clymene was doing—why she hadn't filed an appeal yet. She was gathering her supporters first. The DA said she had a following on the outside consisting of a few friends and people she went to church with. Having the prison chaplain on her side would be a PR coup for her.

"The health department investigated the doctor's office," said Diane. "They found nothing that would account for the infection."

He again shifted uncomfortably in the small chair, putting further strain on his buttons. She could see the white T-shirt underneath. "Would they find anything? I mean"—Rivers shrugged his shoulders—"if it was just that one contaminated needle."

"Of course," agreed Diane—just to be agreeable, "that was a possibility. But the investigation didn't stop there."

"Let's move over here to the table," he said, pointing to a honey-colored maple table with a vase of red silk roses. "Either the chairs are getting smaller or I'm getting bigger." He gave a small self-conscious laugh and squirmed out.

They moved to two straight-backed wooden chairs with vinyl-covered padded seats. They were better than the desk chairs, thought Diane, but not by much.

"I'm sure the prison saves a lot of money on furniture," said Rivers.

"And paint," said Diane because she knew it would make him laugh.

Rivers' laugh was a little more hearty. "Yes, definitely on paint." He sighed. "I'd like to understand this," he said, resting an arm on the table.

Diane nodded. By "this" she understood him to mean the evidence against Clymene.

"Archer O'Riley was old Rosewood—old money. Many of his friends were old Rosewood." Diane had actually met him once at a contributors' party at the museum. He had come as a guest of Vanessa Van Ross, the museum's biggest patron and good friend to Diane. Clymene hadn't been with him.

Vanessa was the first to light the fire under the police when he died. For reasons Vanessa couldn't explain exactly, she had never liked Clymene. "There was something about her that seemed fake to me," was all she could tell Diane.

"One of Archer O'Riley's friends, along with his son, insisted that the police investigate," said Diane. She didn't say that Vanessa had to convince his son at the time.

"O'Riley's infection had spread more rapidly than normal, so the ME's suspicions were already raised. Then she found puncture wounds in the bend of his arm that could not be accounted for as a result of the blood sample taken by his doctor. Two of the punctures were not in his vein, but into the muscle tissue. We—the crime scene team—were asked to search the house. We started in his bedroom," said Diane.

Rivers listened without comment. The intensity of his gaze revealed his interest in what Diane had to say.

"It had been several days since Archer O'Riley was last in his house, and the room had been cleaned. We didn't expect to find anything. But behind the nightstand on his side of the bed, caught between the stand and the chair rail, we found a cotton ball. It had two distinct creases in it—as from wiping a needle-shaped object." Diane made an effort to keep her descriptions objective.

Rivers opened his mouth to speak but said nothing. He motioned for Diane to proceed. He probably thought the evidence so far was pretty weak, but he leaned forward, resting his elbows on the table.

"We analyzed the substances on the cotton ball," said Diane.

"And these substances told the story?" said Rivers.

Diane nodded. "One crease contained trace amounts of corn syrup, cornstarch, carrageenan, L-cysteine, casein hydrolysate, traces of horse manure, and an ample supply of *Clostridium tetani*, tetanus bacteria. The most interesting of these being casein hydrolysate and the horse manure—and the bacteria. The second crease had trace amounts of the same substances but also included Archer O'Riley's blood, rohypnol, and epithelials from Clymene and from her horse."

Rivers was frowning now. Diane wasn't sure if it

was from trying to understand the string of substances she had just rattled off or from a deep concern about Clymene's guilt.

"Can you walk me through what all those things mean?" he asked.

"Corn syrup, cornstarch, carrageenan, L-cysteine, and casein hydrolysate are ingredients in a baby formula," said Diane.

Rivers raised his eyebrows.

"Casein hydrolysate is a good medium for growing tetanus. Horse manure is a good place to get the tetanus bacterium."

"I see," said Rivers. He stared down for a moment at his hands, clasped in front of him on the table.

Diane continued before he could say anything—like, How did you connect this to Clymene?

"There was baby formula in the house. O'Riley's son and his wife have a baby, but the baby's mother said she didn't use that particular brand of formula. Epithelials—skin cells—in the manure were matched to Clymene's own horse."

Rivers looked up at Diane. He looked tired and surprised. "So what you are saying, if I read the evidence right, is that she cultured some tetanus bacteria, gave her husband the date-rape drug rohypnol to knock him out and keep him from remembering she punctured him with a needle and squirted tetanus in him."

"Yes," said Diane. "Add that to the fact that she fabricated a false family history for herself, she never gave us her true identity that could be verified, and her previous husband died an untimely death, and you can see why she was convicted."

He let out a deep breath. "I must say, I'm disappointed."

Diane could see he was. She felt sorry for him. He was a man wanting to believe in people who were constantly disappointing him.

"So am I," she said. "Clymene is intelligent and gifted. You can't help but wonder what she might have become if she had taken a different path in life."

"We'll never know," he said. "She tells people that too much was made of her creative scrapbooking. She's never mentioned the cotton ball."

"You know Clymene loves horses," said Diane. "She went to a lot of trouble to make sure that hers went to a good home. Yet she never made a scrapbook of her riding or of her horse."

Rivers looked at her, frowning, as if trying to understand what that had to do with anything.

"The scrapbooks were just tools of her trade, part of the con. Her horse and her riding were true loves for her. She kept them out of the lie."

He nodded and stood. "I'm seeing the picture now. Thanks for telling me." He reached out and shook her hand as she stood.

"Thank you for speaking with me." Diane wanted to say she was sorry but felt anything she said might be embarrassing to him. Clymene had won him over before he had even realized it. Diane was more convinced than ever that Archer O'Riley wasn't the only person Clymene had killed. She was just too good at her job to have done it only once.

Rivers walked her back to the gate, where she was again let out of the maximum-security section. She was glad to leave the prison and didn't want to go back anytime soon. She had quit human rights work because she was just too sick of mass graves. That's what prisons were like to her—a mass grave of the living. It was too depressing.

Chapter 6

Diane pulled into her parking space in front of the RiverTrail Museum of Natural History. The building almost always impressed her with its massive granite stones and nineteenth-century gothic architecture, looking like a medieval palace. On any ordinary day she would have paused to appreciate the many cars and tour buses that signaled good attendance at the museum. But not today.

On her way back from the prison Diane had stopped at a convenience store to get a cold drink when she saw the headlines on the Rosewood newspaper.

MAJOR SCANDAL AT RIVERTRAIL MUSEUM
Prominent Board Member Says Assistant Director to be Fired.
Director Diane Fallon Not Available for Comment.

Diane grabbed the paper and stood in the store reading it, oblivious to customers squeezing past her to get out the door.

"Son of a bitch," she muttered under her breath,

then paid for the paper, walked out, and got into her car, slamming the door.

Carrying the newspaper rolled up like a club, Diane entered the museum. There weren't any visitors in the lobby at the moment, but a tour was going on just beyond in the Pleistocene room. The voice of the docent telling a group of Japanese visitors about mammoths drifted into the lobby. A blond young woman wearing a white Richard III T-shirt sat at the information desk talking with a lanky, dark-haired young male docent in a matching T. Amber and Hunter, Diane noted mentally. She made it a point to remember the names of all her employees.

"Dr. Fallon," Amber called as Diane walked by.

Diane stopped. "Yes."

Amber spotted the paper in Diane's hand. "I guess you've seen that," she said.

Diane noticed that Amber had a copy of the newspaper just below the desktop. Undoubtedly she and Hunter had been discussing it. Their eyes stayed fixed earnestly on her.

"Yes, I've seen it," said Diane.

"It's not—" Amber began.

"No," said Diane, "it's not true."

"I told you," she said to Hunter before turning back to Diane. "There's a man from the FBI looking for you. I directed him to your office. I didn't know what else to do with him."

Diane could see the worry in both their faces.

"What is his name?" asked Diane.

"Kingsley. Ross Kingsley." Amber enunciated his name carefully. "He doesn't look like he is from the FBI. Don't they always have short hair?"

"He had a beard too," offered Hunter, as if maybe

the guy claiming to be from the FBI was an imposter, possibly a reporter.

"It's not about the museum," said Diane.

She watched them both relax as they realized it had something to do with the crime lab on the upper floor of the west wing. The museum staff called that part of the building the dark side and they called all things relating to the crime lab dark matters. She could see they had just mentally filed Ross Kingsley under dark matter.

"If any reporters come by, call Andie. Don't send them into the office," said Diane.

"Oh, we wouldn't do that," said Amber. The two shook their heads in unison.

Diane walked to her museum office. Her heels clicked on the shiny granite floor, almost keeping time with her rapid heart rate. The brief interaction with her employees hadn't mediated any of her anger and she was glad. Right now she wanted to be angry. She went through the large double doors and down the hall to her office.

Mike Seeger, the geology curator, was there entertaining Andie and Ross Kingsley with tales of his latest adventures in searching out extremophiles. Mike and Andie were wearing the same style T-shirts as Amber and Hunter. Mike greeted her with a wide grin. Andie was frowning.

Kingsley stood and nodded a greeting to Diane. He looked more like a history professor than an FBI profiler in his vest and suit. He started to speak but Andie got there first.

"Dr. Fallon," said Andie and paused as she saw the rolled-up newspaper in Diane's hand. "You've seen the article."

Diane nodded.

"Diane. I was hoping you could spare me a few minutes," said Kingsley quickly.

"I'm sorry, Ross. I have a board meeting in a few minutes. It will have to wait until after that." Diane turned to Mike. "If you have time, will you show Agent Kingsley around the museum?"

"Sure . . . " began Mike.

The telephone rang. Diane imagined that all Andie had been able to do all day was answer the telephone.

"Excuse me, Dr. Fallon," said Andie. "It's the DA. He's called several times. He insists on speaking with you."

"He insists? Tell him unless he wants me to jerk his arm out of its socket and beat him with the bloody end of it, he'll wait until I have time to call him."

"Ooookay," said Andie. She took the DA off hold. "Sir, Dr. Fallon can't be disturbed. She'll call you just as soon as she has a chance." Andie doodled with her pen as she listened. Her springy auburn hair bounced as she nodded into the phone. "I know, sir, but she is in a board meeting. It's likely to last a while, but she will return your call."

There was another pause and Diane could hear the DA's voice but not his words. *Just as well,* she thought.

"No, I'm sorry. I can't pass a note to her. That would disturb the meeting and I can't do that. She will call. I prom— He hung up on me," she said, holding the receiver out for all to see.

"Andie, ask Kendel to come to my office," said Diane.

"I don't think I've ever seen this side of you," said Kingsley. "I'll be glad to wait until after your meeting." He grinned at her, rubbing his shoulder. "But can you give me a hint about what Clymene wanted?"

Diane had started into her office, but she turned to

him. "Clymene is afraid that one of her guards has married someone like herself." Diane turned to her office without looking back.

"Okay, now, you can't drop a bomb like that and leave," he shouted after her.

Diane was already in her office and closing her door. She turned off the water fountain on her desk. Normally she liked the sound of the water running over the stones, but today it was annoying. She should have gotten a jump start on this situation when she read the first article. But she had been knee-deep in other things and Kendel had assured her there was nothing to it.

After a moment Kendel opened the rear door to Diane's office and quietly slipped in. She was dressed in a navy pinstriped suit and a pink shirt. Her brown hair, usually in some kind of twist, was down, just touching her shoulders. Her eyes were red and she looked tired. Her usual countenance, the tough-as-brass assistant director, was absent. Kendel was scared. Diane motioned for her to sit down.

"Diane, I know I told you the other day that this was nothing—"

The phone rang and Diane picked it up.

"I'm sorry to disturb you," said Andie. "It's the *Journal-Constitution*. Do you want to speak with them?"

"Thank you, Andie. Put them through."

She waited on the phone, frowning. This was just the beginning. Kendel sat staring at the photograph of Diane hanging suspended from a rope inside a dark cavern. Diane wondered if that was how Kendel felt, like someone dangling at the end of a rope.

"Diane Fallon?" said the voice on the other end of

the phone. "I'm Shell Sidney from the *Atlanta Journal-Constitution*."

Diane wondered if the reporter's name was really Sidney Shell and she had reversed it in order to have more gravitas.

"I've been trying to reach you in regard to the stolen antiquities."

"Stolen antiquities?" said Diane.

The reporter hesitated a beat. "The stolen antiquities that have been in the news. One of your own board members stated that Miss Williams, the—ah—assistant director, has been fired for purchasing antiquities that she knew were looted. What do you have to say about that?"

Chapter 7

"Your information is incorrect," said Diane.

"Which part of the story are you saying is incorrect?" The reporter asked.

"All of it. The entire story is no more than a collection of allegations, innuendo, and rumor," said Diane in what she hoped was a calm voice.

"What about your board member's statement?" asked the reporter.

"The statement as published was a misquote. I'm sure what she said was that if any employee were found to have dealt in stolen antiquities we would take the appropriate action."

"Are you saying that Miss Williams has not been fired?"

"She has not."

"And you're saying she is still assistant director at the museum?"

"Yes, she is. It is not the policy of the museum to fire or suspend its personnel based on rumors. Surely your newspaper has the same policy concerning its employees."

"Let me get this straight. You are saying that Miss

Williams did not purchase antiquities that were looted from Egypt?"

This is tricky, thought Diane. She had to respond. She had been stung by reporters who printed their own speculation as if it were truth. She had to be wary about how she worded any explanation.

"Before we purchase any antiquity for the museum, we research the provenance," said Diane. "We adhere to the highest international standards for authentication and certification. After an item arrives at the museum, we double-check its provenance before it is entered into our collection. The double-checking is done by a staff of museum employees not involved in initially acquiring the piece. Right now we have several acquisitions from various locations around the world going through that process. To date we have found nothing amiss with the provenances. I can e-mail you a copy of our acquisition policy if that will help."

"Are you saying that this whole thing is a fabrication by someone?" asked the reporter. "Why would they do that?"

"I can't say anything about the motives or behavior of some unknown person," said Diane. "I can only tell you that the articles were written without any attempt by the reporter to verify the information through this office."

"Have you been contacted by the Egyptian government or the FBI?" asked the reporter.

"No," said Diane, "no one has contacted us."

"So you are saying the whole thing is just a rumor?" asked the reporter.

"That is correct. If any stolen or improperly acquired item should come into our possession, our procedure will discover it. That's what it's for."

The reporter gave Diane her telephone number and asked her to call if anything developed. Diane said she would and hung up the phone.

Kendel was standing, examining the Escher prints hanging on the wall opposite the caving photographs. There were three prints in a row: a self-filling waterfall, a castle with endless ascending and descending staircases, and a tessellation of angels and devils. Kendel sat down when Diane hung up the phone.

"I suppose you will get lots of calls like that," said Kendel.

"Andie will field most of them," said Diane, looking at her watch. "In just a few minutes I have to face the board. Do you still stand by your assessment of the provenance?"

"Yes . . . well, I don't know." Kendel slumped in her chair. "In the beginning I was completely sure. This is something I'm good at. But now—I just don't know. I don't understand where any of this is coming from."

"This isn't like you," said Diane. "You are always self-assured. Is there anything you need to tell me?"

"Nothing that would help." Kendel ran her hands through her hair. "Since this article came out, I've been getting calls and e-mails accusing me of grave robbing, stealing, ethnocentrism, and other things too vile to mention."

"That's awfully quick," said Diane. "It was just out today."

"It started with that first article a few days ago," said Kendel. "And my name wasn't even mentioned in that one."

"The article was very vague," said Diane, wrinkling her brow.

"It was precise enough for some people," said Kendel. "I imagine that now there is going to be a flood of hate mail."

"Save all your mail and anything on the answering machine. Keep notes on any harassing phone calls you take in person. Is there anything else?" Diane sensed that there was.

"I got an e-mail rescinding my invitation to speak at the University of Pennsylvania seminars," said Kendel. Her gaze searched the room as though there might be something in Diane's office that would explain all of it. "I've worked hard building my reputation," she said, staring again at the photo of Diane at the end of the rope. She blinked and the tears spilled down onto her cheeks. "And this—it's like being struck by lightning—just suddenly out of the blue, all of this . . ." Diane handed her a tissue and she wiped her eyes. "And I don't understand even how the university found out so quickly."

Diane stared at Kendel for a moment, then glanced at her computer. "The University of Pennsylvania had you listed on their Web site as an upcoming speaker," she said. "I'm sure the reporter did an Internet search for your name and found it there. She must have contacted them."

"If that's true, it was cruel. What did the reporter think would happen? Don't they care if they ruin someone's life?" She wiped her eyes again. "I don't know what to do about this."

"I do," said Diane. She picked up the phone and called Jin. He was probably down in the basement in his new DNA lab caressing his equipment. "Jin," said Diane, "you are on break, aren't you?"

"Sure, Boss, I'm on my own time," he said. That was one thing Diane liked about Jin. He was always quick. She couldn't really use any of her crime scene personnel on non–DNA lab museum business—not at this point. But she could use them on their own time.

"I assume that Neva is on her break too," said Diane.

"Sure is," said Jin. "What can we do for you?"

"I want you to go to the conservation lab and open the crates marked . . . Just a minute." She looked up at Kendel.

"EG970 through EG975," said Kendel. "There are six boxes."

Diane relayed the numbers to Jin. "I need you to process the artifacts. No fingerprint powders or glues—these are antiquities. Use the big camera and high-contrast film for any latents. I also want every piece photographed from all angles, collect any dust and detritus you find, get a sample of the packing material—anything that might help us trace their origin. You can use powders on the outside of the crates."

"I get to use David's cameras," said Jin. "He'll love that."

Diane could almost see him grinning on the other end of the phone. To Jin everything was fun. Maybe she should send Kendel to take notes from him. "Don't forget the lighting in your zest to get into David's cameras," said Diane.

"Boss . . . I know about photographic enhancement and latent prints," he said in mock hurt.

"Good. I want you to be thorough and very fast." The question from the reporter about queries from the FBI nagged at Diane. She didn't want the objects to be confiscated before she had a chance to have a good look at them.

"Thorough and fast," said Jin. "Got it."

"Have Korey there as you work. We need to have

the conservator oversee the process. When you finish, search the National Stolen Art File and see if any of the pieces are in it."

"Will do," said Jin.

After hanging up with Jin, Diane immediately dialed David Goldstein, another member of her crime scene crew, who was supposed to be leaving for vacation today. David had worked with Diane at World Accord International when she was a human rights investigator and had been a friend for a long time. She hated interrupting his time off, but she knew he would love it.

"Diane," he said immediately, "want me to come in and look into that artifact thing I've been reading about?"

"You sound like you've been waiting by your phone," said Diane.

"It's a cell. I always wait by it. So that's why you called, isn't it? I figured you would need me."

"I'm sorry to intrude on your vacation," said Diane.

"It's not an intrusion. You know how I've been dreading it. So is that why you called?" he asked again.

"Yes, it is. You can start by interviewing Kendel."

"Great. I'll be right there. And thanks. You don't know how I've been hoping for something to do."

"I thought you were going to be doing some traveling," said Diane.

"I was, but then what do I do when I get there?"

"Go sightseeing?"

"If I wanted to stand and look at stuff, I could stay at the museum and save on gas money."

"I'll be in a board meeting when you get here. Kendel will be in my office waiting for you."

When she hung up with David, she turned her attention back to Kendel, who sat looking like her world was coming to an end. Normally Kendel was tough. Diane wondered if there was something else, or perhaps Kendel was tough only when she had firm footing. Now, with the rug pulled out from under her . . .

"Kendel," said Diane a little sharper than she meant to, "David is going to investigate. He's the best. I've asked him to speak with you first. What I want from you is two things. First, find where you left your backbone. Then I want you to think about every interaction you had concerning the Egyptian artifacts. Every person you spoke with, anything, no matter how remote, that you noticed during the transactions, any casual person who happened to walk through the room while you were negotiating, anything."

Kendel nodded. "I appreciate your support. Everyone at the museum has been great."

Except for a certain member of the board, thought Diane. "You're innocent unless proven guilty," she said. "Stay here and wait for David." Diane stood up. "Now I have to deal with the board." She picked up the rolled newspaper from her desk.

Chapter 8

Andie looked up from her desk as Diane passed through her office on her way to the boardroom.

"Mrs. Van Ross is with the board members," Andie said.

The situation must be critical, thought Diane. More than any other single person, Vanessa Van Ross *was* the museum. She and Milo Lorenzo had been the driving forces behind its development. She had shown caution not to undermine Diane's authority or to give the impression of undue influence over the operations of the museum. She rarely came to board meetings, trusting instead to give Diane her proxy vote. If Vanessa was in attendance, it meant she was more than just concerned; she was alarmed at the possible harm to the reputation of the museum—Milo's museum and hers.

Milo hired Diane to be assistant director under him. He died of a heart attack before the museum even opened, and the governance he had set up for himself went to Diane—a governance that gave Diane more power than the board. Still, under extraordinary circumstances they could remove her. It was going to be an interesting meeting.

Diane started out the door, hesitated. Clymene's concern for Grace Noel nagged at her. Damn, if she hadn't enough to do. She turned back to Andie and pulled the piece of paper from her pocket with Grace Noel Tully's information written on it that Rev. Rivers had given her.

"Andie, get this woman on the phone for me. When you find her, transfer the call to the office in the boardroom." Andie nodded. "This is the only interruption I want," Diane said.

"Got you . . . MOF. . . ." said Andie, nodding her head up and down as she read the card.

MOF was Andie's abbreviation for *museum on fire*, which meant only in a dire emergency did Diane want to be disturbed.

Diane cocked an eyebrow at Andie. "If the museum's on fire, just let me and the board go up in the conflagration," said Diane.

Andie giggled and reached for the telephone. Diane left the office, still holding the rolled-up newspaper.

The board members were waiting for her in the third-floor meeting room. Diane wasn't in a hurry to get there. She needed to regain her focus. On the way up she reread the newspaper article to rekindle her anger and her indignation. It worked. What could board member Madge Stewart have been thinking?

Diane knew the answer to that question. Madge liked to feel important and in the know. She also liked to blame others for her own lapses in judgment. How she must have enjoyed it when Ms. Boville called for her opinion. No one on the board ever did.

It probably was not simple chance that led the reporter to the one board member who was most likely to speak unguardedly to her. Someone had primed the reporter and pointed her toward the weakest link.

Diane looked again at the byline—Janet Boville. She didn't know her. She wondered if David could wheedle out of the reporter the name of the person who started this whole mess. Perhaps not without extreme trickery.

Madge Stewart was on the board of directors because her parents were friends of the Van Rosses and had donated a substantial sum to the museum. Madge had studied art and she worked as an illustrator for a publishing company in Atlanta. Added to her trust fund, her work should have provided her with a good living. But Madge had reached her mid-fifties, and Diane sensed she was feeling that life was passing her by.

Diane didn't hesitate at the door when she reached the meeting room. She opened it and walked in. They were all there—Vanessa; Laura Hillard, a psychiatrist and Diane's friend; Harvey Phelps, retired CEO; Madge Stewart; Kenneth Meyerson, CEO of a computer company; and the newest members—Martin Thormond, American history professor at Bartram; Thomas Barclay, a bank president; and Anne Pascal, schoolteacher and Georgia Teacher of the Year.

They were divided up—old Rosewood families on one side of the table and more recent residents on the other. *Recent* meant having great-grandparents who weren't from Rosewood. It was odd how social boundaries were subconsciously maintained.

They all looked up as she entered. Laura smiled slightly. Vanessa didn't smile, but she rarely did in board meetings. All their faces reflected the seriousness of the situation. Their frowns deepened when they saw Diane. She must look as pissed off as she felt.

Thomas Barclay looked at her with dark, serious eyes over glasses pushed forward on his nose. His bushy eyebrows met in the center as he frowned. She wondered how many loans he'd turned down with that weighty expression. Laura told her that he had been shocked to discover how much power Diane had and how little the board had. She said he had been lobbying Vanessa to make changes. Were it not that the governance was Milo's plan—and as far as Vanessa was concerned, Milo was a saint—she might have considered it.

Diane reminded herself that most of the people in the room were her friends. Not because she was nervous about what they were going to say to her, but because she was angry—angry with the reporter, with Madge, and with all of them for insisting on a board meeting. Before the meeting was over, she intended to wipe that what-do-you-have-to-say-for-yourself look off Barclay's face.

Diane went to her place at the head of the long, polished mahogany table, unrolled the newspaper, smoothed it down on the shiny surface, and sat down. She looked at Madge, then at the others.

"This article has created a problem for the museum," she said in an even tone.

"It looks to me like Miss Williams has created the problem," interrupted Barclay. "Has she been suspended?"

Diane looked over at him. "Mr. Barclay, you are trying to apply solutions when you don't know what the problem is."

She turned her attention back to the rest of the board. They looked startled. Were they surprised she hadn't come hat in hand? They were all frowning except Kenneth Meyerson, who winked at her. *Don't make me smile*, she thought.

"The museum's reputation is seriously threatened," continued Barclay.

He said that for Vanessa's sake, thought Diane. He knew what phrases would get to her. Diane also knew that Vanessa would listen to what she had to say . . . and Vanessa was no fool. She came from a family of centenarians and supercentenarians and had more than sixty years' learning from their experiences.

"Mr. Barclay, a museum's reputation is always in danger. That's the reality of an enterprise that depends on acquiring objects in a field fraught with looters, smugglers, forgers, grave robbers, and sharks. That's why we have procedures and a code of ethics for dealing with acquisitions."

"Well, it looks like your procedures and ethics don't work." He tapped the table with his middle finger, reaching toward the newspaper in front of her.

"How do you know?" asked Diane.

"What?" he said, clearly surprised by her question.

"How do you know the procedures didn't work?" repeated Diane.

"Look at the news." This time his tapping was more of a hammering. "The newspapers . . . then television . . . now that damn radio talk show . . ."

"You accept that as authoritative? And where did the newspaper get its information?" she interrupted.

He hesitated, glanced at Madge beside him and then at the others.

"Where there's smoke there's usually fire," he said, still giving her his you-don't-get-the-loan look.

Diane saw Laura wince. She knew how Diane hated bad analogies.

"No, Mr. Barclay. Often there's just someone lobbing smoke bombs."

His eyebrows parted as he looked at her for a moment.

Diane didn't wait for a response. "When Dr. Williams finds an object for the museum, she researches the provenance before authorizing a purchase. If she needs to, she hires independent appraisers. Once the item is here, its provenance is audited by our staff. If Dr. Williams' research is in error, the second check will find it. When the Egyptian artifacts came to us they were stored in the conservation lab, where they remain, unopened, awaiting the audit of their provenance. *No one* yet knows if there is a problem with them." Diane cast her gaze around the table at all of them.

"Let me explain to you what this article did." She laid her hand flat on the newspaper. "It reports that a board member, Madge Stewart, admits that Dr. Williams knowingly purchased looted artifacts and that RiverTrail Museum possesses stolen antiquities." Diane stopped to let that sink in. "And the story has been picked up by other news outlets.

"The consequences to Dr. Williams have been severe. She's getting hate mail calling her a thief and worse. The University of Pennsylvania canceled her lecture series. Out of the blue, her reputation is in tatters with no proof whatsoever of wrongdoing. As for the museum—at best we look incompetent, at worst we look disreputable." Diane paused. The board members exchanged glances.

"Why did you think it was true?" Laura asked Madge.

"The reporter told me it was," she said.

"Oh, Madge," muttered Vanessa.

"Christ," said Barclay, snatching off his glasses.

"Why would she say it was true if it wasn't?" Madge

looked around to each board member, challenging them to offer an answer.

"If our goal is to protect the reputation of the museum," said Martin Thormond, "perhaps we should just give the items in question back."

Diane was shaking her head even before he finished. "Protecting the reputation of the museum is more than making sure we don't display stolen antiquities. We must also protect our ability to acquire them. If it's known that all it takes for us to back off an acquisition is an anonymous accusation, then we have seriously crippled our ability to compete in a very competitive world. And I also want to add that an important part of our reputation is how we treat the people we employ. The people here look to me to protect them—and I will."

Diane stood, walked to a bookshelf, and came back with two magazines she laid on top the newspaper. "*Best Aging* magazine lists Rosewood in the top ten places to retire to. In citing the reasons for the selection they named the RiverTrail Museum of Natural History." She pointed to the other magazine. "*Good Working* named RiverTrail in its list of top one hundred best places to work in the Southeast—citing treatment of employees."

Her gaze took them all in before she spoke again. "This is a good museum and a good place to work. Because of the efforts of Dr. Williams and Dr. Seeger, our geology department has one of the best reference collections in the country. Students from several large universities in the region come here to study our specimens. That kind of scholarly caliber was one of Milo Lorenzo's goals for the museum. I will not let all we have accomplished be sabotaged by rumors." Diane wondered if her face looked as hot as it felt.

"Where did the newspaper get the information in the first place?" asked Harvey Phelps. He had been fingering a copy of the newspaper tucked away on his lap. Diane noticed that he had looked sheepish the entire meeting. Another friend who felt guilty confronting her.

Most of the members had remained quiet, perhaps letting Barclay be the bad guy, a role he seemed to relish. Diane supposed they hadn't said anything because all the words they had for her were of reproof and they hadn't wanted to scold her. But they had wanted answers.

"I don't know who the original source was," said Diane. "But I will find out. Someone set out to do us harm. And I will find out who they are."

Harvey smiled at Diane. He tried making it the avuncular smile he usually had for her, but it came up a little short. "What are we doing about the problem?" he asked.

"I've told the registrar's office . . . " Diane noticed a puzzled look from the newer members. "That's where we review provenances," she explained. "I told them to start reviewing the provenance for the Egyptian artifacts immediately. My best detective has agreed to cut short his vacation and find the source of this attack on us."

"Our bank uses a good detective agency I can recommend," offered Barclay.

Diane supposed he wanted to purchase back some of the ground he had lost by now being helpful. She really wanted to ask him what a bank needed with a detective agency.

"David will do an excellent job," said Diane.

"Professionals in the field will do a better job than museum people," he said. "I'm sure your people are good at researching artifacts, but this investigation needs to be out in the real world."

Diane didn't believe that he meant to be insulting. He was just one of those people who was out of touch with anything that wasn't in his world. She folded her arms and looked at him for a moment.

"I think you're forgetting that Diane's also director of the crime lab over in the west wing," said Kenneth Meyerson. "Her people are pretty professional in the real world."

"Yes. Well, I suppose I must have forgotten. One doesn't think of that in a museum," he said.

"How is Kendel?" interrupted Vanessa.

Vanessa liked Kendel—well enough to let the assistant director talk her out of a ten-thousand-dollar diamond to put in the gemstone reference collection.

"Not well at the moment. As you can imagine, this has been devastating," said Diane.

Madge looked up suddenly from somewhere deep in her thoughts. "You don't think she will sue me, do you?" she asked.

"I would," said Diane.

Madge sucked in her breath and her eyes grew large and round. She looked frightened. Diane hoped she would think before she spoke from now on.

"But what should I have said?" asked Madge. "The woman said Kendel was guilty."

"You say you have no comment, and then refer them to me," said Diane. "That would be good for all of you. The charter specifies the director as the official spokesperson for the museum. I'm the one with the most up-to-date information. And we do have policies in place to handle these matters."

They nodded, muttering among themselves in agreement. Barclay sat looking at his glasses. Diane noticed he no longer looked as if he were going to make her explain herself.

The room was tense and Diane wanted to leave it that way. The mission of the board was advisory, and they had offered only recriminations. However, her friend Laura sat smiling brightly. Laura liked to end things upbeat. Diane supposed it was the psychiatrist in her. Diane started to adjourn when she heard the phone ringing in the adjacent office.

"I have to take this call," said Diane. Ignoring the frown Barclay gave her, she left the table and entered the small, bare, little-used office off the boardroom. It had a large window that allowed her to watch the boardroom.

She picked up the phone. "This is Diane Fallon. Is this Grace Noel Tully?"

Chapter 9

"Yes, I'm Mrs. Grace Tully," said the voice on the other end of the phone. "The girl said something about your being the director of the museum?" She emphasized the word *Mrs.* and ended with a slight giggle. Grace had a childlike voice that probably made her mistaken for a kid on the phone.

Okay, Diane thought, *she's not dead. Now what? Tell the woman that I'm happy to find her alive?*

"I'm working with FBI agent Kingsley, the profiler . . ." Diane began.

"Oh, I know him . . . but the girl who called said you worked at the museum . . ." she repeated.

"I'm also director of the crime lab," said Diane.

"Oh, I think I knew something about that. What can I do for you?"

"I was wondering if we could meet and talk about one of the prisoners."

"Well, I'm kind of in the middle of my honeymoon . . ." She giggled again. It was a girlish sound that made Diane sense her happiness even over the phone.

"I did hear that you had just gotten married. Congratulations," said Diane, testing the waters. "How do you like married life so far?" Diane hoped she sounded sufficiently friendly and congratulatory.

Diane watched the board members as she spoke. Madge looked like she would like to curl into fetal position. Laura was smiling, trying to keep the conversation light, Diane guessed—Laura the peacemaker. Barclay cleaned his glasses again. Probably wondering how to recover his alpha status.

"I love it, just love it. Eric, my husband, has a daughter, Julie—just a living doll. I became a wife and a mother. I'm so lucky. I just have to pinch myself every day."

"So you're on your honeymoon?" said Diane.

Grace told her that she and Eric had just returned from Gatlinburg, where they had a shortened honeymoon because they didn't want to be away from Eric's daughter, Julie, for long. "We are leaving in a few days on a sort of family vacation," she said.

"Where are you planning on going?" asked Diane.

Grace laughed again. "Can you believe we haven't decided yet? Eric wants to take a trip across the country and visit the national parks—he's always wanted to see the Grand Canyon. I think that might be a little tiring for Julie. I'd love to take her to Disney World. We've also talked about a cruise."

Grace Noel Tully sounded happy and Diane didn't want to ruin it. Truthfully, she only partly believed Clymene; on the other hand, the thought of the Grand Canyon and an ocean cruise gave her pause. She glanced at her board again and made up her mind.

"Agent Kingsley would like to speak with you before you leave again," said Diane. It was Kingsley, after all, who had sent her to see Clymene. He could take care of the consequences. Besides, she didn't feel competent to assess whether or not Grace Tully had married a serial killer. That was Kingsley's expertise.

"I'm not sure. . . . Eric's been after me to quit and be a stay-at-home mom and I'll admit, it appeals to me. . . ."

"Are you familiar with Clymene O'Riley?" asked Diane.

"Oh, Lord, yes. She's one of the more interesting inmates. Is this about her?" asked Grace.

"Yes," said Diane—only half lying, she told herself. "Kingsley is profiling her and it would help the FBI a great deal if you would speak with him. Briefly," she added.

"Well . . ."

"And I would be happy to throw in free tickets to the museum for you and your family," said Diane.

"Oh, that would be nice. Julie would love that. . . . Well, you could give me your number and I'll see if I can fit it in," said Grace. "I would prefer not to tell Eric. He's very insistent on wanting to take care of me."

Diane gave Grace her cell phone number and told her to call her anytime. She wanted to give her a word of caution but was afraid she would scare her into not seeing Kingsley.

Diane placed the phone on the hook and looked out at the board members before she made a move toward the door. Barclay was smiling. Even Madge was sitting straighter. She walked out the door and took her place at the head of the table. Maybe there was a way to undo some of the cheer that Laura was spreading around.

Barclay and Madge weren't jovial, but they were in better spirits than when Diane had left the table.

Diane didn't believe, as Laura did, that it was always a good thing for people to leave on a positive note. Diane didn't believe that Madge or Barclay needed to be feeling good about themselves until some of the damage to Kendel and the museum was undone. She sucked in a breath of air, frustrated at being unable to make them understand the harm done to Kendel. She was also left with a nagging fear for Grace Tully.

"Tell me," Laura said before Diane had a chance to speak, "why is everyone wearing those Richard the Third T-shirts? Are you planning a Richard the Third exhibit?"

"One is in the works for next year," said Diane. "The planners had Richard the Third T-shirts made for the opening. They're wearing them now to support Kendel," said Diane.

The identical blank stares that Diane saw in the faces around the table would have been humorous in another situation.

Kenneth gave her a self-deprecating grin. "You know, Diane, I'm just a computer salesman. You're going to have to explain that."

"I'm ashamed to say the subtlety is lost on me too," said Martin Thormond, the history professor.

"Isn't he the one who killed his nephews?" said Laura. "How does that support Kendel?"

"I don't understand either," said Harvey Phelps, a slight laugh barely escaping his throat. "My wife and I saw *Richard the Third* in Atlanta last year at the Fox. I can't really see how that's going to give her any moral support whatsoever—if that's the aim."

Diane hesitated a moment. She stood and gathered the magazines and the newspaper from the table, grateful for the nice opening that Laura gave her for another attempt to make them understand.

"You have to keep in mind that Shakespeare's play was fiction based on an unclear history. There's historical evidence to support Richard's innocence. Many believe it was Henry Tudor, Richard's conqueror, who had the princes killed. Richard wasn't blamed for it until about a hundred years after his death."

"I can see where that's the ultimate cold case . . . but for supporting Dr. Williams?" began Kenneth. "I mean, why a long-dead king? I don't get it."

"Richard was loved by his subjects," said Diane. "His reign wasn't long, but in his short time he instituted judicial and legal reforms that we still hold sacred today. He established bail for everyone, not just the wealthy. He outlawed seizure of property before an accused was convicted. He reformed the jury system so that a verdict could not be bought. And he told his judges to dispense justice equally to all classes. Underlying all of his judicial reforms was the revolutionary concept of *the presumption of innocence*—a gift he was denied by history, but one the staff intends to give to Kendel."

Diane paused a moment, gratified to see many of them frowning again. "There are books in the library on his reign if you are interested. Now, I need to get back. Madge, you need to come with me. David will want to interview you."

"Me? Why?" Madge scooted back in her chair as if afraid Diane was going to hit her.

"We need to find out who is behind this," said Diane.

"But . . . I don't know. The reporter didn't tell me," insisted Madge.

"There may be something in the way she asked the questions that could give us a clue. It won't take long and you need to help solve this."

"But I really don't want to take the chance of running into Miss Williams," said Madge.

"Really?" said Diane. "I would have thought you would welcome the opportunity to apologize to Dr. Williams."

Barclay cleared his throat. "If there's any chance that Dr. Williams might take action," he said to Madge, "it might not be a good idea to apologize to her. It would be an admission."

"Indeed," said Diane, eying them both. "Well, I'll leave that to you and your conscience. However, I do need you to speak with David, Madge."

"I'll go with you," said Vanessa. "I certainly need to say something to Kendel." She turned to Diane. Her lips curved up almost to a smile. "I would say that I know how difficult this meeting was for you, but I don't think it was."

Diane smiled back at her. "All in a day's work."

The board members began to drift out of the room. Diane made for the door, escaping with them. Vanessa walked ahead with Madge. Diane had the feeling that Madge would like to break loose at the first opportunity.

"You know," said Laura when Madge and Vanessa were out of hearing, "it's our fault. We don't take Madge seriously at all. It's no wonder she would confide in someone who said they valued her opinion."

"She's an adult," said Diane. "And she is not stupid. I think none of her friends or relatives have ever held her accountable for anything."

Laura looked at Diane. "That's rather harsh. She may have lived a sheltered life, but—"

"You don't have a sympathetic listener today," said Diane. "Try another day. I know Madge Stewart isn't a bad person, but I had just finished speaking with Kendel before I came down here. She's worked hard for her reputation, and to have a university like Pennsylvania take back their offer for her to speak is a blow. And I know what it's like to get hate mail."

"You're right of course," said Laura. "I know Vanessa likes Kendel and she will do what she can for her. But you must look at it from our side. We don't know that Kendel didn't go over the line just a little to get some really nice items. You have to consider that. I'm not saying she was dealing in stolen artifacts to make money, I'm just saying I know that museums are competitive, and curators and assistant directors might sometimes cross the line just a little."

They arrived at the bank of elevators. The others had already gone down, and she and Laura were alone. Diane was poised to push the elevator button but didn't. She studied Laura for a moment. Apparently Richard III hadn't impressed her at all.

"I deal in facts," said Diane. "And right now I don't have any. Anonymous accusations of serious wrongdoing bear investigating but do not warrant a conclusion of guilt."

"I know, and you are right." Laura gestured with her hands as if she were trying to hold something back. "I'm just wondering if you are prepared to be wrong. I know you like Kendel. All of us who know her like her. But she does have a reputation for being a hard-nosed negotiator when it comes to acquisitions."

Diane stepped back from the elevators and took a deep breath. "I'm trying to tell you that it doesn't matter what I feel or whom I like. This is an empirical problem. It will be solved by empirical means. In the meantime, Kendel will be thought of as innocent. If she turns out to be guilty, it will be because we discovered it from evidence, not because of rumors and accusations."

Laura nodded. "Okay. I'm just bringing up some issues. I didn't see the report, but Vanessa was really upset when she saw the noon news on TV. She said it was just a rehash of the newspaper article, but it ended by saying that RiverTrail would be investigated and the reporter couldn't find you to talk to you. You know how that sounded."

Diane laughed. "Like I'd skipped town with the loot? Come on. I thought everyone in the state knew I have two jobs."

"I know, but we couldn't reach your cell phone," said Laura.

Diane reached over and punched the elevator button. "I was conducting an interview inside a prison. They don't allow cell phones."

Laura hesitated a moment. "Diane, I know Thomas Barclay can sound a little gruff, but he's all right. He really does respect you. He just likes to have his hand in things. You know, he thinks he needs to oversee everything."

"You need to warn him about making bad analogies around me," said Diane.

Laura laughed. "At least it wasn't a sports metaphor."

The elevator doors opened and they entered. So this was how Vanessa was handling her concerns, thought Diane. Not in front of the whole board, but privately—friend to friend. It probably meant that Thomas Barclay had initiated his interrogation during the board meeting on his own. Her phone vibrated again. She pulled it out of her pocket. It was a text message from the people checking the provenance on the Egyptian artifacts. They needed to see her immediately.

Chapter 10

Diane parted ways with Laura on the ground floor after declining an invitation to have coffee and cake in the museum restaurant with her and some of the other board members.

"Give them my regrets," she said. "I have Jin and Neva inspecting the artifacts. I need to see if they've found anything." She did not want to mention the cell message to Laura until she knew what it was about.

"Are we okay?" asked Laura, laying a hand on Diane's arm.

"You mean about the board meeting?" said Diane, shrugging her shoulders. "Something like this is likely to come up again in the future. We all need to be calm about it."

"You're right. We live in such a bubble here in Rosewood," said Laura.

Some of us do, thought Diane. As director of the crime lab, her bubble had been burst a while back. She took the elevator to the second floor, where her legal researchers were waiting in the conservation lab.

At first glance the conservation laboratory might look like little more than a room full of tables, each with different works in progress. Closer inspection would reveal varieties of microscopes, a fume hood, a suction table, photographic equipment, and other instruments designed to stabilize, protect, and record the many items brought to the lab.

Korey Jordan, a tall African American in his early thirties, was head conservator. He and his staff stood with Jin and Neva and with Harold and Shirley, the provenance checkers. Before them lay the suspect artifacts. A dead body on the table would not have produced a more solemn group.

Well, damn. She so wanted good news.

Everyone looked up when Diane entered. Each was wearing a Richard III T-shirt—except Harold the registrar, only because he thought Richard III was guilty. Even Jin and Neva wore the white shirts with Richard III's picture on the front. Diane hoped that Kendel was comforted by this show of support by the staff.

"What have you found?" she asked as she neared the table. They parted to let her see the artifacts.

They're beautiful, she thought as her gaze rested on them. A necklace containing the image of an Egyptian deity on a pectoral of gold, lapis lazuli, and turquoise lay on a piece of linen. Next to it on the same piece of linen was a circlet made from gold beads shaped like cowrie shells. Diane recognized it as a girdle to adorn the waist. Next to it was a simple canopic jar with a lid in the shape of a jackal's head. Three other artifacts were of stone. There was a bust of red granite about a foot and a half high with the nose broken off and a quartzite face also without its nose. On the floor still in its crate was a small granite sphinx about three feet in length and almost as tall. The staff were quiet as Diane looked over the artifacts.

Harold stepped forward and gestured to another

table, where he'd placed open folders containing documents and photographs.

"We were evaluating the documents and everything was looking great," he said. "Everything was in order."

Shirley, one of his legal researchers, stepped up and nodded her head. "The documents are fine. They are authentic."

"Then why does everyone look so grim?" asked Diane.

"When we brought the documents down to compare the photographs with the items . . . " began Harold.

Diane saw it before he finished. The folder in front of her contained documents for the girdle. The photograph showed a circlet formed from lion heads made of gold alternating with polished amethyst beads, not the girdle on the table made of gold cowrie shell beads.

She looked at another set of documents. The photograph showed a gold and jeweled necklace containing the image of the Egyptian deity Senwosret III. The necklace on the table was similar, but it wasn't the same.

"These artifacts don't belong to these documents," finished Harold.

Diane looked at the photographs of all six items. They were all similar, very similar at first glance, to the items on the table, but not the same.

Well, damn.

Diane thanked Harold and Shirley for their work. They took that as a dismissal and started to leave.

"Do you want to keep the documents here?" asked Harold.

"For now," said Diane. "I'll return them to you

today so you can continue researching." She paused a moment. "Everyone remember, all information flows from me."

They all nodded. The legal researchers left and Korey's conservation staff drifted back to their own work, leaving Jin, Neva, and Korey with her and the undocumented Egyptian artifacts.

"Have you finished with these for now?" Diane asked Jin and Neva.

Deven Jin, Neva Hurley, and David Goldstein were her crime scene specialists. They all enjoyed the museum as a welcome escape from their grim work of processing crime scenes. Right now they didn't look like they were having fun.

"We've photographed and collected about everything we can," said Jin. He pushed his straight black hair out of his face. "I'll go back and develop the film, but I can tell you now, there weren't any prints."

Diane wasn't surprised. Professional museologists would have worn gloves while handling the artifacts. So would smart thieves.

"We got some dust samples from the stone artifacts," said Neva. "If we are lucky we may be able to find out what part of the world they've been in."

"Go do your best," said Diane. "Do the crime lab stuff first. This is just your free-time activity. And thank you."

"Sure," said Jin. His dark eyes sparkled. "Now that I've had my coffee, I'll get back to the Dark Side."

"Ask Kendel to come to the conservation lab," said Diane. "She should be in my office or hers."

Neva nodded. "We'll check the photographs against the NSAF and see if anything turns up." She and Jin left, hauling David's camera equipment with them.

"You guys can take a break," Korey said to his staff

of conservators. They took off their gloves and walked together out of the lab, leaving their work on the table. "Take a long break," Korey called after them.

"We'll order a pizza," said one of the guys.

"You know," said Korey, "Kendel would know better than this. She would have been nuts to try . . . " He put a hand on the back of his dreadlocks. "Actually I'm not sure what was done. What's the point of this? If Kendel was involved in an attempt at deception, she would have forged the documents. She knows our procedures. She knows the items would be checked against the documents."

"We know that," said Diane. "But I'm afraid the authorities might not stop to look at the finer points. They could just see Kendel's name on the purchase order and think she was trying to launder stolen antiquities with real documents."

"I hear you there. They can be awfully dense sometimes."

Korey was still pissed about the time he was interrogated by the police as a suspect for no other reason than that he was an African American male with dreadlocks.

"How did it go with the board?" he asked. "Scuttlebutt says you ripped them a new one. What's going on with the board, anyway? Is it the new guys?"

"One new member is unaccustomed to the way we do things," said Diane. "But I'm afraid my ripping them a new one is an exaggeration. They all got just a little nervous after reading the items in the paper and hearing the news broadcast."

"Well, I don't blame them there. It was kind of bad," said Korey. He shrugged and turned toward the artifacts. "Too bad we can't keep these. They're really nice pieces."

"They are. But now they don't have a pedigree. I wonder who's doing this? Who tipped the newspaper and who—" Diane stopped when she heard the door open.

Kendel came in. She looked better. She had reapplied her makeup and was wearing a smile. David was good at cheering people up when he tried. One wouldn't think he had that talent, as paranoid and pessimistic as his personality was.

"Neva said you wanted to see me," she said.

Diane nodded.

"I'll be in my office," said Korey. He walked up to Kendel and put a hand on her shoulder. "Hang in there."

She placed a hand over his. "Thanks, Korey. I really appreciate all of you guys."

"I just want to get on your good side for the next time I need to requisition something," he said, then smiled at her and walked on to his office beyond.

"David's a sweetheart," said Kendel. "He got me to remember more than I thought I could about my visits to Golden Antiquities."

"David's good at that," said Diane.

"I've been thinking about this," said Kendel. "There's simply no way I could have made a mistake. I know how to verify provenances. For heaven's sake, I've seen all these on display at the Pearle . . ."

As she spoke her gaze rested on the table of artifacts and her eyes grew wide.

Chapter 11

Kendel stood for a long moment staring at the artifacts on the table, then at the sphinx in the crate. She shook her head, frowning.

"These aren't the artifacts I purchased."

She examined each piece. "There's a passing similarity, but that's all. These are all different dynasties." She looked up at Diane. "I was so excited when I found out that the Pearle Museum had sold some of their pieces to Golden Antiquities—they were all twelfth dynasty. That's what we are building in the Egyptian room—Egyptian antiquities that match our mummy's twelfth-dynasty date." She looked over at Diane. "I've never seen these."

"Did you see anything like them at Golden Antiquities?" asked Diane.

"No, nothing." Kendel noticed the documentation lying on the opposite table. She leafed through the pages and photographs. "These are the correct provenances for the items I bought. These are the documents I verified. Do you think they just sent the wrong items?"

"Maybe," said Diane. "I suppose someone could have just . . . what? Read only part of the tag on an object and decided that was the one. But all six?" She shook her head. "We'll certainly follow up with Golden Antiquities to verify that there was no accidental mix-up. But it looks like someone made an effort to substitute items similar to the documentation."

"You're right," said Kendel. "This is very deliberate."

"And we have to account for the person who called the newspaper in the first place," said Diane. "How did they know something was amiss in the unopened crates?"

Kendel turned to face Diane. "What's this about? Why did someone go to this much trouble?"

"I don't know. But we'll find out," said Diane.

"Have you been contacted by the FBI?" Kendel asked. She fingered the pages, looking again at the photographs and back at the artifacts as if she could will them to change into the right thing.

"No, but I expect to be. I think you need to prepare yourself for that," said Diane.

Kendel nodded. "Talking to David helped a lot. He calmed me down considerably."

"He's good at that." Diane looked at her watch. Ross Kingsley had probably gotten tired of waiting and left. No, he wouldn't have left but probably was tired of waiting, she thought. "Kendel, I have to go talk with someone." She held out her hand, motioning Kendel to follow.

Kendel looked blank for a moment, lost in thought. "I suppose I need to go too."

"Just so you can say you were never alone with the artifacts after they arrived. It probably won't matter, but it might," said Diane.

Kendel looked at Diane with wide eyes, suddenly

unsure again. "Surely they will believe that I didn't have anything to do with this. The provenances are always reverified after they arrive—verified by someone other than me," said Kendel.

"I will explain our procedures in detail," said Diane.

She walked with Kendel, stopping at Korey's office. The office was mostly glass. He saw them coming and came out to meet them.

"Korey, would you repack the artifacts?" Diane asked.

"Sure thing, Dr. F," he said. "I'll do it myself. Andie called up here looking for you. Something about some guy from the FBI."

Kendel sucked in her breath. "Oh, no. I'm not ready for this."

Diane put a hand on her arm. "There's another person from the FBI here for a different reason entirely. I imagine it was he, wondering if I'd gotten lost somewhere among the displays. Why don't you go to your office and relax. Or spend some time meditating among the collections. I find them calming."

"That's a good idea," said Korey. "Let Dr. F figure this out. That's what the Dark Side does."

Diane found Ross Kingsley on the terrace drinking coffee and watching the swans on the pond. The early spring weather was still cool. There were buds on the trees but none had blossomed yet. Diane saw a couple of runners in the distance on the nature trail just before they disappeared around a bend.

"I'm sorry," said Diane taking a seat. "There's a lot going on."

He rose as she sat down and smiled. "So I've been reading." He pointed to a newspaper lying on the table. He set his cup down and turned his chair around to face her. "I've enjoyed your museum. I don't get much time for things like this. It was very relaxing."

"It is—most of the time," said Diane. A waitress came out of the restaurant and Diane ordered a cup of hot tea.

"Mike Seeger gave me a most interesting tour," he said, a knowing glint in his eye. "He's obviously taken with you."

Diane shook her head. "He just gives that impression."

Kingsley laughed. "I won't even pretend to know what that means." He took a sip of coffee. "I've been dying to know what in the world Clymene wanted with you. You said she was afraid that one of her guards had married someone like her? Was that an admission of guilt on her part?"

Diane shook her head.

The waitress came out with a small teapot and a cup. She poured Diane's tea and left them.

"Clymene didn't actually admit to anything, but it was my impression that she didn't care if I thought she was guilty."

Diane gave Kingsley an account of the visit. When she finished, he sat back in his chair in amazement.

"Of all the things I imagined she might want to talk with you about, I confess, that didn't cross my mind. Do you think there is anything in it? She said what— you would think that she could recognize her own kind?"

"Yes. I think that is as close to an admission of her guilt as you are going to get," said Diane.

"Are you going to check on—what's her name?— Grace Noel, I suppose Grace Tully now?" he asked.

"No," said Diane. "You are."

"Oh?" he said, his cup halfway to his lips.

"Some things Grace Tully said made me think that maybe Clymene was right—like maybe her husband is trying to separate her from friends." Diane shrugged. "You are better equipped to determine if she has married a killer than I," said Diane.

The waitress came out and refilled Kingsley's coffee and gave Diane a fresh pot of tea.

"Can I get the two of you anything? Chocolate cake? Apple cobbler?"

"None for me, thanks," said Diane. Kingsley shook his head and the waitress left. "Sure. I'll be happy to speak with Mrs. Tully," said Kingsley.

"That was easy," said Diane.

"What you have told me is sufficiently disturbing to warrant a look. Maybe he simply wants a traditional household with a stay-at-home wife; he may be just a controlling guy—or a killer." He gave a short laugh before he took another sip of his coffee. "Amazing how much credibility we are giving to Clymene's judgment. Tell me what you think about her," said Kingsley, his eyes glittering. "I would like to know your impression. Did you find that you liked her?"

Diane squinted at Kingsley. *Like her.* "I think she is very good at what she does," she said. "I didn't dislike her. I believe she's a killer. She knows I believe that, but . . ."

"But what?" Kingsley leaned forward, smiling.

"But that's it. I didn't dislike her. She won over Rev. Rivers, did you know that?"

"No, I didn't. You spoke with him?" Kingsley said.

"It was a spur-of-the-moment thing, but an interesting conversation. He didn't seem to know he had been drawn in by her until we talked."

"What do you mean?" he asked.

"He wanted to know the evidence presented in

court against Clymene and I went over it with him. His general comments and attitude were very subtly in defense of Clymene."

Kingsley's brow knitted together in a frown. "Did he believe the evidence?"

"Oh, yes. And he was visibly disappointed. I think he himself was surprised at how disappointed. The thing that is interesting to me is I think she knows not only what to say, but what not to say. That's—"

"Explain that." Kingsley leaned forward again. Diane had the impression that he wished he was taking notes or recording the conversation.

"I've spoken before with felons I've helped put in prison. Almost all of them have complained about what an injustice I've done them. And if they know anything about my background, they make some kind of jab about the death of my daughter. They've enjoyed twisting that knife.

"As you said," Diane continued, "Clymene is very low-key about proclaiming her innocence. With me, she made a joke of it. She let me know early in the conversation that her lawyer had researched my background. But she never once even alluded to my tragedy—subconsciously I noticed that.

"According to Rev. Rivers, she didn't proclaim her innocence to him either. With him she was simply helpful. She helped other prisoners in his classes. She didn't proclaim that she had found religion, which, as you know, is common. She listened to what Rivers had to say. That won him over and that is her special gift. Her methods are subtle and their effect is often subconscious. And that is why I think she's dangerous and why I think she has killed other husbands—she is so very accomplished."

Kingsley sat nodding as she spoke. When Diane stopped he was quiet for a long while.

"Interesting analysis," he said. "And I agree with it. It's hard to explain those subtleties to a jury. It's lucky you found that cotton ball filled with all that evidence." He relaxed, sitting back in his chair. "You know, I had to study hard to become a profiler—I still have to take workshops to keep up on the latest information. But Clymene is a natural."

"I believe you're right," said Diane. "I'm still just a little unsettled about what she wanted to speak with me about. You know, waiting for the other shoe to drop."

"You want me to give the DA a report on your visit with Clymene?" said Kingsley.

Diane eyed him suspiciously. "That would be good. I really don't have the time," said Diane. "Thank you. Talking to Grace, profiling her husband, talking to the DA. I don't know what to think. What should I think?" Diane stared at him.

Kingsley blushed under her steady gaze and grinned. "Actually I have a favor to ask."

"Favor? Does it have anywhere near the value of speaking to the DA and Grace for me?" asked Diane.

"No. I definitely will have to sweeten the pot," he said.

Chapter 12

"This sounds like something I would want to say no to," said Diane. She had pushed her teacup away and sat with her forearms resting on the table, scrutinizing Kingsley. She was envious of Clymene's ability to size people up so quickly that it seemed as if she was reading their minds.

"You will say no at first. I know that because I'm a profiler." He grinned.

"Okay, what is it?" asked Diane.

"I'm working on a book about Clymene and some other cases," he said.

"Clymene told me," said Diane.

Kingsley stopped, coffee halfway to his lips. He sat looking at Diane for several seconds.

"Okay, that's a surprise. I never told her," he said.

"Did you tell Rivers?" asked Diane.

"No. No one outside the FBI knows except you." He shook his head and finished his sip of coffee. "It must have been something in the way I asked questions, or my organization of the questions." He shrugged. "I told you she is a natural profiler. Anyway, I'm writing a book—"

"I didn't think FBI agents could do that," said

Diane. "Some prohibition against profiting from your work?"

"I'm writing a textbook to be used for training profilers. The idea is to do in-depth case studies of different types of serial killers," he said. "The classic killers that we already know so much about compared with killers like Clymene who are harder to detect and catch because their patterns aren't as obvious."

"Clymene was motivated by profit," said Diane. "Would she really be called a serial killer even if it turns out her body count is high?"

Kingsley nodded. "I think so, but there is debate about that. Motivation makes a big difference."

The wind picked up, sending them a cool breeze. Diane's paper napkin blew off the table and into the air. She jumped up and snatched it before it got away entirely. She had seen them take off like kites and sail out of sight.

"Let's go inside the restaurant," she said.

Kingsley looked at his watch. "Why don't we have an early dinner?"

"That's fine," said Diane, hoping because it was almost the end of the day that nothing else would happen concerning the Egyptian artifacts.

She nodded to the waitress, who followed as Diane went to an out-of-the-way booth in the back of the restaurant. Kingsley ordered prime rib. Diane ordered marinated salmon. After taking their orders, the waitress brought them both iced tea.

Kingsley took a drink of his tea and set it down. He pursed his lips together as though trying to recall what he was talking about.

"Yes, Clymene is a for-profit killer. I believe she married and killed her husbands for money. But she is distinguished by her modus operandi. Some serial killers get off on a particular killing fantasy, and the method of murder comes from that fantasy. Your typical for-profit serial killer will choose a single method like poison to use in all their murders because once they have used it successfully it is easy and safe for them. Where Clymene differed is she let circumstances dictate the method. The husband's manner of death had an integral connection to some typical activity in which he was often engaged."

Kingsley rested his elbows on the table and steepled his hands. "If we believe that Clymene killed Robert Carthwright, then she did it by causing the antique car he was working under to fall on him and crush him to death. Not an easy or safe method."

"What about the murder of Archer O'Riley—the only murder of which we have proof?" asked Diane. "Did she think his family and friends would believe he simply contracted tetanus while on a dig in a foreign country?"

"Why not?" said Kingsley. "Americans find it perfectly believable that a person might die of some bacterial infection in a foreign country, particularly if the victim is digging around in ancient contaminated soil."

"I suppose so," said Diane. "His son didn't suspect anything sinister."

"It was Clymene's bad luck that Archer O'Riley was a friend of Vanessa Van Ross," said Kingsley. "I doubt the police would have paid any attention to the suspicions of a Vanessa Jones, waitress, or even a Vanessa Smith, bank president. But Van Ross is one of the founding families in Rosewood, and the name carries a lot of weight. She convinced O'Riley's son that something wasn't right about the death and the two of them convinced the police. I don't have to tell you that it's only on television that all untimely deaths get the full treatment of a crime scene investigation unit. That you were called in was unusual. That you found the incriminating cotton ball was another bit of bad luck for Clymene. I'm sure she thought she had been very careful to clean away all evidence."

"I agree with all your points, but this concerns me how?" asked Diane.

The waitress brought their meal and neither spoke for several minutes as they ate. After several bites and comments on the quality of the meal, Kingsley put down his knife and fork.

"Right now, most of this profile of Clymene is just educated guessing on my part. I only have one real murder to go on—that of Archer O'Riley. Before I can go much further on Clymene, I have to know who she is—who she was before she married Robert Carthwright. I need to have more history, more information—probably more victims. I want you to find out her real identity for me."

"No," said Diane.

"See, I told you you would say no at first. Am I good or what?" Kingsley grinned at her.

"I don't have any spare time—I have two full-time jobs and a couple of outside interests that I would like to keep." *Not to mention a guy that I really love that I'd like to see occasionally*, she thought.

"Yes, I remember your caving," said Kingsley. "You really like that, do you?"

"Yes, I really do. There are very few things more relaxing," said Diane.

"*Relaxing* is not a word I'd use—but if that does it for you." Kingsley smiled and looked, as many did, as if he couldn't fathom the calming effects of caving. "And if I remember correctly, you are also seeing an Atlanta detective—white-collar crimes?"

"Yes. When I can," said Diane. "Something I'd also like to continue. And you were right. Your offer to relieve me of having to talk to the DA about my visit to the prison doesn't even come close to equaling so great a task as you are asking of me. Besides, you have the resources of the FBI behind you. Why do you need me?"

"She's a closed case," he said. "She's in prison for life. They aren't going to invest scarce resources running down theories and hypotheticals. If Clymene has other victims out there, I'd like to know, but the DA and the FBI have no official interest in her until evidence of other murders comes to light."

He shook his head and gestured as if he were grabbing at something intangible. "We usually discover serial killers by the body count of victims and a pattern in their murders. Some serial killers we don't catch because they choose the most vulnerable and the most invisible—runaways, prostitutes, illegal aliens—and the body count is less visible, less connected. But even then we get lucky fairly often." He stabbed a piece of prime rib with his fork.

"I believe there are more like Clymene out there who are just so clever, we never connect them to a murder," he said. "And in some cases we don't even know there was a murder. One of the things I want to do is to develop a method to spot those hidden serial killings. To do that I need every detail I can gather about known killers. I need to learn about Clymene's background and if there are any more husbands out there." He stopped and took a bite of his speared meat.

Diane shook her head, uncertain. "Even finding who she really is doesn't mean we will discover all of her identities. One possibility we discussed is that she may change identity after each kill and then move on to another victim."

He nodded. "Yes, and I still think that is a good possibility. But the closer we get to the real Clymene, the closer we will get to the other identities she established." He took a long drink of his tea. "I can see you have a busy schedule, but there are advantages to making me beholden to you," said Kingsley.

"And what would those be?" asked Diane.

He smiled and cut another piece of meat. "If I'm reading the newspapers correctly and picking up on the vibes from your staff, you are going to be visited by the FBI shortly because they have jurisdiction over art and cultural property crime. Now, while I don't have a lot of pull, I do know the agent assigned to this region and I can help ease the way for you." He speared the piece of meat and put it in his mouth.

"That would be worthwhile. But a friend would do that for me anyway," said Diane, grinning back at him.

"True, and I will. However, I can't imagine you not doing a favor in return," he said.

"I'll need all the evidence," said Diane.

"Is this a yes, then?" he asked.

"Yes. I'll give it a try," said Diane.

"Everything we have will be delivered to you."

"I know I'm going to regret this," said Diane, wondering when she would find the time. Of course, there was all that wasted time when she was sleeping. "You know, it seems that someone from her past would have recognized Clymene and come forward by now."

"I would have thought so," said Kingsley. "And she must have worried about that. You know she avoided having her picture taken. Her face in those scrapbooks was usually half covered with a cap or something. She didn't accompany her husband anywhere they might be photographed." He reached inside his jacket. "Did the waitress leave the check?"

"It's all right," said Diane. "Consider it recompense for having to wait all afternoon."

"You sure?" he asked.

Diane nodded.

"Thanks. I should have had a bigger steak." He smiled and put his wallet back in his pocket. "Did you ever meet her before the investigation? I know O'Riley came to some of the museum functions here," said Kingsley.

"No, I didn't. The one time Archer O'Riley came to a function here, he was with his son and daughter-in-law. That was the only time I ever met him." Diane thought for a moment. "There are her mug shots. I saw them in the Atlanta and Rosewood papers."

"Yes, but even I would hardly recognize her from those," said Kingsley. "Her mouth was turned down; she seemed to be . . . squinting, or something." He waved a hand. "It was a terrible photograph."

"Still, some people have an amazing ability to recognize people even from sketchy drawings," said Diane.

"All I know is, no one came forward. Not everyone reads the news, I suppose, and I'm not sure news coverage of the trial ever made it out of the region. I know her lawyer made sure Court TV didn't cover it," said Kingsley.

"You know," said Diane, "her other identities, if she had other identities, could easily have been in other countries. I know she speaks fluent French, and Rivers said her Spanish is quite good."

"That's a possibility. Do you think English is her first language?" asked Kingsley.

Diane nodded. "I do, but I'll ask a forensic linguist

to take a look at some of the journaling in her scrapbooks. I don't suppose you have a tape recording of
her speaking?"

"No. She didn't want me to record our conversa-
tions," said Kingsley.

"Could you get one?" asked Diane.

He raised his eyebrows. "Legally?"

"Of course," said Diane.

"I don't know. Let me think about that," he said.

"A linguist would be able to analyze her speech and
perhaps tell us at least if English is her first language
and might gather a clue as to what section of the country she grew up in."

"I'll see what I can do," he said. "If nothing else,
perhaps a forensic linguist could interview her."

"Have you considered that Robert Carthwright
might have been her first husband to die and that his
death was an accident? She could have liked the benefits a dead husband gave her so much that she decided
to make a career of it," said Diane.

He nodded. "I've thought about that, but I don't
think so. We were saying earlier how good she is at
getting people to like her. I was interviewing another
killer once—a marrying-for-profit murderer something
like Clymene." Kingsley's half smile looked more like
a grimace. He shook his head. "The son of a bitch
killed a woman's husband in order to woo and marry
her; then he killed her for the insurance. She had two
kids. He killed two people and destroyed a family for
a couple hundred thousand dollars and had no remorse whatsoever—total sociopath. I hated that guy.
I had a very hard time being objective while I interviewed him. Even now, just talking about him, I
hate him."

Kingsley leaned forward slightly. "Clymene killed

her husband in a terrible way. Tetanus is a frightfully painful way to die. And she shows no remorse for it. Yet, my feelings about her are different—I don't dislike her. I'm mainly neutral, but there are times when we are having a conversation, I actually like her. As you said, she has these ways of subconsciously getting to you. That takes not only talent, but practice and refinement. She does it to perfection. I think she's killed many more times and I think she started her career earlier than we might have imagined. And I don't think she's unique. I believe there are others like her out there who aren't even on the radar."

The waitress came and offered to fill their coffee cups. Kingsley nodded and pushed his toward her. Diane covered her cup with her hand. "Did I tell you she denied being a sociopath?" Diane said when the waitress left. "She said she isn't one but Tully is and that he is dangerous not only to Grace Noel but to his own daughter. She wasn't being defensive; it was almost like she was just stating a fact."

Kingsley sat for a moment looking thoughtful. "Maybe that's why she's so good," he said. "She doesn't have to fake certain emotions. The problem a lot of sociopaths have is they don't know how normal people feel, or understand the normal behavior that comes from those feelings. They can fool a lot of people for a long time, but not everyone, and often it's family members close to the target victim who are first suspicious of them. O'Riley's son and daughter-in-law were totally taken in by Clymene."

He paused a moment and sipped his coffee. He put in another packet of sugar and sipped again. "I like coffee with my sugar," he said. "Tell me, what was it Vanessa Van Ross saw in Clymene that she didn't like?"

"She had a hard time conveying exactly what made her suspicious," said Diane. "That's why it took so long for the son to go to the police with her misgivings. It was something about Clymene always looking rehearsed, and one unguarded expression Vanessa saw that chilled her. Not much, I know. That shows you how much political weight Vanessa carries with the authorities in this city."

"No, that's not much, but it shows you how Clymene was caught by her own bad luck—not by victimology," said Kingsley.

David approached the table and slid in beside her so abruptly and unexpectedly, Diane jumped. Kingsley looked startled.

"This is David Goldstein. He's one of my crime scene people. Supposed to be on vacation, but I've asked him to work on the artifact problem," said Diane. "David, this is Agent Ross Kingsley."

"The profiler," said David. "I remember."

"Were you able to charm Madge Stewart?" asked Diane.

"I'm sure she thinks we're dating," said David. "But, the reason I sought you out is about Golden Antiquities."

"That's where Kendel acquired the artifacts," Diane said to Kingsley.

"It burned down last night," said David. "The owner, Randal Cunningham, was killed in the fire."

Diane stared at him for several moments. "Are you serious?" she said.

David nodded. "Dead serious."

"Do they know what happened?" asked Kingsley.

David shook his head. "Not that I was able to find out."

Diane started to speak when she saw two more men

in dark suits approaching. Kingsley and David followed her gaze.

"Not FBI," whispered Kingsley. "I know my kind."

David seemed to slump down in his seat.

"Diane Fallon?" asked one of the men, who looked to be in his late thirties and a lifetime weightlifter with no sense of humor.

"Yes," she began.

"Are you Agent Kingsley?" the man interrupted. "We need to speak with you too."

Kingsley raised his eyebrows.

"We are federal marshals . . ."

Federal marshals didn't worry about antiquities, thought Diane. They worried about fugitives.

Well, shit.

Chapter 13

Diane, Kingsley, and the two well-dressed deputy marshals sat at the round oak table in the conference room of Diane's museum office suite. Deputy Marshal Chad Merrick was the larger of the two. He was easily six five, Diane guessed. He had neatly trimmed light brown hair, amber eyes, a broad, plain face, and flawless skin that any woman would envy. Deputy Marshal Dylan Drew was a good five inches shorter than his partner, which put him at six feet—still taller than both Diane and Kingsley. Drew had a shaved head, sharp features, a dark umber skin tone, and hazel eyes—an interesting face. Both men were focused.

"Clymene O'Riley escaped from Greysfort Prison shortly after your visit," said Deputy Marshal Dylan Drew. There was enough expression in his stony stare to convey the impression that he might think Diane had something to do with it.

Diane and Kingsley both sat dumfounded, even though Diane had an inkling of what their presence might mean as soon as she learned they were U.S. Marshals. That was because Clymene was the one thing she, Kingsley, and U.S. Marshals might have in common. But it was still a surprise to hear it stated as real.

Kingsley found his voice first. "How did she escape?"

Drew glanced over to Merrick, who nodded, and back to Kingsley. "As nearly as we can tell at this point in the investigation, she feigned illness and was taken to the infirmary, which is outside the maximum security section. From there the picture is a little hazy, but prison staff thinks she escaped on a delivery truck."

"That seems rather common," said Kingsley. "I would have thought prisons have pretty much blocked that escape route by now. How was she not detected?"

"They have not been able to establish that," said Drew. He turned his attention to Diane. "According to prison records, you were her last visitor. Why were you there?"

"She asked me to visit her," said Diane.

"And you just dropped everything and obliged?" asked Drew.

"No, not at all," said Diane.

"I asked her to go," interjected Kingsley.

"You're the FBI profiler?" said Merrick as if profilers were the academics of the law enforcement world, and who knew what silly things they might be up to.

Kingsley nodded.

"What did she want to see you about?" Merrick asked Diane.

Diane told them about the content of the letter and repeated her conversation with Clymene for the second time that day. The marshals took notes and listened with interest and what looked like a good deal of skepticism.

"And you didn't think it suspicious that she claimed to be motivated by concern for one of her guards?" asked Merrick. The look on his broad, fair face plainly said he did not believe that could be her real motive.

"It didn't matter," said Diane. "She could have wanted to tell me the warden was possessed by aliens and it wouldn't have mattered. It was a rare opportunity to see what she had to say."

"Why was that important?" asked Drew. This time he directed his question to Kingsley.

"Because she shows signs of being a serial killer that we know almost nothing about. She appeared seemingly from nowhere and killed in a very calculated fashion. We don't even know her true identity," Kingsley said. "We're searching for clues."

"What does that mean?" asked Merrick. "She's not Clymene O'Riley?"

"We don't know who she is. The murder investigation found no record of her existence prior to her marriage to Robert Carthwright—the husband who died in a tragic accident before she married Archer O'Riley," said Kingsley.

The two deputy marshals exchanged worried glances. Diane understood—they just realized the object of their hunt was a lot more sophisticated than they had imagined and their job was going to be much harder than they expected.

"No match on her prints, I assume," said Merrick.

"None," said Diane. "She was run against every available database."

"I see," said Merrick. He looked around the room, then back at Diane. "Let's back up for a moment. I'm aware that the crime scene unit is in this building and you are director of the unit. Why are we in the main office of the museum? Do they give you a key?"

"Yes, they do," said Diane. "I'm director here too."

Merrick raised his eyebrows. "We thought you were just having dinner here." He smiled for the first time. "Is there anything you can tell us that might help us apprehend Clymene O'Riley? Any place she might have mentioned that we could look for her? Any person she might turn to? Do you think she will go to see this guard"—he looked at his notes—"Grace Tully?" He seemed to be asking either of them.

"I don't know," said Diane.

Kingsley was shaking his head. "No. I don't think she would."

"Why?" asked Drew.

"Because you would think to go there. Clymene is a planner. She's probably been planning this escape since she was incarcerated and got a good look at her prospects. She already knows where she is running to, and it isn't anyplace we are likely to know about."

"You're saying she's smart," said Merrick.

Kingsley nodded. "Yes. Very high IQ. And very detail oriented. That's one of the things that makes her so dangerous."

"She's fluent in French and Spanish," said Diane.

"That expands the possibilities," said Drew. "Anything else?"

"Yes," said Kingsley. "I'm guessing she's a master at disguises."

"You guess?" said Drew.

"I don't know very much for sure. It was what I . . . we were working on—finding out about her. We believe that Archer O'Riley was not her first victim."

The two marshals were quiet for a moment. Diane guessed they were absorbing the information—thinking about their next move.

"You've given us some leads to work with," said

Merrick. "We thank you for your time." He put two business cards on the table. "If you think of anything helpful, call us."

They were rising to leave when Drew turned and asked, "What do you think she will do if she's cornered?"

"Give up to fight another day," said Kingsley.

"You don't think she'll want to shoot it out?" said Merrick.

"No. She would always have the hope of escape, I think. Clymene is very pragmatic," said Kingsley. "If you do find her, your biggest problem will be to not be seduced by her."

"What?" said Drew. The two of them gave slight, derisive laughs. "What do you mean? I've seen her mug shot. Not what I'd call a babe."

"The mug shot isn't representative of her looks. But it's not just her looks. She has a special gift," said Kingsley. "She knows how to appeal."

"What do you do?" said Merrick. "Wear tin foil on your head when you go see her?"

Diane laughed. Deputy Marshal Chad Merrick had a sense of humor after all.

Kingsley smiled and scratched his head. "We get special training," he said.

"Sure you do," said Drew.

"If all you have is the mug shot," said Diane, "the local paper will have photos from the trial."

"Have you spoken with Rev. Rivers, the counselor at the prison?" said Kingsley.

"He had gone for the day," said Drew.

Diane and Kingsley exchanged glances. "That's how she got out," said Kingsley.

"What?" said Merrick. "You're saying the prison chaplain helped her escape?"

"It's a very good possibility," said Kingsley. "I would look at him."

The two deputy marshals left, turning down Diane's offer to walk them to the door, saying they remembered the way out. Diane and Kingsley stayed in her office.

"I didn't expect this," said Diane.

"No. Now we really need to find out who she is. I know the U.S. Marshals have had a lot of experience at this, but in this particular hide-and-seek contest my money's on Clymene," he said.

"And here I thought she was planning her appeal," said Diane. "Listen, we need to find out if there are any family movies of her—Archer's son might have some. I'd like to get a recording of her speaking."

"If you want to try a forensic linguist," said Kingsley, "we have one. Michael loves to analyze voices."

"That's a good place to start. I have some other ideas too. Jin will love it. Jin is another member of my crime scene crew. He just finished calibrating a new DNA lab here in the forensic unit."

"How is her DNA going to help?" said Kingsley. "I don't see how that will locate her, or where she's from."

"I'm not going to look for her. I'm going to look for a relative."

Chapter 14

Ross Kingsley looked at Diane for a moment with a blank expression, then smiled.

"People with similar DNA to hers," he said, "Like siblings or cousins?"

"Right. I'm hoping the DNA profile of someone related to Clymene is in one of the many databases we have access to. If we can find a relative, then we have a link to who she is and where her family is from. That would give the marshals places to look and give us family history we need."

"I like that. Any more ideas?" asked Kingsley.

"A few. Analyzing her speech should give us some clues. And I need to talk to David. He's my king of databases. I think we can do something with our face recognition software. She may have made her face look a little distorted in the mug shot, but that would not have changed the indexes used by the software. We also have photographs taken by the media during her trial."

"Not many. She kept her face covered entering and leaving," said Kingsley.

"We only need one to find a match," said Diane.

"Even the bad mug shot we have will do if worse comes to worst."

"You thinking she's been arrested before? That there's a picture of her in a database someplace from a previous arrest, maybe under another identity?" asked Kingsley.

"Maybe. Perhaps someplace where the fingerprints from old records have not yet been digitized. But we have lots of databases we can comb through—missing persons, for instance, or driver's license records."

"See, I knew it was a good idea to get you to track down her identity," said Kingsley, grinning broadly.

I'm glad you think it's such a good idea, thought Diane. She wasn't so sure she would have any time to devote to the search for Clymene after dealing with what was becoming a major scandal at the museum. Diane stood up and stretched, kneading her lower back muscles.

"Why did Clymene ask me to come see her?" asked Diane. Ever since she'd learned of Clymene's escape, Diane had been wondering what the point of the visit had been.

Kingsley shrugged. "She knew she was escaping; maybe she just wanted to mess with your life a little. Maybe she really was concerned about Grace Noel and wanted to take care of those concerns before she left. Maybe receiving a visitor put her in the right place or got her out of prison duties that would have delayed her. I have no idea, but it's interesting. We'll be sure to ask her when we catch her."

"Do you think the marshals will find her?" asked Diane.

Kingsley shook his head. "No, but I think we will."

"You have a lot of confidence in my abilities," said Diane.

"I do. But you saw the looks on Merrick's and Drew's faces. They can't conceive of anyone who can outsmart them. A lot of law enforcement personnel have the notion that people in prison are stupid or they wouldn't be in prison. And I'll be the first to admit that quite a few prisoners are a couple of standard deviations left of the mean on intelligence. But quite a few are also like Clymene—very smart and very cunning."

Diane stood up. "I need to go to the other side of the building to my other job. David's probably wondering if I was carried off in chains by the U.S. Marshals."

She looked up at the clock on the wall. It was past quitting time for the museum staff, but Andie would be in her office waiting for her. Diane needed to speak with her so Andie could go home. The muffled ringing of the phone in Andie's office had been continuous while she and Kingsley were being questioned by the marshals. Andie must have had an onerous day herself, fielding calls from concerned, irate contributors, not to mention the media.

"Do you have a night crime scene team?" said Kingsley, standing up and smoothing his jacket.

Diane grinned. "Yes. It's the same one as the day team. We have a night receptionist who receives requests and forwards them to whoever is on call. We take turns. So far the crime rate has been low enough to allow us some sleep." Diane yawned. "Which I'm in need of. The DA has probably worn out his carpet waiting for my call. You going to speak with him tonight?"

"Yes, I will. He'll probably blame both of us for breaking Clymene out," said Kingsley. "I'll have to put on my FBI attitude."

Diane walked Kingsley through Andie's office on his way out.

"I'll give you a call tomorrow," he said, waving as he left.

Diane turned her attention to Andie. "I heard the constant ringing of the telephone. I hope things haven't been too bad for you today."

"Me?" said Andie. "How about you? I didn't have the U.S. Marshals after me. What was that about?" She looked more than ever like Orphan Annie when her eyes were large and round like they were now, staring up at Diane.

"It wasn't about the museum," she said.

"Oh, dark matter," said Andie. "That's a relief."

Not really, thought Diane. "What's been going on here? What have the calls been like?"

"That DA is a pest. I tell you, come next election he doesn't get my vote. We've been getting some calls from people asking about the scandal. I tell them that it's being looked into. Some of them say they are contributors and they want to know what's being done. I just tell them that you are on top of it. Of course, then they want to talk with you and I have to tell them you are busy being on top of things. Some want to give Kendel a piece of their mind. Really, people can be so mean. I want to tell them, like they've got a piece of mind to spare." Andie stopped to take a breath.

"I'll work on an e-mail tomorrow to send to the contributors," said Diane. *When I think of what to tell them*, she thought. "Go home, Andie. I'll see you tomorrow."

Andie grabbed her purse. "Things will be better tomorrow," she said. "I'm sure of it. You always fix things."

"I hope so," said Diane. She didn't feel as though she could fix anything right now. She felt weary to the bone.

Diane walked from her office to the bank of elevators in the center of the museum and rode to the third floor. From there she walked to the west wing. She waved at the night guard as she entered her code in the keypad and opened the door to the crime lab.

The warren of glassed-in rooms looked empty. Then she saw Jin and Neva near the elevator. They were carrying crime scene kits and appeared to be preparing to leave. When they saw Diane they set their cases down and walked along the glassed-in hallway to where she stood. David popped up from a computer station inside one of the rooms. He mouthed a greeting and came out to join them.

"You have a scene to process?" Diane asked Jin and Neva.

Neva nodded. "In White County. How are things with you?"

"Yeah," said Jin, "David said the U.S. Marshals took you and the FBI guy away."

"I said no such thing," said David, frowning at Jin. "I said they left the restaurant together."

"Clymene escaped today sometime after my visit with her," said Diane.

They all walked over to a round table sitting in the corner that they used for debriefing. They all looked so alert. *I miss young,* thought Diane. But then David also looked alert and chipper and he was her age.

"Don't let me keep you," said Diane. "The two of you need to get to the crime scene."

"We'll get there. We want to hear about Clymene first. She escaped? How?" asked Jin.

"Don't know," said Diane. "That seems to be up

in the air at the moment. Jin, I want you to search the DNA databases for anyone related to Clymene."

"We looking for her too?" asked Jin. "You saying we're helping the marshals?" He looked so skeptical that Neva laughed.

"The FBI would like us to find her," said Diane.

"You mean Kingsley," said David.

"Same thing," said Diane.

"Jin, can you do it or not?" asked Diane.

Jin looked wounded. "Sure, Boss. I'll start to-morrow."

Diane shook her head and put her hand to her temples. "Sorry, I didn't mean to snap."

"You look tired," said David.

"I am. It's been a weary day and instead of getting my morning run in, I had to visit Clymene. The woman is a lot of trouble. Now, Neva, Jin—go. David, tell me about your interviews with Kendel and Marge—and the fire at Golden Antiquities.

Chapter 15

"I'll start with my interview of Madge," said David. He stretched out his legs, then after a moment sat up straight and stretched. "Let's go into your osteology office. It's more comfortable and you have that little refrigerator with drinks in it. You know, you need to put in a bar."

In Diane's capacity as forensic anthropologist at the crime lab she had an osteology lab in the west wing with an attached office. She punched in her key code for the bone lab, entered, and switched on the light. A newly arrived box of bones from a cold case in Ohio was sitting on a shiny metal table waiting for her analysis. If she hadn't felt so tired she would have started laying them out while David briefed her. Instead she went to her office.

Smaller than her museum office, it had off-white walls adorned only with a watercolor of a wolf, a green slate floor, dark walnut office furniture, a leather chair, and a long burgundy leather couch that David immediately claimed. He stretched out full length with his head on the arm and his hands behind his head.

"Now, this is comfortable," he said.

Diane went to the small refrigerator in the corner

that was topped with an artificial green plant because she managed to kill real ones. Besides, there was no sunlight in the room anyway. She got Cokes for herself and David. She tossed David his and popped hers open as she sat down in the leather chair near the sofa.

"Did Madge have any useful information?" asked Diane.

"I had to calm her down before I could get much out of her," he said. "She said you told her that Kendel was going to sue her."

"Not exactly right. She asked me if Kendel would sue and I told her that if I were Kendel, I would," said Diane.

"Well, it scared her," said David.

"Madge Stewart is babied too much," said Diane. "It's time she started taking responsibility for her behavior."

David knitted his brows together. "So you're her mother now?"

"No. I'm director of this museum and she made some stupid statements to the newspaper that caused problems that I now have to deal with."

"Just getting things straight," said David. He looked comfortable lying there in his jeans and T-shirt. Diane wished she had taken the couch instead.

"Did you get a coherent answer from her?" asked Diane, sipping on the ice-cold drink. She pressed the cold can to her forehead.

"More or less. She said the reporter called her from the *Rosewood Review* and told her that Kendel Williams had knowingly purchased looted Egyptian antiquities for the museum and what did Madge have to say about it. Madge told her that Kendel would be fired," said David.

Diane rolled her eyes. "Is that it? Did the reporter have any other questions for her?" asked Diane.

"She asked Madge information about herself. You want my opinion, I think the reporter played up to her ego—or lack of it. Then she asked her about your running of the museum," said David.

Diane frowned. In her meeting with the board she had purposefully ignored the parts of the article that raised questions about her management of the museum. She wanted to keep the board members focused on the real harm of the article to the museum and not think that her anger was in response to things Madge had said about her personally.

Truth was, she didn't care that Madge thought she ran a loose ship or that the crime lab was taking too much of Diane's time and that too much responsibility had been shifted to Kendel. She did care that Madge verified the reporter's accusation about stolen antiquities without having any real knowledge and without thinking about the consequences to the museum or to Kendel.

"What about the reporter?" said Diane. "I suppose you haven't had time to speak with her."

David shook his head. "I haven't tried. I called a buddy at another paper and asked about Janet Boville—that's the Rosewood reporter's name. He said she's an ambush reporter, very aggressive, and he had little respect for her ethics. I was concerned that if I approached her the wrong way, the next article would be 'Museum Director Panicking—Harassing This Reporter,' or something equally tabloidlike," said David.

Diane nodded. "I wouldn't have liked that. Did you find out anything else from Madge?"

"Not directly, but Boville had been tipped off by some informant; I think the informant scripted the questions," said David.

Diane sat up straight and leaned forward with her forearms on her knees. "Why do you say that?"

"Because of the questions she asked Madge—about the UNESCO convention and where the museum stands on its provisions. About whether the provenance matched the artifacts. I thought that one was interesting."

"That is interesting. The informant obviously knew they didn't match," said Diane.

"Yes," said David. "Madge was clueless as to what the questions even meant, much less how to answer them."

"How about Kendel?" asked Diane. "Did she have any helpful information?"

"Yes. She provided a model to work from. Now that I know the lay of the land, so to speak, I'll know where to go to investigate." He took a sip of his drink. "The Pearle Museum in Virginia had a nice collection of twelfth-dynasty Egyptian artifacts that Kendel wanted to get her hands on. She had seen them several years ago, and when you guys inherited the twelfth-dynasty mummy, Kendel went back to Pearle and asked if they would like to sell the artifacts. The answer was no." David stopped, sat up, and took another big swig of his drink.

Diane was familiar with the Pearle. It was a good museum, a little smaller than RiverTrail. They belonged to the same associations for small museums. RiverTrail, however, was unique in that even though it had a small number of holdings, it had a very large building.

"But they changed their minds?" said Diane.

"Kendel had asked them to notify her if they decided to sell the items. The director said he would. In the meantime, he took a job with the United Nations."

"I remember," said Diane. "Noah landed a very good position."

"The new director, Brenda McCaffrey, didn't know about the agreement to contact Kendel and she sold the items to Golden Antiquities to make room, and money, for an exhibit she had worked out with the Greek government," said David. He stopped a moment. "You don't need the history of the pieces, do you, like where they were before the Pearle?"

"I've seen the provenance. Go on," said Diane.

"Good, because you know when Kendel gets started telling you about something . . . Anyway, Kendel found out about the sale to Golden Antiquities and she started negotiations with them. Golden Antiquities has been in business for about thirty years. Started by a man named Randal Cunningham, Sr. He's been gradually turning the business over to his son, Randal Cunningham, Jr. for some time," said David.

"Which one died in the fire?" asked Diane.

"I don't know yet. I'll find out more tomorrow. Kendel dealt with both the Cunninghams, Senior and Junior. She said she examined the artifacts and watched them being packed. She said she didn't notice anything hinky during the transactions. Everything was very routine and normal."

"Nothing unusual whatsoever?" asked Diane.

"I had her close her eyes and revisit each encounter to see if she could remember anything that would be helpful. The only thing she said that I found interesting was that each time she was there she had smelled Jean Patou's Joy. It's a very expensive perfume," said David. "But she never saw the wearer."

"Like hundred-dollars-an-ounce expensive?" asked Diane.

"No. Like five-hundred-an-ounce expensive," said David.

"Wow," said Diane. "So, it's rare?"

"No. It's the second-best-selling scent in the world," said David.

"You're kidding. I've never heard of it. Can that many people afford five-hundred-dollar-an-ounce perfume?" said Diane.

"Well, I think it's the second-best-selling overall since it was created sometime in the thirties. I'm not sure where it stands today. But Kendel says it's very popular still—and you don't have to buy it by the ounce. You can get a fraction of an ounce—like a hundred dollars' worth," said David. "You want me to give Frank a hint?"

"No. I'll look it up when I visit Paris this summer," said Diane.

In a bid to talk Frank's adopted daughter Star into going to college, Diane had offered to take her to Paris and buy her a new wardrobe if Star would go to the university for a year and make at least a 2.7 grade point average. She was beginning to look forward to the trip and was feeling very proud that Star, a troubled girl whose parents had been murdered, was turning her life around.

"So Star's made the grade?" said David. "Good for her."

"So far. She still has the rest of spring semester to go. You know, spring break and all. Frank is planning a trip for the two of them during spring break. He's really nervous she is going to want to go to the beach with her friends instead of with him."

"Spring break is a tradition," said David.

"Sure it is, but I think he's right. Next year she'll have more experience being on her own. All this is new to her," said Diane.

"New? She was on her own when she was on the lam with that guy she called her boyfriend," said David.

"I mean being on her own in a responsible manner, then," said Diane. "Anything else Kendel remembered?"

"The whole transaction was smooth. Not even much haggling," said David. "Last meeting they said they would deliver the items within the week. Which they did, except as I understand it now, they weren't the items."

"Maybe she'll remember more now that her memory has been jogged," said Diane. "Can you keep in touch with the arson investigation at Golden Antiquities?"

"I think so," said David.

"Good. Let's go home. I know it's early for me, but I'm tired. A lot happened today. Things will look fresher in the morning."

Diane closed up her office and lab, and she and David walked through the building to the lobby. She waved at the guard on duty and they walked out the door to the parking lot. It was dusk, the moon was full, and everything had the faintly bluish tint of darkness coming. People were arriving at the restaurant for a late dinner, and many cars belonging to the staff were still parked in the lot. Diane looked up at the colossal building just in time to see the day lighting go off and the night lighting come on. She loved the museum and silently promised she would protect it from scandal. Diane waved to David, got in her car, and drove home.

*   *   *

Diane opened her eyes at the sound of someone knocking on her door. Was she dreaming? She got out of bed. *What time is it?* She looked at her clock: 4:14 a.m. No wonder she felt so sleepy. Not enough sleep. There was that knock again.

She slipped on a robe and flipped the light switch. Nothing happened. *Great, another power outage. What this time, another squirrel on the wire?*

She walked down the short hallway in the dark toward the living room. As she passed the kitchen she stepped in something wet and slick. She lost her footing, slipped, and fell hard on the floor, hitting her head against the wall on her way down.

She lay stunned by the fall. After a moment she became aware that she was lying in a wet pool. The coppery-iron aroma was unmistakable.

Chapter 16

Diane was trying to rise to her feet just as the door burst open.

"This is the police," shouted a loud male voice she thought she recognized. She felt a surge of relief.

"Dr. Fallon?" he called out.

"Here," said Diane. He switched on the living room light.

The light worked. What about the electricity? The illumination revealed what Diane knew, what she had smelled—blood. The pool in the hallway ran into the dining area and the kitchen. Diane was covered in it.

"Sweet Jesus," said the policeman, lowering his gun. "What happened, Dr. Fallon? Where are you hurt? Don't try to move."

"I'm all right. It's not my blood," she said. *Then whose is it?*

"Is there someone else here?" he asked. "We got an anonymous call about someone being killed. Is there a body?" He looked around the room, squatting on his haunches as if there might be a body hidden under the couch.

"No—I don't know. . . ." said Diane.

Before she finished, the patrolman began searching

her apartment, trying carefully to avoid the blood—which was impossible. He tracked it into her bedroom.

Diane struggled carefully to her feet. A policeman who had been standing at the door came in to help her.

"Are you hurt? You say this isn't your blood? Do you know whose it is?"

"No," said Diane. "No, I don't."

He pulled out a chair from her dining room table as she carefully made her way, trying not to step in the blood. As she started to sit down, she looked at the seat cushion and stopped. She was soaked in blood. It dripped from her night shirt and robe. The policeman noticed her hesitation.

"You need to sit down," he said. "You have a bruise on your head. Did someone attack you?"

Diane reached a hand up to touch her head but saw that her hands were covered in blood. She sat down on the floor.

"Is there a body somewhere?" the patrolman asked.

"What? No, not that I've seen." *That sounded stupid.* "I mean, I just woke up." *Think, dammit.*

"All clear," said the first policeman. He walked back to them. He was leaving bloody footprints all over the floor. "You got a bulb out in the bedroom."

"You just woke up and found all this blood in your apartment?" The policeman sounded skeptical. Diane didn't blame him.

"Better call Chief Garnett," said the first policeman. "You know he wants to be called about anything involving Fallon, the museum, or the crime lab."

"We need to call the paramedics. She has a serious lump on her head," said the other patrolman.

"Call the crime lab. . . . " She thought for a moment, remembered Jin's home phone number, and gave it to them.

As they made their calls, Diane looked at the blood pattern—pooled in the hallway, running into the kitchen and dining area, pooling up under the table. There was so much of it. A smear of blood led from the main pool out the door. Something—someone was dragged. She looked up at the ceiling. There were three lines of cast-off blood spatter—that would be four thrusts of a knife. First one picked up the blood, the subsequent ones spattered it across the ceiling. On the wall across from the table where she sat there was a smear of blood as if someone had put their hands on it, then slid down the wall. She looked on the floor for footprints. There should have been a lot of them made by whoever was here, but she couldn't make out the originals from the ones made by the policemen and by herself. It struck her that it all looked so ridiculous—and so horrible.

"Are you hurt?" asked one of the patrolmen.

Diane touched her head. "Just a small bump."

"How did you get it? Were you hit?" he asked.

"Hit? No. I fell—slipped in the blood," she said.

"You didn't hear anything?" he asked. She looked at his brass name tag. Officer Ellison. She looked at the other one. Officer Lange. It was Lange she knew.

"No, I didn't hear anything," she said.

"Are you a heavy sleeper?" Lange asked.

Diane shook her head. "No. I'm a light sleeper." She was a light sleeper. Why didn't she hear anything? And why did she feel so fuzzy now. *Drugged? When?*

She looked down at her arms, her clothes. She was soaked in blood. The smell was making her sick, the sight about to cause her to gag. She had to get away from the blood.

"You don't need to be getting up until the paramedics get here," said Officer Ellison.

Diane hadn't realized that she had tried to rise. "Sorry. I feel sick. It's the smell."

"The paramedics will be here soon. Put your head down," he said, nodding at her and putting his own head on his raised folded arms as if she might not understand the language.

She put her forearms on her knees, bent her head down, closed her eyes, and tried to breathe evenly.

The noise level rose and Diane realized that other people had arrived. She thought of her neighbors. Given the number of times violent events had happened in or near her apartment, they had been long-suffering. She was sure that the people across the hall already had their door open a crack. Hopefully they had heard something that might shed some light on what happened.

Two paramedics entered and began taking her blood pressure and asking her questions designed to detect whether or not she was in her right mind.

"Your pulse is low," commented the female paramedic.

"I run," said Diane. "My pulse normally runs about fifty, often lower."

"We're okay, then. Does your head hurt?"

"Yes," answered Diane.

They continued to ask questions and Diane answered. She heard Garnett arrive, followed by her crime scene team.

"Oh, my God," said Neva. She, Jin, and David stood looking at Diane and the pool of blood. "What happened?"

"That's why you're here," said Diane.

"What do you mean?" said David.

"I mean, I don't know," said Diane evenly. "David,

you aren't on call to respond to a crime scene. You're supposed to be on vacation."

"I am on vacation. This is one of the sights," he said. "Like I was going to stay home when the crime scene Jin and Neva were called to was your place?"

"Are you all right?" asked Neva.

"Yes," said Diane.

"You have a big bruise on your head," Chief Garnett said. "It looks like you were attacked." Garnett, as usual, looked like he had just come from the theater or a concert. Well dressed, tall, in his mid-forties, he always appeared elegant, especially with his full head of black and silver hair.

Diane started to explain to Garnett that she slipped and fell in the blood, but her voice was drowned out by the policeman telling someone they couldn't come in.

"What's going on?" a woman's voice said. "Has something happened? If there is danger, we need to know about it."

It was Veda Odell, her eccentric elderly neighbor across the hall who lived with her husband and attended funerals for recreation.

"Just go back into your apartment, please," said Officer Ellison.

"I'll talk to her," said Garnett.

He clearly wanted to control the situation, thought Diane, making all the information come to him.

"Let David do it," said Diane. She met Garnett's eyes. He nodded, probably remembering that David had a special rapport with the Odells, earned from a previous case they had worked on.

David shot her a you-owe-me-big-time glare as he reintroduced himself to Veda Odell.

"Yes, I remember you," Veda said. "David, isn't it? We have some new photographs in our collection I'll bet you would like to see."

"I would indeed, Mrs. Odell. Do you mind if I ask you and your husband a few questions? I know it's early in the morning."

Neva chuckled under her breath and shook her head. "He's going to get you for this," she said.

"Is any of this blood yours?" asked Jin. He stood staring at the red pool.

"No," said Diane. "I don't think so."

"Lord have mercy."

The newest member of the law enforcement entourage to arrive was Lynn Webber, medical examiner for Hall County, just north of Rosewood. Like Garnett, she was never caught anywhere—even at a crime scene—without being well dressed. She was wearing designer jeans, a blue silk blouse that went great with her short, shiny black hair, and a lightweight brown embroidered jacket. She watched carefully where she stepped with her Ferragamos.

"Are you all right?" She turned to the paramedics. "Let me see her vitals."

After exchanging a brief glance, the paramedics handed Lynn a clipboard.

"What are you doing here, Lynn?" asked Chief Garnett. "A little out of your jurisdiction, aren't you?"

"I heard on my police scanner that the paramedics were called to Diane's. . . ."

Garnett jerked his phone from his pocket. He looked around for a safe place to walk and finally decided it was out in the hallway where he had entered the building. Lynn and Diane watched him go. Lynn raised her eyebrows at Diane.

"A long and political story," said Diane.

In an effort to protect the interests of the city and of the museum, Garnett had a standing order that any police business having to do with Diane, the museum, or the crime lab was not be broadcast on the police radio but should be called in by phone. That order certainly extended to emergency services.

Lynn nodded, a knowing look glittering in her dark eyes. Garnett returned frowning. Lynn stared at the pool of blood as if she had just noticed it.

"What happened?" she asked. "Did someone break into your apartment? Where's the body?"

Then she saw the drag marks out the door. She lifted her eyebrows and looked back at the pool of blood. Diane knew what she was thinking, what Jin was thinking as he looked at all that blood.

Chapter 17

The human body has ten pints of blood. If you lose four pints you die. There were easily more than four pints on the floor. All that blood amounted to a dead body. Jin knew it, so did Lynn, so did Diane, so did the paramedics. Diane guessed that Garnett and the policemen knew it too.

Provided all the blood came from one person. Diane hoped it didn't. She hoped that when they canvassed the area hospitals they would find two or three very anemic people who could tell her why they decided to battle it out in her home. *Why didn't I hear it?*

Garnett sent the paramedics outside. Diane didn't hear what he said to them. When they were gone he pulled up a chair and sat down.

"Was this a home invasion?" he asked.

"If it was, they didn't invite me," said Diane.

"You slept through it?" If Garnett, who was both politically and by friendship predisposed to believe her, looked that skeptical, she was in for a difficult time.

"Apparently I did," said Diane.

"You know, if someone came in and attacked you in your home, you are entitled to defend yourself," said Garnett. "I need you to try to remember. We don't want anyone thinking you did this for any other reason." He stopped as if waiting for her to respond.

"Oh, don't be ridiculous," said Lynn, using her mildly scolding southern voice. "If she wanted to kill someone, she wouldn't do it here and ruin her hardwood floors, for heaven's sake. Besides, Diane is just like me. We both know a dozen ways to kill a person without making such a mess—and without detection, I might add."

"I'm not suggesting anything like that and I didn't mean it the way it sounded," said Garnett. "I'm just afraid others might interpret things in the most negative way. You know how newspapers are."

Indeed Diane did. "I know this is strange. I'm not understanding it either . . ."

The paramedics came in rolling a stretcher.

"What's that?" asked Diane. "I don't need to go to the hospital. Neva has to process me and I have to shower and change. I don't know if you have ever had occasion to wear bloodsoaked clothes, but it is not comfortable."

"You can be processed at the hospital," said Garnett. "I'll be in charge here so there will be no—"

"Neva needs to stay here and help process the site." Diane said *site* as if it were someplace other than her home.

"I'll go with you," said Lynn. "I process bodies all the time. They're dead, of course. But I can do yours, no problem. You need to go to the hospital. I don't like some of your readings, and any hit to the side of the head like that needs to be looked at more closely. And I don't like that nausea you've been feeling."

In the end, they won. Before Diane left on the stretcher—which she was sure Garnett ordered in case any reporters were lurking outside—she directed Neva to process outside the apartment and have Jin do the inside. Neva was only too happy to let him take care of the blood. Diane expected Neva would find a dead body somewhere around the apartment building. It was still the early hours of the morning, so with good luck, it would be one of her crew who found it and not one of her neighbors.

Fortunately there were no reporters waiting outside. She was embarrassed to be riding to the hospital, taking up valuable ambulance space and the paramedics' time. She was fine. Garnett simply wanted Diane to appear as the victim in case anyone was watching. Which was true, she was a victim, but not in the way he was staging it. She didn't know how he would spin the presence of all that blood and no body.

As for Lynn, she was going along with Garnett. Lynn knew her way around politics, had sized everything up quickly, and fell easily into helping Garnett. Diane doubted that Lynn would be riding to the hospital with her under different circumstances. But then maybe she would have. Lynn wasn't a brutally scheming person any more than Garnett was—but she was a player. Diane might have felt better about all this attention if it had actually been about her well-being. It wasn't. It was all about the crime lab and maintaining its reputation.

The ride to the hospital was uneventful. Thank goodness they didn't use the siren. Diane was rolled right into an examination room and the paramedics left, taking the gurney with them. She removed all her clothing and sealed it in a plastic bag for processing by the crime lab. It was a relief to get out of bloodsoaked clothes, even if it meant putting on one of the skimpy hospital gowns.

Lynn Webber did know how to process a body. She looked for bruises, defensive injuries, and blood-spatter patterns, and she took numerous photographs.

"With all that blood you couldn't have stabbed any-one and not have cuts on your hands. The knife would have been too slippery to hold," said Lynn.

She was right. Diane's grip would have slipped on a knife and sliced her palm or her fingers, assuming the weapon was a knife. But the victim, whoever the victim was, could have been bludgeoned with some-thing like a tire iron. It would also have made cast-off spatters and a lot of blood. Diane wanted to see the spatter pattern up close. She hadn't been in a posi-tion to do much from her dining room table. Now that she was thinking more clearly, she realized that the castoff was very high, too much of an arc across the ceiling to be from stabbings; more like a beating.

Lynn took a blood sample from Diane and had her collect a urine specimen.

"We need to find out why you slept through a mas-sacre in your home," said Lynn.

"I don't know when I could have been drugged," said Diane.

"Well, obviously someone had access to your house. Did you eat or drink anything before you went to bed?"

"I drank a bottle of green tea," said Diane.

She remembered grabbing it out of the refrigerator. She had to think about that. Could someone have spiked it? She remembered that the lid was on tight. Did she hear the little clicks of the perforated plastic breaking as she unscrewed the cap? She didn't remember.

"How would anyone know I would drink that bottle of tea?" said Diane. "For that matter, what's the point of this—to use my tiny apartment for an ultimate fighting ring because they weren't able to find anyplace else?"

Lynn laughed. "I suppose we'll have to wait until we find a body to answer that. But tell me, what all do you remember? Do you remember going to bed?"

Diane nodded. "Yes, I remember changing clothes and climbing into bed. I remember everything leading up to that. I went to sleep thinking about the Egyptian artifacts. The next thing I remember is the police banging on the door."

"When you got up to answer the door, did you feel any pain anywhere?" asked Lynn.

"No. Just a drowsy feeling."

"If we find anything in your blood," Lynn said, "the lab can test everything you came in contact with until they discover how it got into you."

When Lynn was done it was clear that Diane had no bruises other than the one on her head. The blood patterns on her body and her clothing were consistent with a fall. All that was good. A member of the hospital nursing staff showed Diane to a shower, where she scrubbed the blood from her body and hair.

"Okay," said Lynn when Diane came out. "Let's X-ray your head."

Diane thought Lynn was enjoying this far too much. After having her head examined, Diane was sitting on one of the examination tables waiting for the doctor and Lynn to come with the X-rays. She knew what they would show. Nothing. She had hit her head on a plaster wall on the way down. She had been dazed, but that was all.

As she sat holding the back of her hospital gown

closed, she realized she didn't have any clothes with her. *Why did I let them talk me into going to the hospital?* This was absurd. She didn't even have her purse with her.

I can stay at the museum, she thought. Her office suite had a bathroom, a shower, and a comfortable couch. She had stayed there many times. She even had a change of clothes there. She would go look for a phone. That meant walking around with absolutely nothing on but an open-backed thin cotton gown. Diane slipped down from the table and looked around the white curtain for a nurse.

She was in a large room lined on two sides with a row of cubicles like the one she was in. Some were probably occupied. She padded across the room, holding the back of her gown closed with a hand behind her back. The floor was cold on her bare feet. Just down at the other end of the room was an empty nurses station. No nurse? *What if there is an emergency in one of the cubicles?* she thought.

She walked toward the station. She passed a stack of neatly folded gowns on a trolley. She swiped one and put it on backwards. At least now she didn't have to hold the back closed. At the nurses' station she looked for a bell to ring. There wasn't one. She walked around the counter and reached for the phone. Her hand touched the receiver just as she was grabbed around the waist and mouth and pulled into one of the cubicles.

Chapter 18

Diane kicked at her assailant but her bare feet had little effect. She bit the gloved hand covering her mouth and tried to squirm out of his grasp. His fingers and palm were well protected with leather and padding thicker than necessary for the season of the year. She bit down hard.

"Stop it, or I'll break your neck." His voice was a hoarse whisper.

This is isn't going to happen, she thought. *I won't let it.*

She bit harder and elbowed him in the ribs but felt the blow slide off. She reached over her head searching for eyes to poke or hair to grab. Her fingers found thick, taut material. A ski mask covering his face. She clawed at it and he jerked his head backward, sending them both against the vital signs monitor, tearing off feeds and cables as it fell to the floor. Her mouth now free, she screamed. In her peripheral vision, she saw a knife. *This definitely is not going to happen.*

She entangled her leg in his to trip him. It almost worked. He fell against the bed, pushing it against the curtain. Diane reached down and grabbed one of his ankles and pulled up hard while she pushed away from him with all the strength she had in her legs. He fell but dragged her with him, twisted her over, pushed her to the floor, and pressed a knee in the small of her back. With his powerful hand on the back of her head he pressed her face into the floor.

"You're a dirty dealer," he whispered. "Everybody thinks you're so good, but you're dirty."

Diane reached and yanked a cable dangling from the monitor, hoping it would fall on him or distract him enough for her to free herself. She heard a voice several cubicles away calling for a nurse. She shouted for help as the monitor she was jerking at slammed against her attacker. He got up and ran as abruptly as he had come. Diane struggled to her feet to follow him.

A door near the nurses' station was partially ajar where he had gone through, and she headed for it. It opened into a large storage room with a door on the other end. Diane ran for it. A hallway lay beyond. She looked both ways up and down the hallway and saw nothing. She had been too slow. She hurried back to the examination room. A nurse was there, or maybe a nurse's aide. It was hard to tell.

"You aren't supposed to be back there," she said. The blond woman was about Diane's age and dressed in scrubs with cartoon prints all over them that looked more like she should be in pediatrics. She stood looking at Diane in confusion.

"There aren't supposed to be maniacs running around the hospital either. I was just attacked in here. Get security."

The nurse just stood there smiling kindly in a confused sort of way.

"What's wrong with you? Alert hospital security before he gets away," said Diane.

"If you sit down, I'll get a doctor," said the nurse.

"Dammit, I know one loses a lot of credibility in these idiotic hospital gowns, but I'm telling you I was attacked in that examination room—as you can see by the disarray inside. Call security—now."

"I think if you just sit back down." The nurse looked at the tossed examining room. "We'll have to find you another bed."

"I have one over there." Diane pointed to the cubicle she was previously sitting in. "I'll go back there." She paused and looked the woman over. She wondered if she was a volunteer or maybe another patient who liked to dress in scrubs and wander about the hospital. "Do you work here?"

"I'm a nurse's aide," said the woman, straightening her shoulders.

"My attacker is probably long gone, but let me explain something to you. That room"—Diane pointed to the curtained area that the attacker had pulled her into—"is not to be touched until my crime scene people have processed it for evidence. My name is Diane Fallon and I'm director of the Rosewood Crime Lab. Are you understanding this?"

A worried looked crept into her eyes. "Yes, but I thought you were just bleary from a procedure. Patients get like that sometimes—you know—confused," she said.

"I didn't have any kind of procedure. I was waiting on X-ray results," said Diane.

"Diane, look who I found."

Diane turned toward Lynn Webber's voice. Frank was beside her carrying a suitcase.

"Frank," said Diane. She smiled at him. Relief flowed over her like fresh water. "How—"

"Neva called," he said. "She collected some of your

things for you and said you would need a place to stay."

"I'm glad you're here—" she said.

"Are you all right?" he interrupted. "Your face is red." He walked over to her, set down the suitcase, and took her by the shoulders.

"Did something happen here?" Lynn was looking at her more closely now too.

Diane explained about the attacker, fighting him off and trying to chase him. She kept it short, but the nurse's aide stood openmouthed as she listened.

"I need to see if you're hurt," said Lynn.

"I'm fine," said Diane. Truthfully she ached all over and her face hurt, but she was not going to be examined one more time.

"Did you call security?" asked Frank.

"He's probably long gone," said Diane without looking at the aide. "I'll have Neva or Jin come down and have a look at the scene. They may find something."

She turned to the aide. "I need a container to put my gowns in. I have to take them with me so they can be processed." Diane looked over at an examining table inside one of the curtained cubicles. "Do you have some clean white paper that I can wrap them in?"

"Yes. On the table. I'll get you a piece." The aide went to the examination room and came back with a long piece of white paper and handed it to Diane.

"Thank you." She turned to Lynn. "I assume my X-rays were fine."

"Yes, fine . . . " she began.

Diane picked up the suitcase and took it with her into the examination room and drew the curtain. She laid the small suitcase on the bed and opened it. She found panties and a bra and put them on, slipped on a pair of jeans and grabbed a neatly folded blue oxford shirt. Her fingers shook as she tried to button it. She squeezed her eyes tight to hold back a flood of tears, flexed her fingers, and finished the buttons.

When she was dressed, Diane stood a minute behind the curtain before she went out, suitcase in one hand and the carefully wrapped hospital gowns under her arm. She tried not to shake.

"Let me take the gowns to your guys," said Lynn when Diane emerged. "Why don't you take a couple of hours off before you go to the museum? I know I can't talk you into staying away the whole day."

"Good idea," said Frank, eying her closely as he put an arm around her shoulders and squeezed. "Stay at my house for a while."

"Maybe for a couple of hours," said Diane. She noticed they didn't ask her to stay and talk to the police about the most recent attack. She must look like the wreck she felt.

"Why aren't you at work?" Diane asked from the passenger seat of Frank's new Chevy Camaro.

"I was fifteen minutes out when Neva called," said Frank. "Why didn't you call me?"

"I thought you'd be at work. And Garnett and Lynn were insisting that I go to the hospital. That was just for show. Making sure the news media saw me as the victim. I wish I'd refused."

He stopped at a traffic light and looked over at her and took her hand.

Diane's lip quivered. "I thought the guy at the hospital was going to rape me," she said. Saying it out loud brought her close to tears again.

Frank squeezed her hand. Diane saw his jaw muscle clench. The light changed and he accelerated.

"I wasn't going to let that happen," she said, knowing that most of the time the victim can't stop a determined rapist. She shook her head as if there might be something out of place inside her skull. "I don't know what came over me—I didn't care what threat he made—I just wasn't going to let it happen. And there I was in that stupid gown. Thank heavens I'd found a second one just a minute before and put it on backwards—not that I was much more protected." She took a breath. "And there was that idiot nurse. She wouldn't believe me and just stood there grinning when I told her to go get security. They need to make those gowns in power colors."

"You asked for security? Why didn't you say something back there?" asked Frank.

"Because nurse's aide is a low-paying job and she's probably the sole support of five kids, a no-account husband, and five brothers-in-law and their families," said Diane.

She saw Frank's jaw twitch into a tiny smile. They were silent until he pulled into his driveway. Diane looked at her watch.

"You're going to be late for work," she said.

"It's okay. I want to stay with you for a while. Come in and tell me what happened at your home and at the hospital. You said you *thought* he was going to rape you. That wasn't his goal?"

Diane shook her head. "No, he wanted to kill me."

Chapter 19

Frank's Queen Anne–style house was set off the road amid several huge oak trees. It was an old house that had been well maintained. Its hardwood floors had a high polish. The interior walls were a light yellow-tan color that made the rooms look bright and clean. He had a preference for stuffed chairs and sofas, and oak and walnut furniture that suited the age of the house. It was a house that always reminded her of Frank himself—a sound and comfortable port in a storm.

They sat on one of the stuffed sofas facing a rock fireplace. There was no fire and it looked like a yawning dark entrance to a cave. It looked inviting. Diane hadn't been caving in several months, and a dark cool cavern was appealing right now. Nothing like crawling into the earth to escape your troubles. She leaned against Frank and he held her tight as if his arms might stop her trembling. After several minutes Diane gently pulled away and sat up.

"I'm okay, really," she said, rubbing her eyes with the tips of her fingers, making an effort not to lose control. She couldn't go to the museum looking so vulnerable—not now, not when the entire museum was looking to her for strength.

Frank studied her for a moment and smiled in the way that made his eyes twinkle—which made everything seem all right.

"Good. I'll get us some coffee and you can tell me all about your day so far."

Frank rose from the sofa, leaned over, and gave Diane a quick kiss on the lips. While he was gone, Diane went to the mantel to look at the photographs. She had seen them all many times but she liked looking at them. Frank had a nice family—parents who were still alive and still married, two brothers and one sister, nieces, nephews. He had a photograph of his son, Kevin, from a previous marriage and one of Star, the young girl he adopted after her parents were murdered. Diane took down the photograph and smiled at it. Star, now going to Bartram University, had been working hard, overcoming a lot.

Frank came back with two cups of cappuccino—which was always way too strong. But right now she needed a good jolt. She put the photo of Star back on the mantel.

"Do I need to sip this sitting down?" she said.

"It probably would help." He sat down next to her with his own drink.

Diane blew across the top of the beverage to cool it, then took a small drink. It was hot, strong, and good.

After a moment she began her recounting of the day by telling him about waking up to the knock at the door and then slipping in the blood. She told him about the attack in the hospital in more detail than she had related in the presence of Lynn Webber and the nurse's aide.

"Did you recognize the voice?" asked Frank. As they spoke he sipped his coffee and rubbed the back of her neck with his hand.

"No, I didn't. But calling me a dirty dealer . . . it had to be about the artifacts. Someone thinks I'm dealing in stolen antiquities. That's the only thing that makes sense."

From Frank's blank stare and raised eyebrows, Diane realized he didn't know about the disputed artifacts or the newspaper articles. He usually didn't read the local newspapers until the weekend. Frank worked in Atlanta and the story hadn't yet made it there, at least not on the front page. That would be today most likely—something else to look forward to.

"We have a scandal of sorts at the museum," she said. Diane told him about the wretched newspaper articles and the hastily called board meeting.

"Are you sure Kendel isn't involved?" asked Frank. "Just to play the devil's advocate, could she be using RiverTrail to launder looted antiquities or at least to get a good deal on some Egyptian artifacts for the museum?"

Diane shook her head. "The only Egyptian artifacts we're looking for right now are twelfth dynasty. The same as our mummy. The artifacts delivered to us are from several other dynasties."

"Could she have intended to replace the photographs in the documents and launder the artifacts that way?"

"The photographs wouldn't match the descriptions," said Diane. "She couldn't hope to launder the artifacts at our museum."

"Why?" said Frank. When he decided to play the devil's advocate he was like a dog with a bone. "I would think a museum would be the perfect place to launder looted artifacts."

"Not ours," said Diane. "We're a small museum and we've had one director—me."

"So?" said Frank.

"Large museums show only a fraction of their hold-ings at any one time. The Bickford shows only about a third of theirs. The rest is in storage. Periodically they create new exhibits from their inventory, re-arrange items into perhaps a comparative study—like stone tools from around the world or medicinal plants from various cultures."

"The Bickford? Where have I heard about them?" said Frank.

"That's where we purchased our casts of the Juras-sic dinosaurs," said Diane. "They sent staff from their museum to help us put them together."

"Ah, yes. I remember now," he said. "Go on. You were telling me why artifacts can't be laundered in your museum."

"In large museums like the Bickford it might be easier to integrate looted artifacts into the stored ones—especially with turnovers in directorship. In fact, their current director is leaving. Here at Riv-erTrail what you see is basically what we have. I know all of our holdings, and everything comes through me. For Kendel to be laundering artifacts, she'd have to enlist the staff who work at the loading dock, the provenance researchers . . . or me. It doesn't make sense that she is involved in this."

"Could the loading dock staff or the researchers be in it with her?"

"Obviously not. They are the ones who discovered the discrepancies."

"But someone thinks you are involved?" said Frank.

"It looks that way. And whatever is going on is worth killing me for," said Diane.

Frank set down his cup, leaned over, and kissed

Diane. Diane liked the taste of his lips and the smell of his aftershave. "He didn't kill you," he whispered close to her lips, "and he won't." He kissed her again before he sat back and reclaimed his coffee.

"Whoever tipped off the press knew what was in the crates before they were opened," said Frank. "So the items were switched at . . . what's the name of the seller?"

"Golden Antiquities," said Diane.

"Either they were switched at Golden Antiquities before they left, or the crates were intercepted somewhere between Golden Antiquities and your museum."

"I'm sure it was no coincidence that Golden Antiquities burned," said Diane.

"I agree," said Frank. "They are implicated in some way." He appeared to mull over Diane's answers for a moment; then he changed the subject. "RiverTrail doesn't seem like a small museum," he said.

"One thing, the building is large. Another is we try to make the best use of what we have. Like with our Egyptian exhibit. All we really have is the mummy, its case, and a collection of amulets that were probably wrapped with him. It looks like a bigger exhibit because of the things we added to it, like the life-size reconstruction Neva did of the mummy sitting cross-legged in the middle of the room, the dioramas with models of Egyptian houses and pyramids, the computer three-D graphics of tombs and temples, the cubicles with computer tutorials on ancient Egypt. There's a lot to look at, but not a huge collection of antiquities."

"Curious," said Frank. "Neither problem makes sense—the antiquities or your apartment."

"No, and that's why I need to get back to the museum and the crime lab. I need to know what my crew found," she said.

Frank stood and pulled Diane up with him. "It won't hurt you to wait a couple of hours. Take a nap. You'll think better after you've rested—and eaten something. I'll bet you haven't eaten anything all day."

She hadn't, and until he mentioned it she didn't realize she was hungry. They went into the kitchen and Frank made bacon, lettuce, and tomato sandwiches. No one made BLTs like Frank—the bacon was always crisp, the lettuce always fresh, and the tomatoes always vine ripened.

"Don't you have to go to work?" asked Diane after her last bite.

"I'm looking through computer files on a fraud case. I can do it here. Neva brought some of your clothes and girl stuff and put them in the guest room. Not that you have to stay in the guest room," he said, smiling. "But that's where I had closet space. Go take a nap. Who knows, this thing may have resolved itself by the time you wake up."

Diane took a shower, the second within just a few hours. The guest bathroom had a large showerhead that made the water feel like rain. She stood under the warm water for a long time. When she was clean and dry she slipped on a nightshirt and lay on the down-filled mattress. Frank was right—what she needed was food and sleep. Things would be better when she awoke.

As Diane stirred awake, she heard the muffled sound of Frank's telephone ringing in another part of the house. She got out of bed, dressed, and put on a minimal amount of makeup. Neva definitely deserved a bonus, she thought, looking in the mirror.

Frank was in the living room standing by the fireplace when she emerged. He kissed her cheek and took her hand—but didn't smile.

"Neva called," he said. "The marshals want to talk with you again. It was Clymene O'Riley's blood in your apartment."

Chapter 20

Diane stood staring at Frank in disbelief, barely aware of how tightly he was holding her hands.

"It was Clymene's blood in my apartment? . . . How?" she said.

"I don't know. But Garnett arranged for the marshals to speak with you at the crime lab and not downtown," said Frank. "They're waiting for you."

"Why the marshals? If Clymene died in Rosewood, jurisdiction now falls to Garnett," said Diane.

"Garnett will be there. So will the district attorney. I imagine the marshals are just tying up loose ends before they leave," said Frank. He rubbed the back of her hand with his thumb.

Tying up loose ends—*like finding the body*, she thought. She could just see the headline now: CRIME LAB DIRECTOR BROUGHT IN FOR QUESTIONING IN MYSTERIOUS BLOODY DEATH. She shuddered at the thought and silently thanked Garnett for scheduling the meeting at the crime lab.

"Why is the DA going to be there, I wonder." said Diane.

Frank shook his head. "I have no idea. I wouldn't worry about it. However anyone wants to spin this, it still gets down to the fact that Clymene O'Riley was an escaped murderer who somehow got into your apartment in the middle of the night."

"Just as long as they don't think I invited her and we had a falling out," said Diane.

Frank shook his head. "That's a long stretch." He looked at his watch. "I'll drive you over. Neva said I should let you off at the loading dock at the side entrance to the museum. You are to go to Mike's office in geology first," said Frank. "And I would imagine avoid being seen if you can, though she didn't say."

"What? Did she say why I'm to be so mysterious?" Diane asked.

"No, but apparently it's important," said Frank. He grinned. "I have a pretty exciting job, but around you it pales by comparison."

He let her off at the museum side-door loading dock and extracted a promise for her to call as soon as she could. Diane thought there was just a little too much cloak-and-dagger about the whole thing. However, she slipped into the building, taking back staircases and service hallways to Mike Seeger's office in the geology lab.

Mike was the head curator for geology, one of Diane's caving partners, and a good friend. He also worked part-time for a company that searched for and collected extremophiles, organisms that live in the most extreme environments on earth. It wasn't just his knowledge of geology that made Mike valuable to the company, but his skill as a rock climber and a caver. He had recently returned from one of his expeditions. Mike was also Neva's boyfriend. He, Diane, Neva, Jin, and another friend frequently went caving together.

Diane knocked on his door. He opened it immediately and Diane slipped in. He closed the door behind her.

"God, I love working here," he said with a broad grin. "There's always something adventurous going on." He gave her a quick hug and stepped back to look at her. "You okay, Doc? I haven't had a chance to talk with you since I got back."

"I'm muddling through business as usual," she said.

Mike's office was crowded with crates of rocks—probably volcanic. Each trip, he brought back geologic samples for the museum. These were from his latest. Along the walls he'd hung huge posters of rock formations and caves from around the world. On a bookcase stuffed with geology books was a photograph of all of them at the entrance to a cave.

Mike had the body of a rock climber—lean, no fat between his skin and hard muscle. His boyish face was getting a slight weathered look from all his outdoor activity. He wore jeans and bright white Richard III T-shirt. He pulled up a chair for her and one for himself.

"What's this about, Mike?" asked Diane.

He reached for some papers on his desk.

"Neva said the DA told her and the others not to talk to you or show you the crime scene report." He grinned. "Of course he didn't tell her not to talk to me, nor did they tell me not to show you their notes."

That was Diane's team all right. On occasions like this you had to explain exactly all the things you didn't want them to do, or they would find a loophole in the instructions. She reached for the pages.

"My team can be very sneaky," she said.

"I'll say. They made the notes and gave them to me with instructions before they spoke with the district attorney. David said they would be warned off from talking to you once the DA had been informed. He was right."

A small laugh escaped Diane's lips. "David should write a book—a practical guide to paranoia."

"Jin wanted you to know that he hated calling Garnett," said Mike.

"He had to," said Diane. "He didn't have a choice once he identified the blood."

"Well, he's real bummed out about it," said Mike. "He kept muttering about how he gets this brand-new DNA lab and the first person he gets in trouble from it is you."

Diane shook her head and smiled. "He did the right thing."

She scanned the first page. The information was written in David's neat hand, listing what was found in her apartment. First was the blood. It was Clymene's. Jin had mapped the entire pool and took samples from Diane's clothes. All of it was Clymene's and it was all fresh blood, not stored blood. The blood trail led down the back stairs of Diane's apartment and out to Diane's car, where Clymene's blood was found in the trunk along with one of Diane's serrated kitchen knives. The knife had been washed clean with kerosene.

They had so far found no trace evidence that was helpful. The police were alerted by a call from a man using a cell phone who identified himself as a neighbor. However, all the neighbors said they heard nothing until the police arrived. And last: Diane's tox screen came back positive for a barbiturate—not a high dose, but enough to make her sleep well. No container was found with any barbiturate residue and there were no pills in her house.

She looked at the next page and sucked in her

breath. It was the report on the crime scene in White
County that Neva and Jin had worked the day
before—the body was that of the Reverend William
Rivers.

"Oh, no," Diane said aloud. "She killed him."

Diane read Neva's notes. Rivers was found in his
garage next to his car. Blunt-force trauma to the back
of the head. One blow. Nothing found at the scene.
No unaccounted-for trace on his body. No sign that
Clymene had killed him, but Diane believed she had—
what kind of coincidence would it be for him to be
murdered by someone else on the day Clymene escaped? One interesting item: Neva noted that his car
had been vacuumed. The bag from his vacuum cleaner
was missing.

Diane had forgotten about the White County crime
scene in all the commotion. She just realized that Jin
and Neva couldn't have gotten any sleep.

"Well," said Diane when she finished reading. "I
suppose I'd better go face the music." She stood and
handed Mike the pages. "Better burn these."

Mike laughed. "I'll eat them right after you leave."
He stopped smiling. The perpetual crease between his
eyebrows deepened. "Can I do anything?"

"What do you have in mind?" asked Diane, smiling
at him.

"We could run away together. I know some wonderful exotic places." He grinned again.

Mike made a running joke about having a thing for
Diane. She didn't believe it, or rather, she didn't believe it much. It was more of a friendly flirtation on
his part. She never returned it and he never took it
beyond talk, which she was glad of. She didn't want
Neva hurt, nor did she want to lose Mike as a caving partner.

"The marshals would hunt us down—not to mention Neva and Frank," she said.

"Guess you're right, Doc." He walked with her the short distance to the door. "Good luck."

"Thanks, Mike. I know intrigue isn't in your job description," said Diane.

"Isn't it? I think it is." He opened the door.

"It should be, with everything that's going on," said Diane.

"I read today's paper," he said. "How is Kendel taking it?"

"Today's paper? There's something in it about the museum? Damn. Do you have one here?" she asked.

He retrieved a newspaper from the recycling bin and handed it to her. "I'm sorry, Doc. I shouldn't have mentioned it, with everything else on your shoulders."

"That's okay, Mike. I need to know."

She took the newspaper. It was the *Atlanta Journal-Constitution* and she had made the headlines.

LOOTED ARTIFACTS AT RIVERTRAIL MUSEUM: IS DIRECTOR BACKPEDALING?

Diane scanned the article. It wasn't as bad as the one in the Rosewood paper, but it wasn't good either. Well, for now she'd settle for not as bad.

"Everything is going to be all right," said Diane as she went out the door. "I'll make it all right."

Chapter 21

District Attorney Curtis Riddmann, Deputy Marshals Chad Merrick and Dylan Drew, and Chief of Detectives Douglas Garnett were sitting at the round table in the crime lab when Diane arrived. Her staff was nowhere to be seen. They were probably in the DNA lab in the basement waiting, thought Diane. David was probably kicking himself for not thinking to bug the crime lab so they could hear what was going on. She smiled inwardly at the thought.

The crime lab wasn't cozy. With all the glassed-in rooms, white walls, and metal doors, it had a cold, icy look. Diane pulled out a chair across from them and sat down. She wore an off-white linen pantsuit with an ice blue blouse. She saw a blurred reflection of herself in the glass of a cubicle and thought she looked as cold and sterile as her lab—a thought that pleased her at the moment.

The four law enforcement officials sat looking somber. They were seated at the table close together so Diane would be across from all of them. None appeared to be speaking to the others.

The marshals were in jeans, navy T-shirts, and jackets today. DA Riddmann and Garnett were in suits—

Garnett looking dapper as usual, and the DA trying hard to. DA Riddmann was not a man who wore suits well. His shoulders and chest were too thin, his hips too wide, and his legs too skinny. Riddmann did have a nice head of brown hair, but it tended to overwhelm his lean face.

I should probably have an attorney, she thought. But lawyering up is tricky when you have to consider publicity—it wouldn't be good for the crime lab or the museum. Right now headlines and potential headlines were running everything in her life. She had to figure out how to change that.

Diane had called David before she got to the museum and put him in charge of the crime lab while she was under suspicion. She hadn't liked the sound of those words coming out of her mouth—*under suspicion. Damn. Well, that's what happens when you have a ton of someone else's blood all over your living room floor.*

"Gentlemen," said Diane, "how can I help you?"

Deputy Marshal Chad Merrick spoke first. "We were wondering if there is anything more you can tell us about your meeting with Clymene O'Riley." His smile actually did look friendly.

"No. I told you everything we talked about. It was a short meeting," said Diane. "I got no indication that she was planning an escape."

"Did you leave the prison immediately?" asked Deputy Marshal Dylan Drew.

"No. I went by to speak with the prison counselor, Reverend William Rivers," said Diane. Of course they knew that already.

"Why?" asked Drew.

"I wanted to hear what his opinion was on Clymene O'Riley. It was a strange story she was telling me," said Diane. "He's had more contact with her than anyone since she went to prison."

The marshals didn't even blink. But Diane noticed that the DA looked down at the table. Garnett's expression didn't change either.

"And what did he think?" asked Drew.

Like Diane, the marshals didn't gesture with their hands as they spoke. Merrick had his fingers laced together in front of him. Drew had his arms folded. He sat back comfortably in the chair. Merrick leaned forward slightly. Diane's hands were laced together in front of her also. They looked each other straight in the eye as they spoke. The whole thing reminded her of her visit with Clymene—all trying not to give anything away.

"Rivers wanted to know what the evidence was that convicted Clymene. I went through it with him," said Diane.

"And why did he want that information?" asked Merrick.

"He didn't say," said Diane. "But Clymene had been a model prisoner and very helpful to the other inmates, according to Rivers. He had heard from her and perhaps from other prisoners that the evidence against her was not very good. I believe he had begun to doubt her guilt. But I don't know that for sure."

"Do you think he would have helped her escape?" asked Drew.

"I don't know. I have to tell you, though, Clymene is very gifted. I daresay she could make you like her," said Diane.

The two deputy marshals looked mildly startled and greatly skeptical. From the smirks on their faces, Diane knew they thought she greatly overrated the powers of Clymene O'Riley. Diane smiled back at them.

"And how about you?" asked Merrick. "Do you like her?"

"I don't dislike her. It would be a stretch to say that I like her," said Diane. "She is, after all, a calculating, cold-blooded murderer."

"So, do you think she could have made Rivers help her escape?" said Merrick.

"I don't know. She's not a wizard. She can't make people do things they don't want to do. She can make them predisposed to believe her," said Diane.

"How does she do that?" asked Drew, frowning now like he seriously wanted to know the source of her power.

"You'll have to ask FBI agent Kingsley. He would know more about the psychology involved. He says she's a natural profiler. She has an uncanny ability to size people up," said Diane.

"Why didn't you call me after your visit with her, as I requested?" asked DA Riddmann. Diane could see the marshals were annoyed at the interruption.

Diane glanced at Riddmann. She could also see he was clearly angry with her. "Agent Kingsley said he was going to call you," she said.

"He didn't," said Riddmann.

"Then something must have come up," said Diane. "I'm sure he will."

"Did Clymene perhaps get to you?" asked Riddmann.

"No," said Diane.

"Maybe—" he began, but Merrick cut in.

"I understand you had a bit of trouble early this morning?" he said.

Riddmann started to open his mouth, but Merrick cut him a harsh look. Clearly the marshals weren't letting their jurisdiction go just yet. Probably because they didn't have a body. *Probably wondering where I hid it*, Diane decided.

"Yes, I did," said Diane.

"Would you go over it with us?" asked Merrick.

Diane looked surprised only because it would have looked suspicious if she hadn't.

"You think what happened to me has something to do with Clymene?" she asked.

"Just tell us about it," said Drew.

Diane again repeated the incident of awaking in the wee hours of the morning to the sound of knocking at her door and slipping in the blood.

"Tell me," said Riddmann, glaring over at the marshals. "How much blood is in the human body? You would know that, being a forensic anthropologist, right?"

"We each have about ten pints," said Diane.

"And how much can you lose and still live?" DA Riddmann asked.

"Less than three and a half pints. Any more than that and you are dead," said Diane.

"How much blood would you say was on your floor?" Riddmann asked, leaning forward. From the glitter in his eyes, Diane could see he was warming to the way he was building up his argument.

"I would say four pints or more," said Diane not taking her eyes off his.

"Can you distinguish, say, blood from a blood bank from fresh blood?" he asked.

"Yes. An anticoagulant preservative is added to stored blood," said Diane. "Among other things."

"Okay, now . . . " He sat up in his chair and straightened his tie.

Going in for the kill, thought Diane. What she didn't understand was why. She cast a glance at Garnett while Riddmann's attention was averted to his tie. Garnett was staring at her intently. She knew Garnett would be on her side—at least she thought she did. She did know that Garnett and Riddmann didn't always see eye to eye. In a flash it dawned on her. Councilman Albin Adler.

Riddmann was a friend and political crony of Adler. When Adler's mental and physical health forced him to leave politics amid one of Rosewood's worst catastrophes—an explosion that killed more than thirty students—it left a vacuum his political opponents eagerly filled. Diane knew Adler's friends and family believed she had misdirected paramedics, causing Adler to be left in subfreezing temperatures overnight, resulting in severe harm to him. They were wrong. It was not her fault. But they still blamed her.

And there was one thing about Adler's gang of friends. They were as vindictive as hell.

Chapter 22

"Can I get any of you something to drink?" said Diane. She wanted to add, *while the DA is straightening his tie*, but didn't. Tie straightening was Riddmann's tell. Diane didn't think he knew it. "I have a refrigerator in my osteology office."

There was a round of "no" from the marshals and Garnett—just enough time to interrupt Riddmann's flow. He glared at her. Diane sat looking at him innocently. He stumbled for words for several moments before continuing.

"What if I told you the blood in your apartment was fresh and belonged to one person," he said.

"I would say that person is most likely dead," said Diane.

"What if I said the blood trail leads from your apartment to your car and that a knife from your apartment was found in the trunk along with more of the same blood that was in your apartment?" said Riddmann.

"I would be very surprised," said Diane. "Is that what you are saying?"

He didn't answer. Diane didn't think he would. She was starting to resent being treated like a perp. She would stop the whole thing, but Riddmann would probably make Garnett drag her butt downtown.

"And what if I told you the blood belonged to Clymene O'Riley?" said Riddman.

Diane didn't say anything and again feigned astonishment. "Does it? Are you saying that Clymene was in my home?"

"Are you sticking to your story that you slept through a massacre going on in your apartment?" said Riddmann.

Apparently all of my neighbors did too, she thought. This is where he wanted to entice her to start a cascade of confessions: Maybe I heard something, but didn't get out of bed; yes, I got out of bed but when I saw someone in my apartment I hid; well, maybe I did confront them but I didn't kill them—it was someone else; well, maybe they attacked me and I had to defend myself. And last: well, there I was ankle deep in blood and a body in the living room—what was I to do but dump it?

But there was nothing to confess. The fact was, she did sleep through it. And Riddmann knew she did. So what was this about? Comeuppance for Adler?

"Of course I'm sticking by my account," said Diane. "It's the truth."

"Maybe you just don't remember," said Riddmann.

"What would be the mechanism that would cause sudden amnesia in me?" said Diane.

"People do have experiences they don't remember later . . . for any number of reasons," said Riddmann.

"It would be unprecedented in me," said Diane. "Let's look for horses and not zebras. Blood and urine samples were taken from me at the hospital. Do you have the results?" asked Diane.

He glanced at his watch on his left wrist and back

up at Diane. "You've been having a lot of stress at the museum. Then an escaped prisoner breaks into your home. Perhaps that caused some kind of mental break," he said.

The marshals shifted in their seats. Diane didn't think they were happy with Riddmann's questions. Maybe they sensed another agenda—or maybe they just wanted him to hurry and ask where she hid the body.

"No stress, just bad newspaper articles," said Diane. "If I blanked out every time there was stress at the museum, I would be in a constant state of sleepwalking. I didn't black out; I don't have amnesia. Do you have the tox screens back?"

"It's just a few more questions. What do you think happened?" he asked in a voice meant to tell her he was trying now to be friendly.

This was another of the trap questions. Get the suspect to come up with a scenario that will reveal that he, or she, has more information than he or she should. Diane rolled her eyes—and it set Riddmann off. He slammed his fist on the table.

"Look, we've been very accommodating to you. We could be having this conversation downtown with the press waiting outside. Anyone else, we would have. You've been getting a free ride because of your political connections, your status with the crime lab and with the museum. From your performance here and what I've been reading in the newspaper, you aren't doing a very good job in either."

Diane placed her hands on the table and leaned forward. She would have stood up, but under the circumstances Riddmann might think she was about to attack him. The mention of her political connections and the references to the newspaper articles about the

museum tweaked her suspicions and she could feel
her face flush. It was clear now what was going on.
Vanessa Van Ross was politically opposite from Riddmann's mentor, Adler, and over the years had done
considerable damage to Adler's and his friends' plans
for the city. Vanessa was too wealthy and well connected to take on directly, but attacking the museum
was a different matter. Everyone who knew Vanessa,
knew the museum was like her child. Hurt the museum, hurt her.

"Are you the one feeding the press misinformation
about the museum?" she asked.

Riddmann's eyes widened. He glanced down at his
watch and back up at Diane. He hesitated too long to
speak and Diane knew she was right. Or thought she
was right. But what could this idiot know about Egyptian artifacts?

"Don't think you can deflect attention from yourself
by accusing me," he said.

"I think there have been some misunderstandings,"
said Garnett. "No one is accusing anyone of anything.
We are just fact finding. In answer to your question,
Diane, yes, your tox screen came back positive for
barbiturates. Do you take sleeping pills?"

"No," she said.

"She could have taken them after her run-in with
Clymene," said Riddmann, clearly smarting from Diane's accusation.

Diane had wanted to tell him he should have left
the questioning to the marshals, that he was no good
at it—as his low conviction rate attested to. But she
held her tongue. Her former boss and mentor at
World Accord International was always telling her
that silence is just as important in diplomacy as all

manner of words—especially if the words you choose are wrong.

"Then I would have been sleeping through being forensically processed at the hospital. Apparently I was drugged," said Diane. "I need to find out when and how. If someone had access to my apartment, then they had access to anything I ate or drank."

"Your own people didn't find anything," said Riddmann.

He glared at her and Diane knew that if he hadn't been an enemy before, he was now. That was the trouble with politics; you could just be minding your own business and still end up in the middle of trouble.

"Absence of evidence is not evidence of absence," said Diane. "If someone took a body from my apartment, they could easily have taken the source of the barbiturate."

"Let's get back to the point of why we came," said Merrick. "Drew and I still have some questions for Dr. Fallon. If that's all right with all of you? Now, Dr. Fallon, you said you got no indication that Clymene was going to escape. What do you think she did have planned? From what I'm hearing, she's not the kind of woman who would be content to stay in jail. She asked you there for some reason."

"I thought she was planning an appeal," said Diane.

"She had no grounds," began Riddmann. Merrick's glance at him had the impact of a shot across the bow. He closed his mouth.

"I think she might have," said Diane. "Some problematic information was allowed in at her trial. However, the reason I thought she was going to appeal was that she had been writing briefs for fellow inmates and had been fairly successful. She's a smart lady. I thought her friendship with Rivers was to gain an advocate in her corner."

"The only reason I had to ask the judge to allow that evidence was because your crime scene evidence was so poor," said Riddmann.

Diane and the marshals ignored him.

"Did she say she was going to appeal?" asked Drew.

"No. But it made sense. I believe she would have won the appeal," said Diane.

"But an appeal would have only gotten her a new trial," said Merrick. "Would she have won without this problem evidence?"

"No," said Diane. "The crime scene evidence was strong."

"So, in that case, it makes sense that she would run, given that she wanted out," said Merrick.

"Putting it that way, yes," said Diane. "But as I said earlier, she had a lot of confidence in her powers of persuasion and she would be up against a DA's office with a fifty-four percent conviction rate. The next jury might side with her," said Diane. Okay, she'd said it. Not a wise thing to do. But it was done.

Garnett winced. Riddmann glared at her with such intensity that she thought his gaze might actually burn her skin. The marshals raised their eyebrows slightly.

"The fact of the matter," said Riddmann, "is that we have what can legally be described as a dead body in *your* apartment. *Your* bloody knife in *your* car with Clymene's blood in *your* car trunk. I convicted Clymene herself on less. I'm ordering Garnett to arrest you."

Chapter 23

"Okay, let's just talk about this," said Garnett. He cast Diane a glance that was more frustration than anger, clearly wanting to defuse the crisis. "There's time to sort this out, and Diane isn't going anywhere."

Diane's cell rang just as the DA opened his mouth to say something. She fished the phone out of the inside pocket of her jacket.

"Excuse me," she said as she looked at the display. It was Andie, her assistant.

"Hi. Diane. I didn't know where you were, so I called your cell. Are you all right?"

"Fine," said Diane. It wasn't true at the moment, but Andie was asking about her health.

"There's a guy from the FBI who wants to talk to you about the artifacts," said Andie.

"The FBI. Great. Tell him he has to take a number," said Diane.

"What?" said Andie.

"Just hold the phone a minute, Andie," said Diane.

She put her phone on mute and looked at the others. The marshals looked amused. The DA looked a little happier. Garnett was still frowning.

"Can we wait until I speak with the FBI before you take me downtown?" she said.

"Look," said Garnett. He turned to the DA. "I think it's premature to arrest Dr. Fallon at this point. The barbiturates in her system do give her an alibi, and I would hate to make a mistake that we all would regret. Remember, no one in the apartment building heard anything either—not the neighbors across the hall, nor the ones above, below, or beside her. You will agree that is odd. In addition to the unpleasantness in her apartment early this morning, Dr. Fallon was attacked at the hospital by an unknown assailant wielding a knife. I think we can cut her some slack, especially since I'm sure she is sorry"—he looked at her when he said the word *sorry*—"for not being as cooperative as she could, but that's understandable." He looked at Diane and gestured with his head toward Riddmann.

Diane knew what he meant. He wanted her to apologize to the DA. *Damn*. But the museum and the crime lab were worth more than her pride at the moment.

"Garnett is right," said Diane. "Mr. Riddmann, I'm sorry. You are certainly due more cooperation than I have given, especially in front of guests." She nodded at the marshals. "I'm also sorry for the misuse of statistics. I hate it when other people do it and I regret doing it myself."

Riddmann had been smiling—or smirking—at her, she couldn't really tell the difference, but now he looked confused. Diane turned to the marshals.

"The police commissioner in Rosewood asked the DA's office to accept cases that have weaker evidence than they would normally prosecute. The aim is for Rosewood to get as many criminals off the streets as it can. Although we do get more people off the streets, a consequence is a statistically lower conviction rate for the DA's office." A policy which Diane, herself, disagreed with because another consequence was that too many innocents got convicted. "If Rosewood had the same policy as, say Atlanta, the conviction rate stats would be much higher."

Riddmann looked as though he hadn't realized that before. He probably tucked it away to use in his next campaign.

"I didn't know you were attacked at the hospital," said Riddmann. "With this new evidence, I think we can wait."

"Thank you," she said, and Garnett looked relieved.

"This attack," asked Deputy Marshal Merrick, "do you think it was connected to the incident in your apartment?"

"I don't know," said Diane.

She didn't say that she thought it was connected to the museum, and she wasn't sure she was going to tell the FBI. She believed she had a better chance of solving it than they did. If someone thought she was dirty and was willing to kill her for it, the FBI would, of course, see her as a suspect for buying stolen antiquities. That would be a blind alley, and valuable time would be lost. But leaving out important information when talking to the FBI was very risky business. Diane was beginning to feel stuck—like she was fighting wars on too many fronts.

She got back on the phone with Andie. "Ask him to wait in my office. I'll be right there."

"Where are you coming from exactly?" asked Andie.

Diane smiled into the phone. "I'm in the crime lab."

"Oh, okay. I'll tell him you'll just be a few minutes, then," she said.

"Thank you, Andie." Diane hung up the phone.

"We will be in the area a few more days," said Merrick. "If . . ."

"Why are you still on the case?" asked Riddmann. "We have jurisdiction now."

"Because we don't have Clymene's body," said Merrick. "It makes the paperwork harder."

Merrick turned to Diane. "If your apartment is a crime scene, where will you be staying?"

"I'm staying with Frank Duncan; he's a detective in—"

"We know Frank," said Drew. "We apprehended one of his white-collar fugitives. Good guy to work with."

"If we need you, then you will be either at his house or here, somewhere in this building," said Merrick.

"Yes," said Diane.

She saw them out of the crime lab on its private elevator side, the side that didn't go through the museum. She supposed she should be grateful that Riddmann appeared to be satisfied with her apology, but the whole thing left a sour taste in her mouth. By the time he got to his office, she imagined Riddmann would have the story embellished to the point that Diane got on her knees and begged him to forgive her.

Before leaving the lab and going to her museum office, she called down to the basement. She was right. That's where her crew was waiting.

"How'd it go, Boss?" said Jin.

"I'll tell you later. I have to go meet with the FBI now," said Diane.

"Gee, Boss, you don't get a break, do you?" he said.

"Apparently not. I want you to know I appreciate you guys," she said.

"Sure—" he began.

"Jin, did you find anything about the artifacts— anything on NSAF?"

"The artifacts. Right. The girdle, the one that looks like it was made of cowrie shells, was stolen from the Cairo Museum in 1957," he said. "It was the only one of the artifacts in the database. The stone artifacts had soil residue on them, but I haven't had a chance to process the sample yet. We've been kind of busy."

"I know. Thanks, Jin. It's about time for you guys to go home," she said.

"We'll wait. We want to know what happened with the marshals," said Jin.

Oh, I'm not sure you do, thought Diane. "I don't know how long I'll be," she said.

"That's okay. Neva and David want to know if it's all right if they go back up to the lab," said Jin.

"Yes. Everyone's gone," said Diane.

"Well, tell me this, did they try to hang it on you?" Jin was in his usual joking manner and she could tell he really didn't believe they would seriously consider Diane to be a suspect.

"Yes," she said, "they did."

"Really, Boss?" said Jin. "I'm sorry . . . did they really?"

"It's all right. Thanks to Garnett, I didn't get hauled off to the station." She looked at her watch. "I need to get going. The FBI is waiting. I'll tell you about it later."

Diane left the crime lab and walked across the dino-saur overlook through to the bank of elevators in the middle of the building. She passed several museum staff. A few looked as if they wanted to engage her in conversation but she waved them off, smiling, hop-ing she didn't look as overwhelmed as she felt. She would really like to sit down and take a break, drink some hot tea, skip town. But there wasn't time. She took the elevator down to the first floor and walked to her office. Andie was there engaging the FBI agent in an animated conversation about dinosaurs.

He rose, smiled, and held out a hand when Diane came into the room. "I'm Agent Shane Jacobs. I understand you have some antiquities that may not be yours."

Chapter 24

You have antiquities that may not be yours—it sounded like a principal gently scolding a naughty student.

"I'm afraid we might," said Diane, "I'm sorry to say." She took his hand.

Shane Jacobs had a firm handshake, salt-and-pepper wavy hair, and a slim tanned face with sharp features. He looked younger than Diane by a few years. His dark suit, smooth-shaven face, and short hair made him look like the stereotypical FBI agent. He pulled out his FBI identification to let her inspect it.

"I would like to see the artifacts," he said.

He wasn't somber like the law enforcement officers she had just dealt with, but smiled broadly at her as if he could just as well have been coming to buy the artifacts. He looked at his watch.

"I know it's getting late, but I'd also like to speak with Dr. Kendel Williams and the curator of your Egyptian exhibits," he said.

He seemed friendly enough, but Diane was sure that was just his method of gaining the confidence of the person he was interviewing. She was getting weary of being on the suspect end of investigations.

Diane turned to Andie. "Has Kendel left for the day?" she asked.

"I'll call," said Andie as she picked up the phone.

"If she's in, tell her to wait," said Diane. "If not, call her home and ask her to come to the museum."

Andie nodded. "Got it."

"Is Jonas back?" she asked Andie. Ironically, Jonas Briggs had been at an Egyptology conference.

"I saw him earlier. He was looking for you," said Andie.

"He and everyone else on the planet," said Diane. "We'll be going by his office. I'll stop in."

Diane led Agent Jacobs out of Andie's office and down the hall toward the main bank of elevators.

"The artifacts are in the conservation lab on the second floor," she said.

"I appreciate your cooperation in this," said Jacobs. "As you can guess, I get a lot of 'where's your warrant.'"

"This has been dreadful for us," said Diane. "We would like it cleared up as soon as possible." As she walked, she explained everything that she had discovered so far. "We didn't know anything was wrong until the newspaper articles began coming out. The artifacts had just arrived and hadn't even been opened yet."

"That's odd." It was the only comment Jacobs made. He had not yet even asked any questions.

Diane took him up to the second floor and into the room housing the Egyptian exhibit. She wanted him to see what they had now, so he would understand why they only wanted certain artifacts and not the ones that were sitting in the conservation lab.

Diane loved walking into the room housing the exhibit. It was like entering ancient Egypt. The walls were painted like the walls of an Egyptian tomb. But upon entering, the visitor's gaze first fell on Neva's reconstruction of their mummy, a scribe, they had concluded, sitting cross-legged on a pedestal in the middle of the room as if he were about to take up his sharpened reed and write on the papyrus lying in his lap.

The mummy whose likeness greeted visitors was in a closed anthropomorphic Egyptian coffin housed inside a glass case away from the hands of curious visitors. Above him on the wall were photographs of him before and after he was rewrapped and placed back in his coffin.

Along another wall sat a glass display case for the amulets that had been wrapped with the mummy. Each now had its own pedestal. Acquiring them had been a coup for Kendel. The museum had inherited the mummy—a survivor from a Victorian unwrapping party and handed down through a family until the last surviving member gave it to the museum. Another branch of the family had owned the good-luck amulets from inside the wrappings. Kendel had negotiated their purchase: an alabaster scarab that probably once resided over the mummy's heart, several small alabaster and lapis lazuli fish figurines, an inscribed sandstone cylinder with the name Senwosret III, two faience figures, several limestone figurines, and black steatite *shabtis*.

The exhibit contained a diorama based on life in twelfth-dynasty Egypt, including an entire miniature Egyptian town, highlighting a scribe's house. The Egyptian room was one of the most popular in the museum.

"Our mummy is from the twelfth dynasty," said Diane. "This is a learning museum and we didn't want an unrelated assortment of Egyptian artifacts from all over the historical timeline. We decided to specialize in twelfth-dynasty items. That is what we ordered and that is what the documents said we had. That is not what arrived."

"It's an excellent exhibit," he said, peering at the amulets. He looked up sharply. "So, Golden Antiquities sent the wrong items?" He pulled out a chair from one of the computer terminals and sat down.

Diane took another chair and sat across from him. "Yes, but the items they sent were similar to what we ordered. That's what's so odd," said Diane.

"So someone sent authentic documents to provide provenance for artifacts that were switched."

"But that wouldn't have worked," said Diane.

She went over the same arguments with him as she had with Frank—how more than one person verified the provenances, how she herself signed off on everything that arrived at the museum, how the museum pretty much displayed everything it owned.

"No one could get away with using this museum to launder antiquities," said Diane.

She studied him as she spoke, wondering whether she could trust him. In the end she decided to wait to tell him about her attacker and what he had said. She stood up.

"Jonas' office is across the way here."

Jonas Briggs was in his office and Diane introduced him to Agent Jacobs. He seemed to be waiting for them, the way he answered his door so quickly. Andie must have called. Jonas was a retired professor from Bartram University. He had white hair, a toothbrush mustache to match, and white bushy eyebrows over crystal blue eyes. He was dressed in jeans and one of the ubiquitous Richard III T-shirts.

"This is just terrible," said Jonas. "Just terrible. Kendel and I were looking forward to the new artifacts." He shook his head and offered them a seat.

"Actually, I would like to see the artifacts and the documents first. Will you be here for a while?" asked Agent Jacobs.

"I can be," said Jonas.

"Good. So you are an Egyptologist?" said Jacobs.

"No. My field is southeastern U.S. archaeology. However, I have taken to learning Egyptology. I've always liked it."

"Did you negotiate the purchase of the objects?" asked Jacobs.

"No. I can't negotiate the purchase of a used car," said Jonas. "But I examined the catalog and the copies of the provenances. Everything was just fine."

Jacobs nodded. "I'll come by again after I've finished looking at the artifacts," he said. "Thank you for waiting."

Diane looked back at Jonas as she left with Agent Jacobs. He looked miserable. She smiled at him as if to say, *It will be all right.* She took Jacobs through earth science across the overlook to the Pleistocene room. Jacobs stopped to look over the railing at the mammoth and other giant Pleistocene creatures.

"Are the bones real, or are they casts?" he asked.

"The Pleistocene bones are real. The bones in the dinosaur room are casts purchased from the Bickford," said Diane.

"Good museum. You know they're looking for a new director. Harold Marquering's retiring, I hear," said Jacobs.

"I had heard also," said Diane. "He had only been there, what, six years?"

"About that," said Jacobs. "You have lots of room here."

"We do. We offer lab space to university faculty in exchange for their curative services."

"How's that working out?" he asked, grinning.

From his expression, Diane guessed he had worked with professors before.

"It has its ups and downs," said Diane. "On the whole, it has turned out to be a good deal for us."

From there they went to the conservation lab. Diane introduced him to Korey, who helped Diane lay out all the questionable artifacts and the documentation.

"This item"—Diane pointed to the girdle—"turned up on NSAF as stolen from the Cairo Museum in 1957."

Jacobs took a pair of glasses out of his pocket and looked at the piece. "I believe you're right. They will be glad it finally turned up. I wonder where it's been." He looked over at Diane. "You're aware that Golden Antiquities burned and Randal Cunningham was killed."

"I had heard. Was it the elder Cunningham or his son?" asked Diane.

"The son," said Jacobs. "There was never any suspicion surrounding Golden Antiquities while the old man ran things. Since he turned it over to his son . . . well, it's one of the places I watch."

Jacobs pulled up a nearby stool and took a pair of white gloves out of his pocket and slipped them on. He looked at the pectoral and opened the document that was supposed to be its provenance.

"Okay, the documentation is of a pectoral showing a vulture goddess with wings surrounded by lotus flowers. The documents say it's lapis lazuli, gold, turquoise, carnelian, and amethyst. Very nice. The artifact we have here is Maat in a boat. You know Maat is the goddess of truth, balance, order. Hope we find some truth here, eh?" Jacobs seemed to like to talk as he worked. Diane and Korey stood by and listened.

"The stone pieces here"—he pointed to the stone bust and face—"they are Ramses II, nineteenth dynasty. The documents are for similar items, but of Senwosret III, which would have gone nicely with your sandstone amulet with Senwosret III's name inscribed on it. You say these were at the Pearle?"

"Yes," said Diane. "We had hoped to purchase them directly from the Pearle, but . . ." She let the sentence trail off as he went to another item.

"The canopic jar is also from the nineteenth dynasty," he muttered as if talking only to himself.

He got up and walked over to the sphinx, still in the crate. "Again, the documents say Senwosret III—this is Amenemhat III. He's of the twelfth dynasty too, however. Nice piece. All of them are." He stood up and took off his gloves.

"Other than the Mereret girdle, I don't recognize any of the pieces as being in our database. That doesn't mean they weren't recently looted or stolen. You won't mind if I confiscate them until we can sort this out?" he said almost guiltily.

"No. They aren't ours," said Diane. "But we would like to have the items we ordered, if they weren't destroyed in the fire. Failing that, we would like to get our money back. We have an arrangement with our dealers that we pay a quarter of the price up front and the rest after we receive the items and they are verified. That quarter is a substantial sum for us. And"—Diane waved an arm, encompassing the artifacts—"this has damaged our reputation. We would like that back too. We didn't do this. If you would like to look at our books, I'll have Andie take you to Accounting."

Jacobs smiled. "Ross said you would be cooperative. He thinks very highly of you and the museum."

Diane smiled back, grateful that Ross Kingsley had

spoken to Jacobs. "We've worked a couple of cases together," said Diane. "I appreciate him giving us a good reference."

"When he's up and about he said he will get back in touch with you."

"Up and about?" said Diane.

"You didn't know? Last night on the way home from . . . actually from here, he fell asleep at the wheel and wrecked his car."

Chapter 25

"Fell asleep at the wheel?" repeated Diane. "Is he all right?"

"Fine. Banged up a little—treated at the hospital and released. He seemed rather embarrassed by it. He said he'd never done anything like that before." Agent Jacobs paused a moment. "What?" he said as Diane stared at him.

It happened here, she thought. "Did you and he talk about his latest case?" said Diane. "Clymene O'Riley?"

"A little. Actually he wanted me to tell you something. He mentioned the name *Clymene* and I, in my usual pedantic mode, mentioned that in Greek mythology Clymene was a girl whose father sold her into slavery." Jacobs stopped and pointed at Diane's face and grinned. "Ross had the same expression."

"That may explain a lot about our Clymene," said Diane. "She can't have chosen that name by chance."

"That's just what Ross said," Jacobs replied.

Diane grabbed her cell. "I need to speak with Kingsley," she said. "Korey can show you the way back to either my or Jonas' office. I'll catch up to you in a little bit."

"That information must be really important," said Jacobs.

"Both things are," called Diane as she went out the door.

Before she was out of hearing range, she heard Korey telling Jacobs, "It's like that here all the time."

Diane retraced her steps to the geology section and to Mike's office and knocked.

"Doc," said Mike when he opened the door. "Nice surprise. What can I do for you?"

"I'd like to borrow your office for a minute," she said.

"Sure. Come in. Shall I leave?" he asked.

"I hate to throw you out of your office, but would you mind?" Diane asked.

"No. I have some things to do in the lab. Take all the time you need."

"Mike, thanks," said Diane as he was leaving.

He lingered at the door a moment. "Sure, Doc. You know you can always count on me." He closed the door.

Diane wanted a private place to talk with Kingsley, and Mike's was the closest office. She looked up his number on her cell.

"Diane," Kingsley said, answering. "I'm relieved to hear your voice. I was just reading about you. Are you all right?"

"Yes, I'm fine. I haven't seen the paper; what does it say?"

"Not much, really. Something about a home invasion and an unknown assailant who might be injured or dead. What happened?" he asked.

Good ol' Garnett, thought Diane. He had a knack for totally confusing a news story.

"A lot more than in the papers. How are you?"

"I guess Shane told you about my accident. Asleep at the wheel . . . I—"

"I think you may have been drugged," interrupted Diane.

Kingsley was silent for a moment.

"Drugged?" he said. "What do you mean? How? You mean at the museum?"

"Do you have a bruise or—I know this is going to sound a little appalling—but do you have any clothes with your blood on them from the accident?" said Diane.

"I don't know. Bruises, yes, but my wife took my clothes. What's this about?" he asked.

"I'm sure you've metabolized it out of your system by now, but the blood in a bruise or in your clothes can be analyzed for barbiturates," Diane said.

"Barbiturates. Okay, what's this about?" he asked.

"Last night I apparently slept through a violent homicide in my apartment. At the hospital they found barbiturates in my blood sample. If it weren't for that, I'd probably be under arrest for murder."

There was a rather long silence at the other end of the phone. Diane was beginning to wonder if he had hung up—or passed out.

"You better tell me about this," he said at last.

Diane heard sounds like he was rearranging himself in his chair, or bed. She explained about waking up to the sound of the police knocking on her door and then falling in the pool of blood.

"It turned out to be Clymene's blood," Diane told him.

"Clymene's? I don't understand. Is she dead?" asked Ross.

"She has to be. It was fresh blood and there was too much blood loss for her to still be alive." Diane explained everything she knew about the incident.

"When I heard you had fallen asleep while driving home, it made me wonder if both of us had been drugged at the restaurant. Perhaps someone found it easier to drug both our drinks than to try and make sure I got the tainted drink. That's always tricky. I'm going to the restaurant to question them now."

"Clymene dead? I can't believe it. What was she doing in your apartment?" he said.

"I have no idea," said Diane. "I don't understand how she even got in. I didn't hear anything, nor did any of my neighbors. And the person in the apartment directly below me hears every little footfall."

"The newspaper account was wholly inadequate," he said.

"Garnett tries to keep anything to do with the crime lab, in this case me, out of the papers. He usually does a pretty good job."

"This is strange. In a bizarre way I'm a little relieved. My wife, Lydia, is convinced that something came loose in my brain. She wants me to take all these tests. If I was drugged . . . well, I actually feel a little better."

Diane laughed. "I'm glad you can see the silver lining in this."

"Lydia almost had me convinced, and I was getting a little worried," he said. "You say they almost arrested you?"

"That was mostly political. The DA was very upset with me," said Diane. "And of course I couldn't account for all that blood in my apartment."

"The DA? Oh, I'm sorry, Diane. I didn't call him," said Kingsley.

"That's all right. I'm glad you're safe. I'm also glad you spoke with your FBI friend in art theft about me. I appreciate that."

"Shane's a good guy. Knows a lot about the subject," he said.

"I'll let you know what I find out from the restaurant staff," said Diane.

"Tell me," asked Ross, "how are you doing, really? You had a hit on the head, the paper said?"

"It wasn't serious." Diane told him about the trip to the hospital and the attack there. She left out what the attacker had said to her about being a dirty dealer. She didn't know why, except she didn't want people to start questioning her honesty.

"You were attacked again? The same day? Do you think it was the same person who killed Clymene?" he asked.

"I don't know. I haven't really had time to sit down and think things out," she said. "Like, who had a motive to kill Clymene?"

"I imagine anyone of her victim's family. You know, someone could have recognized her picture from the trial publicity and tracked her down. It may be a family from a victim we aren't even aware of. You really are going to have to discover who she is."

"I know. And I don't know if it was in the papers, but Rev. Rivers was murdered right after Clymene escaped," said Diane.

"Rivers murdered? Oh, no. He was really a decent guy. Clymene must have convinced him to help her escape. I told you she was good—and no good."

"That's what I was thinking," said Diane, "that she got to him. He looked so disappointed when I shared the evidence against her with him."

"I'm really not in bad condition. Tomorrow I'll drive to Rosewood and we can talk about it," he said.

"You don't think you should at least take another day or two to recover?" said Diane.

"I was lucky," said Ross. "I just ended up in a ditch. The air bag was the worst part of it. The hospital didn't even keep me."

"I'll see you sometime tomorrow, then."

After Diane hung up with Kingsley she called Frank.

"Babe," he said, "how are things going?"

"All things considering, they're going pretty well. I avoided getting arrested, thanks to Garnett. Right in the middle of that interview, an agent from the FBI art theft division came to talk to me. I'm still a free woman, so I guess things are going pretty well."

"Why don't I come and pick you up?" said Frank.

"I still have to talk to my crime scene people. And I have an FBI agent wandering around in the building that I need to keep track of. I also have to speak with the museum restaurant people."

She told him about Kingsley's accident and her suspicion about the source of the barbiturates.

"I hardly know what to say," Frank said when she finished.

"I know. It's not easy being me." Diane fingered a geode on Mike's desk. She picked it up and examined it. It looked like a tiny cave filled with sparkling crystal.

"You need to alert your security people at the museum to watch out for you."

Diane could hear the concern in his voice and it made her feel guilty. "Thanks for letting me stay at your house."

"You know you can stay here as long as you like."

She put the geode back down and leaned back in the chair. "I know, and it's tempting."

"If you ever get back here, I'll really tempt you," Frank said.

Diane smiled. "That's worth hurrying up for. Oh, I almost forgot. The marshals said they know you— Chad Merrick and Dylan Drew. Do you remember them?"

"Yes, I do. Rather tenacious. They aren't going to like not having a body."

That's what I figured, she thought.

When Diane hung up, she felt a cold stab of fear in the pit of her stomach. She was quickly losing control of everything around her and the thought panicked her. She gripped Mike's geode tightly, inhaled deeply, and let her breath out slowly. She had to solve the mysteries—all of them—or she could never make her world right. She set the geode down, got up, and headed down to the restaurant, hoping that the young woman who waited on her and Kingsley was working today.

Chapter 26

The museum restaurant with its tall old-brick arch-
ways and vaulted chambers looked very much like a
medieval castle. In the evenings all the tables were lit
by candles. It was a cozy restaurant and served good
food. This evening the restaurant was packed, as it
had been the previous evening when Diane was there
with Kingsley. She glanced around the room and saw
several people she knew. So far no one had noticed
her. She spoke to the hostess and asked if Karalyn
was working tonight. She was. Diane asked to see her
in the manager's office.

"Sure. Is everything okay?" asked the hostess.

"Fine," said Diane, hoping her smile didn't look as
fake as if felt. "Just ask her to meet me, please."

Diane hated this kind of interview. Karalyn was
young and had worked at the restaurant for several
months while attending Bartram University. Diane
couldn't really imagine her drugging the patrons—or
her. Diane walked to the back of the restaurant, looking
straight ahead. She saw someone wave to her out of
the corner of her eye. She pretended she didn't notice.

Diane went into the office, a small room with a desk
piled high with papers and restaurant catalogs. She

pulled out two chairs, sat down in one, and waited for Karalyn.

"Sorry I took so long to see you . . . someone didn't show up for work and I have to fill in for him," she said, a little out of breath.

"Did you lose someone?" asked Diane. She motioned to the chair and Karalyn sat down.

"One of the wait staff didn't show up and the manager can't get hold of him. It's common in this business, unfortunately. Some people don't bother to call." She frowned and smoothed her long skirt.

"Do you remember me and a gentleman eating dinner last night?"

"Sure. He was here most of the day," said Karalyn.

"When we were eating, did you fill the drinks you brought us?"

"Why . . . no, as a matter of fact, Bobby Banks did." said Karalyn. "He's the one who didn't show up. Was something wrong with the drinks?"

"Why did he fill them and not you?" asked Diane.

Karalyn's frown deepened. "He offered," she said. "We were so busy. I just thought he was trying to get on my good side, to ask me out." She paused a moment. "He wasn't, was he?"

Diane shook her head. "No, I don't think he was. Do you have an address for him?"

"Sure." Karalyn jumped up and went to a filing cabinet and started looking through the files.

"Did you or anyone here notice anything unusual about Bobby yesterday?" asked Diane as Karalyn searched for the address.

"No. He was his usual self. Funny and friendly. We all like him. He's a good worker and he doesn't try to steal tips. A little odd, though. Very juvenile acting. Well, this is funny," said Karalyn.

"What?" asked Diane.

"His address: 1214 Rockwell Drive," she said.

"Rockwell only goes to 800. That would put him in the woods," said Diane.

"It would. What's going on?" she said, looking at Diane with a frown.

"What does he look like?" asked Diane.

"Blond hair. Hazel eyes. Slim. Real cute . . . almost pretty in a guy sort of way," said Karalyn. "About five ten, I guess. My boyfriend is five ten and Bobby seems about that tall."

"Does he have a personal space? Don't you guys have lockers?" asked Diane.

Karalyn nodded. "That was an odd thing about him," she said. "He was really into cleanliness."

"What do you mean?" asked Diane.

"He's always wiping down everything. Even his locker." She paused a moment in thought. "He was getting rid of fingerprints, wasn't he?"

Karalyn was getting that sparkle in her eye that Diane often saw in people when they found themselves landed in a mystery.

"Maybe," said Diane.

"Wow, can't you tell me what he did?" she said.

"I don't know that he did anything," said Diane. "I just need to speak with him." She left Karalyn closing the filing cabinet and walked out and through the restaurant.

"Diane."

She recognized the voice of Kenneth Meyerson, one of the board members. She turned to him and smiled. He was at a table with his wife.

"Can you sit down a minute?" he asked.

Diane hesitated, then smiled and sat down. "Just a minute. How are you and Evelyn?"

"We're great. Just going to a concert on campus tonight. Ever heard of a fellow named August Kellenmeyer?" asked Kenneth.

"Oh, Ken, of course she has," said his wife.

Evelyn was a petite woman with pixielike short, dark hair and a heart-shaped face. She reminded Diane of Clara Bow.

"Pianist," said Diane. "Yes. One of my favorites."

"I just wanted to tell you how much I enjoyed the board meeting yesterday," said Kenneth.

"You enjoyed that?" said Diane. "You must be hard up for entertainment."

He chuckled. "Oh, you don't know. Before you arrived, Barclay was telling Vanessa, 'This is what happens when you have no oversight. You've got to change this. The board has to have more power. I'll show you how to handle this.' He hammered his hand up and down on the table like he was swatting flies." Kenneth laughed. "I guess he did show her how to handle it. I thought to myself when he was going on, Diane's going to rip him a new one. And you did."

"I take it you've had a run-in with him before," said Diane.

"Oh, yeah. When I was just starting out I went to his bank for a loan. He treated me like I was hardly worth stepping on. Barely looked at me when he was turning down my application and lecturing me on how there are bigger computer companies out there and who was I to think I could compete with them out of my garage," he said.

Kenneth's computer company was now both successful and international, but Diane could tell he still felt the sting of that rejection.

"I guess you showed him," said Diane.

Kenneth waved his hand dismissively. "He's turned

down so many loans since then, I don't think he even remembers me. It was a long time ago. I just wanted to tell you how much I enjoyed the meeting."

"Why did you guys vote him in?" asked Diane.

"I didn't. You know Vanessa, Laura, and Madge. They are old Rosewood just like Barclay. Laura thinks he's just a gruff avuncular bear. Hell, he's good to his own kind. And Vanessa thought we could use a banker. I don't think they were pleased with his performance, to tell you the truth."

"I certainly wasn't," said Diane. She wished Kenneth and his wife a pleasant evening and left hoping she wouldn't run into anyone else. But as she exited the restaurant she ran into Vanessa and Laura leaving at the same time. Normally she enjoyed visiting with them. But not today. She stiffened as they said hello.

Chapter 27

"Diane," said Vanessa, "Laura and I have been trying to get in touch with you since . . . well, the board meeting . . . and now the papers. Someone invaded your home? Are you all right? Can we talk?"

Vanessa and Laura looked like they were going to the same concert as the Meyersons. They glittered and shined in flashy evening clothes.

"Aren't the two of you going to be late somewhere?" asked Diane.

"We have time," said Vanessa.

Both were staring at Diane's forehead.

"You're hurt," said Laura.

"Not much," said Diane. She looked at her watch. "I really have to go . . ."

"Diane, please," said Vanessa. "Take a little time and talk to us?"

Diane shrugged. "Very little time."

She led them across to the mammals section, unlocking the door with her key. She called security and asked them to keep the day lighting on until she told them otherwise, but to keep the museum locked down. Then she called Andie, who was still at her desk.

"Is Jacobs still interviewing Kendel?" she asked Andie.

"Yes. I put them in your conference room."

"Okay, just checking. Call me on my cell if you need me," she said.

Diane led them through to a seating area in the Pleistocene room and they sat down near the giant sloth.

"Someone is interviewing Kendel," said Laura. "Is that about the Egyptian artifacts?"

"Yes. An FBI agent from the art theft division is here. That's why I don't have much time."

"Are they stolen?" whispered Laura.

Out of the corner of her eye, Diane thought she saw the flicker of a shadow near the flora around the Smilodon, the saber-toothed tiger, across the huge room. She stared a moment. Nothing. She was beginning to become frightened of shadows. *Get a grip*, she told herself firmly and turned her attention back to her two friends.

"The artifacts aren't what we purchased. The FBI is looking into it. It's a long story and I'll brief you when I have more information and more time."

"Diane," said Vanessa, "you're angry, aren't you?"

"I'm just weary, Vanessa. And yes, I'm still angry with Madge and Barclay."

"Madge meant well," said Vanessa. "She just didn't understand the implications."

"Meant well . . ." Diane shook her head. "No one seems to understand the harm she did. This will follow Kendel and the museum forever. You can't get rid of accusations. Had Madge just referred the reporter to me rather than confirming something she had no idea was true or not, the museum could have come out of this looking like a hero rather than appearing as if it has something to hide. Did you see the paper today? Director backpedaling? I've done nothing of the kind. They just attributed Madge's recant as coming from me."

"What if the accusations against Kendel are true?" said Laura. "I know you don't want to consider that—"

"Of course I have to consider it. But whether or not they are true doesn't make what Madge did right. If Kendel turns out to be guilty it will just make matters worse because Madge's behavior will be reinforced, and the next time a reporter calls her they might be accusing Kenneth of illegal business practices, or me of embezzling, or you, Laura, of unethical conduct with patients. And Madge will just confirm whatever the reporter says because she likes her name in the paper and, after all, things turned out just swell the last time."

"Nothing like this is likely to happen again," said Laura.

"Why not? The reporter knows who to call to get a confirmation about anyone connected with the museum. Her duty is done. She checked out her story with an authoritative source and now she can print it," said Diane. "After all, Madge is a board member and an upstanding citizen."

Vanessa and Laura exchanged glances.

"We do see your point," said Vanessa. "And we really do see the harm that has been done by this. I'll do everything in my power to fix it."

Diane glanced at her watch again.

"I can see how this is upsetting," said Laura, "but—"

"Upsetting? Laura, I'm tired and my day isn't nearly over. Clymene O'Riley escaped from prison

yesterday and the U.S. marshals are talking to me because I was her last visitor. Someone broke into my
home and killed her on my living room floor last night.
At least they had the good manners to drug me so I
wouldn't wake up in the middle of it. While I was in
the hospital examining room in one of those ghastly
insufficient gowns with my bare butt hardly covered,
someone tried to kill me. I don't know if it had to do
with Clymene or the artifacts. Riddmann tried to arrest me for Clymene's murder, but fortunately Garnett
stepped in."

Diane took a deep breath. She had never been cross
with either Laura or Vanessa before, but it felt good
at the moment.

"Now, I find not only was I drugged," she continued, "but the FBI profiler I was with was probably
drugged too. And it probably happened in the museum restaurant, because he fell asleep at the wheel
of his car and had an accident on his way home from
dinner here. Oh, and I can't move back into my apartment until the crime scene cleaners remove the two
quarts of blood on the floor. Yes, Laura, it's all upsetting to me."

While she spoke, both Vanessa and Laura paled,
their eyes wide and mouths open, speechless.

"Diane," said Vanessa at last, "I had no idea—the
newspapers . . ."

"You can stay at my home," they both said simultaneously.

"Thank you, really. I appreciate your offers, but I'm
staying with Frank. Now, Agent Jacobs is somewhere
in the museum. I have to go." Her head actually felt
clearer. Sometimes venting was a good thing.

Vanessa laid a hand on Diane's arm. "What does
all this mean?" she asked. "Clymene O'Riley is dead?

I can't say that it makes me unhappy. Archer O'Riley was a good man. I liked him very much."

"She's dead, but we don't have a body. Someone dragged it out of my apartment and dumped it using my car." She paused again and looked over at the saber-toothed tiger. The long, sharp canine teeth reminded her of the knife found in her car.

"What? Why?" said Vanessa.

"I don't know," said Diane. "None of it makes any sense, except to cast suspicion on me for some reason. If the attack at the hospital was related to the homicide at my home, why didn't they just kill me there? I was completely vulnerable. I'm thinking that the hospital attack was related to the artifacts because of something he said. I believe he thought I deal in stolen antiquities, but why, I don't know. Now I really have to go. Follow me and I'll let you out the doors into the lobby."

After Diane saw Laura and Vanessa off, she headed to her office. *The knife,* thought Diane. Why clean it, then leave it in my car with other blood? That doesn't make any sense—nothing did—Clymene's murder in her apartment or the stolen artifacts. She hurried to her office to see Agent Jacobs.

Chapter 28

When Diane walked into Andie's office, Agent Jacobs had just finished speaking with Jonas Briggs. Jonas sat down on Andie's sofa next to Kendel. Diane looked at the two of them. They didn't look beat up, so she supposed it went well. She smiled at them and went into her office, where Agent Jacobs was gathering his notes. He glanced up at her.

"I appreciate your cooperation, really," he said. "You don't know how many times I get stonewalled by museums."

If stonewalling would work, I might do it, thought Diane. "We need this solved," she said. "Do you have any idea who the artifacts belong to?"

"Only the girdle is in the database, but I haven't had a chance to check with my sources for the latest looting," he said.

"Is there any chance we can get the items we purchased? I suppose you don't know if they were burned in the fire?" asked Diane.

"Not all of the building was consumed. The contents are being inventoried. And fortunately a lot of the artifacts are stone, so something will be left. I hate to think of all those antiquities gone forever." He sighed.

Diane could see that he loved his work—saving the world's historical treasures.

"I didn't get a chance to look at your books," he said, "so I'll be back tomorrow."

"Let me know what you need," she said. "Kingsley will be coming tomorrow also. Perhaps you'll run into each other."

Jacobs made a face. "Should he be up and about?"

"Probably not, but this Clymene thing calls like a Siren," said Diane.

Jacobs smiled. "It must. Maybe the two of you can fill me in over lunch. You've gotten my curiosity up."

Diane wanted to ask him what he thought about the investigation here so far, but she knew he wouldn't tell her. She walked him to the door and gave him directions to a good bed-and-breakfast.

She returned to her office to debrief Jonas and Kendel. She pulled up a chair across from them and leaned forward, resting her forearms on her thighs.

"I'm so sorry," said Jonas. "I'm supposed to be curator of archaeology and I've completely fallen down on the job. I just don't know how this happened."

"It's not your fault," said Diane. She reached over and squeezed his arm. "Come on, I get enough illogic from my board. Don't you start."

"It just doesn't make sense," said Kendel. "I told Agent Jacobs that." She sat with her shoes off, hugging her legs.

"We'll sort it out," said Diane. "I promise. There's some sense to it. We just haven't found the key yet. Why don't you go home and relax. Come in late tomorrow if you like."

"He's going to be back tomorrow," said Kendel. "He said he might have more questions. I don't want it to seem like I'm avoiding him."

"Okay," said Diane. "If you need to relax tomorrow, you can use my office couch."

It occurred to Diane that if she had told Jacobs about the attack on her at the hospital and what the guy said, it might have taken some of the suspicion off Kendel. She hadn't thought about that angle. She'd have to tell him tomorrow. Maybe tomorrow her mind would be clearer.

"We'll sort everything out. I have David on it and he's very good," she told the two of them.

Kendel smiled. "He did ask more questions than the FBI agent," she said.

"Is this going to hurt the museum?" said Jonas, still looking glum.

"I'll tell you what I told the board. We are going to run across problems like this sooner or later. We have to acquire objects in a field filled with looters and smugglers, and sometimes it's tough. Right now it's tough, but we'll be okay."

Diane turned to Kendel. "Vanessa said when this is sorted out, she'll do everything she can to restore your reputation. You're the one who has taken the biggest hit on this. We'll do everything we can to fix it."

Kendel nodded. "You know, it's usually people who are afraid of *me*, not the other way around. I'm not used to this. I don't know what happened."

"You were blindsided. You'll get your mojo back," said Diane. "Now, you two go home. You too, Andie."

"I told them you would make everything right," Andie said.

Diane hoped that was true. It was useful for them to believe that she could, if only for a good night's sleep.

"How can we help?" said Jonas.

"Right now, cooperate with Jacobs. He's definitely

going to be looking for a culprit, but I don't think
he's looking to pin it on just anyone," said Diane.
"Remember too, no one has claimed these artifacts as
theirs. Only one piece showed up in the FBI National
Stolen Art File—the girdle—and that was stolen fifty
years ago. So far there's actually no crime. The artifacts had just arrived when the newspaper article came
out. We can prove what objects we intended to purchase. I showed Jacobs our exhibit and told him how
the artifacts we thought we were buying were to fit
into our display. The artifacts that Golden Antiquities
sent don't fit in. We are the victims here because we
didn't receive what we ordered and paid for."

"When you put it like that, it doesn't seem so bad,"
said Jonas. "But I have to tell you, I hate being the
department that has the first scandal."

"It's because of what archaeology has to display,"
said Andie. "Nobody's going to show up and accuse
Mike of stealing rocks."

Diane laughed. It felt good. Jonas and Kendel
joined in with a weak chuckle.

"Golden Antiquities burned. David told me," said
Kendel. "Randal Cunningham was killed. How is that
going to affect us?"

"Not much, I would think," said Diane. "It looks
like Cunningham Jr. was neck deep in something bad.
The FBI were already watching him. Jacobs said the
father was clean, but when the son took over, things
started to get shady."

Kendel stood up and smoothed out her skirt and
slipped on her shoes. "Diane, thanks for sticking by
me. You don't know what it has meant to me. Everyone here . . . I just don't know what I would do without the support."

"Okay, I'm leaving before I cry," said Andie. She

stood up and heaved her purse strap onto her shoulder.

"What do you have in that thing," said Jonas, "rocks from geology?"

"You know those ceramic tiles with wolf paw prints that the museum store is selling? I bought eight of them. They are just the neatest things." Andie grinned.

Diane called security and told them to turn on the night lighting in the exhibit rooms. She had waited to give Agent Jacobs time to get out of the building. To get to the outside doors from Diane's office you didn't need to go through any exhibit rooms, but as Jacobs said, it's a big building, and she hadn't wanted him to get confused in the dark. The night lighting was mainly floor lighting, not particularly good lighting for anyone lost among the exhibits.

"I'll see all of you tomorrow," said Diane. "Get a good night's sleep and remember what I told you. We are the victims in this fiasco. Let's not act like the suspects."

The three of them left and Diane closed up her office. She wanted to take her own advice and go home with the rest of them, but she still needed to talk to her crew. She had spoken with them hardly at all since last night. There were things rattling around in her head, questions she had, and she needed to brainstorm with them.

She turned off the lights in her office and left, taking a shortcut through the Pleistocene room with its huge mega fauna looming in the darkness. The bones of a woolly mammoth were the centerpiece of the Pleistocene room. Standing thirteen feet at his shoulder, he was impressive. He stood in the center at the entrance, greeting the visitors from the lobby. In the dark, he looked like he could be fleshed out and alive. She smiled as she walked past him into the mammal exhibit, heading to the elevators.

The brain and its processing of visual images are amazing things. Diane reacted before she realized she had seen anything reflected in the glass of the wolf diorama.

Chapter 29

Diane's arm shot up in front of her face just as a garrote of rope came over her head. The attacker, a black shadow that she had barely seen reflected in the darkened glass, pulled hard, trying to strangle her. Diane's hand grasped the knot in the rope that was there to make choking her more efficient. She held on tight while pushing it away from her neck, trying to duck out from under it. She stomped hard on his instep and elbowed him in the ribs. She also managed to scream at the top of her lungs.

"Why don't you just die, bitch?" His voice was a whispered grunt.

Diane recognized the voice. It was the same as her attacker in the hospital.

Diane elbowed him again. She still held the rope, but he had her hand against her windpipe, cutting off her scream and her air. She worked her other hand behind the rope and pulled. She took a gulp of air and kicked at him furiously.

"I hate you," he said. "I hate you, bitch. What business is this of yours? You're spoiling everything. You're going to die right here." His words sounded like acid and came out in short, hoarse bursts.

His anger was giving him strength. Diane's panic gave her her own adrenaline rush. She focused only on getting free of him. She dug the two-inch heel of her shoe into his foot as she pulled furiously on the rope.

Suddenly he fell sideways to the floor, taking Diane with him. He hit with a groan. Diane pulled the rope off and was scrambling to get away when she saw the silhouette of Andie furiously hitting him over the head with her purse.

Diane ran to help Andie as the attacker rose to his feet and struck out at Andie, sending her flying into one of the display cases. He ran to the hallway door leading to the restaurant. The doors weren't locked to keep people in, only to keep them out of the exhibit areas when other parts of the building were open to the public.

He pulled his black ski mask from over his head as he pushed the door open and walked briskly into a sea of people leaving the restaurant to go to the concert.

Diane went to Andie and knelt beside her.

"Andie, are you all right?"

"I'm fine." Andie scrambled to her feet. "Let's get that guy!"

She took off through the door after the assailant, her purse flying behind her, before Diane could say anything. Diane followed at a quick pace.

She chased after Andie, even though it occurred to her that the attacker might have gone the other way, against the crowd, escaping out the back of the museum. She smiled politely at the people coming down the long hallway from the restaurant to the front door. Fortunately, no one tried to engage her in conversation. As she stepped through the front doorway, she saw Andie start running across the parking lot.

Damn.

Diane took off after her. In the distance she saw the back of the attacker as he ran into the woods at the end of the lot. Diane increased her pace, vowing to start wearing running shoes no matter what outfit she chose. She caught up to Andie just as Andie was about to follow the assailant into the woods.

"No, Andie. This man's dangerous. Don't go after him."

"But—"

"No buts." Diane put an arm around Andie's shoulders. "Thanks for saving my life."

Andie was breathing hard and started shaking. "I had to come back after a phone number and I heard you scream."

"Wasn't there a security guard at the front desk?" said Diane.

"No." She shook her head. "I guess nobody's going to make fun of my heavy purse again," Andie said.

"I know I won't," said Diane. Off in the distance through the woods she heard a vehicle engine start. "Call security. Don't follow me."

Diane started through the woods. She knew where the car was. There was a dirt access road just beyond a few yards of trees. That's where he parked his car, away from cameras. She ran through the woods as quickly as she could and still stay upright.

Definitely need my running shoes. Heels just won't do.

She arrived at the spot just in time to see the vehicle go around the curve. It was too far away to see a license plate. But she could see it was a dark SUV, a Tahoe, she thought but wasn't sure. The quarter moon didn't provide quite enough light to make out anything but a shape.

She walked back through the woods to where Andie

was waiting. Security was just arriving in a white Jeep Cherokee. Two guards jumped out.

"What happened?" said the older one.

Both were relatively new. Chanell Napier, head of security, had hired them only last month.

"I was attacked in the mammal exhibit," said Diane, boring her gaze into them. "Andie, my assistant, rescued me. There wasn't anyone stationed on the desk in the lobby."

"I'm sorry," said the younger man. "I just went to the office for a minute. It's down the hall. It wasn't that long."

He looked to be about twenty-two, probably a student. Many of the security staff were.

"It was long enough," said Diane. "I'm getting all of you red shirts until you straighten yourselves out." Diane started walking back toward the museum.

"What did she mean?" she heard the younger one say.

"Something from *Star Trek*," his partner said. "I think we're dead."

"I'll need to see the video," Diane called back at them.

She was about to rethink the policy of hiring students. Several times in the past few months people had secreted themselves in the museum after closing.

Jin was out in the woods trying to find tire tracks to make casts. Neva had taken Andie's purse and found two hairs snagged by the metal parts. Diane, Garnett, and David sat and watched the tape of the intruder on the security monitor. Frank stood behind them lending another set of eyes. Unfortunately there was no video of the assailant's face. Not even a fuzzy image for David to clear up.

"This was the same guy as in the hospital?" said Garnett.

"Yes, I'm sure of it," said Diane. "And it sounded personal. At first I thought it had something to do with the artifacts, but now I don't know." She just realized that she may have seen him earlier while she was speaking with Laura and Vanessa—the fleeting shadow she saw among the saber-toothed tiger's flora. She shivered.

"What about the attack in your apartment? You think it's the same guy?" asked Garnett.

Diane hesitated a moment, startled at being brought out of her thoughts. "This guy really wanted to kill me," she said. "I think if he had me as vulnerable as I was in my apartment he would have done it. Frankly, I don't know what this is about. You should have heard him as he was telling me he hated me. It was . . . it was gut level. He meant it."

"Can you think of anyone you've offended . . . lately?" asked Garnett.

"Other than Riddmann, no," said Diane.

Garnett grimaced. "I appreciate you apologizing to him. I know it was tough."

"Not very," said Diane. "I had my fingers crossed." She eyed the video. "Is there nothing that shows his face? No reflective surface, nothing?"

"I haven't seen anything," said David.

"It's just not there," said Frank. "He must have known where the cameras are."

"Is he stalking me?" said Diane.

"He has to be," Frank said. "How else would he know you were at the hospital and how to get to you here?"

"Well, damn," said Diane. "What the hell did I do to this guy to inspire so much hatred in him?"

"I have no idea," said Garnett. "You're going to have to answer that. Go home and get some rest. Maybe something will occur to you in the morning."

"What about the exam room at the hospital?" asked Diane.

"No go," said Garnett. "A doctor came in and overrode your instructions. He had it cleaned up so they could use it."

Diane swore.

"Do we have anything?" she asked.

"We did find black nylon fibers on your hospital gown," said David.

"His ski mask," said Diane. "Probably the same one he wore tonight."

"There were two gowns," David said. "Did you have two?"

"Yes, I was trying to correct for a flaw in the design," said Diane.

She turned from the video. "I'm going to go get some sleep. When you find the guy who attacked me," she said to Garnett, "let me know so I can send him my drycleaning bill. David, what are you doing working in the crime lab? You are supposed to be doing your vacation work."

"I am, but your crime scenes alone are putting a lot of pressure on the unit. I thought I'd lend a hand," he said.

"Go get some rest now. I'm going to," said Diane.

Before Diane would leave she made sure her crime scene crew and Andie went home—except for Jin. He said he was staying in his lab. Jin designed the DNA lab that Diane had installed in the basement of the west wing. In it Jin allowed room for two small bedrooms, each with two bunk beds and bathrooms. Everything in them was either shiny metal or tile and looked so modern it could have been a cabin on a spaceship. Diane suspected that he often spent the night there. David said he probably spent hours just standing in the middle of the lab gazing in adoration at the equipment. Diane halfway believed him.

"Did you lose a whole day of work because of me?" Diane asked Frank on the way to his house.

"No. I got more than a day's work done at home. I had to go over some account books and correlate them with dates, and the quiet of my home is more conducive than my office to that kind of work," he said.

"That's a relief. I hate to think that it's come to the point that you have to babysit me," said Diane.

Frank took her hand. "I'm having the Mountain Rose deliver our meal tonight. I thought while you are a guest I'll take advantage of it," he said, kissing the palm of her hand.

"Wow. I can't wait for dessert," she said.

When Frank was in full romantic mode it was better than a vacation at the beach, or the mountains, or even caving. Certainly better than a good night's sleep. Better than a month of good nights' sleep. Frank had a gift for romance. So when Diane arrived at the museum the next morning, she felt in control of the day.

She parked the museum car—which she'd had museum security deliver to Frank's house early that morning—in her usual spot and went to security first. Chanell Napier was on her two-week vacation and her second-in-command was in charge. C. W. Goodman was waiting for her.

Goodman kept his hair cropped close to his head. It was hard to tell what color it was—premature gray or blond. He was a thin, boney man who had been in security all his working life, which Diane guessed was about fifteen years.

"I figured you would come here right away," he said.

Though he didn't have a hat at the moment, she could visualize it in his hand as he stood in front of her. He looked unhappy as he offered her a chair.

Diane didn't sit in the chair Goodman offered. Instead, she stood behind it and gripped its back with her hands as she spoke.

"I know it's hard to keep people out of a place that, for most of the day and some of the evening, is open to the public. I also know that there are hundreds of places to hide if someone is determined—and this attacker last night was nothing if not determined," she said.

"That's true, ma'am," said Goodman.

"However, I thought there were procedures in place so that no one leaves the front desks unattended in either wing," she said.

"There are, and all I can say is Adam made an error in judgment. He knew he was going to be gone just a minute and didn't want to bother another guard. I think he has learned his lesson. There is no such thing as just a minute. A lot can happen in a minute," said Goodman.

"Yes, it can. Reinforce in the personnel that they need to follow the procedures Napier has laid out." Diane paused a moment. "I know this museum doesn't seem like any kind of security risk, and the temptation to let some rules slide is great. This isn't NORAD, but we still need to take security seriously. We have a lot of valuable things in here and a lot of people that need to be protected."

Diane was sure many in security thought that she

herself was the only security problem. It certainly seemed that way to her. When she finished with Goodman, she went to her office. Andie was already at her desk, as usual.

"Are you all right today?" asked Diane.

"Am I ever. What a rush. I can see why you have so much fun," she said.

Fun. Is that what I have? thought Diane. "Andie, thank you for the rescue. As for chasing the guy, don't do anything like that again. He is very dangerous—whoever he is."

"I know that, but I was just so full of adrenaline," she said.

"I understand, and I really appreciate your coming in when you did. I just don't want you to get hurt."

"Yeah, I know. That's why I didn't tell my mother," said Andie.

Diane smiled. "So, anything going on this morning?"

"We are still getting phone calls and e-mail about the artifacts. Several contributors have called to say they are canceling their contributions. You know, that's hardly fair," said Andie.

"No, it isn't. But that's their choice. Anything else?"

"Yeah, something *really* weird," said Andie.

"Must be, for you to call it weird. Weird is the norm for this place," said Diane.

"Well, you know I open your mail," said Andie.

"Yes, that's part of your job description. I take it you found something strange," she said.

"Well, yes. I opened this envelope." Andie took a fat package out of her drawer and laid it on her desk.

"What is it?" asked Diane.

"It's money. A lot of it."

Chapter 30

"Money?" said Diane. "How much?"

"I haven't really counted it, but there's a bunch." Andie pulled a packet of bills from the large envelope. "There's a lot of these bundles and they're all hundred-dollar bills."

Diane picked up the stack of bills and fanned through it. A lot of pictures of Ben Franklin.

"Is it a contribution to the museum? Is there a letter with it?" asked Diane.

"Not exactly a letter."

Andie lifted a piece of paper from the envelope lightly, holding it by its edge between the tips of her thumb and index finger, and laid it on the desktop. Diane stared at the sheet of plain white paper with one word printed on it in large block letters. BITCH.

"Well, I'm confused," said Diane. "You're right. This is weird, even for us. Is there a return address?"

"No," said Andie. "What do I do with it? I mean, I can't deposit it, can I?"

"No, I wouldn't think—"

Diane was interrupted by the door opening. Andie shoved the packet of money back into the envelope.

"Agent Jacobs," said Diane, "you're up early."

He looked at his watch. "Is it early? I thought I slept in." He looked from Diane to Andie.

We must both look guilty, Diane thought.

"So, can I look at your accounting books?" he asked.

Diane frowned, then picked up the package and the note. "We need to talk first."

Diane's office door was behind and to the right of Andie's desk. Diane led Agent Jacobs through her own office and into her conference room, where he had interviewed Jonas and Kendel. Her conference room looked like a comfortable living room. It was decorated in shades of green. The main focus was a large round oak table with padded oak chairs. Just beyond the table were two plush gold-green sofas at right angles to each other. Both were very comfortable. She had slept on them overnight many times. The walls were the same hue as the sofas. They gave the room a golden glow. There was a full bathroom and closet where she kept changes of clothes. It did not look like an interrogation room.

She closed the door behind them. "Can I get you something to drink?" she asked.

"No, I just had breakfast. Maybe later. Great bed-and-breakfast, by the way." He studied her for a moment. "This looks serious," he said and smiled as if it really were not.

He and Ross Kingsley must be from the school of FBI philosophy that says friendly is okay, she thought as she looked at his sparkling white teeth. She wondered how much of it was his act to make people trust him. She sighed. It didn't really matter. She poured the money out on the table.

He raised his eyebrows in surprise. "What's this?" he asked.

"I really don't know. It arrived in this morning's mail. This came with it." She gave him the note.

"That's it? 'Bitch'? Do you know what it means?" he asked.

"No. I haven't a clue. Not much of one anyway. I was attacked here in the museum last night by the same man who attacked me in the hospital. He called me a bitch on both occasions." Diane told him about the attacks, about his anger, and what he had said—about her being a dirty dealer.

"You think it may be related to the artifacts?" he asked. "Why didn't you tell me yesterday when I was here about the first attack and what he said?"

That's the trouble when you decide to withhold important information from the FBI. They want to know why and you need a really good explanation. Diane took a deep breath.

"I wasn't sure it was related. I had just been attacked in my home; that's why I was at the hospital. Well, not exactly attacked. Let me start from the beginning."

Diane told him about waking up in the wee hours of the morning, about falling in the blood.

"The assault at the hospital was violent, and whatever happened in my apartment was extremely violent—they seemed at the time to be related. The artifacts—well, that wasn't violent. At least not at our end, though something may have been going on at Golden Antiquities. When I woke up yesterday morning I was drugged and confused and it took a while for the barbiturates to get out of my system. Apparently someone had put sleeping pills in both my and, I suspect, Ross' drinks when we dined together. That's why he fell asleep at the wheel. At least that's the hypothesis until he gets some tests back. But, that's why I slept through a violent murder in my living room."

"Okay, I'll admit, that's not a bad answer. Ross was drugged too? Why?" Jacobs asked.

"I think someone wanted to make me sleep soundly. But rather than keep up with who got which drink, they just doctored both of ours," said Diane. "I just discovered that the waiter who filled our drinks didn't show up for work yesterday."

"That's cold. Ross could have died," said Jacobs. He shook his head. "There was only blood, no body in your apartment?"

Diane nodded. "The blood trail indicated the body was dragged outside and put in the trunk of my car."

Jacobs cocked an eyebrow. "They didn't arrest you?"

"The DA wanted to. The barbiturates in my tox screen gave me an alibi of sorts. I'm not out of the woods."

"No one saw anything?" he asked.

"Or heard anything, which is really strange. I can hardly walk across the floor without my downstairs neighbors calling up and telling me to be quiet. And my neighbors across the hall live to eavesdrop on what's going on in my apartment—they even broke in once because they were sure I was harboring a forbidden cat."

He smiled and shook his head. "Do you know who the blood belonged to?"

"The DNA is a match to Clymene O'Riley," said Diane.

He looked startled. "Ross' Clymene?" he asked.

"The very one," said Diane.

"I thought she was in jail," said Jacobs, ". . . or did I hear that she escaped?"

"Yes, she escaped, right after I visited her at her request. That's another long story," she said.

"Well, you're right. None of this makes any sense. Why would Clymene escape and then show up at your apartment?" he asked.

"I don't know. Why would someone else decide to kill her there? The whole thing had to be premeditated and coordinated. And why drug me?" said Diane. "I'm aware that all of this makes me look guilty of something."

"Maybe that's the point. If Clymene blamed you for her conviction, could she be behind the artifact problem? It started before her demise," he said.

"I don't see how . . ." She stopped.

"What?" he asked.

"Clymene's late husband, the one she was convicted of murdering, was an amateur archaeologist. Clymene boned up on archaeology in order to lay her trap for him," said Diane.

"So she could have made contacts," said Jacobs. "See?" He patted Diane on the hand. "You need to tell your doctor all your symptoms, no matter how much you think they are unrelated, and let him make the diagnosis."

Diane smiled. "It hadn't occurred to me that Clymene might have masterminded this. All she would have to do is get Golden Antiquities to switch the artifacts and make a call to the newspapers."

"That's a possibility," said Jacobs. "I'll look into it. I'll see if Randal Cunningham had any dealings with Clymene. Did she have friends, known associates? Some people in prison have a following."

"She had visitors. And there's a possibility she conned Rev. Rivers, the prison counselor, into helping her escape. He was found murdered at his home after she broke out," said Diane.

"Something went bad for her," mused Jacobs. "If it's true that she orchestrated all of this, I wonder what went wrong."

"Orchestrated. That's what's been going through my mind. The whole thing feels like some kind of game. If it were just a simple crime, it wouldn't be so hard to understand. Motives would be more straightforward. I know there is no way either Kendel or I or anyone else at the museum could make the artifact switch work as a moneymaking plan the way it was done."

"Could it be a game Clymene started but now can't finish?" he said.

"Maybe." Diane began gathering up the money.

"I need to take the whole package for analysis," he said.

Diane shook her head. "We don't know if it's related to the artifacts. I'll have my lab do it. Look, yours is backed up and this isn't a priority for the FBI, but it is a priority here. Besides, it might just be a contribution to the museum. Granted, patrons don't usually insult me when they are donating, but some of them are not pleased with me lately."

He smiled and agreed. But Diane knew it was because he had no choice. There was no physical connection to the envelope and money he could make with his case. It just looked suspicious. For that matter, he didn't even know if the wayward artifacts were his case either. It was all just suspicion.

"So, you run the museum and the crime lab. Anything else?" he asked.

"I'm also a forensic anthropologist and have an osteology lab in the building," said Diane.

"I know there's a story here," he said.

"There is. A very long one," she said.

"Maybe over lunch when Ross comes," he said.

There was a knock on the door and Andie entered. "I'm sorry to interrupt."

Diane walked over to her with the envelope.

"David called and you are wanted in the crime lab," Andie whispered. "The federal marshals are here again. So is that FBI guy, Kingsley, and some other folks from the police station. David is afraid they may want to . . . well . . . arrest you."

Chapter 31

"Okay, thank you, Andie," said Diane as she looked into Andie's worried eyes. She was a little surprised that Andie hadn't suggested she go out the loading dock exit and avoid the whole thing altogether. "It's all right. Go back to your desk. I'll let you know if you need to bring me a toothbrush."

Diane smiled at her as she shut the door. Diane stood for a moment and closed her eyes before she turned back to Agent Jacobs.

"I have to go," she said. "I'll have Andie show you to Bookkeeping."

"I have really good hearing and the acoustics in this room are quite superior," said Agent Jacobs. "I'd like to come with you. See how Ross is doing. Do you think you are going to be arrested?"

He said it as if it was such a normal thing. Not cause for alarm or disgrace. Just a simple statement. Diane was wondering if he was that unflappable in his un-FBI persona.

"I think they probably found where I hid the body. I probably left my letter opener stuck in her back with my fingerprints on it," she said. Then she added, "That's a joke."

"I can tell a joke from a confession," he said. "So, you think they found the body?"

"I think that's probably why the marshals are here—tying up loose ends," Diane said. "I guess it's all right if you come along. It'll give you a chance to fight over who gets to take me in."

"You believe that I'm about to arrest you?" he said, amusement twinkling in his eyes. Diane was glad that someone found all this funny.

"I'm sure you catch a lot of people with your friendly charm," said Diane.

"You think this is an act?" Jacobs put his hand over his heart in mock pain. "And here I thought you trusted me."

"I obviously do; I spilled my guts to you, didn't I?" said Diane.

"I see, you just weren't fooled." He was still smiling, but Diane thought he probably had elicited a lot of information with his friendly manner.

She got a light sweater out of the closet and put it on.

"Like all of us, you have a job to do," she said. "Those artifacts came from somewhere and they are unprovenanced. You have to be suspicious. But I hope you see that neither Kendel nor Jonas could have hoped to get by with anything. If anyone could, it would be me. I control everything here. Or at least I thought I did."

"I think it's too early to fall on your sword," he said as Diane led them out the back door of her office.

"I'm not falling on my sword. I just think Kendel and Jonas need to be protected from whatever mischief is going on here," said Diane.

"Ross said you have a highly developed sense of justice," said Jacobs as they walked through a small door into the Pleistocene room.

A docent was telling a group of Japanese tourists about woolly mammoths. One man was arguing about whether or not the giant beasts were really here in Georgia.

"I hope he didn't mean I'm prone to take justice into my own hands," said Diane.

"You mean like killing Clymene? No. He said you believe in a justice system. That's why, when you were a human rights investigator, you collected evidence all those years even when there was no court in which to present it," he said.

So Jacobs knew more about her background than he had admitted, she noticed.

"I'm glad he thinks so highly of me," said Diane.

"He does. All these Richard the Third T-shirts have *fair trial* written all over this museum's identity," he said.

"You're familiar with Richard the Third issues?" said Diane.

"I took a lot of history and art history in college. That's how I ended up in this section of the FBI. These guys were really big," he said as they passed a giant bison.

"You should visit the dinosaur room while you're here," said Diane.

"I will. I'll visit the whole building before I leave."

"Do you know where the artifacts belong?" Diane asked after a moment.

She went through the large entrance to the mammal room, where more tourists were viewing the dioramas of taxidermied and skeletonized animals in artists' recreations of their natural habitats. *This is where I was attacked,* she thought. Here among all the animals. It looked so harmless in the daylight.

"No. It's hard to prove something is stolen when you didn't know it existed in the first place. That's the problem trying to deal with looted artifacts. The thing that made the Getty Museum case so great was one of the principals had photographs in his apartment of the artifacts actually being looted. You don't get that kind of hard evidence often. I need a witness. And with Cunningham Jr. dead, there isn't one at the moment. Cunningham Sr. apparently knows nothing about what his son was into, and a couple of his employees have vanished. I've got BOLOs out for them. So far, nothing. That says a lot. The other employees either know nothing or are not talking. I'm hoping the Clymene thing is a lead."

"I hope so too," said Diane.

They reached the elevators in the center of the museum. Several people were waiting. When the doors opened, more people poured out. Diane was always glad to see the museum so busy. Walking into an exhibit room during open hours and finding no one was disheartening.

All the visitors got out on the second floor. The third floor was dedicated to exhibit preparation, library and archives, and offices. Except the west wing. That was the crime lab.

"You know, you didn't have to cooperate with me," said Jacobs. "You could have stonewalled me."

"We don't want objects that are not ours. We would like to have the ones that are ours. I couldn't see how not cooperating would help in any way."

They were walking past the staff lounge when a hand reached out and tapped Diane's shoulder. She jumped back, ready to fight—or run.

"I'm sorry, Dr. Fallon. I didn't mean to startle you."

Diane caught her breath. "That's alright, Dr. Albright. What can I do for you?"

Dr. Albert T. Albright was the curator of dinosaurs and had helped acquire a couple of very nice velociraptors.

"I had this idea for an exhibit," he said.

Diane could see the excitement dancing in his eyes. She hated to brush him off.

"Dr. Albright, I . . ." she began.

"We make this life-size model of a dinosaur, probably a *T. rex*—that would be the most exciting for the youngsters. Anyway, we use"—he motioned quickly with his hands—"whatever that stuff is they use in Hollywood to make dinosaur skin look real. The exhibit would allow the kids to go through the dinosaur, starting through it's mouth and walk through the throat and down to the stomach—you know, to show digestion—and finally the kids are pooped out the back end. I think they would love it," he said.

"I . . . don't know exactly what to say," said Diane. "I think you need to run your idea by Janine, the exhibit planner. Do you have it on paper?"

"No, I thought of it just now as I was eating some popcorn," he said.

"See what the two of you come up with and I'll take a look at it," said Diane.

He nodded happily and went on his way toward Exhibit Preparations.

Shane Jacobs stood trying to laugh silently.

"You going to do it?" he asked.

"The exhibit?" said Diane. "I'm going to let Janine take care of it. Right now I'm not thinking about new and unusual exhibits."

They walked across the dinosaur overlook and Jacobs stopped to look at the real giants of the museum—the Jurassic dinosaurs. The Brachiosaurus that stood on the first floor came all the way up to the third floor. They were staring at his head. The *T. rex* was only half as tall. That surprised most kids because *T. rex*, with his carnivorous behavior, was king.

"Now, this is fun," said Jacobs.

"It is. I enjoy the dinosaurs," said Diane. She stepped away from the fenced railing. "We're crossing over to what the rest of the museum staff call the dark side, and the things that go on there are dark matters."

She proceeded forward to see what dark matters the marshals and Rosewood police had come about.

Chapter 32

The first thing Diane noticed when she walked into the crime lab was the two tabletop Christmas trees.

"I must have overslept," she said, eying the trees, one with red ornaments, the other with blue. She exchanged glances with Jacobs. He grinned.

The chairs weren't around the debriefing table but were facing a flip chart. It looked like someone was going to give a lecture. Garnett was there. So was Kingsley. They were talking to the marshals. Jacobs caught Kingsley's eye and walked over to him.

David was about to look under a piece of fabric draped over some object sitting behind the trees. Instead he stepped over to Diane and whispered in her ear.

"I didn't know when I talked to Andie that it was Jin who set up this meeting."

"Jin?" said Diane. "Where is he?"

David shrugged. Diane looked over at Neva. She shrugged too.

"What's with the Christmas trees?" asked Diane.

"I have no idea," said David.

Again Neva shrugged. "You know Jin," she said. "I

can tell you he's really got his motor revved up. And you know how that is."

Garnett walked over to the three of them. "You didn't know about this?" he asked.

"No," said Diane.

"Is he allowed to do this . . . call this kind of meeting on his own?" Garnett asked.

She had never told Jin he couldn't. It never occurred to her to say, *Jin, don't call meetings of U.S. marshals and the chief of detectives without my approval.*

Diane pinched the bridge of her nose. The thing about her crew was you had to be specific with instructions.

"I see he didn't ask Riddmann to attend," said Diane, looking around her. "That's a plus."

"I have some news for you about Riddmann," said Garnett in a low voice.

Diane raised her eyebrows. "He's moving to Alaska, I hope?"

Garnett ignored her. "You know how guilty he looked when you accused him of leaking to the press about the museum issue?" he said.

"I remember very well. Don't tell me he's behind it," said Diane.

"No, I don't think he is. At least my sources tell me he isn't. But he did do something to twist the knife a little. He had one of his staff call in to the radio talk show and ask questions designed to embarrass the museum. It was aimed at Mrs. Van Ross."

"Well, he hit his mark. It upset her, which is not a good thing," said Diane. "He has to know that sometimes payback's a bitch."

"That's why he did it anonymously. And it would

have stayed that way, but I have an ear in his department. Just thought you'd like to know."

"You never know who's listening in Rosewood, do you? I'm glad you found out," said Diane. "And I'm glad you told me. That little pissant."

"Any idea what this is about?" Garnett gestured to the Christmas trees and the lined-up chairs.

"Not a clue," said Diane. "Neither does David. When he called I thought you were here to tell me you had found Clymene's body."

"We've come up empty so far on that," he said.

"How about my attacker?" said Diane.

"Nothing yet. I'm still waiting for DNA results from Jin on the hair snagged on Andie's purse."

"It takes time. We just got the lab calibrated and certified and we already have people sending us samples. The backlog of DNA analysis in this country is . . ."

Jin appeared through the elevator doors. He was carrying what looked like handouts. *What on earth?* thought Diane.

"Jin," she said. "What's this about?"

"All in good time," he said, grinning.

He was so hyperactive the marshals might have thought he'd been drinking too much caffeine, but Jin was always like this. Whatever he was up to, he had told neither Neva nor David. This would be interesting.

"Everyone sit down, please. I believe I have chairs for everyone," said Jin as if he were the host at a professional conference.

Diane watched his head bob gently as he silently counted the people and the chairs. Eight people, eight chairs. The marshals were already sitting. Kingsley and

Jacobs sat beside them, then Garnett, Diane, Neva, and David.

Kingsley leaned over and spoke to Diane. "You were right." He pulled up his sleeve and pointed to a bruise on his forearm. "Barbiturates." He looked up at Jin, then back at Diane and grinned. "I'll talk with you after the show."

"I'm sure you all are wondering why I called this meeting," said Jin. "We're going to have a short workshop on genetics."

"What?" said Deputy Marshal Dylan Drew. "You called us here for a workshop?"

"Now, please bear with me, because the payoff is great," said Jin. "There's been some interesting progress made in the world of genetics lately. What I want to talk to you about is epigenetics. Epigenetics studies the changes in gene expression that don't require changes in the base sequence of the DNA itself."

"Okay, son," said Deputy Marshal Chad Merrick, "you've lost me already. What the hell are you talking about and how does it affect me and my partner here? And can you please stop pacing and moving around?"

"He can't," said David.

Neva shook her head. "Nope, he really can't."

Jin ignored his coworkers. "I'm talking about making changes in the way genes"—he seemed to be searching his brain for a word—"the things that make genes function differently—when the basic DNA is still the same."

"Not helping," said Merrick.

"That's why I got the Christmas trees," said Jin.

"I've been sitting here worrying about that," said Drew.

"Say you have a gene for lung cancer but it is turned

off—not doing anything. But because of your environment, say one full of secondhand smoke, a certain chemical group hooks onto your chromosome—like the decorations hooked onto a Christmas tree—and turns the gene on and you get cancer.

"Let's say these two identical Christmas trees were bought at the same place but taken to two different homes where they were decorated differently. The trees look different to us because of what's hanging on them, but underneath they are just alike. That's like two people with the same DNA who have lived in different environments."

Jin held a red tree ornament in one hand and a blue ornament in the other. "For two DNA sample profiles that look just alike on the base indicators, you can do an epigenetic profile, which means taking a little wider focus on the DNA structure, and see these differences," he said, indicating the different colored ornaments.

The hairs on the back of Diane's neck stood up. She glanced over at Kingsley, who looked wide-eyed.

Chad Merrick straightened up in his chair. "This has to do with Clymene or we wouldn't be here. Are you saying that Clymene is a twin?"

"No, not a twin," said Jin, grinning.

Now Diane was confused. That is exactly what she thought he was saying. So did Kingsley and the others.

David looked at her as if to say, *I can't do anything with him.*

The marshals frowned at Jin.

"Let me tell you what got me to thinking about this," he said.

"If it clears things up, go to it, son," said Merrick.

"Too many things didn't add up. For one thing, why didn't anybody in Dr. Fallon's apartment building hear anything? Were they all drugged? Let me tell you, if the odd couple across the hall heard a life-and-death struggle going on, they would have been over there, and so would the people from downstairs. And why was Dr. Fallon drugged to make her sleep through the whole thing? You have to ask yourself that."

Jin paused and looked out at his audience, who were giving him their attention in hopes that it would be made clear why they were sitting there listening to him.

"We study blood patterns in this unit," continued Jin. "If you have enough blood, it can tell you all kinds of things, from the shape of the drops to the pattern on the walls. And Lord knows there was a lot of blood. One thing I noticed was the cast-off blood was more like a beating than a stabbing, but what we found was a cleaned-up knife.

"And what about all that blood? We found no arterial spray, no spurting. Not too unusual. People can just lie there and bleed out after an attack, but what did the perp do while that was happening? Sit in Dr. Fallon's living room and wait? Then finally, at four pints of blood on the floor, got tired of waiting and dragged the body out? Why didn't we find more blood on the way to Dr. Fallon's car? Even if Clymene's heart had stopped, she would still have been leaking blood from her wounds. We only had a smear."

They all leaned forward, attentive now. Diane wasn't sure where he was going, but his analysis of the crime scene was interesting.

"But what really got me to thinking was, why clean the knife with kerosene—which is better than bleach, by the way, for getting rid of blood. Why clean it and then leave it in the trunk to be found alongside the blood? That made no sense. Then it hit me. They weren't trying to hide what was on the knife, but what *wasn't* on the knife." Jin paused for dramatic effect.

"Skin cells. It was a serrated knife. There should have been a lot of skin cells if that was the murder weapon. We found no skin cells."

"I take your point," said Garnett, "but what does this mean?"

"I'm getting to that," said Jin. "All of these questions led me to go back and resample the blood and do an epigenetic profile. And low and behold . . ."

Jin flipped over a page on the chart, showing a drawing that looked to Diane to be an outline of the blood pattern on her living room floor. But Jin had drawn another pattern inside the outline.

"The blood on Dr. Fallon's floor came from two contributors with the same DNA. The blood was poured out of two containers that left overlapping patterns something like this." He traced the patterns on the chart with his finger. "But the real kicker—Are you ready for this? I told you it would be great—both blood sources matched Clymene's DNA . . . but *neither* matched her epigenetic profile. It wasn't her."

Chapter 33

All eight of them sat staring at Jin as he lifted the piece of white fabric, revealing a third Christmas tree. This one was decorated with candy canes. There was silence for several moments. Finally Kingsley spoke up after looking at the three trees openmouthed.

"Are you saying she is a triplet?" he said.

Jin's grin broadened. "She could be one of a set of quintuplets as far as we know. I just have three contributors."

"More important, are you saying she's alive?" said Merrick.

He and Drew exchanged glances and leaned forward as if somewhere in the three trees they might catch a glimpse of her.

"She could have gotten hit by a truck this morning and be dead, but she didn't die in Dr. Fallon's apartment," said Jin. "No one did, as far as the evidence shows. But two very anemic people left there."

"She's alive," said Diane. "And she's bought herself a really big head start."

"You would never even know to look for her again were it not for Jin," said David. "Way to go, buddy. Sorry for thinking you'd finally gone over the edge."

The two marshals did not look happy. "Can you tell us anything that will help us find her?" said Merrick.

"Nothing definite," said Jin. "But I can tell you something interesting." He brought the third tree around and set it beside the other two. "This is Clymene," he said of the tree with the candy canes. "The other two, the one with the red ornaments and the one with the blue ornaments, are her two sisters. There's been a lot of twin studies in epigenetic research. Twin babies have, as you would expect, very similar epigenetic profiles. The older they get, the more different experiences they have, the more divergent their profiles get—that's especially true in twins that have been separated at birth or at some other point in their lives. Clymene's two sisters have similar profiles to each other. Clymene's is very different."

"Clymene was separated from her two sisters at some point," said Kingsley. He was literally on the edge of his seat. "Is that what you are saying?"

"Yes," said Jin. "I don't know if that will help catch her, but I thought it was interesting."

"In a way, it supports what Shane mentioned," said Kingsley. "The Clymene in Greek mythology was a daughter whose father sold her into slavery. She may have chosen that name to commemorate an event in her own life."

"The Greek Clymene also had two sisters, by the way," said Shane Jacobs.

"Well, hell," said Merrick. He turned his attention from Jin to Kingsley. "You said she won't go anyplace we would know to look for her. So we don't know where to start."

Diane noticed that the marshals seemed more willing now to listen to Kingsley's ideas on Clymene, as if suddenly the knowledge the profiler possessed might be of more use than mere academic curiosity. At this point, Diane guessed they would take all the help they could get.

"No, she wouldn't. She will hide in a persona we don't know about," Kingsley said.

"Would she come here after Dr. Fallon? She seems to want to get even," said Merrick.

It struck Diane that he was considering using her as bait.

Kingsley shook his head.

"I think messing with Diane was just icing. Clymene planned this diversion to draw attention away from herself by making everyone focus on Diane." Kingsley nodded toward Garnett. "Which was helped greatly by your DA when he shifted investigative resources from looking for Clymene to trying to figure out what Diane might have done with her body."

"I'll be sure and tell Riddmann that," commented Garnett.

David turned to the marshals. "I'm sure you recalled your BOLO on Clymene once Diane was accused of having killed her."

"Only because you guys said she was dead," said Drew. "We don't normally issue BOLOs on corpses." He wasn't defensive so much as exasperated.

"I think Clymene did a good job of fooling all of us," said Diane. "All cons are good magicians and that's just what she did, a little sleight of hand." She stood up and stretched her legs.

"So," said Merrick. "Where do we look now? Do we plaster her photograph everywhere?"

"Maybe, but it might force her deeper into hiding," said Kingsley.

"I think we should," said Neva. "She has a real problem. She has two sisters who look just like her.

That makes our chances of finding one of them three times as good. All three will have to go into hiding. How far does their loyalty go, to disrupt their lives that way?"

"I think they will be plenty loyal," said Shane. "If they've gotten this deep in it together, it means that they're devoted. You won't break them apart."

"Who are you?" asked Garnett.

"Yeah, who are you?" echoed Drew.

"Oh, of course, you don't know me." He grinned. "I'm Shane Jacobs, FBI agent from the art theft division." He held out his hand, which Garnett and the others shook in turn.

"So, Clymene's been stealing art too?" said Drew with raised brow.

"The girl gets around," said Merrick.

Jacobs laughed. "There is the possibility that in her effort to make Dr. Fallon's life miserable, she misdirected some stolen artifacts to this museum. I have no proof of Clymene's involvement, but I thought I'd crash your party anyway. As for my statement about not being able to break Clymene and her sisters apart, I'm also an identical twin and I know the attachment of twins to each other."

"Really?" said Drew. "Your brother's in the FBI too?"

"He's a professor of art history at Brown," he said.

Drew nodded. "Less stress, I guess."

"Yes, I couldn't handle the politics in academia," said Jacobs.

They all chuckled.

"So," said Merrick, looking from Diane to Kingsley, "Drew and I are open to any suggestions you have on where to start looking for Clymene. You guys seem to know her inside out, so to speak."

"Diane and I have been discussing that," said Kingsley. He nodded toward her as if yielding the floor.

"Clymene and her sisters may or may not be in our databases. But we can search for a relative," said Diane.

"If we don't know who she is, how the heck are we going to find a relative?" said Drew.

"By looking for a close match of her DNA in the various databases we have access to. Instead of an exact match, look for anyone with alleles in common," said Diane. "We might get lucky and one of our databases will contain the DNA profile of a cousin or other relative. They could tell us who she really is."

"I guess the whiz kid over here can manage that," said Drew.

"We can fax or e-mail her photo to estate and family lawyers," continued Diane. "Clymene's husbands that we know about were wealthy men. One of those kinds of lawyers is likely to have met her. That might lead to her identity and give us clues to other victims."

"Great idea, but do you know how many lawyers there are in the country? Even pared down to estate lawyers, that's a lot of e-mails and faxes." said Merrick.

"I know it is," said Diane. "Maybe we can think of a way to pare it down even more."

"Her mug shot isn't that good," said Garnett.

"We don't want to use that anyway," said Diane. "These lawyers are people who don't normally deal with criminal cases. They have chosen to associate with wealthy clients who don't get into that kind of trouble. They would probably dismiss her mug shot out of hand, thinking that it couldn't possibly be anyone they would know. We need to get one of the

photos the media took of her coming out of court—
where she was dressed up and looked the part she
was playing."

Merrick nodded. "Okay. I'm buying all of this.
What else?" he said.

"This is a little more"—Diane searched for the right
word—"a little more Hail Mary. Get someone in linguistics to analyze her core vocabulary if we can find any
recordings of her voice. We can check with the prison—"

"What do you mean her core vocabulary?" asked
Garnett.

"Body part words, colors, action verbs—the words
she would have learned first as she learned to speak.
Her early use and pronunciation of those words would
be heavily influenced by the region of the country in
which she lived and what kind of environment she
lived in. Some of the words might have retained hints
of her original accent. The linguist can also look at
her journal writing in her scrapbooks and any other
writing samples we can find." Diane shrugged. "It
might lead to where she's from, even though her accent will have changed over the years. Clymene speaks
fluent French and Spanish. I think she may have lived
abroad. That would change her accent. As I said, this
one's more of a long shot."

Merrick knitted his brow and shook his head. "If
this woman is as chameleon as you say, hell, she could
have dyed her hair black and gone to work somewhere
as an illegal."

Diane nodded. "She's accomplished at many things,
which gives her many choices."

"Shoot," said Drew, "she could be working here as
one of your tour guides."

Diane laughed, then stopped. "Damn. . . . Not her,
but one of her sisters. Damn."

Chapter 34

All eyes were on Diane as she sat lost in thought, trying to remember everything that Karalyn had told her about Bobby Banks.

"What?" said Garnett. "Are you telling me that one of them is here? Where?"

"I'm not sure," said Diane. "Agent Kingsley and I were both drugged, and it apparently happened here in the museum restaurant. When I went to interview our waitress I found that our drinks were actually filled by another waiter, who didn't show up for work the next day. He was described as being pretty for a male. I was just wondering if it could be one of Clymene's sisters, or Clymene herself in disguise."

"Surely they wouldn't be that bold," said Neva.

"Is it really that easy for a woman to pass as a man?" asked Garnett.

"Not easy, but it's been done. It's easier for a woman to pass as a boy. The wait staff are young, some just out of high school," said Diane.

"That would be bold on her part," said Kingsley.

"What's the waiter's name?" asked Garnett.

"Bobby Banks, and he apparently lives in the woods. At least that's where his address puts him."

"In other words, he gave a false address," said Garnett. "I'll go talk to your staff."

"Ask them if he had an Adam's apple," said Diane. "Guys over fourteen have them; women don't."

"Always?" asked Garnett.

"Nothing's always. But in the great majority of cases," said Diane.

"While you guys do your thing," said Merrick, "Drew and I will get back to some old-fashioned detective work and talk with everyone Clymene was in contact with while she was in prison. Who knows, that might actually work."

"She had to be getting information to and from her sisters someway," said David. "Might check with the other inmates and see if they were passing information along or if someone was getting her throwaway cell phones."

"Gee, why didn't we think of that?" said Merrick. "You know, if we hadn't listened to you guys, we would still be out there looking for her, maybe even found her by now." His words had a little bit of a sting, but Merrick looked good-humored when he said them.

David just smiled at him. "Call me if I can help some more," he said.

The meeting broke up, with the marshals and Garnett going to interview witnesses and Kingsley calling to get a linguistics expert. Diane's staff already had a full load of assignments. That left Jacobs and the misdirected artifacts.

"You still want to see my books?" asked Diane.

"Just to be thorough," he said, smiling.

Diane had made arrangements for a crime scene cleanup crew to clean her apartment. She looked at her watch. She'd agreed to meet Kingsley for lunch and had just enough time to go to her apartment and get some photographs and other personal items she wanted to retrieve.

The crisp white Greek Revival house looked almost luminescent in the bright sunshine. Years ago it had been converted to apartments. Diane didn't know who originally owned it. She would have to ask the landlady sometime. Speaking of the landlady, she needed to speak with her. Diane entered the wide double doors that led to the hallway and all the downstairs apartments. The landlady's apartment was immediately to the right of the front door. She knocked.

The landlady, a small, white-haired, elderly woman, opened the door. She was normally a nonstop talker, but at the moment she was speechless as she stared at Diane with a rather startled look on her face. Diane was beginning to wonder if she had morphed into an insect as she walked up the steps.

"Oh, dear, this is awkward," the landlady said finally.

"Who is it, Aunt . . . oh," her nephew said as he came to the door. "You're right, awkward's the word. Come in," he said with a rather faint smile.

As she entered she heard one of her neighbors from upstairs speaking. Leslie had just had a baby a few months earlier. She and her husband were students at Bartram. They were a nice couple. In the aftermath of a meth lab explosion on a nearby street, they had knocked on everyone's door to make sure all their neighbors had heard the evacuation order. Later the two of them served coffee to Diane and the others whose grim task it was to identify the bodies in the house that blew up while a student party was in progress.

"This isn't right. It's un-American," said Leslie. Her voice was full of feeling. She sounded close to tears.

"I don't even think you can," said her husband. "You're turning this into the Salem witch trials. It's just wrong, and Leslie and I won't have any part of it."

Everyone went quiet as Diane entered the room. She looked around at the landlady's quaint living room. The entire population of her apartment building was sitting either on the rose-covered upholstered sofas, or the matching stuffed chairs, or her needle-point dining room chairs.

Leslie and her husband were standing with their backs against the darkened fireplace. Diane's forty-something downstairs neighbors were sitting on the sofa. Ramona always looked to Diane as if she were about to implode in on herself—there was something tightly constricted about her whole person. She sat with her husband. They were the ones who frequently complained about Diane making too much noise, even though Diane was at home very little.

Diane recognized several other neighbors. One of the most recent was a professor of history at Bartram named Lawrence Donner, a distant relative of the Donner family who lent their name to the ill-fated Donner party. It was Diane's understanding that he was writing a book to clear their reputation of cannibalism. He had moved into the basement apartment vacated by another of Bartram's professors a few months before.

The Odells, her neighbors across the hall known for their interest in everything funerary, sat in two straight-backed chairs. Several others Diane knew by first name only. Most would not meet her eyes. Diane had the strangest urge to laugh. She bit it back.

Leslie looked at her with tears in her eyes. Their

baby wasn't with them. Probably being babysat by her aunt.

"I'm glad you're here," said Leslie. "They need to face you. I just want you to know that we didn't vote for this."

"Oh, dear," said her landlady. "I really like you, Diane, I do . . ."

Diane's cell phone rang and saved the landlady from further embarrassment.

"Frank," said Diane when she saw the display. "Excuse me one moment, please," she said and turned aside to take the call.

"Hey, I just called to say that I'm going to have to stay in Atlanta this evening."

"That's fine," she said. "No problem."

"You sound like you're holding back a laugh," he said. "Having a good time, are you?"

"Well, I think I was just voted off the island," said Diane. She saw Leslie and her husband smile at her.

"What?" asked Frank.

"I'm at my apartment house. I inadvertently interrupted a meeting."

"They're kicking you out? They can't do that." Frank started laughing and Diane thought she was going to lose it.

"I'd better go. I'll talk to you later," she said.

He was silent a moment.

"What?" said Diane.

"You know I love you," he said.

"I'm so glad you do," she said and let a laugh escape her lips. "I love you too." Diane didn't remember if she had ever told him that. She thought she had, but she certainly picked a strange time to say it now. She flipped her phone closed.

The room was still silent, and Diane started to tell

her landlady why she had come to her door when her downstairs neighbor spoke up.

"We might as well say it in front of her. She brings just too much violence to the building. We all had to leave our homes just a few months ago."

Leslie jumped in with a huff. "That wasn't her fault—she had nothing to do with the explosion."

Ramona, the downstairs neighbor, sniffed. "She had something to do with it."

"She was identifying the victims," said Leslie's husband. "You might as well blame us because we were there serving coffee. Jeez."

"Well, there were other times. Many other times," Ramona said.

"She kept a cat," said Veda Odell. "Marvin's allergic."

Her landlady sighed. "Veda, no she didn't. That was me. I was just keeping him temporarily until I found him a home."

Veda looked at her, stunned. "You? You know Marvin's allergic."

Diane was thinking, were she to vote, she would vote to get out of here too. Most of her neighbors were nuts. But she had to admit, there had been many occasions when something bad had happened at her apartment that needed police attention. It wasn't Diane's fault. It had kind of come with her position at the crime lab, but she was sure it had scared the neighbors more than once. She didn't really blame them.

Diane turned to the landlady. "I came to tell you that the crime scene cleanup crew will be here tomorrow. They will sanitize everything."

"Oh, that's good. I was wondering what to do," she said.

"You don't have to do anything. I'll take care of it," said Diane.

"Diane. I really hate this," said the landlady.

"It's all right," said Diane. "It's nice that all of you could meet and get to know each other."

"It is, isn't it?" said the landlady. "This could be a party at a happier time. That boy in 1-D is the only one who didn't come. He must be gone."

"I don't know him," said Diane. "Isn't he new?"

"Yes, he is. Just moved in about a month ago. Bobby Banks is his name."

Chapter 35

"Bobby Banks," said Diane. "What does he look like?"

"Nice-looking boy. He has sort of wavy blond hair, pretty eyes a kind of blue-green color. He has the nicest complexion you've ever seen."

All their eyes were on Diane when she fished her cell phone out of her jacket pocket. She dialed David.

"Hey, Diane, what's up?" he said.

"Get hold of Garnett and tell him to get a warrant for my apartment building, apartment 1-D," said Diane. "Bobby Banks has been living there."

"At your apartment building? Now, that's creepy," said David. "For how long?"

"About a month. Can you and Neva take the scene?"

"Sure. Damn, I probably interviewed him that night. Everyone was home in your building," said David.

Her neighbors were muttering to one another when Diane got off the phone. She slipped it back in her pocket and turned to address them. They all looked rather stunned. She could imagine they were. Things just kept happening too close to their home.

"Why did you do that?" asked her landlady.

"What's wrong?" The fear in her dark blue eyes made Diane feel guilty.

"It's all right," said Diane, although she knew it sounded rather stupid under the circumstances.

"I demand to know what's going on," said Ramona.

"It's all right," she said again, and it still sounded idiotic. "He is just someone the police want to speak with."

"About what?" said Ramona. "You tell us what this is about. We have a right to know. What are you into?"

"My job," said Diane.

"I have connections in the police department," said Loyal, her husband. "They say some escaped convict died in your apartment. It wasn't in the papers because of who you are," he said.

"Your contact is not keeping up with current events," said Diane. "Chief Garnett will be here shortly and will probably want to ask all of you questions about 1-D. Please answer him as truthfully as you can. In the meantime just stay calm. This is nothing to worry about."

"He said the U.S. Marshals questioned you," persisted Loyal.

"Of course they did. It was my apartment," said Diane.

"He said nothing bad is ever written about you in the newspaper because you have connections high up that threaten the newspaper."

Loyal was just a fountain of misinformation. She wondered who his informant was.

"If you've been reading the paper lately, you know that's not true," said Diane. She never thought she would have to bring up bad publicity to defend herself.

"Are you calling the police because we voted you

out?" asked one of the tenants, a man who owned a small jewelry store in Rosewood. He twisted his ring on his finger nervously.

"No, of course not. I can't get a warrant and mobilize the chief of detectives for something like that. This is an ongoing investigation into the events in my apartment. I can't give you any details, but your cooperation will help a great deal."

"Would everyone like some tea and cookies?" said her landlady. "I made some fresh in the kitchen."

Diane stayed until Garnett arrived so no one would be tempted to leave, though she didn't know what she would have done to stop them. She was afraid the more nervous ones would leave home just to avoid talking to Garnett. Being interviewed by a detective sometimes makes the most innocent feel guilty of something. But this collection of people probably felt so guilty for asking her to move out that they would do what she asked.

When Garnett arrived and took over her landlady's living room, Diane left and went upstairs. As she opened the door to her apartment, the smell of decomposing blood hit her in the face. She covered her mouth and stood in the entrance for a few moments. Looking at the stain and smelling the aroma, she didn't think she could live here again anyway. Even after the cleaning crew got rid of the odor, she would still think she smelled blood.

There was a walkway of boards across the dried blood. Jin and Neva must have put it there after they processed the scene. Diane went into her bedroom and looked in her closet. Neva had taken most of her clothes. Diane took a metal box of photographs from the top shelf. Her caving gear was neatly piled in the

corner. She began carrying things to her car. She went
back and checked out her refrigerator. Fortunately she
didn't have much in it. She poured the milk out and
threw the container away. She checked her pantry. It
was pretty skimpy. She had been meaning to get to
the grocery store. Now she didn't have to.

Diane checked out the bathroom. Neva had been
thorough there as well. She had also taken Diane's
jewelry box and the picture of Diane and Ariel that
sat on the nightstand. Neva had done a good job of
collecting the important things. There were her CDs
and stereo, of course, but Diane would hire someone
to move those and all the large things. She thought
she might just dump the sofa and stuffed chairs. She
couldn't imagine ever getting the smell out. She found
a bottle of Febreze in the cupboard and sprayed herself down.

By the time she left, Diane had already removed
herself psychologically from the apartment. It didn't
feel like home anymore. But she wasn't sure where
home was going to be.

She met Leslie and her husband as she was locking
the door.

"I'm so sorry," said Leslie. "I don't know what to
say . . . just that not everyone voted to ask you to leave."

Diane smiled. "Just the majority," she said.

"They can't enforce it," said her husband.

"It doesn't matter. It's pretty messed up in there
anyway." Diane didn't want to say bloody.

"We are going to miss you," said Leslie, suddenly
hugging her.

"Me too," said Diane. Though in truth, she hardly
ever saw them. "How's little Bella?"

Leslie suddenly smiled. "Growing so fast. She already weighs fourteen pounds."

"She's going to be a tall girl," said Leslie's husband. "She's already twenty-five inches."

"When she's two," said Diane, "she'll be approximately one half her adult height. So you'll be able to estimate about how tall she is going to be."

"You're kidding, at two?" said Leslie.

"Come by and see me at the museum sometime," said Diane.

"We will. We've visited the museum and loved it. I'm glad there's something like that in Rosewood."

Leslie looked like she was going to get teary eyed again. Diane could see she was very tenderhearted. It's always uplifting to be around nice people when your job is to hunt so many bad people.

"This is all right," said Diane. "There have been a lot of . . . well, events. And I imagine they've scared some people."

"Maybe," said Leslie, "but to blame you for the explosion. That was ridiculous."

"Ramona just wants your apartment. She thinks it has two bedrooms. She's the one who spearheaded this," said Leslie's husband. "We just now heard her talking to the landlady's nephew."

"She's going to be in for a surprise," said Diane. "It's just one bedroom and has a very small kitchen. I believe it's one of the smaller apartments."

Diane said good-bye and walked downstairs with a few more items she wanted to take with her. She met Garnett on the first floor. Several of her neighbors were leaving the landlady's apartment. Some were going back to their places; others went out the front door. Only a few met her eyes. Diane guessed those were the ones who'd voted to keep her.

"I didn't get much information from this group. I

think Bobby Banks kept a low profile—by the way, he is a he," said Garnett.

"Oh, he had an Adam's apple?" said Diane.

"A penis," said Garnett. "The men's room has urinals."

"Okay, that's also mainly a male characteristic," said Diane.

Garnett coughed and laughed at the same time. "I thought you were on to something," he said.

"So did I," said Diane. "He still may be associated with Clymene and company in some way."

"I think so too. I heard these folks are running you out of your apartment."

"My life is a little too eventful for them," said Diane. "This episode was the last straw, I think."

"I'm real sorry to hear that," said Garnett. "Anything I can do to help?"

"No. I appreciate your offer. I'll be fine. I'm staying at Frank's since the event the other night. I've been sort of toying with the idea of buying a house. This might push me into it."

Neva came out into the hallway and walked toward Diane when she saw her. "Did they really ask you to leave?" she said.

"News travels fast," said Diane.

"Your neighbors were talking about it when David and I arrived," said Neva. "That's just . . . just plain mean."

"I'm apparently a hard neighbor to live with. Finding anything?" she asked.

"Blood," said Neva.

Chapter 36

"You found blood?" said Garnett. "So this kid . . . Bobby Banks is involved with Clymene?"

"We've found a few drops on the bed frame. And a couple of drops in the bathroom. It's not much. He could have had a nosebleed, but . . ."

"But what?" said Garnett.

Diane noticed the landlady watching them behind her partially closed door.

"Is there a clear path in the apartment?" Diane asked, meaning, had David and Neva processed a place in the apartment where they could walk and not contaminate evidence.

"Sure," said Neva.

Neva led the two of them back to 1-D. Diane heard the landlady's door close softly behind them. Once inside, Diane glanced around at the apartment. It wasn't much different from hers in layout, larger perhaps. The sofa, chairs, table, and lamps were new but very cheap. There were no paintings or photographs or accessories of any kind.

"Spartan," said Garnett.

"Isn't it?" said Neva. "Bed and bath's the same. Nobody really lived here. He just stayed here."

"You had a *but* you were going to tell us about," said Diane.

"We found an IV needle wedged in the floorboards," said Neva. "I think this is where they donated the blood and rested up afterward. I think Clymene and her sisters were in the bedroom when David came to the door to ask if the guy in the apartment had heard anything."

David entered from the kitchen. "Neva tell you what we found?" he said. "They were here. Right here. I talked with that kid there in the doorway. He told me he'd been studying and didn't hear a thing."

"I wonder why he didn't just say he heard a ruckus, to bolster the image that Diane was doing something in her apartment," said Garnett.

"Then he would be the only witness," said David, "and we would have come back to him and found him missing. This way, he's like everyone else in the building."

"Smart group of people," said Garnett. "I wonder where they're from."

"I'm going to find out," Diane said as she turned to leave. "You guys are doing a good job, by the way."

She left Neva, David, and Garnett and went back to the museum and made an appointment for movers to pack everything up in her apartment after the cleaning crew finished.

Since Frank wasn't coming back to Rosewood this evening, she thought she might stay at the museum on one of her couches. Perhaps she could just move into the museum. Maybe create a small apartment in the basement somewhere in the east wing. She shook her head of the thought. She was mentally creating a life where she would never leave the museum.

When she got back to the museum, she had a note

from Kingsley saying he was sorry to miss lunch, that
he had to go back to Atlanta but would return tomorrow. Jacobs was probably somewhere in the building
trying to find out if they were thieves. Which reminded
her that she needed to bring the board up-to-date on
the disposition of the artifacts. She sent an e-mail to
the members asking them to come to a board meeting
at the end of the day.

After sending the e-mail, she started searching the
Internet to find out how to contact estate planning
attorneys and family lawyers. There were several professional organizations that had lists of attorneys in
estate planning, or family law, but only addresses were
listed, no e-mail addresses.

She picked up the phone and called the museum's
attorney and asked about lists of lawyers from professional organizations and their e-mail addresses.
She told him what she wanted to do, carefully explaining that this was a woman who was stalking and
preying on wealthy clients of attorneys. He suggested
that if she left the message and photograph on various attorney Listservs, it might reach a broader
audience.

Diane found a fairly good photograph of Clymene
on the local newspaper's Web site. After getting permission to use it, she created a message asking for
help in identifying the woman in the attached photograph. She went back and forth on how much she
should reveal, and decided to give a moderate amount
of information, but mention that she was thought to
have preyed upon men with large estates. She then
e-mailed the owners of the Listservs and asked if they
would post the message for her, explaining to them in
greater detail the importance of finding Clymene. She

expected to be turned down by half. She was surprised when none did.

With that out of the way, she told Andie she was going over to the crime lab for a while. She used the back way to avoid meeting anyone that might slow her down. The downside was that she missed seeing most of the exhibits and she enjoyed that, even in passing.

No one was in the crime lab. Jin, she assumed, was down in his DNA lab. Neva and David were still at her apartment building. She had been trying to convince the police commissioner and the mayor that she needed to hire more personnel, but they always turned her down. Right now she was stretched thin, but she couldn't use this as an example of why she needed another person. The police commissioner would just tell her that catching Clymene was the responsibility of the U.S. Marshals. And he would be right. But Clymene had targeted her, and in doing so had targeted the lab.

Diane entered one of the warren of rooms in the crime lab that housed one of the many computers. This one had face recognition software and a capacity for long searches.

Sophisticated face recognition software can pick a face out of a crowd—a clever thing for a computer to do. It has to recognize that a face is not a gourd, or a bole of a tree, or a rock, or a cloud, or anything else that happens to look similar to a face. After that bit of cleverness, the software then can compare that face with images that are stored in a database.

A photograph could be scanned into the software and it would search a database for a match. Diane scanned Clymene's mug shot, which would work just fine because the software didn't look at expressions. It took measurements between various landmarks on the face and created an index number. It then looked for faces with similar indexes.

When Clymene was on trial, the DA didn't bother looking for who she really was. He said he didn't need to know ancient history to convict her. So a deep background investigation was never done. Diane would correct that error now. She decided to search both American and international databases.

With a second computer Diane sent the mug shot to Colonel Alex Kade. Diane had become acquainted with him when he matched a missing child's photograph with a facial reconstruction Neva did of a skeleton found in the woods near Rosewood. In his retirement he searched, with the blessing of the FBI, for missing children in a database he created from pornography sites on the Web. His daughter disappeared when she was fifteen. They found her years later but not before she had suffered severe abuse and had contracted a fatal disease that took her life. He said if he could have just found her earlier he could have saved her. Now he tried to save other children.

Diane explained to him in an e-mail that this wasn't a child and it was too late to save her, but that the woman might have been separated from her family as a child and that it was critical for Diane to find out who she was. She didn't tell him Clymene's name.

He e-mailed back almost immediately and said he would look. Diane thought that he must be at his computer all the time looking for lost children. He had software whose algorithm could account for the age difference so that an adult Clymene could be matched to a child Clymene or a teenage Clymene. *Software just gets more and more clever,* she thought.

Next she called David. He and Neva were on their way back.

"I'd like to use Arachnid," she said.

David didn't say anything for a long moment. "I suppose this is what it's for," he said.

Chapter 37

Arachnid was David's baby. He compared it to Rosemary's Baby.

"It's essentially evil," he said.

"No," Diane had told him. "It is not evil. Someone could put it to evil use, but then the evil would reside in the use of it, not in the system itself."

Her argument fell on deaf ears because David was paranoid. He admitted it and embraced it. The irony of Arachnid was that David had created what he was afraid of. Big Brother. This was not lost on him, and he felt guilty about it. But there it was, sitting in the basement, the ultimate spider.

Diane wanted carrels in the museum for people to rent and work on scholarly things. The entire basement and subbasement were being renovated for storage vaults and work areas. The DNA lab and David were the first occupants. David rented space for his photography. He occasionally taught classes in photography in the museum, so it made sense that he should have space. He had a darkroom, a workroom, and a study. All very small, but big enough for David's needs. Arachnid was in the study.

David was the insect and spider expert in the crime

lab. If insects needed to be reared to discern time of a victim's death, David was the one with the rearing chambers. He liked bugs. He didn't particularly like spiders.

"They just look evil," he told her on many occasions. That is why he named his creation Arachnid—that and its basic function, to search the Web.

David had married search engine algorithms and face recognition algorithms. He thought it a terrible invasion of privacy, but he had done it anyway because he loved algorithms. He swore Diane to secrecy—neither Jin nor Neva knew about Arachnid.

"It's probably illegal. If it isn't, it should be," he had told Diane.

Arachnid searched the Web for images, picked out faces, and compared them with the photo to be identified. If the faces of Clymene or her sisters were anywhere on the Web, Arachnid would find them.

"You know, you could make a lot of money with this software," she told him.

"Blood money," he had said.

Diane had rolled her eyes. "You know someone is going to come up with this. It just makes sense. They probably already have."

"I'm sure some black ops have invented it too, but it's still evil. We can only use it for good."

"David, you worry me sometimes," Diane told him.

"I worry myself," he had answered.

Diane walked down to the basement and let herself into David's space. Arachnid was sitting there looking like a sleeping cyclops. That's what monitors looked like to Diane. Some kind of one-eyed creature. Arachnid's monitor was black, which added to the illusion. She turned the computer on and waited. The face of a spider came on the screen and told Diane how to proceed, asking her each step if she really wanted to do this, that once it's done, she couldn't turn back the clock.

"David," she whispered, making a face, "I swear, you're nuts."

She scanned Clymene's mug shot into Arachnid and told it to search. This would take a while—possibly a long while. Diane locked up his study and left.

While she was downstairs, she went to the DNA lab. It looked like a futuristic medical facility. Everything was glass, metal, or white. Jin was sitting outside the lab at a desk with a computer.

"Hey," he said, pulling out a chair for her. "I've got the computer searching for relatives." He pointed to another computer running in the corner. "Some people post their DNA to look for family and for various other reasons. I'm looking through those files too." He paused while Diane sat down. "You think we'll find her?"

"I don't think she has a chance," said Diane. "With the number of things we're trying, one is bound to turn up something. Do you know how the detectives in White County are doing with the Rivers murder?"

Jin shook his head and shoved his black hair behind his ears. "We've given them everything we found at the crime scene, which wasn't much. I think everyone is assuming Clymene was the perp and they aren't following any other leads. I heard you got kicked out of your apartment."

"How did you find out?" she asked.

"Neva called. You going to stay with Frank?" he asked.

"For a while. I haven't decided. I might like to get a house," she said.

"I think it's a good thing," said Jin. "Your neighbors are nuts. You got those people who like funerals and death memorabilia living across the hall and now you have a member of the Donner family in the basement . . . you need to get away from there."

Diane smiled. "The apartment was very small and I would like to have a yard."

"Oh, speaking of dirt, I have the analysis of the soil on that sphinx. The region came up Egypt. Specifically in the area of Abydos. It didn't have the amount of dust on it to suggest it had been lying around in a warehouse for fifty years. I think it was looted fairly recently. The stone face and the bust both had a mixture of dust that didn't point to any identifiable region of the world."

"We know the girdle was stolen from the Cairo Museum fifty years ago, and the sphinx may have been looted recently. That really doesn't tell us anything, does it?" said Diane.

"That the artifacts are all over the board," said Jin. "I guess they were selected because they kind of look like what the documents describe. But why do it?"

"I don't know." Diane looked at her watch. "I have a meeting with the board."

"Again?" said Jin.

"I called it this time. I thought if I keep them up-to-date they won't get so edgy."

"Good luck," said Jin.

Diane took the elevator to the third floor and walked to the meeting room. Most everyone was there and it was still early. *Must be anxious to hear the latest,* she thought. Barclay looked sullen. She wondered if Vanessa had spoken with him.

"Since everyone is here, I'll go ahead and start early. I wanted to bring you up-to-date on the progress so far with the Egyptian artifacts," she said. "The artifacts that arrived here do not match the artifacts we purchased and do not match the documentation. The documentation does match what we were buying, and those items, wherever they are, are legitimate."

"So this was a mistake?" said Harvey Phelps.

"I don't know if it was simply a mistake. One of the pieces turned up in the National Stolen Art File as being stolen from Egypt fifty years ago. We don't yet know where the rest are from. One shows signs of perhaps being recently looted, but that's not confirmed."

"Where does that leave us?" asked Anne Pascal. She had a quiet voice and a kind face. She hadn't said much in the last meeting. Perhaps she felt she could get a word in during this one. But then, Diane was being cynical.

"It leaves us without the artifacts we were in the process of purchasing and for which we made a partial payment," she said. "I think the FBI agent will help us locate them. There is a chance they were burned in a fire that consumed the antiquities dealer we purchased them from."

"Did you check out this place before you bought from them?" Apparently Barclay couldn't hold his tongue any longer. *Still has to scold. It must be embedded in his personal makeup. Must scold every day.*

"Golden Antiquities is—was—one of the most reputable dealers in the state. However, it just passed from father to son when the elder Cunningham retired. The younger Cunningham might not have been as honest as his father. However, he died in the fire. And the FBI is having a hard time finding witnesses."

"What has the FBI person said about Kendel?" asked Laura.

"He has interviewed her. He hasn't indicated to me

that he is interested in her as the culprit who did this."
Diane looked around the table at each of them.

"One thing; I did discover who called the Lanie
LaRu radio program and asked if we were laundering
stolen antiquities," said Diane.

"Who?" said Vanessa.

"My source tells me DA Riddmann asked someone
in his office to make the call. He wanted to poke
Vanessa in the eye, and he thought trashing the museum on the radio was just too good an opportunity
to pass up," said Diane.

"That runt," said Vanessa. "I should have known."

"What can we do about it?" asked the history
professor.

"Nothing," said Diane. "We just have to absorb
some fallout."

"We need to discuss the damage all this will do to
the museum," said Vanessa.

"I don't think it will do any damage," said Diane.
"Not in the long run. We have gotten a couple of calls
from people who don't want to contribute any longer,
but I think all that will change as soon as this is
straightened out."

"Well, I think you are doing a terrific job," said
Kenneth Meyerson. "You seem to have won the FBI
agent over to our side."

"That's hard to tell with law enforcement agents.
The best thing right now is to be as straightforward
as we can with him."

"What about you?" said Harvey. "I've been reading
in the paper that your home was invaded and you
were attacked. Are you all right?" His white bushy
eyebrows were brought together in a frown.

"I'm fine, thank you. It's an ongoing investigation
so I'm not free to talk about it," she said.

"Is all this publicity going to affect the museum?" said Barclay.

"It hasn't yet," said Diane.

"You seem to have too many irons in the fire. I think we need to think about a new director," he said.

They were all startled by the loud slap on the table. It was Vanessa.

"That is not a topic for the board," she said.

Her voice was up a few decibels and had such an I-mean-business quality to it that no one spoke. Not even Diane.

"I'm just saying we should think—" began Barclay after a moment.

"Diane is running the museum exactly as Milo would have it. That is why he gave the director so much power—to cut out nonsense. We are supposed to advise and assist. That's the way it is."

"Okay, Vanessa. I realize this is your museum, but things must be done right," he said.

"They are done right," said Anne Pascal. "This is just the best place. If you will allow yourself time to go to each room and look, really look at the exhibits, I think you will see that. This is a repository of knowledge. You can't run it like a bank."

"Well said, Anne," Kenneth said.

"I agree," said Vanessa. "That is what Milo envisioned—a repository of knowledge. If Diane will adjourn the meeting, we can let her get on with her work."

"Okay, the meeting is adjourned. I'll update you with e-mail as I find out more about the disposition of the artifacts."

Her cell rang and she fished it out of her pocket. It was Andie. Diane had a phone call from an estate attorney.

Chapter 38

Diane hurried to her osteology office on the third floor of the west wing. It was a quick trip from the third-floor boardroom. She sat down and took a deep breath before she picked up the phone.

"Thank you for waiting," she said into the phone.

"I want you to know that was a wholly inappropriate message you left on the Estate Attorneys Listserv. That list is for discussing professional issues. It is not there to do your job for you."

"Excuse me, and you are?" said Diane. Disappointment stung her throat. She thought it was the first hit in the search for Clymene. It was someone else who wanted to scold her.

"I'm Attorney Emma T. Lorimer, and I want to know what right you have to plaster this woman's photograph all over the Web saying she's a criminal."

"She is a criminal," said Diane.

"Has she been convicted?"

"Did you read the message? Yes, she has. Convicted, imprisoned for murder, and now she's escaped from prison. This is a dangerous woman who preys on wealthy families. Do you know her?" said Diane.

"No, I don't know her. I called because I am incensed that you would use a private list in this way."

It was strange to Diane that someone would take the time to call her about what they felt was an unauthorized e-mail. There had to be something else going on.

"The woman who is now going by the name Clymene O'Riley is very adept at getting people to trust her. Do you know who she is?"

"No. Why do you keep asking me?"

"Because you took the time to call. I appreciate your championing the innocent. There are more innocents accused of crimes than people realize, but this woman is not one of them. Do you know her or someone who looks like her? Her sisters look very much like her."

"For the last time, no, I don't know her. I'm just infuriated that you would spam my list and fill my mailbox with crap like this. It isn't what estate law is about."

"I didn't spam the list. I asked permission from the list owner," said Diane.

"Well, he used bad judgment in granting it."

"Maybe he just wanted to protect your clients from a predator."

"Just don't do it again."

The phone went dead with a loud click.

"Well, hell," said Diane.

Diane Googled Emma T. Lorimer to discover where she was from. She found an address for her in Richmond, Virginia. This was probably just someone with a strong sense of political correctness, but she also may be someone who recognized Clymene's photo. Diane copied the information from her screen.

She walked back over to the board meeting. Not

that she wanted to interact with them again, but she had rather rushed out on them. They were still there, arguing about putting a letter to the editor in the newspaper.

"What do you think?" Harvey asked Diane. "We were thinking a little letter might reassure some of our contributors."

"I think it might be more reassuring to write to each contributor personally and let them know we're investigating. When we know more, we can write a public letter."

"Well, we agree on something," said Barclay. "I've been telling them you have to watch what you say publicly."

"On that note, then," said Harvey, grinning, "why don't we all leave while we're ahead?"

"I'll write a letter and send it to each contributor," said Diane. She was happy too, to have some common ground with Barclay.

Vanessa talked Diane into having dinner with her, Laura, and Harvey in the museum restaurant. It was a pleasant meal, mainly because they didn't talk about any problems. As Diane rose to leave, Vanessa put a hand on her arm.

"Is all this about me?" Vanessa asked. "Is someone trying to hurt me through the museum?"

"I don't know," said Diane. "Riddmann was trying to get at you, but my source tells me he isn't behind the artifact problem. He was just taking advantage of it."

"I've made a lot of people mad in my time," said Vanessa.

"We all have," said Harvey.

"It could be me," said Diane, "or Kendel, or Jonas for that matter. He's the curator of the archaeology section. It's probably something completely different. Whatever it is, I will find out."

Diane went up to the osteology office and phoned Deputy Marshal Merrick. She got his voice mail. She explained that it was probably nothing, but Attorney Emma Lorimer might know Clymene. She gave him the details and repeated that it was probably nothing—just a feeling on her part.

It was still early and she had done all she could for the moment regarding Clymene. She would be spending the night in her museum office, so she decided to stay a while longer in the lab and work on the box of bones sent to her from Ohio.

She lay the bones out and saw several things immediately. The bones were young—the victim was between twelve and fifteen years of age. Both radii had healed spiral fractures. She saw healed ribs and finger bones. This was an abused child. She was female and she was malnourished. These were the saddest set of bones Diane had seen in a while. She recalled that the sheriff who asked her to look at them said the bones had been on the shelf in the medical examiner's office for fifteen years. A hunter had found them in the woods those many years ago.

The skull was in a separate box. The face was completely shattered. Diane stood looking at the shattered bone and decided she was going to find out who the little girl was even if it took another fifteen years. She began by piecing the facial bones together.

Diane worked until the early hours of the morning. She had pieces of the face setting up in a sandbox while the glue dried. It was almost finished. When the glue was dried and she had the skull whole again, she would use the laser scanner and have the computer reconstruct the face. She would also age it to see what the girl would have looked like as an adult. Who knew, she might have looked like her mother or an aunt and somebody might recognize them in her. Diane took a sample of bone to be packaged and sent to a lab in California. Maybe they could tell her where the little girl grew up.

She washed her hands, took off her lab coat, and turned off the lights. Her museum office was on the other side of the building and down on the first floor. She started to call a security guard to walk her to her office but decided that she wasn't going to live like that. This was her museum and she wasn't going to be afraid of walking through it. Only the exhibit rooms would be dark. The custodial staff would be working. She would be fine.

She locked her door and waved at the crime lab security guard. She walked across the dinosaur overlook and past the staff lounge, where the custodians were cleaning. She waved to them on her way to the elevators.

Diane made it to her office without incident. It angered her that she even had to worry about it. She changed into pajamas, made up the couch, and snuggled in for the night.

She awakened at the sound of Andie coming into the adjoining office. She looked at the clock—eight o'clock. Four hours' sleep. That ought to be enough for anybody. She got up and collected clean clothes and stepped into the bathroom for a shower, anxious to get to the various computers to see if anyone in the cyberworld had seen Clymene O'Riley.

Chapter 39

"Andie," Diane said as she walked through to her office, "I'm going to be in the crime lab most of the day. Call me there if you need me."

"I heard the shower running. Did you spend the night here? Are you homeless?"

Andie looked very retro today. She wore what Diane's mother called a sack dress—very sixties, straight, no waist. It was pink with black trim and large black buttons down the front. She had new black patent leather Mary Janes on her feet. Diane smiled.

"No, I'm not homeless. Actually, I guess I am, now that you mention it. I'm staying with Frank and he had to remain in Atlanta, so I slept in my office. I like your dress."

Andie stood up and took the skirt of the dress in her hands as she turned. "I love it. I got it in the cutest little vintage dress shop that just opened downtown."

"What happened to Agent Jacobs yesterday? I didn't see him when he left," said Diane.

"He looked at the books and said he'll be back in touch." Andie shrugged. "I figure since he didn't handcuff anybody on his way out, that was good."

"Hopeful, anyway," said Diane.

Diane was trying to remember if she had told him about the soil sample from the sphinx. She hadn't. She took her cell out of her blue twill jacket. Agent Jacobs had given her his cell number and she had programmed it into her phone. Never know when you'll need the FBI on speed dial. Diane supposed that was a good sign too, giving her his private number. She punched the speed dial number and he answered almost immediately.

"Dr. Fallon," he said. "What can I do for you?"

"The soil sample from the sphinx is from the region of Abydos in Egypt," she said. "Jin thinks it may have been dug up recently. There was very little other contamination to suggest it had been sitting in a warehouse or some other place for any length of time."

"That's good information. Thanks," he said.

"You're welcome," said Diane.

"So," said Andie when Diane was off the phone, "you know where the stuff came from?"

"Not exactly. But we are a fraction closer."

"What about that money?" whispered Andie.

"I don't know." She stood up and slipped her cell in her pocket. "Call if you need anything. I'm going up to the crime lab."

Her crew was there—Jin, Neva, and David. Jin had news; Diane could tell by the look on his face, as if the news would fly out of his mouth at any moment or he would choke. But before she sat down with them for a debriefing she went to check on the progress of the searches. The face recognition software was working away, applying its formula to each face in the official databases at lightning speed, but so far there was nothing. Diane felt a stab of disappointment. She checked her e-mail. Nothing from Colonel Kade yet either. She was hoping to wake up this morning and everything would be solved—or at the very least there would be a clue. Of course, there was still Arachnid. She would go down later and see whether it had found anything.

Diane did have some results from her query of Internet Listservs—five e-mails from disgruntled lawyers. They were short, basically polite, but terse statements, like "this isn't appropriate" or "I've spoken with the list owner." One was more explicit, asking her if she knew "how f**ing long" it took him to download the picture. Diane thought that only five complaints out of the hundreds of attorneys on the various lists was pretty good, especially from a group of people who file complaints for a living. There was no telling how many complaints the list owners got. But she imagined they were used to putting out fires.

Her crew had been looking over her shoulder as she checked the progress.

"Nothing, huh, Boss?" said Jin.

"It's early yet," said Diane. "You guys want to tell me what progress we've made so far?" Diane got up from the chair, and after casting a wistful glance at the face recognition program still running, she went to the debriefing table and sat down.

"What I want to know," said David as he sat down, "is what's with the money? There's four thousand dollars in there. Did someone just send it to you?"

"What money?" said Jin and Neva together.

"Yes, someone just sent it to me," said Diane. "With the note. I don't know if it's supposed to be a bribe, a payoff, or a donation from an angry contributor who still wants to give but is pissed at me."

"What are you talking about?" said Neva.

"Yesterday, when we had a room full of law enforcers—with guns," said David, "Diane hands me this envelope filled with packets of one-hundred-dollar bills."

"You're kidding," said Jin. "Someone sent you bundles of money?"

"Yes, and I haven't a clue what it's about. We can add it to the long and growing list of things I don't know anything about." She looked at David. "Were you able to find anything on it?"

"Yes, I did. You know that tiny piece of paper with blood on it I gave you, Jin?" said David.

"That piece was cut from money? Is that legal?" asked Jin.

"It was cut from one of the wrappers," said David, glaring at him. "Apparently the guy got a paper cut."

"Wow, Boss, that's my news," Jin said. "We're making some progress, now." He rubbed his hands together.

"Well finally," said Diane. "What is it?"

"The blood on the money wrapper has the same DNA as the hair pulled off Andie's purse, the one she hit your attacker with."

Diane stared at him. She wasn't sure her surprise was because the attacker and the money sender were the same, or because they had actually found out something.

"Are you sure?" she said.

"Of course I'm sure," said Jin. "And neither one is Clymene or even related to her."

"Is he in the system?" asked Diane.

"No," said Jin.

"Why is he paying you?" said Neva. "That's so strange."

"I don't know. Did you find anything else? Fingerprints?" she asked David.

"No, and I found that odd. How did he get the paper cut if he had gloves on?" David said.

"You know," said Jin, "not everyone leaves prints. If you have very dry skin, or handle a lot of paper in your job, or—"

"I know," said David. "Your prints get sanded off, so to speak. I know that. It's still strange that there weren't any prints from anyone."

"What about the postmark?" asked Diane.

"Rosewood," said David.

"Was there a—" began Jin.

"No, there was no return address," said David.

"Just asking," he said.

"What about the note?" asked Diane.

David smiled. "That was a little more helpful. The writing is simple block letters. The pressure was very heavy. I think this is an angry guy."

"What did the note say?" asked Neva.

"Bitch," said David.

"And you needed to look at the amount of pressure he used to figure out he was angry?" said Neva. She grinned at David's scowl.

David ignored her. "What was kind of interesting was what was indented in the paper. He wrote the message on a piece of lined school paper that had been underneath a page that had been written on."

"I'm assuming you used the electrostatic machine," said Diane.

"I did but really didn't need to because the pressure was hard there too," said David.

"What was it?" asked Diane.

"Words," said David. He jumped up and went to his desk inside one of the glass rooms and came out with a piece of paper. "Back, red, blue, have, dog, play, and face."

"What the heck is that?" said Jin.

"Spelling words," said Diane. "First grade, if I'm not mistaken."

David nodded and put the paper down. There in a neat but unmistakably child's printing was a vertical list of words.

"That's good," said Neva. "You can narrow down a community with that information."

"I know. Now all I have to do is figure out what I'm going to say—hello, I'm from the Rosewood police and I need to get a list of your first-grade spelling words." David started to laugh before he even finished. Jin and Neva started, so did Diane, and for a moment the four of them sat at the table laughing.

"When I figure out just how to go about it, I'll find out what school and maybe what classroom this kid is in."

Diane was starting to feel like they were making progress after all. She started to ask about Jin's DNA search when she saw a red glow coming from David's glassed-in workspace.

Chapter 40

"What is that?" asked Neva, pointing toward a red glow illuminating the inside of David's cubicle.

David grimaced, alarm evident in his dark eyes. He stroked his bald scalp and the fringe of hair circling his head and looked at Diane.

What? she thought. Then it occurred to her—Arachnid. Arachnid had found something. She started to open her mouth, then shut it.

"What's wrong?" said Neva. "Is the building on fire?"

Diane could see David's dilemma. He was actually proud of his program and wanted to show what he'd done. But he also didn't want anyone to know about it.

"Okay," said Jin looking from David to Diane. "You two are really freaking us out here. What's going on? Do we need to evacuate? Has some toxic chemical breeched its containment? Are the dermestid beetles loose? What?"

Diane didn't say anything; she just looked at David. He sat down and put his hands flat on the table.

"If I tell you, you have to promise to keep it a secret," he said to Jin and Neva.

Neva glanced at Diane and gave her a what's-he-up-to? smile.

"We promise," said Neva.

"Jin?" said David.

"Sure," he said.

"Sure what?" said David.

"Okay," said Jin. "Cross my heart and hope to die, stick a needle in my eye. Is that what you want to hear? You've got me curious now. You'll never get any peace from either of us unless you tell us, I swear."

"Okay. I wrote some software. It's in the basement," said David.

"What?" said Jin. "You wrote some software—it's in the basement? Those two sentences don't go together. What are you talking about?"

"I wrote a facial recognition program that searches the Internet for image files, picks out faces, and compares them with a target face. It's called Arachnid."

"And you kept this a secret?" said Neva. "You should sell it."

"It must only be used for good," he said. "In the wrong hands it could be evil. Besides, something like it is probably out there already in dark places, collecting pictures of all of us."

"So the red light means it found something?" said Neva.

"It found something," said David. "I told it to call my computer up here when it did. I didn't think the light would be so . . . so glowing."

"You put Clymene's picture in, didn't you?" said Jin. "Come on, let's go look at it."

They took the elevator down to the basement and headed to David's space.

"I thought you did photography down here," said Jin as David was unlocking the door.

"I do. I also have my laboratory," he said in mock Boris Karloff voice.

David led the way to the room where he kept Arachnid. When he opened the door the first thing they saw in the dark was a closeup photo of a spider's mouth parts on the monitor.

"Jeez, David," said Neva, "now I see why you said, 'It's in the basement.' " Neva did a better Boris Karloff impersonation than David.

David flipped on the light and went to the printer.

"Oh, my God," he said. "Arachnid did find something."

They laughed at his surprise. He fidgeted nervously and handed the printed page to Diane.

"Isn't that her sitting at the table?" said Neva, pointing to the face of a woman seated at a banquet table with an older man who had his hand over hers. There were three other couples at the table with them.

Neva had a good eye for faces. Diane had to look closely. The woman in the photograph had short dark hair in a swept-up style, giving her quite a different look from the woman Diane had sat across from in prison. Or the woman who sat in court. But it was Clymene's face.

"Does it also collect information that goes with the photograph?" said Jin.

"Of course. It wouldn't be much use otherwise," said David.

He sat down and punched a few keys and the printer started printing more pages. Diane snatched the pages as they came out.

"This was taken at the Commonwealth Lawyers Convention in 1997, Richmond, Virginia," said Diane.

Neva read the caption. It listed the names of the people in the photo.

"Mr. and Mrs. Grant Bacon," said Neva. "We have one of her aliases. Too bad they didn't give her first name."

"It could be one of her sisters," said Jin.

"That's true," said David, "if they are identical in features."

"Well, Clymene or her sister, you've got one of them," said Neva.

As the three of them were talking, another name caught Diane's eye.

"She did know her," said Diane.

"Who?" asked Neva.

Diane told them about the call she received the day before from the estate attorney complaining about the e-mail Diane had posted on the Listserv.

"It was this woman—Emma Lorimer," Diane said, pointing to the name in the caption. "I need to fax this to the marshals."

"They have several people to talk to now," said Jin. "That should make them happy."

"Arachnid did a great job, David," said Diane. "Things are coming together finally. With all the searches, we are bound to find out who Clymene really is."

Diane raced up to the crime lab and called Deputy Marshal Merrick.

"I got your voice mail," he said. "I'll ask the locals to have a talk with this Emma Lorimer."

"I have an alias for Clymene," Diane blurted out. "Mrs. Grant Bacon. I also have names of people she was with at a lawyers' convention in 1997—including Emma Lorimer."

"You're kidding. Do you think that's who she really

was before she married Robert Carthwright?" he
asked.

"I don't know. And it's possible that it is one of the
identical sisters, but it's a place to look," said Diane.

"We've been coming up dry on this end," said Merrick. "Do you know if this Grant Bacon is alive or
dead?"

"No, I don't know. That's the next thing I'm going
to look at. Is there a place I can fax you these pages?
I'll send them right away."

He gave her a number.

"Keep me informed," he said. "Let us know immediately if you find out anything else."

"I will. We have several things working here."

Diane was putting the pages in the fax machine as
she spoke. While the pages were transmitting, she got
on her computer and looked up Grant Bacon on the
Web. Too many hits. She looked up *"Grant Bacon"
Virginia* and searched. That narrowed it down considerably. She started scrolling through the listings. Still
too many. She put in *"Grant Bacon" obituary* and hit
ENTER. There was one entry. Grant Bacon, Richmond,
Virginia, died in a boating accident in 1998. He was
survived by his wife, Kathy Delancy Bacon, and two
sons from a previous marriage. Diane printed out the
obituary and faxed it to the marshals as well.

She then called Ross Kingsley.

"I have a name for you," she said when he answered.

"For Clymene?" he asked.

"Yes."

"I knew you could do it. Tell me," he said.

The excitement in his voice was electric. Diane was
surprised her ears didn't crackle.

"It's probably one of her aliases," said Diane. "It

could be one of the sisters. The name is Kathy Delancy Bacon. She was married to a Grant Bacon. I
have a picture of the two of them at a banquet for
lawyers. Give me your fax number and I'll send you
what we've found."

He gave her a number. "Did you look up the husband?" he asked, more soberly.

"I'm sending you his obituary also," said Diane.

Kingsley sighed. "How did he die?"

"Boating accident. There are no details," she said.

"I can look them up. Diane, this is great. I am
amazed," he said.

"Frankly, so am I. The marshals are checking it out.
There are other people in the picture too." She told
him about Emma Lorimer.

"Now, that's interesting. She denied knowing her, yet
she actually called to defend her. I think I need to speak
with this woman myself. I'm really interested in the way
Clymene gets under people's skin. When was this?"

"The picture is from 1997. He died in 1998," she
said. Diane entered Kingsley's number in the fax machine and sent the pages through again.

"The woman is still loyal after ten years. Where is
this?" he asked.

"Richmond, Virginia," she said.

"Richmond. If Clymene's from that region, perhaps
she has some lingering accent. The prison didn't have
a tape of her voice; we're still looking. I have a linguist
named Marley working on her journal entries. Maybe
he will be able to find something in her writing. Of
course, you're moving so fast it may turn out there is
no need for the linguist. How did you find this information?" he asked.

Diane had been dreading that question. "Just Internet searches," she said.

"This is a good lead. It's a good thing Lorimer called. It was an excellent idea to send out those pictures and e-mails to the lawyer lists. I'd be willing to bet you'll get some more hits before the day is through."

He assumed that she had looked up Emma Lorimer on the Web and happily found Clymene, thought Diane. Good. She didn't like keeping the truth to herself, but David would absolutely freak out if she told the FBI about Arachnid.

Diane looked at her watch. She was hungry but it wasn't even close to lunchtime; then she realized she hadn't eaten breakfast. She was about to get up and go to the staff lounge for a snack when Jin knocked on her door and peeked in.

Chapter 41

"Jin," said Diane. "More news?"

They had so many feelers out now that information should begin flowing in. It was the first time she had actually felt optimistic about finding Clymene. It was true what she had said to Jin earlier; Clymene didn't have a chance. Diane waved a hand to the chair in front of her desk. Jin bopped into her office and threw himself into the stuffed chair.

"You know, Boss, that spider program of David's is something. Why is he keeping it hidden? I mean, besides the fact that he probably thinks the men in black will come get him."

"I think it offends his root sensibilities. He believes the Internet should respect people's privacy. When users post photographs it's for people to look at and not to exploit in any way."

"We didn't exploit; we just looked for Clymene. It would have been the same if we did it manually. It would just take years. David's funny sometimes, have you ever noticed that?"

"Occasionally," said Diane, smiling. "Did you come in for a reason or are you just wandering around the building?"

"Oh, yeah, sure. This is good. We're finding so much good stuff, looking for Clymene's starting to get fun. The blood on the bedframe in apartment 1-D in your former apartment house belongs to Clymene Red," he said.

"Clymene Red?"

"Yeah, remember the Christmas trees? There's Clymene Prime—she's the murderer. And there's Clymene Red and Clymene Blue, the two sisters I named after the colors of the ornaments."

Diane nodded. "Okay. So the blood on the bed is one of the sisters," said Diane.

"Yes," said Jin. "But the epithelials in the IV needle we found belong to Clymene Blue, the other sister."

It gave Diane a chill to think they were living just a floor below her all that time and she didn't know it. She wondered how long Clymene had been planning her escape.

"Good work," she said. "Did you find anything else in the apartment?"

"No, and David vacuumed the place good. You know how he is. The three Clymenes washed that place down with bleach before they left. They missed the blood on the bed, and we almost did too. It had dripped and run under the frame. The needle was caught in the corner between the floorboards. Lucky for us, they just didn't see it. Clymene and company are not perfect," said Jin.

"Any sign of the young male who was with them?" asked Diane.

"No. Nothing from him or Clymene Prime in the apartment," said Jin.

Diane started to comment when the phone rang. She picked it up.

"Fallon."

"Dr. Fallon, this is Alex Kade." He had a slow drawl and a gravely voice. "How are you doing today?" he said.

"Colonel Kade. I'm fine. I hope you have some news for me," she said.

"I do. But please call me Alex," he said. "*Colonel* was a lifetime ago."

"I will if you call me Diane," she said.

"Deal. I think I found your woman." He paused. "You said it's too late to save her?"

"She's alive, but . . ." Diane let the answer fade away.

"I don't need to know. I'm sorry I wasn't around to save this little girl," he said.

"I don't think she was ever reported missing. We think, though this is not confirmed, but we think her father sold her," said Diane.

"Aw jeez. Aw jeez."

Diane could hear the pain in his voice.

"She looks to be fifteen or sixteen. I'm sending you just her face. I don't think you need to see the rest of the picture. I'll send the whole pics along if you need them, but—"

"I don't really want them in my head," said Diane. "Is there any information with the pictures?"

"I do have some information. This set of pictures has been on the Internet porn sites for years. A favorite collection, it seems. It was originally posted by a man who called himself Jurgen Heinrich, but his real name was Simon Greene. He's from the U.S. but lived all around Europe in the seventies, eighties, and early nineties. Had family money but made his real fortune selling sex slaves. He was a mean one. I'd like to have had him at the end of my fist."

"Is he still out there selling slaves?" asked Diane.

She had called up the browser on her computer and found Alex Kade's e-mail. She looked at the pictures. He had cropped out everything but the head and tops of the shoulders. Diane was glad. As she listened to Kade, she looked at the face in the images. She was so young, but it was Clymene. Clymene when she was about fifteen. In the photographs her mouth was always in some kind of seductive pout, but the eyes told the story. They were angry.

"No. Greene was murdered. One of them misdemeanor homicides, if you ask me. Someone doused him with kerosene and lit a match to him. He lived for a few months before getting an infection and dying. A bad end to a totally miserable human being."

Clymene's first murder, Diane was willing to bet. Kingsley had told her the first murder usually set the pattern for the rest. This Heinrich, or Greene, died violently and painfully. Clymene may have changed her method of killing to suit the situation, but the death of Archer O'Riley was painful. Her previous husband, Robert Carthwright, died a painful death too. The odds that his death was an accident were dropping by the day. She killed wealthy men in a painful way. Her twist was to marry them first to get their money.

"I appreciate what you do," said Diane. "I know it has to be the most repugnant and emotionally draining undertaking."

"I have some pictures people send me of them and their kids reunited. I posted them so I can look at them while I work at the computer. That gets me through. I know a little bit about your background and former line of work. That wasn't easy either."

"No," said Diane simply.

"The hard thing is that I know even when I find them and they go back home, their life will never be the same. They've always got to live with what was done to them. I saw on the news the other day about a new drug. Propranolol? It's for high blood pressure, but they're saying it might get rid of bad memories and traumatic events. I was thinking, when these kids come home, if they could be treated with something like that they might have a better chance at life," he said. "Have you heard of that? You think it's possible?"

"I haven't heard of propranolol, but I'm sure something like that's possible," she said.

Diane wasn't sure she believed that, but Alex Kade was a man who desperately wanted to give back a normal life to kidnapped and abused kids and their families. That was his hope and Diane didn't want to take that away from him with doubts about the efficacy of such a drug.

"Is there any information on what happened to the girl?" asked Diane.

"No, not a thing," he said.

"This helps a lot," said Diane. "Thank you."

"Glad to be of service anytime," he said.

"Was that the guy who looks for missing children?" asked Jin when Diane hung up the phone.

"That's him. He found Clymene at around the age of fifteen," she said. "Kingsley and I are thinking that her father sold her to the sex trade."

"Kind of makes you feel sorry for her," said Jin. "Like all she's doing is getting even."

"I think on one level she is getting even. But she's a rational adult now and she knows what she is doing is wrong. If she applied her considerable skills to doing good, like Colonel Kade, think of all she could do."

"I guess so. Hey, you want to go eat? I'm starving," he said.

"Yes, I do," she said. "See if Neva and David would like to join us. I haven't asked David if he found anything more about the artifacts."

"Maybe Arachnid could be modified to look for stuff like that too," said Jin. "What do you think?"

"You can bring it up with David," she said. "I'll meet you at the restaurant. I need to call Garnett first."

Chapter 42

Garnett was in his office and Diane was put through immediately.

"What's up?" he said. He sounded busy.

"Just updating you with some information," she said. "I can call back if this isn't convenient."

"No, this is fine. Just doing a little paperwork. One of the necessary evils of this job," he said. "But I really hate it."

Diane filled him in on everything they had discovered about Clymene. "I know this is in the marshals' jurisdiction, but I just thought you would like to know the latest," she said.

"That's quite a bit of information your team's dug up," he said. "My detectives here didn't have any luck finding anything about her. Of course by that time she was already in the system and the DA had other murders to solve. I'd be interested to see how you did it," he said.

"A lot of luck."

Here she was, fibbing again to protect David's project. She told Garnett about the lawyer who called to scold her about e-mailing the Listserv and finding said lawyer in a picture with Clymene in one of her other lives.

"Of course, I'm assuming it's Clymene. It could be one of her sisters. At least we have some names and people to talk to. That's more leads for the marshals."

Garnet was silent and Diane could hear paper rustling.

"So, if it is Clymene," he said after a moment, "she's probably been doing this a long time. That was what? Ten years ago? No telling how many bodies she's racked up."

"She probably started before ten years ago," said Diane. She told him about Colonel Kade and his mission to find missing children. "He searched for Clymene on Internet porn sites—making adjustments for a younger age." She described what Alex Kade found.

"You're having quite a bit of luck," he said. "Of course, you have a lot of resources we don't have here. I'll remember this next time we have a missing person."

"My staff is very talented and creative," said Diane. "I'm very proud of them."

"That stuff Jin did with the blood analysis was pretty good. The mayor and the commissioner were very impressed," said Garnett. "They like having a DNA lab."

Diane wondered if they realized the DNA lab, like her osteology lab, was part of the museum and not owned by the city. They should know it, since they didn't pay for it. But they sometimes forgot trivial details like that and took a proprietary attitude toward anything in the west wing.

"His analysis was impressive," said Diane. So was his presentation, she thought. "I'm glad the marshals got a look at what we can do."

"My bosses liked that idea too. They have aspira-

tions of being Atlanta, but I guess you know that."
He laughed. "You using some of that face recognition
software?" he asked. "They particularly wanted to
know about that. Seems the commissioner saw it on
television the other night."

Diane rolled her eyes. Television had a lot to answer for. "We're searching the national and international databases. So far we've come up empty on
those. What I'm hoping is that another estate attorney
will contact us."

Diane updated Garnett on the findings in apartment
1-D and finally about the hairs from her attacker
matching the blood on the money wrappers.

"What money?" he asked.

"I didn't tell you about the money?" said Diane.
"Right, I told Agent Jacobs. You know, between you,
two marshals, and two FBI agents, I'm having trouble
keeping track of who knows what and who has jurisdiction over what, not to mention who is investigating what."

"You are getting a lot of law enforcement attention
lately. The mayor was a little upset over the item in
the paper about the museum and those . . . looted
antiquities, I think is what it said."

"Did you tell him he doesn't have a dog in that
fight?" said Diane.

"The problem with the mayor is he thinks all dogs
are his," said Garnett. He chuckled. "Jacobs, now,
he's investigating that thing about the artifacts, right?"
said Garnett.

"Yes," said Diane.

"And he thinks Clymene has something to do
with it?"

Diane could hear the confusion in his voice. Nothing
they had discovered pointed to that.

"Just an angle he's looking at," said Diane. "Clymene does know something about archaeology and might have the contacts to mess with the museum. There's no evidence of that whatsoever. So far everything's a dead end in that investigation."

"So, what about the money?" he asked.

Diane told him about receiving a padded envelope filled with packets of one-hundred-dollar bills.

"So the guy's attacking you and sending you money. He sounds conflicted."

Diane smiled. "He does, doesn't he? I have no idea what the attacks or the money are about, but we're following some leads," she said. "I think I have you up-to-date on what's going on here. We still have several searches going on. I'll let you know if something comes of them."

Diane and Chief of Detectives Douglas Garnett had a good working relationship, and that still sometimes surprised her. In the beginning, before the crime lab, she hadn't gotten along with anyone in the police department or the mayor's office. It had to do mostly with her not being willing to sell the museum property to a real estate broker.

The broker told anyone who would listen that unless she sold the property, the city was in line to lose new jobs, extra taxes, and other promised benefits. Diane pointed out that the museum provided jobs and two private businesses—the restaurant and the gift shop. If she had to move, she would move out of the county and all those people would lose, including the city. She was amazed that they wouldn't listen to her, until the real estate broker was shown to be a crook. But now she was forgiven. The mayor found her useful, and she got along well with Garnett, who was a good buffer between her and the rest of the powers in Rosewood. Today everything worked. In the back of her mind, though, Diane was always waiting for the other shoe to drop.

At her stomach's insistence Diane stopped contemplating the fickle power structure of Rosewood and went down to eat lunch with her crime scene staff. The restaurant always provided such a pleasant respite. The murmur of the luncheon crowd today sounded soothing. Diane was greeted at the entrance by a waitress carrying vases of spring wildflowers to the tables.

Over a salmon salad Diane told Neva about the bones she was trying to identify of the little Ohio girl and asked Neva to find time to make drawings of her—not just her face, but of her standing.

Diane could describe for Neva how the girl would look with one leg a little shorter than the other. How she might rub her fractured forearms because they would hurt, how her eyes would look afraid, and how her face would show pain. Diane's facial mapping software did a great job, but Neva's drawings put life into the image. Diane didn't want the little girl to get shoved aside because her justice wasn't as urgent. It was urgent and it was important.

After lunch Diane checked in with Andie and started back up to the crime lab. In the lobby she met Kingsley coming through the door among a group of schoolkids rushing and screaming around him, their teacher calling for them to get in line.

"Can't stay away from the museum?" said Diane.

"There's just so much going on here." He grinned at her. "I have some news." He motioned to the lobby elevator. "Shall we go to the other side?" he said.

When the doors opened, before they could get on, a small kid of about five rushed past them and stood in the back of the elevator laughing. One of Diane's docents, a young woman by the name of Emily, came in after him, grabbed him, put him under her arm, and hauled him out.

"Emily," said Diane, shocked at the way she handled the boy.

Emily turned and grinned at Diane. "It's all right, he's my brother. That's our mother over there with the scowl on her face."

The kid giggled and tried to wiggle out of her grasp.

"I'm going to feed you to the dinosaur," she said.

He laughed harder.

"And I think my job is tough," said Kingsley.

Diane shook her head. "They sometimes run away and get lost in the museum. Drives the docents nuts."

Diane pushed the elevator button for the third floor.

"I have some news too," she said when the doors shut. "I'm not sure what I've told you, but we have information coming in a little faster now."

The doors opened and they got out on the overlook to the Pleistocene room.

"Jacobs is very impressed with your museum," said Kingsley, walking over and looking down at the mammoth. "He said he will be greatly disappointed if it turns out you are involved in buying and selling looted antiquities."

"I would think by now he would have discovered that we aren't," said Diane.

"He believes you're an honest museum. He's just cautious. Plus, he says he's at a standstill." Kingsley laughed. "He's hoping Clymene did it."

"Me too, at this point, but I really doubt it. All this seems a little too much for even Clymene to organize," said Diane. "Of course, there are three of her."

"Three Clymenes." Kingsley laughed again. "Who would have thought it?"

They walked through the exhibit preparation room and were stopped by Janine.

"I don't think we should have a dinosaur that poops kids," she said with her hands on her hips.

Kingsley looked startled and laughed.

"I didn't think so either," said Diane, "but talk to Emily Fellows and see what she thinks."

"The docent?" said Janine.

"Yes. The docents are around kids a lot."

"You want to do it?" asked Janine.

"Not necessarily. I think it's a ridiculous idea, but then, I'm not five. I'll leave it up to you," said Diane.

"I'll talk to her." Janine shook her head and walked away.

"Do I want to know what that was about?" said Kingsley.

"Museum stuff."

They stopped once more so he could look at the Brachiosaurus, then moved on to the osteology lab and Diane's office, where she had the pictures from Colonel Kade. There was something she wanted to look at in the pictures that nudged at the back of her mind.

Chapter 43

Diane sat down behind her desk in the osteology office. Kingsley pulled the upholstered burgundy chair nearer to her desk and sat down.

"This is nice," he said, settling into the deep comfort.

"It is. It's a nice reading chair."

Diane called up her e-mail and printed out Alex Kade's message to her containing the photographs and the summary of information he had told her over the phone.

"I think you will find this interesting," said Diane. She handed him the material.

Kingsley was smiling when he sat down, wondering about the conversation about exhibit preparations, no doubt. His smile quickly turned to a frown.

"This explains almost everything," he said. "This man Heinrich, or Greene, or whatever you want to call him, was her first kill. He has to be. I'd bet my reputation on it."

"That's what I thought," said Diane.

"Diane"—he gently struck the pages with his hand—"this is just the kind of thing I had hoped for. How did you find this?"

She told him about Col. Alex Kade and his crusade.

"He deserves all the credit," she said. "He cropped the photographs out of consideration for my sensibilities. He said he would send the complete pictures if we need them."

The marshals wanted only to find Clymene to put her back in prison. Kingsley wanted more than that. He wanted to understand what had created her. For that he needed detailed information about what she had experienced.

"I'll take his e-mail address from here." He gestured at the page. "And ask him to send the pictures to my office. You know, I feel sorry for her. She was what, fourteen, fifteen? What kid should have to go through this?"

"I feel sorry for that little girl in the pictures. The adult has a choice," said Diane.

"Does she? Does she really have a choice when— if we are right—her father sold her to a maniac who enslaved her in the sex trade?" He sighed. "Who really has choices?"

Diane didn't argue with him, but she didn't agree with him, at least not completely.

"I wish we had her real name," he said.

"I've been thinking about that. Did you ever see Clymene's cell?" asked Diane.

"Yes."

"How was it decorated?" she asked.

"Simply. She had pictures of flowers in vases. I think she tore them out of magazines."

"Were they irises, roses, and lilies?" asked Diane.

Kingsley looked surprised. "Yes . . . they were. Only those flowers."

"Those are the three sisters' names," said Diane. "Clymene's name is Iris. Her sisters are Rose and Lily."

"It makes sense—triplets, flowers. Easier than names that rhyme," he said. But how the devil did you come up with that?"

"At lunch I saw the waitress putting wildflowers on the tables and it tickled something in the back of my mind . . . something I had seen. Look at the pictures Colonel Kade sent. Every picture has an iris in a clear vase in the background. When I spoke with Rev. Rivers, we were in the chapel. He said most of the flower arrangements were by Clymene. The arrangements were of three flowers—irises, roses, and lilies."

"So all we need now is a last name," he said, grinning. "See, you did this very fast. I knew I was right in bribing you."

Diane gave him half a smile. The phone on her desk rang and she picked it up.

"Fallon," she said, still smiling at Kingsley.

"Dr. Fallon, I'm Trenton Bernard, an estate attorney in Seattle. I'm calling in regard to your e-mail. It says you are the director of the crime lab in Rosewood, Georgia?"

"Yes, Mr. Bernard. Do you mind if I put you on speakerphone? I have Ross Kingsley, an FBI profiler, with me and we are both working on the case."

"I suppose that's all right. I have to say, this is very strange," he said.

Kingsley's attention perked up when he heard his name. He leaned forward as Diane switched the phone over to speaker.

"Hello, Mr. Bernard," said Kingsley. "Thank you for speaking with us."

"Do you know the woman in the photograph?" asked Diane.

"I know someone who looks very much like her," he said.

"How do you know her?" asked Diane.

"She was married to a client of mine. But I have to tell you, this can't be the same woman you e-mailed about. The woman I know is just the nicest woman. However, I was persuaded by my secretary that I should probably call because the woman in the photograph looks so much like her," he said.

"Can you tell us about her?" said Diane.

"Her name is Estelle Redding. She and my client Glenn Redding were married about three years altogether. Glenn is now deceased," he said.

Kingsley raised his eyebrows at Diane. Diane nodded.

"He was one of Seattle's most prominent citizens and they were a good couple. Very much in love."

"How did he die?" asked Kingsley.

"It was tragic. He had bypass surgery and contracted a staph infection. They just couldn't get it under control. As soon as they thought he was getting over it, it would flare up again. Hospitals are so bad these days for staph infections. Now I hear that sports locker rooms have the same problem. It's frightening. Poor Glenn suffered terribly before he died."

"When was this?" asked Diane.

"He died in 2001," he said.

"Who inherited?" asked Diane.

"Estelle inherited the bulk of the estate. I know that sounds suspicious, but it wasn't," he said.

"Why do you say that?" asked Kingsley.

"About a year before Glenn died, he came in to change his will. It stands out clearly in my mind. Estelle was with him. He had children from a previous marriage—two sons and one daughter. They were all grown. He was furious with all of them because of some irresponsible behaviors, which I won't go into.

He wanted to cut them out of the will. He was adamant. Estelle told him that they were his children and even though he was angry with them now, he wouldn't always be. And that they may be irresponsible now, but they wouldn't be forever. She told him to make some provision he could live with, but he shouldn't cut them out. Estelle had a very calming effect on Glenn. She was that way. Then I remember she stood up and said that the two of us could figure out something that would work and she was going shopping. Now, does that sound like a woman who is a gold digger?"

"What did Mr. Redding do?" said Diane.

"He had a few special bequeathals and a few charities he wanted to give money to, but the bulk of everything went to Estelle, along with a letter saying that when she felt the children were mature and responsible, she was to give them their portion."

"Did she?" asked Diane.

"She was angry at the boys. They had demanded money before their father was even buried. After the will was probated, she came to me and said she was going to wait on the boys to see how they turned out, that she was still angry with them. However, she set up a generous trust for the daughter with a bonus if she graduated from a good college. She also did something which I thought was very kind and not many women would do."

"What was that?" asked Kingsley.

"Glenn and his first wife had a very acrimonious divorce. Just before he died, she was diagnosed with breast cancer. It went into remission for a while but returned with a vengeance. Estelle told me that she knew Glenn hated Marilee when he was alive, but where he was now he would approve of what she was about to do. She gave Marilee two million dollars so she could be comfortable before she passed. Now, does that sound like a woman who would do the things described in your e-mail?"

"That was very kind and decent," said Kingsley. "How much money was in the estate?"

"Roughly two hundred million dollars total value. Some in cash and the rest in investments and real estate," he said.

Both he and Diane looked at each other. Kingsley shook his head. "Wow," he silently mouthed to her.

"What did Estelle look like?" asked Diane.

"In the face, very much like the photograph in your e-mail. Not as much makeup. And her hair was platinum, I think it's called. She was quite a striking woman."

"Would you know if she liked flowers?" Diane asked.

"Yes, she did. Her greenhouse was filled with roses, lilies, and irises."

"Does she keep in touch?" asked Kingsley.

"She did up until about two years ago. She said she was going to travel. Go to some of the places she and Glenn went to. She called several times and asked how the boys were doing. Unfortunately, I could never give her good news."

"Thank you for speaking with us," said Kingsley. "We may be calling to speak with you again."

"I hope I've been helpful," he said. "As I said, I cannot believe that she is the same woman you are inquiring about . . . but I thought that I should call."

"You have been very helpful," said Diane. "You did the right thing. Thank you."

Diane hung up the phone, sat back, and looked at Kingsley.

"What do you think?" asked Kingsley.

"I think she's a clever girl. I believe she maneuvered her husband ahead of time in the decision about the will. It's like the card trick where I keep asking you to pick a card out of several that I show you. When I finally reveal the card you chose, you are surprised and wonder how I knew, when all the time I was guiding you to the card I wanted you to pick."

"I agree," said Kingsley. "That's exactly what she did. She had Redding primed before he went into the attorney's office. She made herself so reasonable and trustworthy, talked about all the different ways he could handle the will. By the time he got to the lawyer's office, he probably thought the whole idea was his. What about the gifts to the daughter and the mother?"

Diane shrugged. "Cooling the mark. Showing how generous she really is, to take attention off the fact that the boys weren't getting anything and she was getting so much. And it could be that she identifies with the daughter and maybe the mother."

"You're good at this," said Kingsley.

"I'm becoming cynical, is what I am," said Diane. "We were right; she had killed before. This deadly staph infection of Redding's sounds very much like the tetanus method she used with Archer O'Riley."

"I noticed that too," said Kingsley.

"You said you have some news," said Diane.

"I do. I showed a linguist the written entries in Clymene's scrapbooks. There isn't much, but he identified some wording in the archaeology-theme scrapbook that is pretty specific to a place. In one of the photographs the archaeology crew are receiving mail. The text says, 'The mail was just called over.' "

"I've never heard that expression," said Diane.

"It's unique to the Outer Banks of North Carolina," he said. "I think we may know where she is from."

Diane looked up as the door opened. Jin's head peeked in.

"Hi. I found a relative of the triplets. Interested?"

Chapter 44

"So," said Frank, sitting down on the couch and pulling Diane into his arms, "you're going on a road trip tomorrow."

"Plane trip. New Bern, North Carolina. About five hundred miles from here," said Diane. "Kingsley wants to interview her as soon as possible and not give her any advance notice. He doesn't want to give her the chance to back out of seeing us, or possibly even notify Clymene."

"And she is?" he asked.

"Carley Volker. She had her complete DNA profile posted on one of those ancestry Web sites. Jin did a good job finding her. It's not as easy as simply matching charts. There's a lot of mathematical probability that goes into finding common alleles among relatives."

"So tell me what you know," he said.

Diane liked to talk cases out with Frank. He had a way of asking questions that made her think.

"Not a lot that we know. A lot we have some good guesses about. One of the problems is that they are identical triplets. Some of the photographs we're finding may not be Clymene, but one of her sisters. Hell, for all I know they may all be in this together—three little black widows all raking in the money."

"So, what do you think you know?" said Frank.

"For the sake of argument, I've decided Clymene must be about thirty-five years old, so that's my base."

Diane sat up and took a sip of wine. She had made one of her famous three-cheese-and-meat lasagnas for dinner and Frank had opened a bottle of wine. She took another sip before she spoke again.

"In 1987, Clymene was with a man named Simon Greene, aka Jurgen Heinrich, possibly somewhere in Europe. He was using her in porno movies. Kade couldn't find any earlier photographs of her, but that doesn't really mean anything."

"So, 1987 is the first date she appeared on your radar. She would have been how old then?" said Frank.

"Fifteen. We suspect her father sold her around that time, possibly much earlier. He probably saw her as just a spare. After all, he had two more just like her," said Diane.

"You feel sorry for her?" asked Frank.

"I feel sorry for the terrible things done to her, the chance for a normal life taken from her," she said. "I feel sorry for that little fifteen-year-old. I don't feel sorry for the murderer she's become."

"Why don't you go over your timeline with me?" he said, rubbing her shoulders.

"In 1991 Greene was murdered, burned alive. We think by Clymene, but we have no proof," said Diane. "She would have been nineteen at the time—old enough to defend herself and to make it on her own."

"It could be argued she was just defending herself.

Found the opportunity to escape from her captor," said Frank. "If it were Star, I would expect her to fight . . ."

"I know," said Diane. "And I agree, if the killing had stopped there."

"That was 1991. What next?"

"The next time we pick her up is six years later in 1997 and her name is Kathy Delancy Bacon and she is married to Grant Bacon of Richmond, Virginia. He died in a boating accident."

"Wealthy husband number one," said Frank.

"Four years later, in 2001, she is Estelle Redding and married to Glenn Redding of Seattle, Washington. He dies of a rampant staph infection and leaves her two hundred million dollars. In 2004 she is Clymene Smith Carthwright and married to Robert Carthwright of the Atlanta Carthwrights. He dies when a car he was working on falls off its jack and crushes him to death. Then in 2006 she is Clymene O'Riley, married to Archer O'Riley here in Rosewood, and he dies of tetanus. That's her history as we know it," said Diane.

"The events in your timeline are located all across the country and in Europe. You said the epigenetic profile prepared by Jin indicates that Clymene was separated from her sisters and moved around for a number of years, but that the other sisters stayed in closer proximity to each other. That would lend support to the conclusion that the woman in your timeline of events is in fact Clymene and not her sisters," said Frank.

"I feel fairly confident the timeline belongs to Clymene, but I like to keep my mind open for other possibilities. Clymene does have an unusual capacity to surprise."

"More wine?" asked Frank.

Diane shook her head and snuggled back into Frank's arms. "This is cozy," she said.

"You know, you could have it on a more regular basis," he said.

"What do you mean?" she said.

"You know what I mean. You need a home. Move in here. This is a big house. You can have your own space if that makes you feel easier about it. You can have the whole upstairs if you want it."

Diane was silent for several moments. It sounded like such a commitment—moving into Frank's house. On the other hand, it felt really good nestled against Frank. She would like coming home to that.

"I'm not hearing you say anything," he said. "You need a place to stay while you look for a house. Just take your time looking. Try it out here for a while. You might like it. Besides," he added, "I need someone who can cook lasagna like that."

Diane laughed and started to push him away, but he kissed her.

"This is nice," she said after a moment.

"It's more than nice," he said. He rubbed his thumb across her lips. "It feels right, doesn't it?"

"I'll stay here while I'm looking," she said.

"Okay, I'll take that as a yes," he said and kissed her again.

"I already have a lot of my things here," she said.

"See, it's already working out," said Frank.

"You're good to talk to," she said. "This thing with Clymene and the artifacts have my mind completely occupied."

"You think she's a sociopath?" said Frank.

"She says not," said Diane.

"Would you believe a sociopath?" asked Frank.

"That's the thing about Clymene. It's easy to fall

into believing her. And it's not the big things; it's the smaller ones, the subtleties, like her giving the money to Redding's daughter and ex-wife. Was that sincere or just part of her act to make people believe in her? The same with her concern for Grace Noel and Eric Tully's daughter. She really did seem concerned for the daughter, and I believed it, but subtlety is Clymene's special gift," said Diane.

"Interesting case. I can see why Kingsley is fascinated by her. She must be a profiler's dream girl. I'm going to get some ice cream," he said. "Want some?"

"Yes, please. What kinds do you have?"

Diane knew he had more than one flavor. Frank always got more food than he needed, just so he'd have lots of choices. She supposed that was why he had such a large freezer on his back porch.

Frank's kitchen matched the rest of the house. The cabinetry was dark wood similar to the Queen Anne style of the house. His appliances were bright white and the floor was a deep green slate. It was a comfortable kitchen to cook in. Certainly more comfortable than the small kitchen in her apartment.

"How about rum raisin?" he said.

"Sounds fine."

Diane watched as he got two pints out and opened them and gave her a spoon.

"Out of the carton?" she said.

"Of course. Only way to eat ice cream." He grinned, and they sat in the kitchen around the island and ate ice cream.

"I won't be able to eat all of this," she said.

"Save it for later. How is your artifact problem coming?" he asked.

"It's not. It's at a complete standstill. The good news is that nothing directly implicates the museum or any of us. The bad news is that it doesn't clear our reputation. Frankly I'm not sure what the FBI guy is doing. He's spent a lot of time on the Clymene case."

"The Clymene case? Why?" asked Frank, savoring a spoon of ice cream.

"Actually, that's not true. He and Ross Kingsley are friends and he visited with Ross a while. He got the idea that Clymene might be behind the artifact thing. She does know about archaeology, but . . ." Diane shrugged.

"You don't think so?" he asked.

"I don't know. It's as good a theory as anything else we have, which is nothing," she said. "It's felt like a game from the beginning. So did the thing with the blood in my apartment. I couldn't shake the feeling that everything going on was a series of moves in a game." Diane shook her head. "This ice cream is really good."

"You've never had this flavor?" he asked.

The phone rang. It felt like an unwelcome intrusion. Diane realized she liked being alone here with Frank. He answered the phone and gave it to her.

"Anne Pascal," he said.

"One of my board members." She took the phone.

"Diane. Hi. David Goldstein gave me your number. He asked me to help find out what teacher was using that list of spelling words. Your life is so interesting," she said.

Yes, my life is a Chinese curse, she thought. "We very much appreciate your help," said Diane. "Were you able to find anything?"

"Yes, I did. I began by matching the words to a book. Spelling words usually come from a particular book the kids are reading that week. I made a call to a school librarian friend of mine and we figured out the book David's list of words came from is *Jack Story and the Big Red Ball*. Then I called some reading teachers and asked who was using that book recently, and . . . Well, the end result is I found out those were last Monday's spelling words in Mrs. Coker's class at Jewel Elementary in Adamsville. I talked with her and asked for a list of her kids, but she was kind of funny about that because the list was going to the police. I'm sorry."

"That's all right. That's understandable. I'm amazed that you were able to find the teacher and classroom. You've been a tremendous help," said Diane. "I don't think we could have done it without you."

"Oh, it was fun. Kind of put on my Miss Marple thinking cap, you know. Thank you for asking me. And I also want to tell you how much I've enjoyed being on the board of the museum. I just love that place," she said.

"I'm surprised you aren't wondering what in the world I got you into," said Diane.

"Oh, no. I have to say, I've really enjoyed your interaction with Thomas Barclay. He's on the school board too, you know. He loves to browbeat teachers. I've heard 'when I was in school' so many times. I don't know why some people who are successful in one thing think they know how to do everything. I'm afraid he just sees teachers as overeducated babysitters," she said. "But I didn't call you to rant about Thomas Barclay."

"I'm hoping Barclay will adapt. The museum board isn't like the other boards he's served on," said Diane.

"You'll let me know how this thing with the child and the spelling words turns out, won't you?"

"Yes, I certainly will," said Diane. "Thank you again for your help."

"One of my board members," said Diane when she got off the phone. "She found the teacher who assigned the list of spelling words indented on the paper used to write the note that came with the money."

"That lived in the house that Jack built?" said Frank. "What money?"

"I haven't told you about the money? The guy who's been attacking me sent me four thousand dollars," she said.

Frank stared at her for a moment, ice cream dripping off his spoon. "Four thousand dollars? Why didn't you tell me? You didn't have to cook dinner; you could have taken us out to someplace nice," he said. "Why did he send you money?"

"I don't know, but he included a note with the word *bitch* written on it in capital letters. On the page of the pad above the sheet he wrote the note to me on, a kid had written a list of first-grade spelling words and it made an indentation in the notepaper," she said. "Using some fancy equipment, David was able to read the words from the indentation and he asked our schoolteacher board member for help in finding out where the spelling words came from."

Diane realized that a lot had happened since she last spoke with Frank. She told him about the DNA found on the hairs caught in Andie's purse matching blood found on one of the money wrappers.

"It looks as though he thinks you're blackmailing him," said Frank.

"It does look that way," she said. "I have no idea how I could have left that impression with him. All I did was bite, kick, and scratch him." She put the lid back on her ice cream container and put it back in the freezer.

"So, you think he has a child in the first grade and

you're trying to track him down by finding the child," said Frank.

"That's the plan. I thought I might recognize the name of one of the children in the class."

"Your board member said the list came from a teacher in Adamsville," said Frank. "That's the same county as the prison."

"Yes, it is," said Diane. She washed her spoon and put it away. "So there is a connection there."

"You might see if the teacher has a child with the last name of Tully in her class," he said.

Diane stared at him. "I didn't think of that. Until tonight I'd put Grace Noel in the back of my mind. Eric Tully has a daughter about that age. Do you think Clymene could have somehow . . ." Diane paused, still staring at Frank.

"You said everything felt like a game—like everything that's happened was a move. I think your instincts are right. Everything has been a game to maneuver you into a corner so Clymene could get away—and maybe exact a little revenge to boot."

"You think Clymene is manipulating Tully?" said Diane.

"This is just a guess," said Frank. "I may be all wrong."

"But it makes sense," said Diane. "Do you think she is behind the artifact problem too?"

"I don't know. That seems like it would involve more people to carry out. I bet that Clymene only trusts her sisters—and this lone male, whoever he is. I can't see her trusting a third party much at all, certainly not with anything that could be traced back to her."

"I need to call Garnett," said Diane.

She went into the living room and dialed Garnett's cell phone. As it started to ring, she noticed the time. He was probably at home eating. She hung up.

"I'll call his office and leave a message," she said.

As she reached for the phone, it rang.

"Go ahead and answer it," said Frank. "You live here now."

Diane picked up the phone and said hello.

"Hey, is that you, Diane?" It was Garnett.

"Yes, I'm sorry, I just noticed it's your suppertime," she said.

"That's all right. What's up?" he said.

She told him about the line of evidence pointing toward Eric Tully as her attacker. "I know there's a lot of ifs here, but I thought it's worth checking out."

"I agree. I'll have someone go pick him up now," he said. "Maybe his blood and hair will be a match and we can lock him up."

"I'll be out of town tomorrow," said Diane. "Kingsley and I are going to North Carolina to speak with one of Clymene's relatives."

"Found one, eh? I assume you've told the marshals," he said.

"Kingsley told them. They will be flying to North Carolina as soon as they check out a sighting of Clymene in California."

"California? That's a ways off," he said. "What's that about?"

"I don't know. The flow of information between me and the marshals only goes one way," said Diane.

"I hear you there," he said. "Are you staying with Frank?"

"Yes, until I can find a place. I might buy a house, I just don't know," she said.

"Have a safe trip," he said.

She got off the phone and told Frank the police were going to question Eric Tully.

"I hope that puts an end to his harassment," she said. "I can juggle only so many balls at once before they all come crashing down around me."

Chapter 45

It wasn't a long flight, but Diane didn't like flying. Intellectually she understood how planes stay up in the air, but in her heart she really didn't believe in the Bernoulli effect or momentum transfer. Flight might as well be magic as far as she was concerned, and the magic could be withdrawn at any moment. She wasn't exactly white-knuckled, but she was on the lookout for the goblin on the wing.

"You don't like flying?" said Kingsley.

"Not very much, and if you start a lecture on how safe planes are compared to automobiles, I'll hit you. Automobile accidents are survivable; airplane crashes are not," said Diane.

"And you have no control up here," he said. "I think that is the source of your discomfort."

Diane looked from the window over at him and found him grinning.

"I may hit you anyway," she said. "Why aren't we in one of those neat little FBI jets?" she said.

"You know, TV has really ruined my job for me. Planes are expensive to fly and I don't have access to one at the drop of a hat. Nor can I do perfect on-the-spot profiles by glancing at a crime scene. I have to research it, think about it, and sometimes I'm wrong. Profiling isn't supposed to be an exact science, just a tool to use in the furtherance of criminal apprehension."

"Oh, you don't like to fly either, do you?" said Diane.

"Not particularly, no," he said.

The flight attendant brought drinks and both Diane and Kingsley accepted a bottle of water.

"I did some homework yesterday," he said. "I have more detailed information on how Clymene's husbands died. I thought you might be interested."

Anything to take my mind off flying. "Yes, I would," she said.

He gave her several sheets of paper. "I've summarized each husband's death. Grant Bacon is the first we know about and one of the most interesting."

Diane read Kingsley's notes. "It says he got hung up in his boat's propeller while he was trying to repair it. How can that happen?" she said.

"They don't exactly know. According to the police report, he was untangling his mooring line, or whatever you call it, and somehow the boat's motor got started. He was tangled in the rope and fairly chopped up when they found him. The whole thing is a mystery."

"Was Clymene—or rather, Kathy Bacon—suspected?" asked Diane.

"No, she wasn't. This is the interesting part. Everyone reported that the wife, as she was often referred to, was a mouse. Grant Bacon was a batterer and he liked submissive women. By all accounts, she was very submissive."

"If she was battered, that would make her a suspect," said Diane.

"She had an ironclad alibi. She was with a number of notable people at the country club when it happened," he said.

"Her sisters helped her," said Diane. "One of them must have."

"That's what I figure," he said. "Either as the murderer or the alibi. Grant was into a lot of shady dealings, made a lot of money. But she didn't gain much by his death because of a prenuptial agreement she had signed. So no one really looked at her as a suspect."

"This doesn't sound like Clymene," said Diane.

"It gets better. I talked to the lawyer who called you from Richmond, Emma Lorimer."

"She talked to you?" said Diane.

"The marshals had softened her up quite a bit. Besides, you don't refuse to talk with an FBI agent, even if he is just a lowly profiler," he said with a chuckle.

The plane hit a bump in the air, and Diane gripped the armrests.

"What did she say?" said Diane, ignoring the churning in her stomach.

"Lorimer is involved in helping abused women escape—you know, underground railroad. She said Kathy Bacon came to her in a panic with the story that Grant's son had started abusing and threatening her. Lorimer said Kathy, or Clymene, asked her to tell her what to do. Lorimer put her in the escape system with a new birth certificate, social security number, and everything."

"That was clever of Clymene," said Diane.

"Wasn't it? Clymene disappeared into the system and the only one who wanted to know where she went was the son."

"Why?" asked Diane.

"Well, and this is the twist, it seems that all of his father's offshore bank accounts had been emptied—about a hundred million dollars."

"A hundred million?" said Diane. "That's a lot of money. So the prenup didn't mean a thing."

"Not so far as Clymene was concerned," he said. "The jurisdiction of the probate court didn't extend to the Cayman Islands, and she apparently had the account numbers and the access codes."

"Do you think Clymene knew he was an abuser before she married him?" Diane asked.

"Clymene knows how to read people. Of course she knew, and she played the part for him," said Kingsley. "She was married to Grant Bacon the least amount of time of all her husbands. She gave Emma Lorimer a huge sum of money for the underground railroad before she left. Lorimer said she tried not to accept it, but Clymene insisted, saying she could earn her way from here on out, and she wanted to give something back."

"Was she sincere, or was that just part of the act?" said Diane.

"I don't know. At best, a little of both," said Kingsley.

Diane looked at the page of notes on Glenn Redding of Seattle, Washington. There wasn't much that she didn't already know. Foul play wasn't suspected at all in his death. At the bottom of the page Kingsley had a figure for how much money she had inherited from Redding—two hundred million.

"She gave the daughter ten million and set aside another fifteen million to be given on completion of a university degree," said Kingsley.

"Did the daughter get a degree?" asked Diane.

"She did—the University of Washington, in communications. She got her money. You can see why the lawyer, Trenton Bernard, didn't suspect Mrs. Redding. It looked as though she was doing what she was asked by her late husband."

"Clymene's good," said Diane.

"I tallied up how much money she received from her husbands—three hundred and eighty-five million dollars," said Kingsley. "That comes to about nineteen million dollars for each year from the time she was fifteen."

"I didn't realize it was that much. Clymene is a wealthy woman," said Diane. "Her sisters must help her hide it. I know the Rosewood police couldn't find any trace of her finances."

"There is another clever move," he said. "Our Clymene paid her taxes."

"What?" said Diane, looking up from the pages to Kingsley. "She paid taxes on hidden money?"

"After each death she stayed around long enough to pay taxes before she disappeared. She learned from Al Capone's mistake, I guess. As near as I can tell, we can't get her or any of her aliases on income tax evasion," said Kingsley.

"What about the hundred million in the emptied offshore accounts?" said Diane.

"Her next tax return says she earned a hundred million in an at-home business. She paid the taxes," said Kingsley.

"She's full of surprises," said Diane.

The plane landed and they disembarked at Craven County Regional Airport and rented a car. Diane drove. Kingsley was right; she much preferred being in a machine she could control. He read the map they had printed off the Internet while Diane found the route on the GPS that came with their rental car.

Carley Volker did not live in the city of New Bern, but about ten miles out. Diane had never been to New Bern but she knew something of the area. It was a pretty town with a lot of history dating back to the 1700s. There were hundreds of sunken ships all up and down the coast, some of them visible from the shore. The Outer Banks of North Carolina were also Blackbeard's stomping ground. There were many things she'd like to see, and here they were, looking for Clymene. All in all, she'd rather look for Blackbeard's treasure.

"What did you tell Carley?" asked Diane. Kingsley had called her while Diane was getting the rental, a Mitsubishi Outlander.

"That we are from the FBI and the Rosewood, Georgia, police department and would like to see her. I thought it might confuse her if I told her we were from the FBI and the Museum of Natural History."

Diane laughed. "Did you tell her what it's about?"

"A little. I told her in general terms it's about a woman who escaped from prison. I told her we located her through the DNA she posted. That's all. I didn't want to dwell on the fact that she might have a homicidal maniac in the family tree.

"Turn left here," said Kingsley. "It should be right over this rise."

Diane looked down at the GPS map display. It agreed with the printed map Kingsley was using.

Diane had expected a quaint older home but realized when she made the turn that they were entering a new subdivision of boxy, vaguely Victorian-style houses. They were pretty, but close together. The houses were new enough that the landscaping still contained small, spindly trees, flowers that had not yet bloomed, and grass that was just coming up through straw covering. The house Carley Volker lived in was gray with white trim. They turned in the driveway. Diane put the SUV in park and turned off the ignition.

Carley came out the front door of the house and met them. She was much younger than Diane expected. She looked to be in her early twenties, gold-blond hair, blue eyes, and slim. She wore blue jeans and an apricot-colored T-shirt. She grinned broadly.

"Come in. It's such a pretty day, Mom's serving tea on the deck."

"Thank you," said Diane. She reached in her pocket for her ID and showed it to her. "I'm Diane Fallon, and this is Agent Ross Kingsley."

"Hello, Miss Volker," said Kingsley, holding out his identification.

She looked at each and grinned as if indulging them. Clearly Carley was too trusting.

She led them up the steps and through a gate to a deck at the back of the house, where her mother was setting out glasses of iced tea and cookies.

"See that window up there?" Carley pointed to a bay window on the second floor. "That's my room. It has a great view of the marsh and the intracoastal waterway. We just moved here," she added.

Diane saw that Kingsley was thinking the same thing she was. Carley was giving away too much information about herself. How nice to live in the innocent world she did, but how dangerous. *Maybe I'm too cynical,* thought Diane.

Diane looked across at the green marsh grasses waving in the breeze and the waterfowl about to make a landing. It was a pretty view, a restful view.

"Hi, I'm Carley's mother, Ellen Volker. Carley is so excited that someone saw her posting."

Ellen Volker was an older image of her daughter, not quite as slim, and her hair was starting to get gray. She seemed just as glad as her daughter to see them.

"Did your daughter explain why we're here?" said Diane.

"Something about a woman who escaped from prison. I'm not quite sure I understood. Please sit down and have some tea and cookies."

"Mom makes the best cookies," said Carley, pulling up a chair. "So. You found me through my DNA profile I posted. Does that mean that this is someone I'm related to? I'm trying to research my family tree. I'm also doing something called deep ancestry. Do you know what that is?"

Kingsley shook his head. "I don't have a clue, but I'm sure Diane does. She's a forensic anthropologist."

"Are you really? That's so interesting. So you know about finding your earliest ancient ancestors," said Carley.

"I told Carley that just doesn't seem possible. There would be so many of them," said her mother.

"The deep ancestry project shows you which haplogroup you belong to," said Diane. "Where your branch of the earliest humans originated and where they migrated to."

"Isn't that exciting, Mother?" said Carley.

"I'm sure it is, dear," she said.

Diane could see she still didn't quite understand what it was her daughter was looking for.

Kingsley pulled a folder from his briefcase and put a picture of Clymene on the table.

"We are trying to find out who this woman is," said Kingsley.

"And she's related to me?" repeated Carley.

"Yes, your DNA profile shows that you are related," said Diane. "I'm not sure of the exact relationship, but I believe she is your mother's first cousin. If that's the case, it would make her your first cousin once removed."

"See," said Carley's mother, "I just don't get that removed business."

She was interrupted by an older woman rushing up the steps to the deck in an obvious state of irritation.

"Carley, what have you done? I told you not to go looking for relatives," she blurted.

"Gramma," said Carley.

The woman turned to Diane and Kingsley and pointed a shaking finger at them.

"Go home. You aren't wanted here. Go home now."

Chapter 46

The woman who stood with her finger pointing toward Diane and Kingsley was about a seventy-year-old version of Ellen and Carley Volker. Strong genes. Diane noted that she didn't look so much angry as frightened.

"Mamma, these are our guests," said Ellen. She smiled weakly at Diane and Kingsley.

"I told Carley she didn't need to be looking for relatives. I want them to go now."

"Why, Gramma?" said Carley.

"Never mind why. You don't need to know why. Just tell them to go," she said. She slumped in a chair as if exhausted. "I heard what you were up to," she said, glaring at her granddaughter, as if Carley had been trying drugs rather than trying to trace her family tree.

Normally, Diane would excuse herself and let them sort out their problems in private, but it was obvious the grandmother knew something. Diane hoped it was about Clymene. She and Kingsley sat quietly watching the drama.

"You have to tell me why, Gramma," said Carley. She was a pretty girl. Diane tried to find Clymene in their faces. She wasn't there—the hair color and skin tone were, but not the look.

"I don't have to tell you why, child. Just do as I say," she said.

"Carley, maybe . . ." began her mother. Ellen Volker was clearly in a quandary with her mother's obvious distress and the possibility of having to kick guests out of her home.

Carley's face was firm. "Mother, you always say this is my home. If that's true, I should be able to have guests."

She laid a suntanned hand on her grandmother's arm. "Gramma, if you would just tell me what this is about. Is it because we have relatives who have been in prison? You can't be ashamed of things you can't control. Look at how many people around here claim to be related to Blackbeard," she said.

Carley's effort to get her grandmother to smile failed. Gramma looked at Carley.

"Ashamed? Oh, child, you just don't know. Why do you have to be so stubborn?"

"She gets it from you, Mother," said Ellen. She straightened up and tried to put on a smile. "Where are my manners? This is my mother, Sarah Wallace. Mamma, this is Diane Fallon and Agent Kingsley," she said.

Diane and Kingsley took out their badges again and showed them to the grandmother.

"FBI?" she said.

"How did you find out I had company coming to talk about our family tree?" said Carley.

"You told your friend Jenny and she told her mother, who told me," her grandmother said. "Does it matter?"

"It does if I want to plug up the leak," said Carley.

"Carley," chided her mother gently. She looked at Diane and Kingsley. "I can't imagine what you must think of us."

They smiled at her.

"Mrs. Wallace," said Diane. "We're looking for a woman who has escaped from prison. She was there for killing her husband and she has killed others. We don't know her real name, but we think she is a cousin of your daughter. That would make her your niece, wouldn't it?"

Sarah Wallace sat without saying anything, looking less frightened and more angry.

"Mamma, is this about your sister?" said Ellen Volker.

"Don't you mention her name," said Mrs. Wallace.

"It's been so long I'm not sure I remember," said Ellen Volker. "Mamma has a sister she hasn't spoken to in over thirty years."

"Shh!" she spat to her daughter. "Do the two of you have to have such big mouths?"

"Mamma!" said her daughter. "I've never seen you like this, least ways, not in front of strangers."

"Mrs. Wallace," said Kingsley. "This is very important. We have to find this woman. The United States Marshals already know that you are a relative, and they will be coming here too."

"Marshals?" said Carley and Ellen together.

"Gramma, you'd better talk," said Carley.

"Look what you've done," said Sarah Wallace. "I'm trying to protect you and look what you've done."

"Mother! Maybe if you hadn't been so secretive and told us why you were so set against her genealogy research, Carley would have understood. She's an adult now and you can't treat her, or me, like a child and keep secrets that you say are for our protection.

If we're in danger, we need to know so we can do something. For heaven's sake, don't tell us we're in danger and then not tell us what we're supposed to look out for. You are being ridiculous and mean about this. Talk to these people."

Sarah stared at her daughter. Diane got the idea that it took a lot to get Ellen Volker mad, but when she got mad, her family paid attention. The grandmother shook her head. "Maybe you're right."

She poured herself a glass of tea and took a drink as if it were whisky.

"I have a sister, Jerusha, who's nine years younger than me. I don't know if you remember her, Ellen."

"Yes, I remember. I was a teenager when you two had the falling out," she said.

"Falling out? Is that what you would call it? I suppose I should have told you the story a long time ago. If I had, we wouldn't be here arguing."

"Well, tell us now, Mamma."

"Jerusha married a man named Alain Delaflote. Our parents didn't like him or his family, and neither did I. But Alain had good looks and money, and that was all that mattered to my sister. Of course, she was beautiful too, all blond curls and Scarlett O'Hara waist. She married him in a big wedding—long gown, doves. Lavish does not begin to describe it. I thought it was embarrassing."

"Do you have pictures?" asked Carley.

"I have nothing to remind me of her," said her grandmother. "She is dead to me."

Carley looked wide-eyed at her grandmother. "What happened?" she whispered.

"If you'll be patient, I'll tell you," said her grandmother.

Diane wanted her to hurry and get it out, but she

could see Kingsley leaning forward, hanging on every word.

"Alain was in the shipping business, as was his father before him and his father before him. They have been around these parts forever and most people think they are some of the most respectable people on the Outer Banks. Little do they know what they have living among them.

"My husband lost his job one time—he was an accountant before he retired—and Alain offered him a position in his office doing bookkeeping. My sister never let me forget their *largesse*, as she called it. I can hear her now, the way she pronounced it, always more accented than the rest of the words in the sentence, as if she were stuck on one sheet of her word-a-day calendar."

Gramma took a sip of tea and grabbed a chocolate chip cookie. She ate all of it before she resumed her story.

"My sister got pregnant. It wasn't easy for her. She had triplets." Sarah smiled. "Cutest little things you have ever seen and just as identical as you could imagine. She had to keep colored ribbons tied to their wrists to tell them apart. I helped her with them. That was about the only time we got along was taking care of those babies. Alain was indifferent to them. He would pat their heads, smile when someone complimented them, but I didn't see any real love. Not like your daddies loved you two."

"Were their names Iris, Lily, and Rose?" asked Diane.

Sarah nodded. "Yes, they were. Iris, Rose, and Lily Delaflote."

The sun went behind a cloud and it got a little cool.

Diane noticed that a few mosquitoes were flying about.

"One day by accident my husband saw one of the transactions and found out what kind of cargo Alain Delaflote dealt in," said Sarah. "That knowledge changed our lives."

Chapter 47

Sarah eyed her granddaughter for several seconds. Finally Gramma reached out a hand and touched Carley's smooth, tanned arm and rubbed it.

"That's why I was trying to protect you," she said. "I didn't want you to ever be kidnapped and sold into slavery."

Carley clearly wasn't expecting that. Her laugh was almost a musical giggle. "Oh, Gramma, they don't have slavery anymore. This is the twenty-first century," she said.

Sarah Wallace's gaze lingered on her granddaughter a moment longer. She frowned. "You ask those two if there's still such a thing as slaves," she said.

Carley looked over at Diane and Kingsley with an indulgent smile. The kind arrogance of youth, thought Diane as she took a breath.

"Twelve point three million people are enslaved around the world in forced labor, forced military service, or forced sexual servitude. The largest category is sexual enslavement," said Diane.

She paused as Carley and her mother, Ellen, stared at her. The grandmother quietly sipped her tea.

"I used to be a human rights investigator," Diane added.

Diane watched Carley's face change from a smile to that openmouthed, round-eyed expression she often saw when she gave those statistics to people who were unaware of some of the very bad things in the world. Diane hated that she was taking away a little piece of Carley's innocent idealism.

"Is that true?" Carley whispered. "Really, there are slaves in the world? Not in the United States, though?"

Here goes another piece of idealism, thought Diane.

"There are about ten thousand people enslaved today in the United States. About forty-nine percent are in sexual servitude; the rest are in some form of forced labor."

"That's what Alain dealt in," said Gramma, setting her iced tea down with a clunk on the glass-topped table. "The community around the Outer Banks thought he was a public-spirited man. They gave him awards for his community service." She snorted.

"Public service. What the man did was sell teenage girls. He would have these extravagant parties for girls from orphanages and homes for delinquent girls. He would always have teenagers, nothing else, strictly teenagers. His official line was that they were harder to place than younger children and needed the extra help. Sometimes these parties would host parents looking for children to adopt. But you see, these *prospective parents* were really people shopping for slaves. They would pick out what they wanted, place the order with him, and he would fill it—with the help of some corrupt officials, of course. Sometimes the places he got the girls didn't have the kind of girl somebody wanted, and local girls would disappear after some of these parties. Not right away—he knew that would attract attention—but in a few weeks or a few months. Sometimes it was a young tourist who would go missing. Officially, the parents were told their daughters drowned in the ocean or ran away. I know now that just about every one that went missing was kidnapped by my brother-in-law.

"Like an idiot, when my husband told me what he discovered, I told my sister what Alain was doing. I told her she had to take her children and leave. She just laughed at me and said, 'He wouldn't sell his own children, silly.' I just stared at her. I couldn't believe she knew about it. I thought she misunderstood what I said. I said, 'Jerusha, he's selling the kids he's supposed to be helping.' She got that look she got when she disagreed with me. She would put her head down and glare at me. Then she told me if God had blessed these children, He wouldn't have taken their parents. I couldn't believe she said it. I didn't know how to respond.

"The next day, Alain came to my house. I remember it like yesterday. Ellen was fifteen. It was summer—1975. Ellen and her friend Laney had just got back from seeing *Jaws*. They were wearing shorts and sun tops, sitting in the grass talking and giggling. I was on the porch reading a magazine. Alain came up on the porch all friendly. He didn't threaten or anything like that; he just looked over at the two of them and said how nubile Ellen and Laney were, how they were almost ready for plucking.

"A chill went up my spine like I've never felt before. I couldn't say anything. All I could do was sit there staring at him. He just turned and walked away. That evening my husband was late, and I was scared to death. Scared that they killed him. When he finally did come in, I told him we were leaving the Outer Banks, I didn't care if we had to wash toilets or panhandle for the rest of our lives, I wasn't staying here. He agreed to go and we moved to Tennessee. It was a good move. We did well there. Earl and me both found good jobs. After a while he opened his own office. I have never again to this day laid eyes on my sister," said Sarah.

They all sat in silence for several moments. Carley looked at the thin, gold chain bracelet on her arm and back up at her grandmother. She put a hand over hers. It was Ellen who spoke first.

"I remember moving that summer. I was so mad at you and Dad for taking me away from school and my friends. Why didn't you tell me? I never understood why we up and moved with no warning."

"You were just fifteen, Ellen. What was I going to tell you?" Sarah said. She looked at Diane and Kingsley. "You said a woman escaped from prison. Is this her?" She picked up the photograph and looked at it. "She looks kind of like my sister. Is she one of the triplets?"

"We believe it's Iris," said Diane.

"You said she is a murderer?" she said.

"She was convicted of murder in Georgia, sent to prison, and recently escaped," said Kingsley. "We believe she was sold by her father when she was about fifteen. We think what she went through turned her into a serial killer."

The grandmother looked shocked. Frankly, Diane found it hard to believe that anything about her sister's family would shock her at this point.

"Poor little Iris." She shook her head. "I told my sister. I told her. She wouldn't listen. Stupid, stupid woman. They were the cutest little girls, just like three little peas in a pod."

"Do you know what happened to any of the family?" asked Diane.

"I never tried to find out. I never wanted to be in their crosshairs again. I was afraid to move back to this area, but Earl wanted to retire here and Ellen had married a boy from here. I just prayed they'd forgot about us and we would never run across them. We never have."

"How old would Alain Delaflote be now?" asked Diane.

"Let's see, he was five years older than my sister; that would make him about sixty-five. Young enough to still be in business," Sarah said. "Can you arrest him? I wouldn't want him coming after Carley. She's a little older than he likes, but . . ."

"We will certainly take a careful look at them," said Kingsley. "We will not tell him you talked to us. We won't mention you or your family."

"Thank you for that," Sarah said.

"Do you know where they live?" asked Diane.

"Like I said, I have never tried to find them. They used to live out on Mosshazel Island. Back when they moved out there it was the only privately owned island on the coast. You follow Highway 70 about thirty miles beyond Beaufort to a little village called Croker. They had their own private ferry used to run from there to the island. It might still be there. They had one of those big white-columned houses in the middle of the island. There was a little village on the island called East Croker. Not much to it."

Kingsley rose as if to leave. "Thank you for speaking with us," he said. "I can see it wasn't easy, but we really need to find Iris. We'll investigate the whole Delaflote family and look into the lost children."

"Do you think you can find any of them?" she asked.

There was so much hope in her eyes that Diane hated to say *no, I doubt we have a chance in hell.* She didn't know what to say.

Kingsley spoke first. "I don't know. But Iris escaped from her captors. There is always hope."

They left Carley's house, thanking the three women and taking cookies Carley's mother wrapped up for them.

"Carley's life changed today," said Diane.

"It did, didn't it? I think things are better out in the open. At least now she knows to avoid anyone named Delaflote," said Kingsley. "So, do you want to ride out to the island?"

"Not without backup," said Diane. "Are you nuts?"

Kingsley laughed. "I guess you're right. It's exciting to be so close. Let's look for a motel near this place—what did she say, Croker? We'll call the marshals. Maybe they're finished with chasing their wild goose and will hurry out here."

Diane followed Highway 70 south to Morehead City and on to Beaufort. It was a little over fifty miles. She wanted to find a motel in Beaufort. According to her GPS maps it was the last large city they would pass near. But Kingsley wanted to get closer.

"Why?" asked Diane. "We aren't going over to the island. You heard what she said; you have to take a ferry. That means there's no quick getaway in case of emergency."

"I know, but there are other tourist towns beyond Beaufort. They will have motels," said Kingsley.

Diane threw up her hands and agreed. Beaufort was a little more than an hour's drive from New Bern. She drove about twelve miles beyond Beaufort. It wasn't a straight drive. This part of North Carolina was a water world. They crossed large rivers and small creeks and passed through many small tourist towns.

Many places Diane would have liked to stop and just look at the scenery—the water, the boats, the ships. The low green landscape was less lush than the vegetation she was used to in Rosewood; the trees weren't as tall. Nor was it as subtropical as the barrier islands of Georgia. It was beautiful away from the towns, very peaceful looking. She would have stopped to look, but she was tired from their long trip. Maybe they could find a good place to watch the sun set over the sound. Sunsets here were supposed to be pretty spectacular.

"You can pull in at this convenience store ahead and we can stock up," said Kingsley.

"You don't want to find a restaurant?" said Diane.

"Not really. Do you? I'd rather just get some snacks and find a place to stay."

Diane filled up the gas tank while Kingsley went in for food. When the tank was full she moved the vehicle to the side of the store and went in to pay. Kingsley had two bags full of food—junk food, from the glimpse she caught of the contents of one of his bags.

"I got us some of those dip dogs," he said.

"Some what?" said Diane.

"Corn dogs, you may call them," he said, grinning as he went out the door.

There were few people in the small store, so Diane was able to pay quickly and grab a Coke and a bag of peanuts. She paid for the gas and snacks and slipped the peanuts in her pocket.

She walked out to the SUV and fingered the UN-LOCK button on the key chain. A bottle of water rolled from behind the SUV and bumped into her foot. She turned to look and everything went black.

Chapter 48

Diane heard a groan coming through the pain and fog in her head.

"What the hell?" It was Kingsley.

She opened her eyes and tried to move. Her hands were bound behind her back and her ankles were tied together. She stayed still a moment and breathed deeply, assessing her situation.

They were in the rear compartment of a minivan with its backseats stripped out. It was new by the look of it. The windows were dark but she could see out the front. It was still daylight. The driver was young. She could see his cheek and his blond hair. The kid. The one who drugged them at the restaurant and the one who was renting an apartment in her building. It had to be him. *Hell, has he been following us— from Rosewood?*

She looked at Kingsley. He was equally bound and apparently equally dazed. Their eyes met and Diane motioned with hers for him to look at the driver.

Kingsley glanced over his shoulder at the kid and looked back at Diane.

"Is he . . . ? Kingsley whispered.

Diane nodded. "Bobby Banks? I think so."

"Hey, kid," said Kingsley. "Have you been following us? You're really good. I didn't see you and I'm pretty good at spotting a tail."

"Just keep quiet," the kid said.

"Where are we going?" said Kingsley.

"Don't make me mad," he said.

While they spoke, Diane tugged at the ropes that held her. Kingsley was doing the same. They were tight but Diane thought if she tried she could bring her arms down and around her butt and legs to get her hands in front of her. As quietly as she could, she wiggled and maneuvered until her hands were in front where she could reach the rope with her teeth.

Kingsley was trying to do the same but with less success. He wasn't quite as flexible or as slim as Diane. She was almost loose when the van stopped abruptly. The kid looked around, then grabbed something beside his seat and rushed back. Kingsley tripped him with his feet and the kid went flying on top of him.

"You bastard," the kid screamed. He had a temper.

Diane reached around to grab his neck, trying to pull him off. Suddenly there was a loud pop, and a cry came from Kingsley.

Diane pulled at the kid. He whipped around and punched her hard on the side of her head.

"See what you made me do?"

Diane tried to shake the stars out of her head. She looked over at Kingsley and called to him. She could see blood on his shirt inside his coat. He was shot somewhere in the upper left chest, near the shoulder. She glanced at the gun in the kid's hand. It wasn't Kingsley's gun, which the kid surely had taken from him. It was a small caliber; that was good. With Kingsley's gun the wound would have been so much worse.

"I need to see about him," said Diane.

"Well, see about him. You did this. I didn't." He went back up to the front. "I'm watching you. I can see you in the mirror. If you try anything funny again, I'll pop you," he said. He made the motion of shooting her with the gun in his hand before he turned around and put the van in gear and stepped on the gas.

Suddenly the van rocked back and forth. Diane could see they were driving onto the back of a ferry. They were going to cross the water. Great. Kingsley was shot and now they were really cut off.

"I have to drive the ferry, but I can see you. If you try to move out of the van, I'll pop you good. Bam-bam-bam."

He hadn't retied Diane's hands behind her. She was grateful for that. He felt cocky and secure because he had shot someone, she thought. Maybe that was good.

The van rocked again but more gently as the ferry started out over the water. Her head throbbed and she felt sick.

Just focus.

Her hands were still tied, but with them in front she could at least look after Kingsley. She squirmed her way to him, bound as she was, and opened his coat and shirt to look at the wound. It was bleeding freely.

"Can you turn and let me see the exit wound?" she said.

Even with both of them trying, she couldn't get his coat moved so that she could see the wound.

"I think it's a through shot," she said to him. "From the placement, I don't think it hit your shoulder girdle," she said. "Wiggle your fingers."

She watched as he obeyed her.

"Can you move your shoulder?" she asked.

He shrugged and moved it back and forth. "Hurts like hell," he said.

"Doesn't seem to have broken any bones," she said. "That's good."

She felt a wave of nausea sweep over her.

"You sick?" he whispered.

"I'm fine. How about you?" she asked.

"I'm a good sailor," he said. "No nausea. Just a bullet hole in me. I'm sorry . . . we should have stayed in Beaufort."

"I'm not sure what happened. Was he following us all this time?" she asked.

"I don't know," he said.

She needed to bandage his wound. What with? She would use her jacket, but she couldn't get it off. She looked around the van. There were plastic grocery sacks. She emptied them onto the floor. Nothing useful, no paper towels, just cakes, nuts and fruit. Just the snacks. Okay. She stuffed the nuts and a couple of bananas in her pocket.

It was then she realized she felt her cell phone in the front inside pocket of her jacket. Why didn't he take it? He must have felt for weapons and would know it was there. He took Kingsley's Beretta. Why didn't he take the phone? Because he didn't need to. No towers, no signal—no service.

She had an idea about the phone. Not one that would get them out of the immediate situation, but one that might help in the long run.

Okay, think. She ignored the throbbing in her head and the queasiness of her stomach and tried to look at all the resources they had.

"How do you feel?" she asked.

"All right, considering," he said, smiling.

She scrambled down to his feet and took off his shoes and socks. She took the time to put the shoes back on before she continued. She didn't want to take the chance that the kid would suddenly decide to dump them somewhere and Kingsley would be without shoes.

"What are you doing?" Kingsley whispered.

"Your socks are the only thing I can get at right now to dress your wound," she said.

"You know, I don't really like the sound of that," he said. "My socks?"

Diane smiled briefly. At least he was alert and not focused too much on pain. She thought it was a good sign. She folded one of the socks and put it next to the wound. She folded the other one.

"I'm going to have to try and scoot my hands up your jacket and shirt to put this in place," she said. She rolled him over.

I'm an idiot, she thought. *Letting myself get in a situation like this. I should have my PhD revoked.* Then, *Keep alert. Forget about the pain in your head.* While he was on his stomach, she untied his ropes.

"I'm watching you," said the kid.

She looked up front. He had popped his head inside the window and was pointing a gun at her.

Diane froze. "I know," she said with all the calm she could muster, "but I have to dress his wounds. He's too injured to do anything. If he dies, you are going to be in a great deal of trouble. I think you know that. And I am still tied up and you still have two guns."

"Tie him back up when you finish. If you don't, I'll shoot you too. Then where will you be? I'll tell you where, in the water, that's where, feeding the fishes." He laughed as if he had just told a terribly funny joke.

"I understand. Just let me tend his wound and I'll tie him back up," she said. *God, he's a little maniac, unpredictable and with a temper,* thought Diane. Her hands shook as she reached for Kingsley's jacket. *Stay calm, stay calm, stay calm,* she kept telling herself.

"You'd better. Remember, I'm watching," he said, grinning at her and pretended to shoot, mimicking an explosion noise before he disappeared from the window.

The ferry rocked back and forth on the water and Diane felt sick. She concentrated on breathing evenly.

Kingsley helped her take off his jacket and shirt, wincing at the effort. Blood was running from the entrance and exit wounds, but they were small and Kingsley could move his arms and shoulders. It was painful, but it was possible. She used strips of his shirt to fashion bandages. She put his jacket back on. She untied and retied his feet, then she tied his hands in front of him.

"I've tucked the end of the rope under the loops here where it's hidden," she said, her mouth close to his ear. "If he checks your hands, he'll see that the ropes are tight. But if you pull on this loop here, free the rope and pull on it, it will come undone," she whispered.

"That's right, you know your knots." He grinned.

Diane thought he looked pale.

"I did your feet the same way," she said.

She got busy and untied her feet and retied them in the same manner as she watched their captor at the helm of the small flatbed ferry.

"I want you to look very sick whenever he sees you," said Diane. "That way he won't consider you a threat."

"Yes, ma'am," he said. "That won't be too hard."

"Now we need to eat this food," she said.

"Okay, I was following you up until that point. Why do we need to eat the food?" he asked.

"Because I don't know when the marshals will get here or when we can escape. I think we both know we are going to Clymene's house. Do you want to eat or drink anything she prepares?"

"Oh, good point," he said. She gave him a banana.

Diane hoped she could keep hers down. Just focus on the goal, she thought, and breathe slowly and deeply.

They were quietly eating the food when the kid peeked in.

"What are you doing?" he asked, pointing the gun.

"Eating," said Diane.

"Oh, okay," he said and went back to the helm.

Diane wondered if Kingsley could swim. If she could get loose she would swim back and get help, but she could do nothing with her hands tied up. She looked at him. He really did look sick. She began trying to untie her rope with her teeth. She was making progress when she saw the kid coming back.

"We're about to dock. There will be a little jolt, but that's all." He grinned at them. "How we doing back there?"

"Just fine," she said.

They felt a small bump and saw him get down to secure the ferry. She tried to hurry and finish untying her hands, but the kid was quicker than she was. He climbed in the van, walked over to Diane, and put his gun to her temple.

"I don't want any trouble. None." His voice was very quiet. "You understand, don't you?"

"Yes," whispered Diane. Her voice shook as she spoke, and he laughed.

"Good. I will shoot you." He shoved the muzzle of the gun into her temple until she winced in pain. "You know I will."

He hit Kingsley in the shoulder with his fist and

went back to the driver's seat as Kingsley yelled in
pain. Diane could see his eyes in the mirror. He
looked amused.

"Arrested development," whispered Kingsley. "I
think Rosewood is as far as this kid had ever been
before now. God, that hurt. Damn little bastard."

Diane watched out the front window as they drove
along a winding dirt road. When the house came into
view she was startled. She expected a rundown old
mansion past its prime and falling into decay, with
hanging vines and huge trees overrunning the place.
What she saw was beautiful. The winding paved driveway led up to an oversized freshly painted Greek revival house with large white columns. The front
gardens were filled with bed after bed of roses, lilies,
and irises in full bloom. A black jaguar was parked
in front.

The kid took an offshoot road, drove to the back
of the house, and stopped in front of a rock building
that looked like it might have been lifted out of *Wuth-
ering Heights*.

"Here we are. It ain't home, but who the hell
cares," he said, laughing. "You can untie your legs
now."

Diane made it look as if it was an effort to untie
the rope as she pulled the end of the loop, releasing
the bonds on Kingsley's legs. She did the same with
hers. Bobby Banks didn't watch closely. He kept looking up at the house as if something up there worried
him. When their legs were free he led them to the
building, locked them in, and left them alone in the
dark.

Little light seeped in past the shuttered windows.
Diane tried the door but it was bolted shut from the
outside.

"Don't undo your bonds yet," she said. "Wait until you have somewhere to run to."

"I do still have some wits about me," Kingsley said. But it wasn't a defensive comment, Diane noticed.

She and Kingsley tried the windows. All were nailed shut. Her eyes were adjusting to the darkness. It was too much to hope that he had put them in a tool shed. It looked like Daniel Boone's bedroom. There was a twin bed with a gray wool bedspread, rough-hewn furniture. It was some kind of rustic one-room guesthouse with no bathroom.

"What is this, a playhouse?" said Diane.

"I don't know," said Kingsley.

"Why don't you lie down on the bed?" said Diane.

"We need to get out of here," he said.

"Yes, but you need rest and it would be good for them to think you're worse off than you are," she said. "If someone comes, they need to find you lying down."

Diane led him to the bed and made him lie down. He was just settled when she heard voices outside that sounded like they were coming their way. She took her phone from her pocket and checked the signal bars. No service, as she suspected. She put it on mute anyway and quickly put it under the chest of drawers, display side down, and stood up to meet whoever was coming to get them.

Chapter 49

Diane was sitting on the bed with Kingsley when the door opened. She could see that it was two people but the light behind them kept her from seeing anything but silhouettes. She waited as they walked in. One was the kid; the other was a woman. The woman turned on a battery-operated lantern and put it on the table. It was a dim light, but Diane could see them clearly. Clymene.

She looked at Diane and Kingsley as if they were interesting specimens and nothing more.

"And why did you bring them here?"

She was dressed in a simple white cotton sundress with a small embroidered jacket. Banks carried a bucket that he set down on the floor. Diane saw that it had toilet paper and a bottle of something in it.

"I saw him," Banks said. "I was going to Jeeters and there he was coming out the door. I couldn't believe it. I had to do something."

Damn, it was an accident of fate, thought Diane.

"Why did you bring them here?" she repeated calmly.

"I didn't know what else to do. Now he's shot. It

wasn't my fault; it was theirs. Do you think she'll get mad at me?" he asked.

"Let me tell her about this, okay?" she said.

Listening to their conversation, it suddenly occurred to Diane that this was not Clymene. The "her" they were talking about was Clymene. "Are you Lily or Rose?" she said.

The woman looked startled.

"Rose. How bad is your companion?" she said.

"Bad enough. I'm concerned about his temperature. I'm afraid the bleeding will start up again. He's recovering from a car accident he had a few days ago, and now this. He needs to see a doctor," said Diane.

"You are a doctor," said Rose.

"I'm not that kind of doctor," said Diane.

"You know anatomy. I'm afraid you will have to do. Do you need dressings?"

"No. If I change them, he'll start bleeding again," said Diane. "You know it's not a good idea to keep us here, don't you?"

"Yes, I do," she said. "He shouldn't have brought you here. But what's done is done."

Diane had been watching Rose and the guy she thought was Bobby Banks. They favored each other.

"Is he your son?" asked Diane.

"My son?" She looked startled again. "No. Joey's my brother."

Joey. Diane could see him as a baby kangaroo.

"You will have to stay in here while I sort this out," she said. "In the meantime, do you need food?"

"They just ate," said Joey.

"Did they? Well. I guess we won't prepare anything for them," said Rose.

The two of them left and locked the door.

"At least they left the light," said Diane. *And their*

names, she thought. Not a good sign at all—like it didn't matter.

A new wave of fear swept over her. She ignored it and looked inside the bucket. There was one roll of toilet paper and a bottle of hand sanitizer. Well, you couldn't say the Delaflotes weren't good hosts. She wished she were MacGyver. She was sure he could do something with hand sanitizer. Maybe blow open the back wall or something. Diane went to the door to see if there was a crack or hole where she could wedge some tool she hadn't found yet between the boards and pry them open.

"Splitting them up may get us somewhere," Kingsley said.

Diane walked back to the bed and put a hand on his head. It seemed warm. She untied his hands.

"I'll just tell them that since we are locked up and you are sick, it won't make any difference if your hands are untied and you will be more comfortable," she said. "Less strain on your injured shoulder."

"It is more comfortable." He rubbed his wrists.

"How do we split them up?" said Diane. "Jacobs said they are probably inseparable."

"He's right, to a point. The key, I think, may be with the boy. He's what, eighteen or nineteen going on thirteen? I'll bet he was born after Clymene was gone. I don't know where his mother fits into this, if she's alive, but it was Rose he went to get. He sees Rose as a mother figure. I'll bet she sees him as more of a son than a brother. I think Rose and Lily raised him. When did Clymene come back into their lives? We don't know, but her two sisters had already bonded with him. To Clymene he is just a kid. I'm just guessing."

"It sounds reasonable . . . but how do we exploit it?" asked Diane.

"I don't know. Just seize an opportunity when it presents itself. We know he screwed up big time and he's concerned that 'she' will be mad. I'm betting that the 'she' he's concerned with is Clymene and he is afraid of her. She's laid all these careful plans and this little runt comes along and screws everything to hell. Rose was concerned enough to tell Joey that she would be the one to talk with Clymene. If we can make Clymene attack him and get them to defend him, we may be able to separate them enough that they will want to save themselves and the boy and sacrifice Clymene. It's a thought."

Kingsley stopped talking. She thought he had fallen asleep. She searched the room, this time opening all the drawers, taking the light and examining the inside of each. Looking for even a nail file stuck between joints. All the drawers were empty. Nothing.

Diane sat down on the only chair in the room, a plain wooden chair with no cushion. It squeaked when she sat down. She was feeling guilty about Kingsley. Maybe if she hadn't struggled with Joey the way she had, he wouldn't have been shot. She had been clumsy and slow and used bad judgment. The only thing she could do now was get him out of here.

She took the lamp around to all the corners of the room, looking for anything. She looked under the bed. The floors were wooden, dark with age like the rest of the room. She walked back and forth, searching for anything that may have been dropped, listening for a squeak in the boards. Most of them did squeak, but she couldn't pry any of them up. She went along the walls looking for loose stone. She found a couple, but they were not loose enough. Maybe she could use the chair leg. She went back to the chair to see how easy it would be to take apart and use a leg as a tool or a weapon.

"Don't you think you need your rest?" said Kingsley.

"I need to get us out of here," she said.

"This isn't your fault. It's mine, if anyone's," he said.

Diane pulled the chair over to the bed and sat down.

"Whoever's fault it is, we need to get out," she said. "You told the marshals you thought that if Clymene were cornered, she would give up to fight another day. Do you still believe that?"

"Yes, I do. But I have to tell you, now that I'm here in her clutches, I'm not quite as sure," he said. He reached for her hand. He felt warm.

"My wife is expecting me to check in with her. I'm sure Frank is expecting you to check in with him. I don't know about Frank, but if my wife thinks something is wrong, she will worry the FBI until they do something. Several people know we went to see Carley Volker, including the marshals. The Volkers will tell them Gramma gave us directions to the island. If we can stay alive, we will be rescued. I think the best thing for you to do is to rest like I am. I'm fine; I'm just conserving my energy."

Diane got up and tried looking out a slit in the closest window. She could just see a sliver of ground. Maybe she could pry the boards off this window. There was something she could see out there if she could just get the right angle. She tried to remember the image she saw driving up to the building. A field? A pond? Not that anything outside could help her in here.

"Come lie down beside me. You said we needed to eat and drink because it would be our last opportunity. That's also true of rest," said Kingsley. "You don't have to sleep. Just rest."

He was right. She was just using up energy. She put the chair by the door just so they could hear the noise if someone opened it. Kingsley scooted over and Diane lay down. It was not a comfortable bed and she was tense. She tried to relax.

"I implemented a plan just before Rose came in the door," she said.

"Oh? What was that?" he asked.

"I put my cell phone under the chest of drawers," she said.

"That's such a clever plan. I wish I had thought of it," he said.

Diane started to laugh. So did Kingsley. The bed shook.

"Please," he said. "It hurts to laugh."

"Joey didn't take our cell phones because we get no service out here and he thought they were useless to us. What he didn't think of was the GPS. Mine has a chip in it."

"That's right. Mine does too." He reached in his pocket and dug it out. "Maybe if we put it somewhere. Or maybe I should just put it back in my pocket. If both our phones turn up missing, they might get suspicious. You can say yours was in your purse."

Diane tried to relax, and it must have worked because she was awakened by the sound of the chair scraping across the floor.

Chapter 50

"Were you trying to keep us out? That was pathetic."

It was Joey. He had Rose with him.

Diane sat up. Kingsley stayed lying down.

"I would like you and Agent Kingsley to join us in the dining room."

It wasn't Rose. That was Clymene.

Kingsley noticed the difference too. He sat up beside Diane.

"Clymene," said Kingsley.

"My name, as you apparently know, is Iris. That is what I prefer to be called."

"Hey, you untied him. . . . " began Joey.

"Hush, it doesn't matter," said Iris.

"As you may notice, Joey has a gun, and he's rather reckless with it, so don't try anything," she said.

Iris stood aside and let them pass. Diane toyed with the idea of jumping one of them, but the last time she'd tried something like that, she had gotten Kingsley shot. She was hoping that going to the main house would afford other opportunities that were less risky.

The inside of the house was much like the outside. It was not decrepit, or shabby chic, or even gently worn. It was a showplace. There was no one particular style, just high-end furniture that looked comfortable and was beautiful to look at. There were vases of flowers everywhere, as well as pictures of flowers. All irises, lilies, and roses. In her mind's eye when Carley's grandmother was telling them about the family, Diane had pictured the house having dark rooms. The house wasn't dark; it was well lit and bright. She wondered whether Iris brought that to the house or it was always this lovely. With grounds that looked the way theirs did, and the house so clean, they had to have help. That made Diane feel more optimistic. There had to be other people around.

"What was that place we were in?" asked Diane.

"A place of contemplation," Iris said. "Please . . ." She gestured toward a door.

It opened into a dining room. There was a long, light oak table with matching buffets and china cabinets. Iris' sisters were putting food on the table. All three sisters were dressed alike. Diane thought they were a little old for that.

"Rose said you had eaten, but you may want to eat again. All of us are great cooks," said Iris.

"I'm not really dressed for dinner," said Kingsley.

Iris smiled. "We will forgive you."

"Neither of us feels very well," said Diane.

"Please, let's be honest. You're afraid that I'm going to poison you," said Iris.

"Yes," said Diane, "there is that. We are also sick. Your brother knocked both of us unconscious and shot Kingsley."

"Point taken," said Iris. "Please sit down. I'm interested to know how you found me. I don't mind telling you I'm impressed," she said. "I had such a good plan."

"And it worked for a long time," said Diane. "But with a little Internet research it's amazing what you can do.

They all sat down and the three sisters and Joey filled their plates with some very delicious-smelling roast beef, potatoes, and roasted asparagus.

"Are you sure?" said one of the sisters. She smiled. "I'm Lily. We haven't met."

Carley's grandmother was right. They were like three peas in a pod. They looked so much alike. Except that Iris had a small scar near her hairline and her nose was slightly crooked. She had been knocked around.

"Why did you kill Rev. Rivers?" said Diane. "He was a very nice man and he genuinely liked you."

The three sisters looked at Joey. He looked at his plate.

"It was an accident," he said. "I'd never hit anyone before. I did better with these two," he said in his own defense.

It worried Diane that they were being so forthcoming—as if she and Kingsley weren't going to live anyway. But the more information she could get, the better. And who knows? Perhaps conversation with them would open a rift among the sisters.

"You are right. He was a nice man and he kept his word to me. He was only meant to be knocked out. I regret that he was killed." She paused to eat some of the food on her plate.

"I'm interested in how much you know," said Iris. "Agent Kingsley, you aren't looking too good. Rose said you were in an accident—besides being shot, I mean."

"Yes," he said. "Little Joey's drug made me fall asleep at the wheel," he said.

Iris looked at Joey and he seemed to slink down in his seat.

"Why did you drug him?" said Iris.

Joey looked at Rose, and she smiled at him.

"Well, their table had another waitress. They were very picky about me waiting on someone else's table. The best access I had was with doing the refills for their waitress. I couldn't be sure which glass was going to Diane, so I had to drug both of them."

"That was one of the first clues," said Diane. "That was how we found out there was a ringer among the wait staff. The restaurant was the only place both of us could have been drugged. Then I discovered his name—Bobby Banks—and there was a Bobby Banks in my apartment building. . . ."

Iris shot Joey a look that was starting to appear angry. He cringed.

"You were supposed to change your name," she said.

"I didn't think it mattered. All my identification was for Bobby Banks, my driver's licence and everything."

"It obviously mattered," said Iris.

"I had to show my driver's license to the old land-lady," said Joey.

"Oh, so then you had to use that name." She looked back at Diane. "That doesn't explain how you came to be here."

"Iris," said Kingsley.

Diane thought his voice sounded strained and weak. She could see he was tempted by the glass of water in front of him. But he resisted, keeping his hands in his lap.

"You have to realize that people know we are here," he said.

"Don't worry about that. I have an escape plan," she said.

"For all of you?" he said.

"My sisters weren't involved," she said, "and you can't prove that they were."

"They were contributors to the pool of blood in my living room," said Diane.

Iris smiled. "Maybe. But we are identical."

All three sisters smiled at Diane.

"I *can* prove it," said Diane. "And you are not identical, not anymore."

For the first time, Diane saw fear pass over Iris' eyes, and she didn't think Iris was faking it. She wondered whether Kingsley saw it too. That meant something to Iris—to be identical to her sisters.

"You're lying," said Iris, calmly.

"Am I?" said Diane. "How about this. Lily and Rose donated the blood for my living room; you didn't. While they recovered in apartment 1-D, you and pal Joey here let yourselves into my apartment—probably with a key lifted from the landlady. That's happened before. You and Joey set the stage to look like you were killed there and your body was dragged out to my car. You wiped down Joey's apartment with Clorox. But you missed a drop of blood on the bedframe and a needle in the floorboards, both containing your sisters' DNA. How am I doing?"

Iris was very still. Lily and Rose looked at her, alarm evident on their faces.

"You're guessing," said Iris.

"Lots of things change DNA. You were identical when you were born. But after you are born you have different experiences that leave markers on your genetic code. We can read those differences. Lily's and

Rose's genetic profiles are very similar to each other, with only small differences. But because you lived in Europe, and Seattle, and Richmond, and a host of other places and had such different experiences and environmental exposure, your genetic profile is very different from theirs. That's how we could separate your DNA from theirs."

"That's not true," said Iris.

Diane had made another hit. She saw that she had shaken Iris' composure.

"Iris," said Kingsley, "right now there are only two marshals looking for you. If you don't let us go, that number will increase exponentially. And they won't be looking for just you, but all of you. They even know about Joey."

"You just want to get away," said Joey.

"Hell yes," said Kingsley, "but find the flaw in my logic. My desire to live doesn't change the facts of what I said."

"How did you find us here?" asked Rose. "Specifically here. That wasn't in our DNA, was it?"

"No, that was written in your scrapbook," said Diane.

All three looked at Joey.

"I didn't put that in the scrapbook, honest," he said.

"In the archaeology scrapbook you wrote next to a picture that the mail was just called over," said Diane.

"So?" he said.

"That phrase, *to call the mail over,* is unique to the Outer Banks and the surrounding area," she said.

"But how did you know it was this island?" said Joey.

"We didn't," Diane lied. "You brought us here. We just stopped at a convenience store to load up before we went to the motel to wait for the marshals, to begin a canvas of the area."

Iris threw her napkin down on the table. "All my planning . . ." she said.

"Iris," said Rose, "Joey did the best he could."

"Well, we have a problem, don't we? And we need to fix it," said Iris.

"We can hold them hostage," said Joey.

"I don't want to hear from you," said Iris. "If it weren't for you, we wouldn't be in this mess. The FBI won't deal with hostage takers. We have to think of something else. We'll put them in one of the up-stairs rooms."

Chapter 51

It was Iris who took them up to the rooms. She had Kingsley's gun with her and from the way she held it, Diane believed she knew how to use it.

Diane supposed Iris wasn't trusting anyone but herself to do anything right. She and Kingsley had definitely ruffled her feathers, and they had done a fairly decent job of starting a schism between Iris and the other two. Diane tried to think of some way to widen it as she was climbing the stairs. Perhaps that was why Iris was taking them up instead of allowing the others to do it. Iris was afraid that Diane and Kingsley might make some progress.

The upper floor was as elegant as the rest of the house. Diane told her so. The wide hallway had several seating areas and a library at the end in an alcove.

"Lily, Rose, and I decorated the house and grounds. Mother had such poor taste. You should have seen it. Of course, she's the woman who slept with my father after he sold me. That's how we got little Joey." Iris sounded bitter. "He also gave her a fur coat to make up for her loss."

"I'm sorry that happened to you," said Diane.

"So am I," said Kingsley. "I can't think of anything more terrible."

They stood there in the big elegant hallway near a pair of large double doors, Diane and Kingsley almost huddled together and Iris holding the gun on them.

"One of my father's clients was here looking for his quota of nubile young things and he caught sight of Rose. We had just turned fifteen. He offered my father a million dollars for her. Father agreed; after all, he had two more. Rose was terrified. Mother cried but did nothing. I offered to go in her place. Father didn't care; he couldn't tell us apart anyway.

"Now you know my story. Profiler Kingsley, you are going in this room. Open the door."

"Let us stay together," said Diane. "You can see we're a pretty pathetic pair, and he needs care."

"Don't try to poor-mouth yourselves. I know what you are capable of," she said. "Open the door."

Kingsley opened the door. The room had a huge four-poster bed, plush maroon carpets with a maroon and gold brocade bed set and matching curtains. It was a little too ornate for Diane's taste, but it was better than the building out back.

"Nice prison," said Kingsley. He walked in and Iris locked the door behind him with the key she held in her hand.

"You will be down here," she said to Diane.

Diane started down the hallway, trying to formulate a plan. Kingsley was out of the way and it was just the two of them. Iris was strong, but so was she.

"Don't try anything," said Iris. "I won't mind shooting you. I can read your mind even from behind."

"I wouldn't dream of trying anything," said Diane. "You have a logical mind about you. I was hoping you would see that killing law enforcement officers puts you in a whole different ball game from the men you killed."

"I'm aware of that. Hardly seems fair to the rest of the population, does it?" she said.

"Iris, look," said Diane. "Kingsley tells me that most people who are tagged as serial killers escalate in violence against their victims. You didn't. He says you are different. You are not one of these people . . ."

"Are you trying to save me? How do you know I'm not escalating?"

"Because neither Bacon, Redding, Carthwright, or O'Riley was killed as violently as that Greene-Heinrich person," said Diane. "Their deaths were terrible enough, and maybe Bacon's was as violent, but the others weren't."

Diane watched Iris carefully as she spoke. Iris was clearly shocked.

"You know about all of those?" she whispered.

"There may be more, but those are all we've found so far," said Diane.

"How?" she said hoarsely. "How could you know about Simon Greene? He's the man my father sold me to. No one knows about him."

"You aren't the only one Greene abused," said Diane. "He's notorious."

Iris was quiet. Diane was hoping she would let her guard down so that Diane could . . . do something . . . what? Outrun a bullet? The Beretta would make a much worse wound than Joey's little gun. Iris' gun hand never wavered.

"Open the door," she said. It sounded more like a request than an order. Diane complied. This room was completely different from the last one. It was done in black and shades of browns and tans. No ruffles, brocades, or tassels, just sleek, tailored designs. Diane didn't like it either.

"We've been very frank with each other," said Diane. "Will you answer two questions for me?"

"Perhaps," she said. "If it won't take long. I have an escape to execute."

"Did you have those stolen artifacts sent to the museum to get even with Vanessa Van Ross?" asked Diane.

"I didn't have anything to do with your museum problem. I was getting even with Vanessa Van Ross by targeting you. You mean more to her than the museum, according to my analysis, though I failed to uncover why."

"So all that blood and my being accused of killing you was to get even with her?" said Diane.

"No, that was to fake my death and poke you in the eye while doing it. I called Eric Tully on the phone pretending to be you and told him to send me fifteen thousand dollars or I would turn him in."

Diane frowned. "That explains a lot. He only sent four thousand and tried to kill me twice."

"I suppose he was low on cash," said Iris.

"What about Grace Noel and Tully's daughter? Were you just trying to con me?" said Diane.

"No. I figured that whether Tully killed you or not, he would get arrested and Grace would see him for what he was. The kid would go to her to raise—or to another relative if they could find one. Grace isn't the brightest, but she would be good to the little girl," said Iris. "Now, if I've told you everything you want to know. Get in the damn room."

Diane walked in and Iris started to close the door. She hesitated and turned back to Diane.

"Rich men are all the same. You may not believe

that, but I know it. They are no different from my
father. Power doesn't corrupt so much as money does.
Vanessa thinks her friend Archer was so good. We
were walking on the beach in Malibu when these
young girls passed by in their string bikinis. They
weren't much more than fifteen or sixteen. He said,
'My, aren't those nubile young things?' That was my
father's favorite word, *nubile*. Men are all alike, and
rich men are the worst because they can buy anything
they want. You tell that to your friend Vanessa.''

She slammed the door. Diane heard the key turn in
the lock. She stood a moment and listened to Iris'
footfalls go down the hall. The first thing she did was
start searching the room. The drawers were filled with
linens, sheets, holiday tablecloths, and napkins—
nothing hard that she could use as a weapon. Maybe
she could tie the sheets together and climb down to the
ground. She went to the window and threw open the
curtain. The window was nailed shut and boarded up
on the outside.

Diane looked at the curtain rod. Now, there was a
possibility. She climbed up on top of the vanity and
took the heavy metal rod off the brackets, slid the
rod apart, and slid the curtains off. Now she had two
weapons. It was sort of like a lance. The finials made
fairly good points. Probably wouldn't puncture the
skin, but she could certainly knock the wind out of
someone with it—hit them right in the solar plexus
and they wouldn't get up for a while.

She laid the rods on the bed, went to the closet,
and threw the doors open. It was a large walk-in
closet, large enough for a small bedroom or a large
bathroom. She turned on the light at the switch just
inside the doorway. Garment bags hung on the rods

on both sides. More rods. She examined them, but they were permanently affixed to the walls.

Clear plastic boxes were stacked up under the clothes. Diane leaned down to see what was in the boxes. Guns and ammunition, she hoped. There wasn't quite enough light, so she grabbed one of the lids and started to open it when a hand shot out and grabbed her arm, digging deep into the skin through the fabric with its nails. Diane yelped and jumped back. The hand held on. It looked mummified, but it was alive and grasping. Diane grabbed the arm with her other hand and pried the grip loose just as a shriveled face appeared from between the bags.

"Help me."

It was a hoarse whisper.

"Please, help me."

It was a very old man, his eyes were red rimmed, and he had a trickle of saliva running down his chin.

"Please . . ."

He was suddenly propelled backward and disappeared into the wall.

Chapter 52

Diane stood dumbfounded, staring at the swinging garment bags. She gathered her wits about her and knelt down, pulled out the boxes, and pressed on the wall. There was a give in the bead board. She heard a loud, high-pitched, but muffled voice behind the wall.

"Please, help me. Help me, please," said a mocking voice. "Do you think anyone came to help Iris when she called out for help, Alain, dear?"

Diane heard slapping sounds and more yelling.

"Mr. Delaflote . . . Mrs. Delaflote?" Diane called out. "Is that you?"

"Who is that? Who knows our name? Get away from here. You'll make them mad. Don't make my flowers mad. Tell them I didn't let him get away."

Diane heard a rattling coming from her bedroom door. She stepped out of the closet and grabbed one of the curtain rods. She slipped the other one under the bed. She turned out the lights in the room and stood off to the side, ready to strike.

The door opened an inch.

"Diane?"

"Kingsley?" she said.

Diane turned on the light. Kingsley slipped in and Diane closed the door behind him.

"How did you get in here? For that matter, how did you get out of your room?" she asked.

"I picked the lock. These old locks are easy for a clever fellow like me. Granted, it's not as clever as putting a cell phone under a dresser." He grinned at her. He looked better than he had at dinner.

"How are you feeling?" she asked.

"I've had better days, but I'm all right," he assured her.

"I think I've found Ma and Pa Delaflote," she said.

"Really? Are they alive?" he said.

"Alive, but payback is definitely a bitch. He hasn't aged gracefully." she said. Diane told him about the encounter. "They are right behind that wall." She pointed into the closet.

"Damn. Did the girls lock them both up, or . . . or what?" he said.

"I think so," said Diane. "I'm not really sure. It looked like only Mr. Delaflote wanted to escape."

"I like your weapon, by the way," he said.

Diane fished out the other side of the curtain rod and gave it to him.

"I had curtain rods. I should have thought of this," he said.

"You picked the locks," said Diane. "We have weapons and I have a lot of false bravado. So now what's the plan?"

"See if we can find a way out. My windows are nailed shut, are yours?"

"Yes," she told him.

"Let's see if we can find a back stairway," he said. They peeked into the hallway. Empty. They stepped into the corridor, closed the door behind them, and walked gently to a door across the hall and tried to open it. It was locked. They tried another one. Locked as well. They made their way to the stairway they had originally come up with Iris. The two of them stopped and listened. Diane wondered if they could hear her heart pounding. She swallowed hard and took a deep breath.

They heard voices, but none near. They were muffled and sounded heated. The triplets were having an argument. *Good*, thought Diane.

"Should we try to get out the front door? Back door?" whispered Diane.

"Do you remember if the steps squeaked as we came up?" he asked softly.

Diane thought for a moment. "Yes, but maybe if we stick close to the wall they won't squeak as much. The house must make noises all the time. I don't understand why they didn't hear Ma and Pa just now. Maybe they won't hear us."

Diane led the way. Kingsley followed close behind. They hugged the wall with each step. So far, so good. When Diane entered the house she had been relieved to find it bright and well lit. Now she wished it were dark. Each time the steps creaked, a tremor of fear went though her. The lightheartedness she felt when she first saw Kingsley was giving way to dread.

As they descended the staircase the voices grew louder and clearer.

"None of this is his fault, Iris. He made the best decisions he could. It isn't his fault he ran across that Diane person. She figured this out. I think she would have anyway, even if Joey had made no mistakes. She knew too much about you . . . about us."

"That doesn't matter now," said an identical voice.

"We need to get out of here and quickly. Whatever we do with them, the marshals are going to come anyway."

"This has gone so wrong."

"You did this, Iris. This is your mess."

"You don't mind spending the money."

Diane couldn't distinguish the voices; they all sounded like Clymene.

The triplets were in the dinning room and the door was closed. Diane motioned to the back of the house. Kingsley nodded. They tiptoed past the door and down a hallway to the back, where Diane hoped to find the kitchen and a knife along the way out.

Through a set of double doors they walked into the kitchen. It was a modern kitchen with a large island in the middle. There was a breakfast nook in the corner. Joey was sitting with his back to them, eating a bowl of ice cream.

He heard the noise, turned around toward them, and looked startled at the sight, but he was slow to react. Diane ran at him, using her curtain rod as a lance. She didn't think it would do much more than stun him, but she put her momentum behind it. She aimed for his chest. He dodged, and the point of her improvised spear punched into his throat and he fell to the floor gagging on ice cream. She and Kingsley rushed past him for the door.

"Can you run?" asked Diane as they went down the outside steps.

"What does it look like?" he said. "Do you know where we're going?"

"Head for the woods," she said.

They ran across the field that Diane had seen when they drove up. It was bordered by a tall wire fence she might be able to climb over, but it was too tall for Kingsley in his condition. She spotted a gap under the fence where it crossed a shallow ditch. They ran for it. It was a low opening, big enough for animals to get through, but was it big enough for them?

They made it to the fence. Diane kicked at briars that grew into the wire. She lay down on her back and wiggled into the opening, pushing at the fence, trying to make the hole larger. After what seemed like too long, she pulled herself out the other side of the fence. She turned to help Kingsley. That's when she saw the triplets running across the pasture after them. Joey wasn't with them. Two were carrying guns.

Kingsley lay on his back and wiggled from side to side under the fence as far as he could. He reached for Diane with his good arm. She locked arms with him and pulled hard as he wiggled and pushed with his feet. She knew he was in pain but they both ignored it as he strained to get under the fence. Finally he slid through and stumbled to his feet.

"Run like hell," said Diane.

They ran. Diane heard shots and saw the ground spit out a piece of turf several feet from her. The stand of trees she was aiming for wasn't tall and thick like Georgia woods, but it would have to do.

Diane ran faster and realized she was leaving Kingsley behind. She slowed down and grabbed him by the arm.

"Go on," he said.

"No, come on. Run as hard as you can. They can't get under the fence easily in those dresses. We have to get out of range of their guns. You can rest up when we're safe; now, get the lead out," she said.

He picked up his speed. They were almost to the woods.

"Faster," she said. "Keep going."

There were more shots and one pinged off an outcrop of rocks a few yards away. But they reached the trees.

"Keep running," she said.

"Need to stop. Go on," he wheezed. "My lungs are aching."

"It doesn't matter. Run," she said.

Ahead there was a road of sorts and a marsh on the other side. She heard a vehicle coming up the road. She ran toward it to flag it down, then stopped. It was the minivan Joey had brought them in.

"Damn," she said. *Where are the damn marshals?* She needed time to think. To get her breath.

There was noise behind them. It was the triplets. They had found a way around the fence and were coming in their direction. The van was coming toward them. Across the road was a marsh. No escape in the marsh. The only alternative was to run up the road. And be chased by the van? That wouldn't work.

Diane picked up a rock and waited for the minivan to draw closer, hoping that if she waited until the last second and threw the rock at the windshield it would make Joey dodge. Kingsley followed suit.

Joey aimed for them.

"Get behind a tree," said Diane. "Now."

"What are you—" he began.

"Now!" she said.

Kingsley threw his rock toward the oncoming van with no result. He ran to the trees for cover. Diane waited. She saw Joey. His face was contorted in anger. Diane waited. She saw the van accelerate. She stared him down. He gunned the engine, driving directly at her. She threw her rock into the windshield square in front of Joey's face and jumped away at the last minute. The van crashed into the trees, exploding the air bags. Diane was beside the van almost before it stopped. She jerked open the driver's side door, pulling Joey to the ground. She felt between the seats for his gun and grabbed hold of it just as she felt Joey bite into her leg.

"Son of a bitch," she screamed and kicked at him.

Kingsley appeared from around the front and kicked him hard in the side of his head. Joey let go of her leg and lay on the ground, not moving.

"Give me the gun," said Kingsley.

"Why?" said Diane.

"Because I'm probably a better shot with a gun," he said.

Diane handed him the gun. He checked the bullets.

"Now you take cover," he said.

Diane got behind the van and watched Kingsley. He rested his arm on the door of the van and took aim as the sisters came running out of the woods. He shot and one of them fell.

"Rose! Oh, Rose," a voice shouted.

Diane saw a patch of red spread on her upper left torso as she lay on the ground. Diane couldn't tell if she was dead.

"Damn you!" either Lily or Iris screamed at him.

The two of them simultaneously dove for a shallow ditch a few feet from them and started shooting.

Kingsley dropped to the ground along with Diane. She heard the bullets hitting the van and passing through. *This is no cover at all,* thought Diane. *If they aim just a little lower, we're dead.* She touched Kingsley's sleeve and started crawling on her belly backward toward the opposite side of the road where it fell off into a drop of about a foot. Not much protection, but better cover than what they had at the moment.

The firing stopped abruptly.

"Put your guns on the ground and lie down with your hands behind your head," Kingsley shouted at them from his vantage. He was in the road halfway between the van and the low shoulder where Diane had taken cover. "Do as I say."

"Don't trust that they are out of bullets," Diane said to him. "I think they are trying to draw us out in the open."

"I agree," said Kingsley. He crawled backward to where Diane was hiding.

From her vantage point, she could see under the van out across to Iris and Lily's hiding place. She couldn't see them, but as she stared, she caught sight of their clothes. They weren't able to completely hide either. Diane turned her head to Kingsley and started to say something, but saw that he was aiming. He fired and they heard a yelp and a scream and more shots.

The shooting stopped again, and this time Diane thought they were probably out of ammunition. But she didn't stand up to test her theory.

"Rose may still be alive," shouted Kingsley. "Do you want to risk not getting her help?"

There was silence for a moment, then one of them called out. "Don't shoot."

"Throw out your guns and stand up where I can see you. Put your hands behind your head and kneel on the ground," said Kingsley.

Diane saw two guns come flying out of the ditch and the two of them stand up, lacing their hands behind their heads before falling to their knees.

Diane cautiously went to pick up the guns. They were empty. She patted the women down while Kingsley held his gun on them. If their gazes could shoot bullets, she and Kingsley would be dead.

A bullet had grazed Iris' shoulder blade and there was a small red stain on the back of her dress.

Diane and Kingsley made Lily and Iris carry Rose as they marched them and a dazed Joey down the road. Just as they arrived back at the house, the U.S. Marshals came driving up along with two FBI agents—and Frank.

Chapter 53

Kingsley elected to fly back to Atlanta to have his wound seen about. Diane understood. Sometimes you just want to go home. They left the cleanup with the marshals. The local doctor said Rose would make it. Joey's gun hadn't made a very big hole in her, nor had Kingsley hit anything vital.

Kingsley was in the window seat asleep on the plane. He looked better since the paramedics had pumped him full of their good stuff.

Diane watched the blue sky and white clouds, glad to be away from Clymene's island.

"Thanks for coming to rescue me," said Diane.

She snuggled up to Frank, feeling safe and secure—it was not simply that he came looking for her, but that down deep, she knew he would and that he would find her.

"It looks like you and Kingsley had things in hand," he said.

"How did you find me?" she asked.

"The police couldn't locate Eric Tully and I was afraid he might have followed you, so I took a flight here. It looks like that flight was very popular for law enforcement. The marshals and the FBI were on it too."

"I thought maybe you located me by my phone." Diane was a bit disappointed.

She rubbed her leg where Joey had bitten it. Fortunately her pants were between her leg and his mouth and he hadn't broken the skin. But it made a terrible bruise and hurt like hell.

"Your phone?" he said.

"Yes. I forgot to retrieve it," she said. "I thought maybe you located me by GPS."

"You mean this one?" He smiled knowingly and took a phone from his pocket and handed it to her. "It was in that little house out back," he said.

"You did find me by my phone. It makes me so happy when a plan finally comes together," she said.

"You want to eat out tonight or go home?" he said, putting an arm around her and kissing her temple.

"I want to go home," she said. "If I had ruby slippers, I'd click my heels three times. Besides, I want to finish my ice cream." She went to sleep on his shoulder.

An ambulance was waiting for Kingsley, along with his wife. She was one of the most striking women Diane had ever seen outside a movie screen. She had smooth black hair, green, almond-shaped eyes, and an olive complexion. Diane heard her scolding Kingsley as they were putting him in the ambulance.

"Mrs. Kingsley," said Diane. "I'm Diane Fallon. I'm glad to meet you."

"Lydia, please." She smiled. "I've told my husband that going out with other women will only get him into trouble."

"It certainly did that," said Diane. "Next time, you're on your own," Diane called to Kingsley as they were shutting the ambulance doors.

As Frank drove Diane home, he told her that the store they stopped at on the Outer Banks had called the police when no one claimed the SUV parked out front. The police traced it back to the rental company, who traced it back to the FBI. A lot of people had been looking for them.

It was dark when they arrived home. Frank parked the car in the driveway. Diane looked out the window at the house. The lights were on inside. It was her home now—at least until she found her own house. When she got out she didn't see the shadow behind the tree until it was too late. He raised the gun and Diane thought she was dead. Her reflexes weren't working anymore. When the shot rang out she thought she must have been hit, until the shadow man fell to the ground.

Frank rushed around the car and took a gun away from a woman Diane also hadn't seen in the dark. She was plump, with dark curly hair and a dimpled chin and tears running down her face.

Frank then retrieved Tully's gun and checked his vitals. He shook his head at Diane.

"I followed him here because I thought he was seeing someone else. Clymene said he was a liar and I didn't want to believe her. Little Julie told me he abused her mother. I didn't want to believe her either. What makes a person be like him?" She looked from Diane to Frank for an answer. Diane didn't have one.

Diane looked at the dead man on Frank's lawn. It was happening here at his house just like it did at her apartment building. They took Grace Noel Tully into the house and called the police. Diane didn't eat her ice cream.

Epilogue

Diane was sitting at her desk typing a thank-you letter to the Egyptian ambassador. Agent Jacobs gave all the suspicious artifacts back to Egypt, even though he never found out where exactly they came from. The murder of Randal Cunningham, Jr., was so far unsolved. Even David couldn't find out anything, a situation he regretted, not only because it was unusual for him, but because he missed a chance to impress Kendel.

The Egyptian authorities made RiverTrail out as heroes for finding their lost artifacts. Vanessa and the board were happy with that. Diane, not looking a gift horse in the mouth, didn't question their good luck, though she thought perhaps Jacobs and maybe Kingsley had something to do with it.

Jacobs found some of the artifacts they had ordered—the twelfth-dynasty artifacts. They were in the fire at Golden Antiquities. The stone artifacts survived. The sphinx of Senwosret III was broken in half. The stone face and bust, like the sphinx, were covered in soot. The canopic jar had burst into small pieces. The gold artifacts were lumps of melted metal. Gone to history.

There are two main philosophies of conservation—preservation and restoration. Years ago restoration was the most popular. These days it's preservation—keeping artifacts at the state they are in currently, but not making them look like they once did before they were worn by time. Restoration often means adding modern material to the artifact, in fact, changing it from what it was.

Korey Jordan, her head conservator, was a preservationist. But he decided to try to restore these burned artifacts because they were so recently damaged and because the entire museum was grieving over their loss.

The phone rang. It was Andie.

"I've got a transfer from the crime lab. You have a phone call from a Sheriff Maddox in Ohio," she said.

"Put him through," said Diane.

"Sheriff Maddox. Did you get the drawings of your little Angel Doe?" she said.

"That's what I called to tell you about, Dr. Fallon. When we got those pictures, in particular the one with her standing in that little dress, my deputy, who's six four and weighs two hundred and eighty pounds, just bawled. Putting a face to her is really going to make a difference. People are going to respond. We are going to find out who this little girl is."

"Neva Hurley, one of my crime scene crew, is an artist. She did the drawings," said Diane.

"Aging the face for the other drawing the way you did was a great idea. What I'm going to do is put it in the paper with the others and say we're looking for someone who looks like this as a witness."

"That's a good idea. I think someone probably will respond," said Diane.

"I just wanted to thank you. This other information

you sent, that analysis of her bone that said she grew up in central Ohio . . . well, uh, we're a small county with a small budget and . . ."

"That is paid for by a grant my osteology lab has," said Diane. "I located a man's son for him, and out of gratitude he funded the lab for the museum and he set up a trust fund for extras like this, so we can go the distance to identify someone else's lost child."

"Poor fellow. He must have loved his kid. That was mighty generous of him."

"Drop me a line if you identify her," said Diane.

"I surely will, and thanks again."

Andie brought the mail in to Diane and Diane gave her the signed thank-you letter to send out.

"Kendel is still upset," said Andie. "She thinks this still makes her look guilty and everyone is helping cover it up."

"I know. I don't know what to do about it either," said Diane. "It's going to take a while to get her reputation back. I think the fact that we aren't going to quietly fire her will help."

Andie went back to her office and Diane took out the mail and looked through it.

Andie called again.

"Ross Kingsley wants to speak with you," she said.

"Put him through," Diane told her.

She got the copy of *Museum World* and took off the brown paper wrapper. There was a picture on the cover of the Bickford Museum along with its acquisition of a piece of moon rock. Diane had heard about it and she was jealous. So was Mike. He was ready to go search for extremophiles on the moon. She picked up the phone.

"Kingsley," she said. "How are you? Recovered, I

hope. If you're calling to go on a road trip again, you can forget it."

He laughed out loud. "I'm doing great. I'm back at work. Joey's little mouse gun didn't do much damage. I thought you might want to hear about Clymene and her family. I still can't think of her as Iris."

"Go ahead," said Diane. She flipped through the pages of the magazine, looking at the pictures. She heard him sigh.

"Where do I start? Ma and Pa are being evaluated. We don't quite know what to do with them. The sisters had made a lavish apartment for them on the upper floor and locked them in it. Their punishment for being the worst parents of the century was to be forced to live together. When they got too rowdy, they were put in the outbuilding we were in and made to contemplate their behavior. The father, Alain Delaflote, had a mild stroke some time ago. I'm wondering if it was induced somehow, but no way to prove that at this point."

"This is so bizarre," said Diane.

"That's not the word for it. I'm talking twilight zone. You remember how lovely Sarah Wallace is—and she is nine years older than her sister, Jerusha Delaflote."

"Yes, I thought Sarah Wallace was a very attractive woman," said Diane.

"Well, did you ever see a movie called *What Ever Happened to Baby Jane*? Bette Davis played Baby Jane, an aging former child star."

"I've seen it," said Diane.

"Jerusha is Baby Jane. And at five years younger and a hundred pounds heavier than her husband—well, you said it, payback's a bitch."

"I'm glad I didn't wait around for them to be brought out of the secret room," said Diane. "How is Rose?"

Diane came to the article on the Bickford Museum and its new director, Brenda McCaffrey, formerly from the Pearle, and raised her eyebrows.

"She's doing well. The doctors had to repair her shoulder joint, but she's already made a full recovery. The various jurisdictions where Clymene and her many deceased husbands lived are trying to make their cases to prosecute Clymene, but they are not making much progress. Too much of the evidence is just circumstantial. They don't have any cotton balls like you did."

"How about the baby kangaroo?" said Diane, though she was now only half listening.

"Joey's in some hot water. He's been arrested for killing Rev. Rivers and for drugging us. Lily and Rose are being charged with kidnapping and assault on police officers," he said. "It's all a tangled mess."

"But very interesting for your book," said Diane.

"Very. Instead of a couple of chapters on Clymene—I suppose I should call her Iris—it's going to be a whole book. Seriously, I think we make a good team," he said.

"I thought we were pretty pathetic," said Diane. "I mean, curtain rods were the best we could do?"

Kingsley laughed again. "You may be right," he said.

After they hung up, Diane called Agent Jacobs.

"Diane. Hello. Good to hear from you," he said.

"I wanted to thank you for helping us out with the Egyptian government. They were most gracious."

"I really didn't do much," he said. But Diane thought otherwise.

"I was wondering if you would do me another favor," she said.

"If I can," he said.

"Find out who was on the short list to be the new director of the Bickford," said Diane.

"Sure, I can do that. I know a few people on their board. I'll call you right back," he said.

"Thanks," said Diane.

She called the director's office at the Pearle Museum. The secretary answered. "Hello, Dr. Fallon. Our interim director is out right now. I guess you heard Dr. McCaffrey's good news," she said.

"Yes, I was just reading about it in *Museum World*. I thought I would send her a congratulatory gift."

"That's so nice of you. I'm sure she will appreciate it," she said.

"Do you know what kind of perfume she wears?" asked Diane.

"Sure do, Jean Patou's Joy. She loves it. Very expensive," she said.

"Thanks," said Diane.

"We here at the Pearle are just so sorry about those Egyptian artifacts burning up in the fire at Golden Antiquities," the secretary said. "A lot of people here didn't want to sell them in the first place, and to think they have been destroyed."

"My head conservator is going to try and restore some of them, but you know how that is," said Diane.

"I do," she said.

"Thanks again," said Diane, and she hung up.

Her private line rang and she picked it up. It was Agent Jacobs.

"You'll find this interesting," he said. "Kendel Williams and Brenda McCaffrey were the only two contenders for the Bickford directorship," he said.

"Neither was notified. They were about to send out requests for interviews when the shit hit the fan at RiverTrail. That took Kendel out of the running."

"You'll find this interesting. Brenda McCaffrey's favorite perfume is Jean Patou's Joy," said Diane.

"Is it, now? The whiff Kendel smelled at Golden Antiquities. Well, I may not go down in defeat on this after all. Thank you," Jacobs said.

"I know that's not exactly proof," said Diane.

"Now that I know where to look, I'll get the evidence. The Bickford would be a nice place to be if one were dealing in looted artifacts," he said. "Thanks, Diane. Feel free to do me a favor again sometime."

"My pleasure," she said.

Diane hung up the phone and went to see Kendel.

Also available in Beverly Connor's
Diane Fallon Forensic Investigation *series*:

ONE GRAVE TOO MANY

Leaving a troubled past behind her, Diane Fallon is starting over as director of the River Trail Museum of Natural History in Georgia – until former love Detective Frank Duncan tracks her down. He needs her unique experience as a forensic anthropologist to examine a bone found in the woods.

Diane can't resist Frank's request – on both a professional and personal level. Because the secrets of bones are in her blood – and their whispers offer a dead family's only chance at justice...

DEAD GUILTY

In the shadow of Diane Fallon's new forensic lab in Georgia, a land survey crew has discovered three bodies hanging in an isolated patch of woods. The sensational case has aroused the interest of the media, unnerved the locals – and inspired a gruesome game between the killer and Diane.

It begins with taunting e-mails and chilling phone calls. Where it leads is a personal investigation as each bizarre clue brings Diane closer to danger...

DEAD SECRET

In the depths of an unmapped cave, forensic anthropologist Diane Fallon makes a chilling discovery: the decades-old skeleton of a caving victim. Soon, the remains of two more bodies are found – one in an old car submerged in the waters of an abandoned quarry, another buried in the Georgia woods.

At first, with nothing to link the victims except desiccated bones, Diane can't fathom the connection. But someone else does. It's the key to a mystery that reaches back seventy years in a heritage of love, greed, and murder – and an unearthed family secret that still holds the power to kill.

DEAD PAST

Diane Fallon's crime scene unit is facing one of its worst ever cases: an explosion in a converted house has claimed many lives – from the students attending a party in one of the upstairs apartments to the junkies running a meth lab in the basement. Diane and her team will be sifting the evidence for days, searching the scene for any slight clue to the identities of the unrecognisable bodies.

The incident has a devastating impact on the local community – with most people knowing at least one of the victims. One of the party survivors was even a member of Diane's staff – lucky enough to escape with her life. Diane is determined to discover the root cause of the explosion. But she must do so while avoiding the frenzy of media interest, local government officials keen to assign blame and the political machinations of a chief fire inspector who will stop at nothing to get Diane's job…